A TOUR OF DUTY

THE THIRD PRINCE: THE MICHELL RICE STORY

MICHAEL R. BUTNER

iUniverse, Inc.
New York Bloomington

A TOUR OF DUTY
THE THIRD PRINCE: THE MICHELL RICE STORY

This is a work of fiction. All of the characters, names, incidents, organizations, and dialogue in this novel are either the products of the author's imagination or are used fictitiously.

iUniverse books may be ordered through booksellers or by contacting:

iUniverse
1663 Liberty Drive
Bloomington, IN 47403
www. iuniverse. com
1-800-Authors (1-800-288-4677)

ISBN: 978-1-4401-8711-7 (pbk)
ISBN: 978-1-4401-8709-4 (cloth)
ISBN: 978-1-4401-8710-0 (ebook)

Printed in the United States of America

iUniverse rev. date:11/10/09

This book is first dedicated to the men and women of the CIA.

For three generations they have been viewed as a dark, clandestine force whose motives have always been suspect. This is far from the truth I have witnessed. On continent after continent and in secret battle after secret battle it has been my privilege to have seen these people as the most selfless warriors who have ever breathed. I have seen them give their all—their lives, their loves, even their very identities—so that others can live free. The debts they are owed will never be repaid.

Second, this book is dedicated to my patients, people who have done more to heal me than I have ever done to heal them.

And third, this book is dedicated to my wife, the one person who, more than any other whom I have ever known, has been the embodiment of courage. Without her urging, this book would have never been written.

Michael R. Butner

PART ONE:

CORONATION

Prologue

(Excerpts of a lecture given to the War College in Fort McNair, 1974 by Brigadier General Wilson Gabriel Strong)

"Gentlemen, the subject of today's discussion is the classification of the three basic types of soldiers that are under our commands.

"First on that list is the adrenaline addict.

"This man is one who is habituated to violence.

"Combat and its trappings supply this soldier with a primal rush very similar to that of any addictive stimulant. This 'high' is a mixture of excitement, power, pleasure, and perceived superiority. It is so essential to this man's ego definition that it is as necessary to him as air, food, or water.

"This man may be antisocial, insubordinate, narcissistic, and resentful of authority, but he has a need for stimulation that is so paramount that it dominates everything else. It is the ordering of this craved-for violence that allows a commander a way to make this man into a malleable tool.

"The primary issue here is one of control, not motivation.

"This soldier has a fairly fragile ego. He defines himself by what he does and has little self-insight. In a sense, he's our Doberman, our attack dog.

"Using this analogy, this soldier is best coddled and petted by the guise of military structure. He is made a part of elite units that furnish him with an identity. Rank, unit distinction, and military custom all make him feel special and separate from his peers. This isolation simultaneously reinforces his ego and allows us, the commanders, firmer rules of engagement. In short, here control and morale become the same thing, and the blending of the two gives us efficient command.

"This second kind of soldier is driven by the everyday pressures of life. He wants to survive, to be happy, to prosper. He tends to be shortsighted in his vision, self-centered in his efforts, and usually limited in his endurance.

"Here the command challenge is not control. This man's own weakness takes care of that. Rather, the command challenge is motivation, and surprisingly, the weaknesses I've just listed are the key.

"This second soldier is controlled by his own needs. To direct him, a commander must set up a series of small tasks whose end points are easily seen. Frequent reinforcements help keep this man focused. Personal progress and well-being are more important to him than understanding the *big picture*. This man just needs to see his own world becoming a better place. So long as this happens, he will buy into the system and do our bidding forever.

"The commander of this second type of soldier needs a big dose of humility. Most of us come from this same bolt of cloth, and consequently, our chief enemy is disillusionment.

"We, the commanders, see a bigger portion of the *picture*. If we become discouraged by what we see, we will become cynical. Cynicism will alienate those in our command, and our effectiveness will be lost. In cynicism's place we must radiate a sense of strong, caring leadership. Perhaps the picture of a strong, high school athletic coach, emulated by his charges, best typifies the image we must project.

"And that brings us to the third kind of soldier. He is the most rare. He is the self-actualized man, the man who chooses to expend himself for others.

"This third man's selflessness is something fundamentally different from the first two kinds of soldiers. They value themselves more than the mission. This man puts the mission first. This disregard of self gives this third man focus, decisiveness, and endurance that far outstrip that of the first two soldiers. This third soldier wastes no energy or hesitation on self-worry and has all of his resources available for action. In short, he is a living weapon, the most potent one in all of our arsenals.

"The first rule of command of this last soldier is that you cannot control him.

"This man answers to a higher power than any of us. Rather than order, here a commander must convince and show the *right* of the situation. Once this man accepts the cause, he becomes a self-motivated, self-contained force who doesn't need other motivation or control. The mission, in effect, becomes both the means and the end.

"The second rule of command with this third type of soldier is that the commander must represent what is right and just.

"In this the commander takes on a piece of the god this man worships. This is a heady experience where one's own ego can be an easy stumbling block. This last soldier won't respond to fraud. If the commander is not selfless himself, this man will not follow. So the commander must either be one of these rare men himself or else be a very convincing actor. Either case is a tall order, but when a commander pulls it off and wins the respect of one of these last men, the reward is the most awesome command experience there is. It is a little like being a god...

"All of this, then, is why you are here at this session of the War College. You are here to learn how to command and use all those in your charge. You are here to come to know yourselves well enough to see through your own self-made myths. In short, you are here to learn honesty. It is honesty that is the key to successful command."

Chapter One

The Boeing 707 roared off the runway and leaped into the Alaskan sky. The sound blasted the air and muted everything. The passengers plastered themselves to the plane's small windows. As the plane rose, every man strained for his last glimpse of home. For some the look would have to last for a long time. For others it would have to last forever. It was late fall in 1967, and the jet was headed for Vietnam. Its occupants were all U. S. Marines.

Shortly after takeoff the big jet was swallowed up by the high cloud cover, and all signs of the ground disappeared. Cushioned by its cruising altitude, the plane throttled back its engines. The resulting relative quiet allowed small conversations to spring up, but the cabin was still fairly quiet. Men flying to war were sometimes boisterous and sometimes quiet. This company, except for four whiskey-soaked marines at the front of the plane, was quiet.

The difference in all this was the changing pace of war. Previous flights had been full, carrying almost exclusively replacement combat infantrymen... untested, brash young men who tried to hide from their fear in the shadow of a bottle. Those neophytes to war had not yet fully understood that they were going to a jungle that would likely consume them.

This particular flight was only partially full and carried some of the war's veterans... medical technicians and Special Forces personnel returning to Vietnam, all who had already seen death. The knowledge of what they were returning to made them a little more sober.

Most of the jet's empty seats were back in the tail section where there was no talking at all. There one lone Marine sat alone. He was a solidly built nineteen-year-old that somehow looked forty. He had light brown-hair and gray eyes. On his chest were a parachutist's wings and an expert marksman's bulls-eye medals. This man's name was Mitchell Rice. He was a marine scout/sniper, the war's greatest enigma and most deadly combatant.

"Move over, marine!" snarled the biggest of the four drunken marines, a newly minted corporal, as he tried to elbow an unyielding Mitch away from his window.

"Come on, you motherfucker! Move your worthless, private's ass! These stripes," he pointed to the chevrons on his shoulder, "mean I don't have to sit in the aisle if I don't want to! Move, you jack-shit!"

As Mitch slowly got up and gave the drunk his seat, his usually steely eyes flickered with what seemed to be little sparks of red.

"That's right, baby doll! Move it on out of there! This seat is *mine*!" the corporal bellowed. "And take your pathetic can of Coke with you! Real men drink bourbon!"

Mitch caught the tossed can with hands so quick that not even one drop spilled onto the floor.

"Get out of my face, you tit-sucking, limp dick! I bet you couldn't even get your own mother off even if she was begging for it!"

The whole plane suddenly became deathly quiet. Even the sound of the jet's engines seemed to have somehow slipped away. An attractive brunette stewardess, a thirty-something-year-old veteran of military flights, headed their way to try to calm the situation. A Special Forces sergeant who knew trouble when he saw it followed right behind her.

"Look!" snarled the corporal as he planted his big paw on the just-arrived stewardess's chest and squeezed hard. "This is what a woman really wants!"

Mitch's right hand struck out like a bolt of lightning. Saber-like, it buried itself right under the burly corporal's diaphragm. The drunk's hand instantly fell away from the young woman's now-bruised breast. Recoiling, the corporal gasped without breathing and cold, sour booze suddenly spurted out of his mouth.

"You okay?" Mitch asked the woman as he moved between her and the corporal in an attempt to shield her from the putrid whiskey pouring out the corporal's mouth. "When he is able to breathe again, I think the corporal here will want to apologize for being such a jerk."

"Stand down, marines!" barked the sergeant as he tried to move around the stewardess.

Mitch moved half a step back but still maintained a controlling stance over the still breathless corporal who was now kneeling in a pool of his own vomit.

"Are you okay, miss?" the sergeant asked the woman as he helped her into his own seat. "I'm sorry. I didn't realize just how out of it Corporal Jenson was. I'll have his ass when we get to 'Nam."

"I'm okay, sergeant," she answered, wincing as she re-arranged the front of her blouse. "It's probably my own fault for giving him and his buddies the extra sauce. I knew they were already lit up before they even got on the plane."

Mitch took another half-step back, his eyes burning holes into the helpless hulk who had finally choked in a part of a breath.

"Get up here, you three!" barked the sergeant at the corporal's three drinking buddies. "You worthless idiots get the clean-up duty for this mess!" The sergeant reached down and yanked the corporal upright. "You oughta be busted and thrown into the brig for this one, Jenson! I've told you before to lay off the hard stuff! You can't hold your liquor for shit!"

Mitch moved back completely to his seat, letting the other three marines pass by with their vomit-soaked, coughing load. The fire in Mitch's eyes continued to burn.

"I'm okay, marine," the stewardess said to Mitch as she gingerly stood up, pushing back the goose bumps on her arms. "Thanks for the help," she said simply. "That guy's a mean drunk."

Mitch shrugged, now suddenly a nineteen-year-old very much out of place. "You're welcome, ma'am. I hope you're not hurt too bad."

"I'm fine," she answered. "No harm done."

It took a few more minutes for everything to return to normal, but only a few. And after that, the few minutes turned into hours.

Mitch, still solitary and almost invisible as snipers always were, spent the time lost in his own thoughts. His eyes, no longer full of hot fire, had returned to their variable gray and blue hues, almost reflecting the same light and dark colors a line of Missouri thunderstorms would spawn in summer. No one saw the few drops of moisture that ran down his face. But since no downpour followed, he was ignored.

The drunken corporal, now smelling of liquid soap, snored quietly, having been towed to his seat by his now completely sober drinking buddies. He would spend no time in the brig. The jungle where he was going would be confinement enough.

The Special Forces sergeant had returned to his fellow sergeants at the center of the cabin. They, unlike Mitch, were not the living weapons of the war. If Mitch was the personification of the sudden, violent death that all soldiers feared, the sergeants were the specialists that served the weapons. They were the technicians of the war's electronics, medicine, mechanized weapons, and small unit tactics. It was theirs to deal with death and dying, not personally, one violent death at a time as it was Mitch's duty, but rather they did it incidentally, almost as an afterthought. For them all the bleeding and dying would always be secondary to their taking and holding ground. But for Mitch everything was secondary to the killing. His sole purpose was the focused, purposeful act of the sudden extinction of another human life. His motto was "one shot, one kill."

The flight attendant, ignoring her breast's soreness, continued her laps up and down the plane's aisle bringing whatever smiles and pleasant words she could, much like a nurse making rounds on her ward.

And over all of this, the plane's engines droned on in their quiet roar. The jungle that was Vietnam and all of the horrific beasts it held were still to come. The flight and all of its noises became, like all the flights before it, a sad cacophony of fear, quiet conversations, and silent despair. It was a wake of sorts, a place and time where youth and innocence once again learned how to die.

The Boeing landed in Vietnam without incident, and in fairly short order, Mitch went from Saigon to DaNang, a major Marine base north of the capital. In DaNang, Mitch quickly acquired all his field gear and re-qualified for field placement as an active sniper. About two weeks before Christmas he left DaNang and slipped into AnHoa, his actual home base. The pace of war around him promised that he, already someone far older than his years, would continue to age very rapidly.

The area around AnHoa was called "Apache Country," and as the named implied, it was a dangerous landscape. All of the base's large artillery batteries, huge ammo dump, everyone of the multiple bivouac areas, the base's airfield, and even its hospital were all dedicated to keeping the countryside peaceful. But unfortunately, that was something not even the base's great firepower could always pull off.

At the very center of AnHoa, nestled deeply behind the base's biggest barricades and tallest sandbags, lay an unmarked group of tents that was Mitch's new home. It was "sniper country."

By this time in the war, the reputation of the Marine scout/snipers was already such that the Vietcong routinely posted large bounties for their assassination. Young VC were easily convinced to try to win their families' financial security by turning themselves into walking, human bombs. They were called "sappers," and they were just as deadly as any well-aimed mortar or rocket shell. Even the theft of a sniper's rifle could fetch more than $2,000, and the bounty for some of the more feared snipers ran as high as $10,000. Consequently, the security needs of sniper country were great.

Because of all this sniper operations in Vietnam had developed as something unique. The two-man sniper team was the smallest military unit capable of independent action. It answered to no commanders other than Headquarters. Two-man teams went afield in unannounced hunter-killer excursions, worked with larger patrols, or were randomly assigned to work out of smaller outlying fire bases. The lack of predictability was essential to a team's survival.

The downside of their special status was that sniper teams were sometimes shunned even by the commanders whose very battalions they protected. Mitch was soon to learn very graphically that his special status was both a boon and a curse.

Mitch's team partner was a long-time veteran sniper named Dave Tooks. Tooks was a legend in Apache Country. He was the kill leader of all active snipers, with over seventy-five confirmed kills. Charlie had the highest bounty on Took's head than he had ever offered for one man's death—at least $15,000. It was a dubious honor. Just the Zippo lighter Tooks carried (an engraved award for being the highest scoring sniper at DaNang during the last qualifying competition) was worth more than $1000. Consequently, Dave Tooks was a very valuable commodity, and Mitch was his new spotter. That made Mitch both Dave Tooks's apprentice and his bodyguard.

"Come on, partner! Let's saddle up!" Tooks yelled at the entrance to Mitch's tent.

It was just dawn, and Mitch had been barely sleeping. Took's sudden order caught him in that gray world where dream and reality meet.

"Oh God!" Mitch screamed. Wild-eyed, he instantly shot to his feet with his rifle already on his shoulder.

"Goddamn it, marine! Stow that weapon!" Tooks yelled, throwing himself onto the ground.

Mitch came completely awake, shuddered, and pushed on the rifle's safety. Tooks got up, slowly dusted himself off, and came right up to Mitch's face, locking onto his eyes.

"The sarge thinks it's time for you to get your candy-assed feet wet. So we're taking a little ride to Delta Company," Tooks growled. He broke eye contact and dusted himself off some more. "It's only about twelve miles so we're going to hitch a ride in the back of one of the supply trucks."

"What's out there, gunny?" Mitch asked, shrugging and picking up his field pack all in the same motion. He guessed somehow he wasn't going to get chewed out.

"Probably not one goddamn thing!" Tooks cursed. "Delta Company has the reputation for being the quietest place in this whole damn country!"

Mitch scowled. He was having problems processing everything that was happening.

"No one's paying you to think, marine! That's my job! You just make damn sure you follow my lead!" Tooks erupted.

Mitch took a breath and felt better. He was going to get a chewing. That at least felt more like normal. His sense of reality was starting to come back.

"No fuckin' screw-ups!" Tooks continued. "Charlie doesn't give a rat's ass that Delta Company is out of the fuckin' war! He'll light you up the first chance you give him!"

Mitch shrugged again and choked back the urge to smile. He had been here before. Sergeants were all the same whether they were Dave

Tooks or Mitch's dad. The only way to shut them up was to be perfect. Twelve thousand miles and a whole new war hadn't changed a thing. Somehow the realization was both comforting and familiar.

"No one but the skipper and the sarge know we're goin'. And it's sure as hell that no one at Delta Company is expecting us. So it's all goin' to be fun and games." Tooks turned to Mitch. "You just stay on the lookout for beggar kids that come up behind the trucks. Sometimes they say hello by throwing a friggin' grenade in your lap."

Mitch stumbled. His eyes hadn't yet adjusted to the bright morning sun.

"You got a problem, marine?" Tooks demanded.

"No, gunny. No problems," Mitch said, bristling slightly as he quickly regained his step. "But I don't get it. If Delta Company's such a quiet place, why's the hottest shooter in the place going there? Does the skipper think I'm so green that I need to be bottle-fed?"

Tooks snorted. "Shit! You fry me, Rice! The skipper doesn't give a fuck how hot a shooter you were in training. This isn't about you. All those records you set at Pendleton don't mean a thing out here." Tooks's voice dropped a tone. "And it isn't about me either. We're just grunts who do what we're told. If the skipper says we go, then we go."

Mitch stopped in his tracks. "Gunny, I didn't mean I was the "hottest shooter." That's you, not me. I may not have all my shit together yet, but I do know who you are. That's all I meant."

"Ah, let's cut the crap, Rice," Tooks countered, half- stepping back, half-smiling. "You and me… we're a team. That's all that matters now. Your scores… my kill record… none of that matters now. It's just you and me. Beyond that, you just need to know that the skipper is no idiot. He's given us a mission, and I'll tell you about it as we go."

Took's reached out and touched Mitch's M14. "You just keep this thing ready to go. Before this is all over, we're both going to need all the firepower you can muster with it."

Mitch, his eyes now fully adjusted to the light, caught Tooks's stare. "It's going to be that bad, huh?"

"Yeah, marine. It's going to be that bad. It always is around here. That's how we earn our pay."

Mitch nodded. "I got it, gunny. You lead, and I'll follow. And I'll try not to screw up."

Tooks's half-smile melted into something else. It was a look Mitch had seen before. It was the same look his dad had given him when Mitch had left for basic training, a look of concern, worry, fear, and maybe… love. Mitch started to chill.

"You're goin' to do fine, Rice," Took answered, breaking eye contact. "Look, we all know you're the hottest goddamn prospect ever to come out of Pendleton. Shit, the skipper's so friggin' shook up about you that he's told me to give you a crash course on this place so you can get your own bolt gun in a couple of weeks. He knows your record, and so do I. So if you loosen up a little, I'll back down my bullshit. Okay? We gotta make this thing work between us."

Mitch nodded and took a deep breath. Everything was going too fast. He knew the significance of the bolt gun. In that he and Tooks had common ground. The Remington bolt action rifle each team leader carried was the very soul of the sniper. It was murderously accurate and coveted as something precious. The team spotter never carried one and usually served in the assistant's role for months before he finally got a chance to have one of his own. To be considered for one so soon made Mitch feel numb inside.

Tooks chuckled. "Don't take any of this as a compliment, Riceman. Things are gonna get real hot around here pretty damn soon, and the skipper just wants you ready. Besides," Tooks snorted, "he thinks I'm getting a little short in my thinking. He wants a new, sharp fire-eater around to keep me on my toes. It would look bad on his record if I got wiped this close to the end of my tour."

Tooks shrugged, losing his half-smile. "So, Riceman, you kinda got it wrong. Sure, I'm your teacher, but you're the babysitter. After this mission, I'm out of here. The skipper wants you to keep me alive, and he wants me to leave him a good replacement." His grin returned. "So, you see… you're screwed."

Mitch snorted. "I thought you said you'd cut the bullshit, gunny. You need a babysitter like I need a heavier pack to tote around in this steam oven. If you don't want to tell me what's going on, then that's just fine. I'll just go along and keep my mouth shut."

Tooks held onto his grin. "Have it anyway you want, marine. Just keep your head out of your butt and pay attention to me. Our taxi's right over there. Let's go earn our pay."

During the ride to Delta Company, Tooks said very little. Mitch was quiet too, but he had remembered to chamber a live round into his M14. He was standing up in the shadows of the bed cover, just back a little from the truck's tailgate. Everything in the dusty road behind them fell under his careful gaze. Tooks had made his point, and Mitch didn't intend to get fragged by some grenade-toting beggar.

Dave Tooks was a legend, and legends, Mitch knew, weren't wasted on do-nothing fire bases, not even if they were just weeks away from going stateside. The mere fact that they were going to "check the place out" meant something bad was there. Tooks had said as much.

"*Shiiiiit!*" Tooks screamed suddenly.

A young Vietnamese girl, maybe ten years old, was running up behind the truck. She had a primed hand grenade in her hand, and Mitch and Tooks were her targets. Tooks started to reach for his bolt gun, but the little girl was too fast. She was already halfway through her throw.

The next moment was both frozen and instantaneous. Mitch's M14 roared, flinging its spent brass right into Tooks's face and filling the truck bed with its blast. Simultaneously the attacking girl jerked backward as a small hole blossomed at the neckline of her black shirt. A spray of blood and tissue shot instantly out from her back. The little girl dropped her arm and died in mid stride before the grenade ever left her fingers.

"Grenade!" Mitch screamed.

Tooks had already thrown himself down behind the truck's tailgate, and Mitch landed on top of him. The grenade fell to the ground right in front of the dead girl. The blast from it tore off part of the canvas covering the truck bed and deafened both of them. It also ripped the ten-year-old girl literally limb from limb, tearing both her right arm and head completely off her dead torso. Her disembodied face, frozen and stunned by her instant death, stared at her missed targets and rolled over and over, bouncing in the suddenly blood-soaked, scorched dust. The blast of Mitch's rifle still filled her eyes.

For a second both Mitch's and Tooks's ears screamed with a high-pitched ringing. In the next second the suddenly accelerating truck nearly threw them both over the tailgate. (The truck's driver knew the drill, and he was getting out his vehicle of the kill zone as quickly as possible. The young girl might have a back-up.)

Three minutes later the bouncing truck slowed down, and the whole episode was over. The bloody encounter would become just another soon-to-be-forgotten event in a war full of nameless tragedies. Life and death had been crammed into mere seconds… but for Mitch, those seconds had been an eternity.

Mitch and Tooks picked themselves up and looked at each other.

"Damn! You're hit!" Tooks yelled, seeing a small stream of blood dripping from Mitch's chin.

"Nah, I just crammed my face into that ammo crate when I hit the deck. It's just a scratch."

Tooks scooted over to him and saw Mitch's analysis was correct. "Hell, it looks like you're going to be broken in pretty fast at this rate, Riceman. Here, put this gauze on your chin. Everything here gets infected real fast."

Mitch complied, but he stared out the back of the truck as he did so. The scene of the attack was nearly out of sight, but it still filled his burning eyes.

"You okay, marine?" Tooks asked.

Mitch didn't seem to hear. He had a "thousand-yard stare," the look of a man who had just killed his first fellow human being. And that person had been a ten-year-old child.

"If you hadn't waxed her, Rice, we'd both be dead men now," Tooks said gently. "I couldn't get operational fast enough."

Mitch turned his suddenly hollow eyes away from the road. "Does it always hurt this bad?"

Tooks paused. "All I can tell you, Riceman, is that I've seen the last look of every VC I've ever waxed. After a while, the hurt isn't as bad, but it never goes away."

Tooks saw Mitch blink. "Look, Rice," he said. "That was a tough way to start, but that's the way it is here. You never know who Charlie is. Say your good-byes, and let her go. Don't let it eat you up. If you do, there won't be anything left."

Mitch glanced down as he engaged his rifle's safety.

Tooks picked up his long rifle and muttered. "Damn! That was some snap shot! Where'd you learn to do that? They don't teach that quick draw stuff at Pendleton." Tooks touched Mitch's shoulder. "You saved my ass, Riceman. Thanks."

Mitch shrugged. "My dad was a drill sergeant. Even when I was a little kid, he used to say something like this would happen some day. So he drilled me and drilled me on how to shoot instinctively. First, it was on targets. Then it was on squirrels." Mitch looked at Tooks. "We used to squirrel hunt a lot together. I loved it. But dad always gave me hell when it took me too long to get on target."

"Well, thank god for squirrel stew and drill sergeants," Tooks whistled. "I'm glad we're a team, Riceman. Real glad."

Delta Company came into view.

"Mitch," Tooks said, "listen real good while we're here, and I'll try to teach you enough to stay alive. After today, I sure owe you that."

Delta Company occupied the top of a small mountain that stood nameless in the Vietnamese highlands. The fire base was set up roughly in a square with each side measuring some two hundred yards in length. The perimeter consisted of three rows of concertina wire spliced with Claymore mines. A short open stretch followed the wire which led to a bunch of anti-tank barricades. Behind them were the machine guns. The guns, all M60s, completely covered the boundaries of the fire base with overlapping fields of fire. They (and most everything else in the base) were protected by large piles of sandbags. The ground was too rocky for any trenching. Only the ammo dump for the company's six 155mm guns, the command bunker, and the aid station were underground.

The north, west, and east sides of the base were heavily fortified and easily covered by the base's big guns. The south side was close to a very steep cliff that dropped off several hundred feet to the valley below. This side was unapproachable and covered only by a token spread of M60s.

At the center of the fire base, but somewhat more southerly positioned, stood a tall observation tower. Even at night the marines there could see their surroundings easily because the tower held a "big eye," a huge night vision scope. The scope made the night glow with an eerie green light for the Marine observers and took away any advantage darkness might give Charlie. On top of that, the base also had ground-based fire control radar. That radar could plot the course of any incoming shells that Charlie might send. It took only a few incomers for the radar to make Charlie the target for the base's high explosive or steel flechet-filled antipersonnel shells. (Charlie especially hated these "bee hive" rounds. The heavy shells could shred whole companies of men in a single blast.) All of this technology and firepower were the supposed reasons why the base hadn't been attacked in recent memory.

Major Sam Farcas, the base's commander, frowned as he saw two snipers entering his compound. "AnHoa must be really pressing to send the likes of you up here," he snarled as Tooks and Mitch approached. "My patrols haven't had any enemy contact in over two weeks. What does Headquarters expect you two to do here?"

Feeling the chill of Farcas' greeting, Mitch glanced out of the corner of his eye just in time to see Tooks's expression freeze.

"Well, what the hell!" the major snorted. "Why don't you two take over the night shift in the tower? My men could use a break, and besides, aren't you snipers are supposed to be the experts with night vision equipment?"

Mitch followed Tooks's lead and stiffened his jaw.

"That is," Farcas continued, "if you don't mind making an actual *contribution* to this base's function. Surely AnHoa wouldn't mind if you two actually did a little work."

"We'll be happy to take your tower duty, sir," Tooks said slowly, "but we'd also like to look around outside the wire during the day. We'd like to tag along with your boys on some of their patrols."

Mitch heard the icy anger in Tooks's answer. There would never be any love lost between the gunny and the major.

"Like hell you will!" Farcas shot back. "My patrols haven't had a casualty in two months. I don't want anything upsetting their concentration. If you go outside the wire, you go alone! I don't need any fuckin' *prima donnas* messing up my patrols!"

Mitch saw Tooks tightened his grip on his rifle. The gunny probably had never been so insulted in all his twelve years in the Corps. Snipers were always an asset wherever they went. Almost supernatural in their abilities to see trouble coming, the snipers' special kind of killing firepower was something every combat force begged for. To be considered a liability was more of an insult than Tooks could stomach.

"Whatever you say, sir," Mitch said, speaking for his seething partner. "We'll just find a place to stow our gear, and we'll be ready for whatever you say."

Mitch pulled Tooks out of the way. It was either that or maybe witness a murder.

"We'll report in thirty minutes, sir, if that's okay."

Farcas turned away. He had seen what was in Tooks's eyes, and he wanted none of it. "That will be fine, marine. Report to the lieutenant."

Several minutes and two dugouts later, Mitch broke the icy silence. "Gunny, did the skipper send along any goose down parkas for us? If this place is as cold as that reception, we're going to need them."

Tooks looked at Mitch's little grin and growled. He was back in control. "Okay, wise guy, enough of the smart -ass humor. What's your take on all this?"

"Is this quiz time?" Mitch quipped, still trying to keep it light.

"Damn it, Riceman!" Tooks exploded. "I don't need your crap too! I've had enough of that already! If I ask your opinion, then I want your opinion! This is the real world now, not some training exercise! So get your shit together!"

Mitch dropped his grin. "I haven't exactly had my best day either, gunny." Mitch paused while he and Tooks eyed each other. After a moment, Mitch simply said, "Look, I know you're the boss, gunny. If you want my opinion, here it is."

"Okay."

"This place is a cluster fuck," Mitch said slowly. "Other fire bases have pretty much the same setup as this place, and Charlie plasters them all the time. You know it, I know it, the skipper knows it, and whoever the hell is above the skipper knows it."

"So?"

Mitch hesitated. "Well, let's do it this way. We'll take this job on like we would any other field assignment. First, we'll scout out the base itself and get a feel for it. Then we'll check out the countryside. From what you've said, no place around here should be as hazard free as this place seems to be. That means either someone here is on the take, or else is the best goddamn liar I ever heard of. I guess the skipper would want us to find out which it is and then quietly get the hell out of Dodge."

"Jesus H. Christ, marine! You pretty much got it! You might have a future in this man's war after all!" Tooks smiled grimly. "Just remember, Riceman, we don't have any friends here."

"Yeah, life's the shits," Mitch answered. "It's just like they told me at Pendleton, you and me is all we got." Mitch's jaw tightened. "But you and me is all we need. So screw all these other mothers if they want to give us grief."

Tooks's grin got a little more genuine. He tapped Mitch's shoulder. "You *are* goin' do just fine, Riceman. Come on. Let's check our weapons."

Over the next few days, Tooks and Mitch put in some long nighttime hours in the fire base's watchtower. During the day they slept some and visited with the local marines. For the most part, they learned the local marines were sound enough, just under- motivated. They, like their base, were just out of touch with the war. It all seemed impossible because every night they heard raging artillery duels just a few valleys over. How Delta Company stayed out of the meat grinder was a mystery.

Early each morning, the base sent out a patrol, each time with a different squad going. The squad rotation was supposed to spread out the risk, but Tooks discovered there was one particular sergeant, a guy named Davis, that went out almost every time.

Tooks learned this Sergeant Davis had a reputation for being a real snake-eater. He was attached directly to Major Farcas and didn't have his own platoon. The local marines thought of him as being the major's eyes outside the wire. Tooks explained to Mitch that the practice wasn't exactly wrong. It was just unusual.

For five days, Tooks and Mitch continued their nighttime duties and saw little or nothing of the major. On day six, they were both ready for a change.

"Mitch, tonight we're not going up in that miserable tower. We're going to take a little walk and stretch our legs."

"It's about damn time!"

"What'd you say, Riceman?"

"I said," Mitch growled, "that this place is FUBARed! I've sat for so long my butt's callused! Enough of this cabin fever shit!"

Tooks had known what Mitch had said the first time, but he liked the poetry of the second statement too much to complain about it.

This base was "fucked up beyond all recognition." Tooks was even more fed up with it than was Mitch.

"Where are we going, gunny?" Mitch asked.

"Well, rookie, how does this sound to you? We'll go outside the wire just after dark. We'll look over the neighborhood a bit, and then lay low until morning. Then we'll shadow the daily patrol when Davis brings it out. I'm curious about this guy's moves. He's either damn good or damn bad. We need to know which."

"Sounds okay to me. How long are we staying out?"

"That depends, but at least two, maybe three days. I don't want us to come back right after the patrol. They don't need to know that we've been watching them. If we come in after three days with nothing to report, we'll write our ticket out of here and take our butts back to the skipper. Then he, General Westmoreland, or Jesus Christ himself can have this hole! We'll get back to the real war where we belong."

"Amen, gunny!" Mitch answered.

Tropical darkness came on schedule that night. It was the nineteenth of December, and the weather was hot and humid. The night held no moon so the two scouts slipped out of the fire base without any disturbance.

They walked carefully parallel to, but not on the route that the patrols usually took on their way into the bush. Neither Tooks nor Mitch wanted to do anything that might tip their hand to Davis or any of his boys. Those marines were still too much of an unknown quantity.

On the jaunt to the wooded valley below, Tooks and Mitch encountered nothing more threatening than a habu, a kind of hoodless cobra indigenous to the area. Mitch might have stepped on the snake had Tooks not pointed it out to him. It seemed that it took a special kind of vision to navigate the jungle at night, and Tooks obviously had the knack. Mitch hoped it was something he would learn quickly.

The little team explored quietly for about three hours. They ran across no booby traps and no evidence of any enemy activity. It was as if the war had forgotten the valley. All they found was an obvious series of trails outlined with Marine Corps litter. If Charlie ever wanted to take control of the valley, he probably wouldn't have much of a problem doing so.

Toward morning, Tooks and Mitch split up and took different hiding places where they could watch for the patrol. They were about one hundred yards apart, each one watching a different branch of a trail. Mitch took the east trail, and Tooks the west. Between them stood a small hill. For some reason, the hill's top had been cleared of the usual underbrush. The hill-top clearing was a little out of place.

In the darkness, Mitch found a depression that suited his purposes. He wove a large mat of native grasses and brush. After arranging the area just so, he slipped into the hole and pulled the mat over his head. It was as if he had disappeared from the face of the earth.

The vigil was long and hot. Daylight came, and the temperature rose. Mitch sweated, lay still, ignored the mosquitoes, and endured. He should have had trouble staying awake, but he didn't. Between the bugs and his recurring flashbacks of the decapitated girl on the road, there was no chance for sleep.

Around 0800 Mitch heard some commotion from the other side of the hill. It appeared that the patrol had chosen to go west. Around 0830 he heard voices up in the clearing. Some were certainly Vietnamese, and at least one was American. Mitch tried, but he couldn't quite make out what was being said. Around 0900 the voices faded away, and it was as if nothing had ever happened. When 1100 hours finally rolled around, Mitch had been in his hole for nearly eight hours. It was now so hot that even the bugs stopped flying.

Around noon Mitch finally gave in and reached for his canteen. He had been told at Pendleton "if you don't want to lie in your own piss, don't drink." But after eight hours of melting, it was time to take a drink. Even field rations and hot canteen water tasted good if a person was hungry and thirsty enough.

Around 1500 hours Mitch heard some rustling in the grass. Coarse, muffled whispers of the base's patrol followed almost immediately. The men had grown tired of the usual rules of patrol silence and were just walking carelessly toward home. They were hot, tired, and dirty, but they were obviously otherwise intact. The entire squad meandered past Mitch's depression and never realized he was there.

The last man to pass Mitch was Sergeant Davis. He looked just like all the rest of his men except he was carrying an extra medic's pack laced under his normal field pack. He was the only professional-acting soldier in the whole patrol, and he passed so quietly that Mitch almost missed him completely.

But that was all. The rest of the afternoon and evening were quiet, and only the return of the whining mosquitoes broke the silence.

In the early hours of December 20, at the prearranged time, Mitch slowly came out of hiding. To his right he heard the chirp of a tree frog that was just a little different from all the other jungle sounds. He replied with the same sound, and suddenly there was Tooks, floating like a shadow out of the darkness. They exchanged reports, and Mitch related the three episodes that had broken the day's silence.

"Did you see Davis when he came by this afternoon?" Tooks asked.

"Yeah. He was the last man."

Tooks frowned back. "Doesn't it seem a little weird that a sergeant would be bringing up the rear on any patrol?"

"Yeah, I guess so," Mitch answered. "I would have thought any noncom worth his salt would be more in the middle of his men. That way he could better co-ordinate both the front and rear." Mitch shrugged. "I guess I've heard of sergeants sometimes taking the point, but never the drag… at least not in this kind of heat."

Tooks nodded. It seemed like he was agreeing with Mitch. "Did you see Davis's pack?" he asked.

Mitch nodded. "Yeah. Was there anything special about it?"

"You tell me."

"I think everything looked pretty much normal." Mitch paused. He felt Tooks's gaze. "Well, I guess he did have an extra medic's pack laced on, but that's all that was different."

"What would you say if I told you that back there in that little clearing was a neat pile of perfectly good U. S. Marine Corps bandages and assorted medical supplies that belong in that pack?"

Mitch looked up the hill. "The pack looked full enough when he walked past me."

"Yeah, it was. It was full of heroin."

Tooks was silent for a long second while Mitch processed what he'd just said.

"Yeah, that's what I said. Our Sergeant Davis is a goddamn mule. He's carrying out the best China white this country has to offer, five kilos worth at a time. I even got his picture stuffing the junk into his pack after he finished talking to some locals."

Mitch turned back to Tooks. The hard realization of what he had just heard had started to sink in. "That's why this place is so friggin' quiet? It's a drug exchange point for the local underworld?"

"Yep. And you can bet they even have Charlie paid off. Nothing interferes with the flow of the junk!"

"Do you think the major is part of the deal?" Mitch asked.

"What do you think?"

"Damn!" Mitch whispered, "If you're right, how are they getting the stuff off the base? I don't think there are that many users there."

"Oh, I think the local grunts are innocent enough," Tooks said. "But the major is as dirty as sin! He's probably worked something out with the daily supply choppers. It would be easy to get a package the size of a medic's day pack out to DaNang, and from there, anything's possible."

"You got the exchange on film? I didn't even know you had a camera."

Tooks smiled dryly. "I still have a few tricks up my sleeve, Riceman. So be respectful. Here, take this film. I have another roll just like it." He looked straight at Mitch. "I don't have to tell you what would happen to us if the wrong people at Delta Company found out about these pictures, do I?"

"No, gunny, you don't. If anyone there knew about this, we'd both be in a world of hurt!"

"That about says it," Tooks agreed.

"So what's our next move?" Mitch asked.

"Under the circumstances, I think we'll go in early this morning, probably right about daybreak. I'd like to get a picture of Davis loading the junk onto the chopper. Then we'll bid our farewells and get back home to the skipper. I think some trucks are due this afternoon. Once we're back home, we'll give these pictures to the skipper. Then this miserable place is his problem. Mission accomplished!"

"Sounds good to me," Mitch muttered. "I just wanna go home."

It was a good plan, but once they got back to Delta Company, the word quickly came down from Major Farcas that there was no room on any outgoing truck or chopper for them. Mitch thought that was weird. First the man didn't want them on the base, and now he was trying to keep them there. Tooks told Mitch the guy was just an arrogant bastard who was jerking them around. Tooks said not to worry. Their scheduled pickup was now December 23, and there was no way "the son of a bitch has a clue that we know what's going on!"

Tooks and Mitch took advantage of the extra time to rig Mitch's spotting scope as a telephoto lens for Tooks's camera. When the right helicopter from DaNang came, on December 22, they quickly filled two more rolls of incriminating film, leaving no doubt about the major's involvement. That left just one more night shift in the tower before the two could go home.

"I'll take the first shift, Mitch," Tooks said. "You can bring your tired ass up the tower at 0200 to relieve me. Tomorrow we're out of here!"

"Great! The graveyard shift again!"

"Yeah, Riceman. It's the shits when you don't have rank, isn't it?"

"Oh well. Anything to get out of this place," Mitch surrendered.

That night Mitch slept with his boots on. He also slept with his M14. He had mounted his night scope on it for reassurance, but even that didn't help him sleep. Mitch didn't like the way the assignment had worked out. Somehow having his first trip into the bush turn into a surveillance job on his own troops just rubbed him the wrong way. Besides, every time he began to slip very far into sleep, he saw the surprised look of the Vietnamese girl just as she died. The portrait of the headless girl was too much. It jarred him awake every time he nodded off.

The moonless night had been very quiet. Around midnight Tooks was in the tower with two other marines. He watched the more accessible north and west perimeters. The two marines watched the other sides.

"Gunny, I'll never understand how you snipers can stay awake for so damn long! This night duty sucks!" muttered the private who was watching the southern portion of the base.

"Oh, it's not that bad," Tooks answered. "Think of it this way. Most sergeants like to sleep so they're hardly ever up in the middle of the night. They're never around to bother you. The night shift has a lot fewer hassles than the day shift."

"Yeah, I guess you're right about that part," The private seemed to cut himself short.

"What's up, marine?" Tooks asked.

"Shit! I think someone's out there on the wire!"

"Here! Give me that scope!" Tooks demanded.

Tooks peered through the powerful night scope. Sure enough, there was a black pajama clad figure stealing over the wire.

"Damn it! That's a sapper! And he's going *back* over the wire! That means he's already deposited his goodies somewhere here on the inside! We're about to get our asses pounded! Here, take the scope and check the other perimeters while I call the command bunker!"

Tooks reached for the phone that connected him with the command bunker. He also had a field radio that could reach DaNang as well as AnHoa or any fly boys in the area. His first thought, however, was for the base and that was why he reached for the phone.

"What the fuck? We have what inside the wire?" yelled the suddenly frightened lieutenant who was in charge in the bunker.

"That's right, sir. I think you should get your gun crews ready pronto! We're seeing Charlie in large numbers just back behind the edge of the bush. They are getting ready for…"

The blast ruptured the darkness with a vicious fire. A large satchel charge had been placed at the base of the observation tower by the outgoing sapper Tooks and the two marines had just seen. Its blast took out the tower's legs and turned the observation shack into scrap wood. The two marine privates with Tooks were dead before they even started to fall, and Tooks was stunned so badly that he didn't feel a thing when he smashed into the flaming rubble on the hard-packed ground below.

The blast jerked Mitch awake. It reverberated in his head as screams and fires erupted everywhere at once. He hit the deck in high gear and tore around a sand bag barrier. Just in front of him he saw a black figure scurrying towards one of the M60 machine guns. It was another sapper, and he had another large satchel explosive. The flames from the tower were bright enough that Mitch didn't need his night scope. He threw his rifle to his shoulder and snap-shot a round into the back of the attacking figure. It was an easy shot.

"Goddamn it, Tooks! Where are you?" Mitch screamed, but he couldn't even hear himself.

All of the M60s all along the perimeters opened up. Red tracer tracks shot across the night in answer to the attacking NVA's green tracers. Several more large explosions shook the ground. Mitch wasn't sure if the command bunker and the ammo dump were hit or not. Fire, explosions, and screams--everything that made up death's chaos--were everywhere.

Mitch had just rounded another corner when he stumbled on some debris and fell. Just as he hit the deck, a flash of green tracers tore over his head and slammed into the sandbags behind him. His name had been written all over those bullets. Only his fall saved him.

Mitch stayed down and crawled away from the incoming shells. He found some cover in a depression and flipped on his night scope. The North Vietnamese attackers were streaming through the southern wire. Mitch could see the NVA easily, but the nearby explosions and his own panic threw his crosshairs all over the place. It took several moments, but he finally calmed down enough to return fire.

It took a few shots, but Mitch's training finally kicked in. The rifle stopped shaking and once again became an extension of his arms. And with that, the North Vietnamese attackers started dying, their death screams adding to the cacophony of the man-made hell.

The sudden NVA attack was fierce, but the coordination it needed for success wasn't there. The first sapper that had taken out the tower had done his work too fast. The man must have had second thoughts about the suicide portion of his mission and had taken off for a return over the southern wire instead of staying with his charge. Those few extra moments had been enough for Tooks to blow the alarm horn and wake everyone up. As a result, the base's marines were able to catch most of the other sappers still carrying their explosives.

But even so, some of the suicide bombers did successfully get through the desperate marine fire, and their blasts did dire damage. The command bunker was hit, killing the men inside and destroying the base's primary radio. Two of the machine gun emplacements were also silenced. But it wasn't enough. The charges meant for the ammo dump never got there. Mitch's furious rifle fire stopped them cold. That bought the gun crews enough time to bring their cannons to bear on the perimeters, and they filled the air with their murderous "beehives." The steel- flechet-filled cannon shells buzz-sawed through brush, trees, and flesh. Nothing above ground escaped.

As the attack stalled, Mitch got up and ran toward the remains of the tower. He had taken only a few steps when a thunderous blast flattened him. The NVA were replying to the base's cannons with heavy rockets. The near miss leveled the dugout where Mitch had been sleeping and knocked him silly. His nose was bloodied, and his senses reeled.

It seemed like forever, but in less than two minutes Mitch was back on his feet. More rockets came in as red and green tracers continued to lace together, weaving a deadly web of fire. And all the while flares continually popped open above the base, and cannon blasts flashed like monstrous strobe lights. The whole scene was surreal and deadly.

Mitch, still partially shell-shocked, could barely stand in the onslaught, but he did. It took all he had, but he made it to the burning remains of the tower.

"Tooks!" he cursed. "Goddamn it, gunny! Where are you?"

Mitch threw burning lumber and ruptured sandbags aside as he choked back sick vomit. He had to find Tooks. Jerking burning lumber away, he suddenly felt another hand under the wreckage. "I got you, gunny! It's Rice!" He pulled with all his might and instantly stumbled backwards. The hand hadn't been attached to a body. Falling, he saw that it had belonged to one of the privates who had been in the tower. Groveling on his knees, he couldn't hold the vomit back any longer.

"Damn it, Riceman! I'm over here!"

Mitch turned and saw the broken form of Dave Tooks crumpled at the base of a sandbag barrier that had been part of the tower's base. Mitch wiped his face and scrambled to him.

"Don't move me, Riceman! I'm all fucked up!"

Mitch gently checked his partner out. Tooks lay at an odd angle with his legs all askew. Blood stained his shirt just above the belt line. "Oh hell!" Mitch gasped as he saw that Tooks's left foot was gone and that the remaining stump was pumping his blood into the hard ground.

"Yeah, it is hell, isn't it?" Tooks whispered, struggling to take a long breath. "My back's busted. I can't feel anything from the chest down."

"Damn it, gunny! Hold still while I get a tourniquet on your leg! I think I see your boot over there!"

"Riceman! Get a grip!" Tooks gasped as Mitch tied off his bleeding leg. "Look, we both know I've had it! Charlie has this place nailed! I saw a bunch of them coming in over the wire on the south side just before the tower came down!" Tooks could barely breathe. "Are all the machine guns operational?"

"The one closest to us is firing. I got a sapper just before he took it out. I don't know about the other positions."

Tooks's eyes began to clear. Mitch had injected him with morphine right after he'd applied the tourniquet, and the drug had begun to take hold.

"Is that the field radio over there?" Tooks asked.

Mitch pulled some debris aside and found the radio. It was still working. He pulled it to Tooks's side.

"Where's my rifle?"

"I don't know, gunny." Mitch nestled the radio in place. He didn't see the bolt gun anywhere.

Tooks reached for his. 45. The pistol, its holster, and his entire web belt were gone, blown away by the blast.

"Here. Take mine," Mitch said.

Mitch handed Tooks his own. 45. Tooks tried to refuse it, but Mitch clamped it into his chilled hand.

"Okay, Riceman, we'll do it your way. I got it," Tooks said, squeezing the pistol. "But right now you have to get your M14 heated up and cover the southern perimeter. I'm going to call in some fire support. I think 'Puff the Magic Dragon' is in the area. I heard him jerkin' off on the air a little while ago. I'll get him to concentrate his fire on the south. If the big guns stay up, they should make it hot for Charlie on the other three sides. We might make it yet."

A violent cough cut short Tooks's voice. Bloody froth ran from the corner of his mouth.

"Riceman, I'll get Puff, but you'll have to hold the south until he shows up. So get to work, sniper! Earn your pay!"

Mitch reached for Tooks's hand, but all he felt was the. 45.

"Get the fuck out of here, marine! I'm not dead yet! Give me that radio!"

Mitch handed Tooks the handset. As he did so, Tooks coughed again, but this time there was no froth. It was all blood.

"Mitch," Tooks gasped with a different voice. It was as though he was suddenly very tired and a long, long ways away. "I'm all fuckin' used up. You're the whole team now. You have to shoot for both of us."

The blood was really bright red now. "Cover for me, Riceman. I can't go any more."

Something snapped inside Mitch. A great wave of anger rose up from somewhere inside. It was a hot, raging fire that burned red, and it seared away all the fear and confusion that had just filled his eyes. And as the fire burned, Mitch's mind became clear. He *would* make Charlie pay. So long as he returned fire, he and Tooks were still a team. Mitch whispered a silent, bitter oath. It was the time for killing.

"I'll do the shooting, gunny, but you hold on! I'll be back for you!"

Tooks waved Mitch to go on. Time was short for both of them.

Mitch crouched down and ran hard for the southern machine guns. As he ran green and red tracers laced intricate patterns of instant death all around him. He should have dived for cover, but he didn't. The overhead flares were burning out, and the roar of the 155's firing point- blank said plainly that there was no more time. So Mitch kept running.

The M60 position thirty yards to the west of Mitch's desperate dash ripped a continuous spray of red fire in answer to the green wave of VC tracers that threatened to engulf it. Mitch bypassed that position. His objective was the silent gun placement further south. The NVA were coming in waves from the south so that's where Mitch went.

Scant seconds later Mitch threw himself into the dead machine gun nest. The gun seemed intact, but every man there was dead, riddled by the shrapnel of either a well-aimed rocket or mortar fire. Ignoring the silent M60, Mitch knelt down behind the emplacement's sandbags, flipped on his night scope, and then looked up over the top.

He saw four running figures carrying AK47s about seventy-five yards away. Two seconds later all four were dead. Mitch shifted his focus fifty yards farther out. He saw more figures on the wire than he could count. The M14 barked, and two more figures went down, the one bullet blowing simultaneously through both men's chests.

Mitch shifted slightly and fired fifteen more times. Fifteen more North Vietnamese died where they stood in the wire. The attackers hesitated, confused and crushed by Mitch's invisible wall of lead.

As they hesitated, Mitch slammed in a second clip, moved twenty feet east to a blast crater, and killed seven more attackers. The red fire in his eyes glowed so bright that he didn't even need the night scope.

He and Dave Tooks were still a team, and together they were holding the southern wire.

The NVA captain whose company Mitch was decimating was desperate. The first part of the night had been perfect. The foolish Americans had not heard his men climbing the southern cliff, and all of the rest of the attacking forces had been in place on the other perimeters on schedule. But after that, everything had gone wrong.

The southern company was supposed to be the actual cutting edge that would gut the Americans, but the blasts from his suicide bombers had been wrong and had not taken out enough of the base's firepower. The companies on the other three sides were doing the best they could, but the Americans' damnable cannons were cutting them to shreds. The attack was stalling badly everywhere.

The NVA captain cursed feverishly. His orders had been very specific. His men had to take the south side of the base and take out the American's ammo dump. Consequently, he ordered all of his reserves to hit the wire.

Mitch had just emptied another clip. His M14 was boiling hot from the continuous rapid fire, and his night scope was badly blurred with after images from the tracers that continued to buzz everywhere. But in Mitch's mind, everything was clear. He and Tooks were still a team, and he was living out his credo. He killed with every shot. He was death itself.

By now Mitch had sent eighty NVA to their graves. He had shifted his ground four times — one clip of twenty rounds and twenty deaths for each position. His last move was just ahead of two rocket-propelled grenades that deepened the crater he had just left. Flipping his scope on again, he saw two NVA just sixty yards away. They were hunkered down behind the remains of the southern M60 position where Mitch's killing rage had begun. They were readying two more of the grenades for launching.

"Damn you!" Mitch muttered as he found the two in his scope. "Goddamn you!"

The first shot entered the NVA sergeant's forehead. The corporal with him turned when he felt his comrade fall away. The last thing the corporal saw was his friend's brains oozing out the back of his head.

To his left, Mitch heard marine voices. It was the eastern M60 crew. They were in trouble. "Medic! Dear Jesus! I'm hit! Medic!" Their gun had just jammed, and one or two of the three-man crew were hit. Mitch saw seven NVA just thirty yards from them. The black-clad attackers were beginning their death run on the gun.

Something suddenly slammed Mitch down, knocking his helmet off. For a moment, he couldn't see anything. Reaching upwards he felt the sudden spurt of blood that blinded him. A tracer had grazed him, searing his skin as it tore a furrow across his forehead. He wiped the blood clear and saw a NVA coming up to the edge of the eastern M60 gun emplacement.

Mitch's M14 went off almost by itself, and the NVA fell onto one of the wounded, screaming marines. The hand grenade the NVA had been holding fell outside of the emplacement and exploded, killing the six other attackers.

Mitch tried to fire again, but he couldn't. Suddenly all he could do was tumble backwards. The green tracers were coming again and were pulverizing the sandbags where he had been resting his rifle. The ruptured sandbags spurted their contents outward like a sandblaster, scorching and ripping Mitch's already bloodied face.

All of this happened because the flames caused by the attack had found new wooden structures and had finally risen high enough to light up the whole base. Mitch's last move had been silhouetted. From his position beyond the wire, the NVA captain had realized a sniper was killing his command, but he couldn't locate the killer. The fresh flames had answered his prayers. Where there had been darkness and shadow, there was now vivid light. Mitch suddenly became an easy target, and the captain's heavy machine gun had finally found him. Its green fire incinerated the sandbags where Mitch was making his stand.

With the sudden relief from Mitch's killing fire, the captain again ordered the remainder of his force to hit the wire. Reports from the other perimeters were beyond desperate. His men had to penetrate the wire and take out the American guns. The battle was in the balance.

Suddenly overhead there came a strange droning sound, almost the roaring of an ancient dragon. The attackers at the wire hesitated, and that hesitance was fatal.

The droning sound was "Puff," the C-47 gunship Tooks had sought. It was a modified cargo plane that carried six electric Gattling guns and a whole cargo compartment full of ammo. The plane found the rest of the southern attacking NVA exposed, easy prey for its fire breathing weapons. It turned on its side and incinerated every square inch of the southern wire.

The NVA captain looked on in horror as the rest of his attacking force died, ripped and dismembered by the flying dragon ship. With carnage and failure before him, he screamed at his heavy machine gun crew to turn their gun skyward. The three-man crew threw the muzzle skyward. But before they could touch the trigger, they all died their own instant deaths, each one's forehead ripped wide open. The sniper was not dead after all.

The NVA captain threw down his field glasses and manned the heavy gun himself. Cursing the sniper from the depths of his soul, he raked Mitch's sandbags mercilessly.

Mitch, however, wasn't where the captain had seen him a few minutes before. Using Puff's attack as cover, Mitch had shifted farther to the east. His eyelids were so swollen he could hardly see, but he could still make out the muzzle flash of the North Vietnamese machine gun. His next shots weren't his best ones, but they were good enough. His rounds shattered the NVA commander's left arm and ate up the mechanism of his weapon, squelching its green fire forever.

"Puff," unaware of its near-target status, continued to belch its fiery breath all over the wire surrounding the base. When it finished, there were no attackers left. The few stragglers that remained gathered the few wounded that could walk and slipped back into the darkness. Two men, one alive and one nearly dead, and one ancient, mythical, fire-breathing monster had destroyed them all.

As the gunship made its departure, Mitch worked his way back to wreckage of the tower. There was still a little sporadic fire so he had to be careful. First he went to the eastern M60 site.

"Hey, marines! You guys on the M60! Are you operational or not?" Mitch yelled from about thirty yards away.

"Who the hell wants to know?" screamed back the terrified gunner.

"Mitch Rice! Keep your eyes open! I think Charlie's had it, but there might be stragglers! I'm going back to the tower!"

"Shit! I think it's one of those snipers we had in camp," yelled one of the grunts to his gun mate.

"Hey, sniper! The tower's FUBARed! There's nothing there!"

Mitch's rage was not yet expended. "Look, you worthless mothers!" he cursed. "Just tell me if you're operational or not! I don't have time for this shit!"

The gunner looked at his loader. "Hell, maybe that's one of the new sergeants."

"Yeah, you're right," the other said. "Hey, sarge! We had a major jam! But we're up and running now! What's happened to the guys on the other M60?"

Mitch's fury spoke for itself. "Stay awake! You lard asses nearly got yourselves greased! Watch the wire, and I'll send you more ammo!"

"Thanks, sarge!"

Mitch worked his way back to the southern gun that had been taken out early in the fray. Along the way, he picked up some dazed marines. When they got to the dead gun, they kicked away the two dead NVA. One of the young marines stared at their corpses.

"Someone really nailed these motherfuckers! Look, their heads are blown off!"

Mitch ignored him. "Check out that gun and set up your position!"

"Damn, I think this thing still works," replied one of the more experienced marines.

"Show me a short burst!" Mitch demanded.

A staccato burst of fire flew south. The gun was operational.

"Good! Now hold here!" Mitch ordered. "I'll get you more ammo!"

The ragtag crew nodded. "We'll hold it, sniper, but send help fast!"

Mitch nodded and left. He was now at last free to find Tooks. His course took him back past the blown out dugout that the two had called home. Mitch went as fast as he could, but he was pretty beaten up. His helmet was missing, and his face was bleeding from several puncture marks where the sand had scorched him. His forehead still oozed where the heavy tracer had grazed him. His jungle suit was torn in several places. Blood and sweat-soaked dirt covered him completely. He both looked and smelled like death itself.

But Mitch wasn't dead. His body was torn and battered, but his eyes still burned. They were sunken back into his head, burning with a horrible, cold fire. He had given himself over to the fight and had become death itself. His mind had functioned as it was trained to, but his soul had become a furnace. And that was where he now burned, embroiled in his own hell. Only finding Dave Tooks alive would lessen the searing pain.

"Gunny, where the hell are you?" Mitch yelled as he threw the tower's broken debris aside. He searched the wreckage of the tower for several minutes, but Tooks was not where Mitch had left him.

From the side of Mitch's field of vision there suddenly was a blur of motion. It was the butt of an AK47, and it caught Mitch squarely on the back of his head. The last living attacker, a man who had been knocked out by the same blast that had destroyed the tower and started the attack, had regained consciousness. The man knew his cause was lost, but his resolve was sound. He would kill at least one more American before he was finished.

The blow from his rifle butt took Mitch completely down. The NVA decided not to waste his ammo so he came up to Mitch with his bayonet poised. He drew his rifle back for the killing thrust, but suddenly a very bright light blinded him. The man stumbled back and fell into total darkness, a. 45 caliber hole visible just above the bridge of his nose.

Dave Tooks was under the wreckage that Mitch had just cleared away. One of the heavy NVA rockets had buried him there and had taken out the field radio. Tooks had tried to pull himself out, but without the use of the lower half of his body, his efforts had been useless. Mitch had just uncovered him when the NVA had dealt his blow. Tooks was barely alive, but he still held Mitch's. 45 in his ice-cold hand. And that was enough to save Mitch's life.

Mitch fell just besides his partner. Tooks reached out and touched him. Mitch was breathing, but he was out cold.

"You poor, dumb bastard! You're goin' to have a horrible headache when you wake up!" Tooks whispered.

Struggling, Tooks reached out to his bolt gun which he had found in the rubble. He pulled the magazine floorplate outward and stuffed his Zippo lighter into the empty magazine well. Next he pulled Mitch's M14 to him. Pulling the butt plate open, he discarded the oiler and cleaning patches. In their place in the storage cavities, he slipped two small round film canisters. Finally, he shoved both rifles over towards Mitch, first the M14 and then the bolt gun.

"Well, Riceman, I guess you're getting a bolt gun sooner than any of us planned. Semper fi, marine."

And with that Dave Tooks's battle was over. Breathing a long sigh, his battered soul took wing.

Chapter Two

The morning of December 23 was already far advanced. The Huey from AnHoa was inbound to pick up Mitch and Tooks. Ostensibly, the helicopter was supposed to be the daily mail chopper from DaNang, but a switch had been made. The substitute chopper was supposed to have been both Mitch and Dave Tooks's ticket to Hue. There they would have been debriefed by a SOG colonel, Colonel Wilson Gabriel Strong. Mitch's skipper at AnHoa had been on the horn early that morning to Colonel Strong telling him of Delta Company's brush with near extinction. It would have been understandable if Strong had called the pick-up chopper off, but he was a man of his word. Consequently, the decision to extract Mitch and Tooks was upheld.

The Huey carefully picked its way down into the firebase. The place was horribly torn up. Nearly all of its structures were either blown away or were still burning, including the command bunker and the aid station. Only the 155mm gun emplacements, the ammo dump, and the machine guns were intact. Every marine who could stand was either manning one of the guns or trying to clean up the mess. Unfortunately, a lot of men weren't able to stand. Rows of full body bags lined up outside the temporary aid station spoke volumes of the price that had been paid for the base's survival.

Once the helicopter landed, no one really questioned its purpose. It was just assumed it had come to med evac out a load of wounded.

And that was what it would do, but only after Mitch and Tooks were found.

The two snipers were not at the landing pad like they were supposed to be so the flight engineer was elected to go find them. He assumed the worst and went right to a tent surrounded by the body bags. There he found not just the dead, but also the wounded. They were all awaiting the choppers that would take them to the field hospitals at AnHoa or DaNang. The flight engineer looked around and saw one of the wounded men whose face was all bandaged up. The man cradled a sniper's bolt gun in his arms almost like it was a baby.

"Are you Tooks or Rice?"

"I'm Rice. Who's asking?" Mitch growled, trying to push the bandages back so he could see better. His head pounded, and his face was on fire.

"Be nice, sniper. I'm your ride out of here. Where's Tooks?"

Mitch looked up with empty eyes. "Tooks is over there." Mitch was pointing to a body bag. "He didn't make it."

"Damn!" the engineer swore. "Marine, I'm sorry."

Mitch stared out through his bandages. His eyes came into focus. "If you're taking me, then you're taking Tooks too! We're still a squad until the skipper says we're not! I won't leave him behind!"

Mitch added emphasis to his demand by trying hard to get to his feet, but the effort was too much. The whole aid station started spinning to his right, and he fell back to his knees. Vomiting followed as the merciless vertigo took over his entire being.

"Okay, marine, okay. I get the message," the flight engineer said. "Take it easy. I'll get you both home." The man stepped around the mess and steadied Mitch's shoulders. "Are you sure the medics have cleared you for evac?"

"Like hell we have!" answered one of the medics who was coming to mop up. "This idiot had his brain scrambled with the good end of a VC's rifle! For all I know, he has a subdural hematoma under that armor plated thing he calls a skull!"

Mitch vomited again.

"Look, fly boy," the medic said. "Why don't you load up Tooks and come back for this guy. His name is Rice. All of Tooks's personal effects are with him in the bag except for his bolt gun. The kid won't turn loose of it. Come back in a few minutes, and I'll try to have him in a uniform that doesn't smell like puke." The medic took the engineer's place at Mitch's side. "We've already changed him twice. I really don't want him here the way he's acting. The surgeons at DaNang need to check out his head."

The flight engineer nodded and grabbed one of the marines who was milling around the aid station. Together they gathered up Tooks's remains and headed for the Huey. Once there, and after the marine had left, the engineer zipped open the body bag. Dave Tooks's body was pretty torn up. The tourniquet Mitch had applied was still on Tooks's lifeless stump. It was clear Dave Tooks had not gone out easy.

The engineer, helped by the rest of the helicopter crew, continued to search Tooks. Before takeoff they had been briefed by Colonel Strong himself. Somewhere on Tooks's body or in his gear there had to be some film, and the colonel needed it. So they looked everywhere, but they found no film. They couldn't even find Dave's engraved Zippo lighter.

"This looks bad," the flight engineer said to the pilot. "How much was Tooks's lighter worth to Charlie?"

"I don't know. Last I heard, maybe $2000."

"Well, whoever got the film got that lighter too. The bastard!"

"This sucks!" said the pilot. "Maybe the other sniper'll be able to fill in some of the blanks." He was zipping up Tooks's body bag. "This guy was too good to go out this way! This place is the shits!"

"Amen to that, good buddy," the flight engineer agreed. "I'm going back for the youngster. As soon as we're back, I want to get out of this fuckin' place! Something around here is very unhealthy! I would rather watch Strong piss napalm than get grounded here!"

Mitch walked to the chopper under his own power. He carried both his M14 and Dave's bolt gun. The long rifle was the baton Dave had passed him, and he wouldn't give it up.

The Huey lifted off as soon as everyone was belted in. No one said much to Mitch. Colonel Strong would do the questioning back in Hue.

"That sniper looks like shit," the pilot said into his mike as they flew south. "What'd he do last night? Kiss a sand blaster?"

"Yeah, and then some," the flight engineer said. "The guys around the aid station said there were two companies of dead VC on the south wire. A lot of them were all torn up by 'Puff', but a whole bunch were one-shot kills."

"Sniper work?"

"That's what the medic in the aid station said. That Rice kid back there worked over more than a hundred bad guys last night."

"No shit?"

"No shit!" the engineer said. "And I saw the size of the dent in his head where Charlie planted his rifle butt. That kid must have a squash like cement to take a lick like that and still keep tickin'."

"You mean he planted the VC who did that to his head?"

"That's what the medics said. The kid greased the little SOB with a. 45."

"Shit! Remind me not to get into a head-butting contest with him when this is all over. I guess those guys are called "jarheads" for a reason."

"Yea, verily. So be respectful. This kid played some serious hardball last night. We'll see what Colonel Strong can do with him when we get home."

Mitch, who sat in the back of the Huey, pulled the bandages back so he could see more. He thought he had heard the two up front say something about Hue when they were lifting off. He guessed that's where they were going. Mitch knew the guys flying the bird weren't normal med evac personnel. Whatever Dave Tooks had gotten him into had something to do with whoever or whatever was waiting for him in Hue.

Mitch shifted on his flak jacket. (He had already learned that in a helicopter you didn't wear your flak jacket. You sat on it. You did, that is, if you ever wanted to have children.) He moved a little closer to Tooks' s body. Mitch had his M14 slung on his back, but he held the Remington bolt gun in his arms. As long as he had it, Dave Tooks was still alive.

The Huey settled down toward a small compound outside of the old provincial capital of Hue. The little compound was located just south of the Perfume River, across the bridge that was on the outskirts of the city. Mitch tried to remember all he could from tactical maps he had studied at AnHoa. He thought someone had said a lot of Europeans lived in Hue City, left over from the time of French rule. That was about all he could remember.

"Come on, marine. I'll take you to our beloved leader. He wants to talk to you," the flight engineer said, leading Mitch away from the chopper pad. "I guess I'm your tour guide for this gig."

Mitch nodded, but didn't follow.

"Don't worry, Rice. We'll take good care of Tooks. We know who he was, and what he did. We take care of our own around here just like you marines do."

Mitch clenched his jaw and fell in beside the engineer. He still had both rifles, and the look in his eyes made it clear that no one should ask him for either one. The team was still a team.

The base around Mitch was actually little more than a constabulary compound. It sat just off the road that led into Hue. It was close to the ruins of an old fort that had once guarded the city from river-borne invaders. The flight engineer said he didn't know how old the fort was, but he guessed four or five hundred years. The compound was surrounded by a simple run of concertina wire and was manned by ROKs (Republic of Korea armed forces). The ROK's had a reputation for being really bad actors, and no one, including Charlie, wanted to mess with them. Just visible, way down the road, was a large, cathedral-looking church.

"What's that down there?" Mitch asked.

"That's a Catholic church, Rice. The French were here for a long time before we came. Hue is their old capital, and that place is one of the fancy churches they built after World War II. I don't know the name of the place, but the locals call it "Phu Cham." What the hell that means I haven't a clue, but later you might have a chance to ask the colonel. He goes over there sometimes."

Moments later, Mitch was ushered into the presence of Colonel Wilson Gabriel Strong. Strong was Army, and Mitch wasn't sure how an Army officer ended up with the command of a Marine sniper. The two branches of the service didn't fraternize that much. Mitch guessed that military intelligence must transcend service connections.

Still carrying Tooks's bolt gun, Mitch entered the bunker where Colonel Strong had his office. It took a couple of seconds for Mitch's eyes to adjust to the bunker's darker interior, but only a scant instant to snap to attention when he caught clear sight of the colonel's imposing six foot three, lumberjack-like figure. Mitch felt the colonel's burning, blue eyes scrutinize every inch of him even as his crisp baritone intoned, "At ease, marine." Mitch knew he was under inspection.

"Private, what do you have for me?" Strong asked simply.

Mitch understood that the colonel wanted an answer for the mystery of Delta Company. That was why Mitch and Tooks were there in the first place. Mitch knew what he was supposed to do, but he couldn't do it. He was completely numb. With the previous night's battle still ringing in his ears, he could barely speak let alone remember where the film canisters were.

"I'm sorry, sir. I had the film you want in my jungle suit," Mitch croaked, "but the medics cut it off me after they found me. I don't know where it is now." Mitch insides were turning upside down. He realized he had just completely failed Dave Tooks.

Colonel Strong sighed. The man looked to be in pain. Mitch saw him shake his head and then simply commanded, "My sergeant will take your rifle, private. I don't think you'll be needing it in here."

"Yes, sir." Mitch answered.

A South Korean sergeant appeared out of nowhere and held out his hands to take the Remington. Mitch brought the rifle up, but he was grasping it so tightly that his knuckles turned white. He just couldn't give Tooks's bolt gun away.

"Don't worry, private. I know this was Tooks's rifle and that you're responsible for it until you return to AnHoa," the colonel said gently. "Tooks worked for me before. I know how attached you snipers get to your weapons. The sergeant is a very accomplished armorer. He'll take good care of the rifle."

Mitch still held onto the bolt gun. His eyes had a vicious wildness, something that was almost a red fire, in them. The ROK sergeant stepped back.

"Here, son, give me the rifle," Colonel Strong said, coming right up to Mitch. "Your buddy was my friend too, but he's gone. Let him go. You can't carry him any longer."

Mitch looked at the colonel with eyes that were suddenly desperate and starting to tear. "Yes, sir," he whispered.

Mitch brought the bolt gun around to inspection position and automatically ran his right index finger into the chamber to make certain that there wasn't a hidden round stuck there. In doing so, his middle finger pushed against the magazine follower. There was resistance.

"What is it, private?" the colonel asked. "Is your weapon clear?"

"With the colonel's permission, I need to check the magazine. Something's in it," Mitch croaked again, his voice barely intelligible.

This was bad, Mitch knew. Marines always knew what was going on with their weapons, and this time Mitch obviously didn't. Sure, it was *Tooks's* bolt gun, but Mitch should have known what was in the magazine. This was really bad.

"That's okay, private. Go ahead and clear the weapon. I don't want anyone getting excited over an accidental discharge."

Mitch popped the floor plate of the magazine and out fell Dave Tooks's Zippo lighter.

"What's that, Rice?"

Mitch held the silver lighter carefully. "Sir, this is the trophy lighter the gunny won at the last sniper competition at DaNang."

The colonel came right up to Mitch. "Let me see that, marine."

Mitch slowly handed off the lighter, but he instinctively brought the bolt gun closer.

"That's a bit of an unusual place for the gunny to keep his lighter, isn't it, private?"

"Yes, sir. It is." Mitch didn't know what else to say.

Strong turned to the Korean sergeant. "Sergeant, bring in all of Sergeant Tooks's personal effects… and let the private keep the rifle."

Mitch relaxed a little, but he still held the Remington in a death grip. Mitch was trying to hold on, but it wasn't working. Tooks was slipping away, and from somewhere deep inside, Mitch felt an awful wave of nausea coming up.

Strong turned away from Mitch and went back to his metal desk. "Bring the rifle over here, Rice, and sit down." Strong had seen how blanched Mitch's face was and now saw the sweat dripping through his bandages. "Here, have a drink."

Mitch sat down and took the offered glass of water. It tasted good. Somehow its coolness both relaxed his hands and lessened the nausea.

An awkward silence followed, but finally the colonel spoke. "Tell me about last night, private."

Mitch didn't know exactly where to begin. His face and head throbbed severely, but he tried. He began with the blast that brought down the tower since that was when his role in the previous night had started. Some twenty minutes later he had related the essentials of the preceding evening's conflict.

Strong looked at the sandblasted face of the nineteen-year-old. It was obvious that the young man had distinguished himself in defending the firebase and that he was considerably the worse for it. It was also obvious Dave Tooks had been out of the conflict from the very beginning. Yes, Tooks probably saved the private's life in the end, but the whole battle had been Rice's. The explanation for the placement of lighter was still not evident.

"What do you make of all of this, private? Why hide the lighter in the Remington's magazine?"

"Sir, I'm not exactly sure. I do know the gunny wanted you to see the pictures we took of the heroin exchanges and…"

Strong jerked straight up. "What did you say?"

"Excuse me, sir. I'm sorry. I guess I really got my head scrambled. Two days ago, Sergeant Tooks and I shadowed one of Delta Company's patrols in the bush. The gunny said he got pictures of a Sergeant Davis dumping out the contents of a medic's pack and filling it with what looked like heroin from a cache there on the hill. Yesterday morning, we used my spotting scope as a telephoto lens to get pictures of that pack being loaded into a chopper that was outbound to DaNang. I'm sure Sergeant Tooks wanted you to get those pictures. I don't know why he hid his lighter in his rifle instead of the film."

Colonel Strong settled back into his seat.

Mitch went on. "Sir, I didn't see the gunny's bolt gun when I first found him in the wreckage. I guess he found it after I got hashed by Charlie. I just remember waking up at the gunny's side. He still had it in his right hand, but it looked like he had tried to push it over to me. My. 45 and my M14 were there too. I collected all of the weapons before I would let the Delta Company guys move us to the aid station. I guess the gunny slipped the lighter into his rifle when he knew he wasn't going to make it."

"Did he have the film on him when the attack began?"

"Yes, sir. I'm sure he did."

"Well, we've now been through Tooks's stuff three times, and there's no film." The colonel rubbed his chin. "Where are your own weapons, Rice?"

"My. 45's here, sir." Mitch reached down to his web holster. "My rifle's outside with your people. I couldn't get both it and the bolt gun in here without a knock-down-drag-out fight. So I decided to keep the bolt gun, and they backed down."

The colonel smiled a little and then asked. "Could Tooks have reached your rifle before he died?"

Mitch hesitated. "I guess so, sir. It was there beside the Remington when I came to."

A look of realization came over Mitch's and Strong's faces at the same time.

"Yes, private. Let's look at your rifle. I think your squad leader was trying to tell us something."

In short order, Mitch had his rifle. He field stripped it quickly, but nothing was evident. Not even the magazine held anything. For a moment Mitch and the colonel just looked at each other. Then, with his headache suddenly abating, Mitch brightened. He reached for the butt plate of the rifle, raised the metal plate, and opened the recesses where the weapon's maintenance tools were kept. Out popped two rolls of film. Mitch handed each one to the colonel.

"Sir, I think Sergeant Tooks wanted you to have these," Mitch said.

Colonel Strong nodded and took the film. "Thank you, private. I think you're right." Turning to his desk, he punched a hidden button. Another sergeant instantly appeared.

"Sergeant, see that this film gets developed pronto! And make sure that no one screws up!"

"Yes, sir!" the sergeant snapped, and in the next instant, he was gone with the film.

Mitch's head, clear a moment before, started throbbing mercilessly once more. His face paled almost to the point of transparency, and then the vomit came. In the next instant, right there in front of the colonel, god, and whoever else was watching, Mitch retched up everything he had. Even his soul turned loose, and then the world went black.

When Mitch regained consciousness, he was lying on a cot. It was still morning, but it was the twenty-fourth, not the twenty-third. He could hear the colonel talking to someone in the next room. Mitch tried to look around, but his vision was blurry, and his stomach queasy.

He had vomited more in the last two days than he had in the last ten years.

Suddenly, he felt a wonderfully cool compress on his forehead and face. The fire there cooled. His vision cleared. He looked up and saw a young woman sitting beside him. She was American and probably the most beautiful creature he had ever seen. As she reached over to reapply a fresh washcloth, Mitch reached up and took her hand.

"Oh, you're awake!" the woman said. "You've been out for quite a while. The colonel was getting worried."

She started to get up, and Mitch released her hand.

"I'm going to tell him you're awake. I think he was going to air evac you out to a hospital ship where there are neurosurgeons. I'm not sure if he'll still want to do that now or not."

With that she was gone, and Mitch was alone in the room. He tried to sit up on the cot and found he could just barely manage it. He was still there sitting on the edge of the cot when the woman returned with the colonel.

"Good. I'm glad you're coming around, Rice. You had us worried," the colonel said. "The medics tell me that you've got a pretty bad concussion. That's nothing to mess around with."

Mitch tried to stand but faltered.

"Sit down, marine! And don't even think about throwing up on me again!"

Mitch blanched. "I did that, sir?"

"Yes, private. That's right," chuckled Mitch's unnamed nurse. "You got away with a stunt all the rest of Vietnam is envious of. You tossed your cookies all over the meanest full-bird colonel there ever was and lived to tell about it."

"I thought we agreed not to talk about that," Colonel Strong said, suddenly seeming a little sheepish.

"Oh, I'm not talking!" the woman laughed. "Not in a million years!"

"Right! In a pig's eye! You'll be blabbing about it all the way back to the orphanage," the colonel muttered, but he really didn't seem that upset.

Turning to Mitch, he said. "Private Mitchell Rice, please meet Miss Sarah Thornton. Sarah, this marine is Private Mitchell Rice. He's a little the worse for wear."

Mitch tried to smile at the woman, but he wasn't sure his face was up to it.

Strong went on. "Sarah and I are good friends, private. I think you two might become friends too. You have a lot in common. You're both from Missouri. You're from Kansas City, and she's from Cape Girardeau. It might be good for the two of you to get to know each other." And with that, the colonel turned on his heel and left.

The next few minutes were rough. Mitch's head spun, but not from pain. He was just confused. The last two days had been a whirlwind. How had he ended up here on this cot, and where had an American nurse dressed like a nun come from? He rubbed his forehead.

"Do you want another washcloth?" Sarah asked.

"No, thanks. I'm just trying to figure this out."

"Well, that's a good sign that your brain isn't totally scrambled."

Mitch looked at her and, suddenly the woman started laughing.

"If you ask what a girl like me is doing in a place like this, I'll give you another concussion!" she grinned.

Mitch let himself back down onto the cot. "Okay, I won't ask. But who are you, anyway?"

The next thirty minutes were some of the best Mitch would experience in Vietnam. Sarah was a special breath of fresh air. He just sat there and listened as she quietly rambled on. Her voice was better than music.

Mitch discovered that Sarah Thornton was twenty-three-years-old. She was the fourth daughter of a prominent surgeon in Cape Girardeau, Missouri. She had a degree in teaching, but some six or seven months ago she and her father had a fight. She hadn't been able to abide by the plans he'd made for her. It seemed Sarah and her father were both strong-willed people who were just a little out of sync with each other. Her dad thought she should continue teaching, marry, and settle down. But that wasn't what Sarah wanted. True, she didn't know just what she did want, but teaching wasn't it. Laughing, she told Mitch that her somewhat plain figure and mousy brown hair "would probably keep me out of the movies," but she knew she wasn't ready for the quiet life her father had planned for her.

When she had seemed out of options, her big sister, a nun in the Benedictine order, had called. Her big sister had said Sarah needed a different challenge, and so she suggested Sarah volunteer to work with the Benedictines in a mission setting. Sarah had agreed.

So a couple of months later, with her dad screaming and her mother approving, Sarah had come to Vietnam. Once there she met Mother Edwina Marie, the mother superior of a group of Benedictine nuns who ran an orphanage in Hue. Hue was a long way from Tonsonot, but Mother Marie had made the trip to personally pick Sarah up. She and Sarah then returned to Hue where Sarah began working as a sort of lay postulant/Red Cross worker.

Mitch listened in fascination. "That's quite a story."

"You don't believe me?"

"Sure I believe you. Heck, last year I was in a minor seminary. Everyone thought I was going to be a priest. Look at me now."

Sarah seemed stunned. "You were in a seminary?"

"Sure. Dad had been a sergeant in Korea. I guess he and Mom didn't want their baby boy getting shot full of holes like most of my dad's unit had been. I think they thought the seminary was a good, safe place to hide me." Mitch shrugged an embarrassed little shrug. "Besides, having a son become a priest is a big deal to a Catholic family. They were really pissed when I left the seminary and enlisted."

"I'd bet you would look better in a Roman collar than you do in all those bandages," Sarah said simply.

Mitch looked away. "The collar was too tight a fit for me, I guess. I know I really disappointed them, but this is the best I could do."

Mitch didn't see it, but for a second Sarah's eyes looked like she was going to start crying. But she didn't. Instead, she went on with her story. She explained that she had quickly come to love the nuns and the orphanage's children.

"How did you handle the language problem?" Mitch asked. "Those kids don't speak English, do they?"

"No. A lot of their dads are American, but none of them stuck around long enough to teach the kids anything. I guess I just picked up the language from the kids. They're pretty good teachers."

"How did you make connections here?" Mitch asked, motioning around the room.

"You mean with Colonel Strong?"

"Yeah."

"Mother Marie introduced me to him. She thought I could help soften him up when we came around looking for handouts. She's a hard one to say no to."

"Oh," Mitch mumbled. Up to that point he'd thought Colonel Strong was the hard one to say no to.

Somewhere around that time in the conversation, Mitch began to suspect that there had to be some other connection between Sarah Thornton and Colonel Strong. The tone of her voice just changed too much when she mentioned him.

"Mitch, if the colonel will let you, why don't you come over to the orphanage tomorrow? Tomorrow's Christmas Day, and we're going to have a little party for the kids."

Mitch was stunned. He had forgotten that this was Christmas Eve. "Okay, I'll try, but I don't think I can promise anything."

After all that had happened, spending Christmas in a Vietnamese orphanage with a bunch of nuns seemed about as good an offer as any he was going to get.

"Good. I'll tell Mother Marie, and she'll save a place for you at supper. Come around 4:00."

Colonel Strong came back into the room, and their conversation stopped. "Private, go with the sergeant. He'll show you where to drop your gear. After that, report to the medics. They need to work on your face some more." Turning to Sarah, he said. "Mother Marie's waiting outside. She needs your help with the packages." He paused. "Thanks for your help here, Sarah. It was a long night."

"My pleasure, colonel."

She turned back to Mitch. "Please try to come to the orphanage tomorrow. It *really* will be a great party."

The colonel made a stern face at her, but she ignored him and scampered out. It *had* been quite a night.

Chapter Three

The silent scream burned like white fire. It was the panicky cry of sudden death, the anguish of a soul being ripped away. Mitch saw the decapitated girl lying on the road. She was a dismembered corpse, but her open, dead eyes recognized him anyway. He was her executioner. Her long, unblinking stare of accusation marked him like a branding iron, searing his very soul. He would not be forgiven.

The first picture faded and was replaced by another. He was tied to a stake, held captive before a wall of accusing faces. Every face was framed by the crosshairs of his riflescope, but it was he, not they, who was the target. He was the criminal, and they were his firing squad. They took aim, and their vengeance was without mercy.

Mitch started crying, sobbing in his sleep. He was falling into a fiery pit and had no way to stop. He screamed his heart out, grasping helplessly for the shadows that flew by. Dave Tooks was there, trying to reach him. Mitch felt the man's dead grasp, but it couldn't stop his horrible fall. He slipped right through Tooks's lifeless fingers and tumbled into the lake of fire below. The flames consumed everything. Only his screams remained.

Mitch partially woke up, jarred out of the nightmare by his own voice. He still felt like he was falling, and he reached out for anything to slow his plunge. All he could find was his rifle. He grabbed it, clutching it almost like a life preserver, somehow hoping the thing would keep him afloat. Wave after wave of guilt and despair crashed over him. His own tears were an ocean that closed in over his head, drowning him in a sea of guilt.

Mitch was still sobbing, but now he was now mostly awake. He knew the nightmare would replay itself if he slept again so he reached up to rub his eyes more awake. His face was still badly swollen, and the sudden but merciful pain of his own touch jarred him completely alert. He rolled over the edge of his cot and sat up. As he moved, the events of the previous day… everything from Dave Tooks's lighter to his throwing up all over Colonel Strong… scrolled through his memory. His head spun, and the cold vomit came up again at the back of his throat. He had to find the latrine. He didn't want to vomit all over himself again.

The tropical sun jerked over the horizon as he stumbled down the path. The sun hurt his eyes. His face was so swollen he could barely squint.

"Damn, marine! You look like you lost an argument with a wildcat!" exclaimed a nameless soldier Mitch stumbled past.

Mitch couldn't answer. His voice was still too hoarse from his nightmare.

"Hey, man! Watch it!" Mitch nearly fell, and the stranger caught him.

"Marine, you smell like puke! Why don't you take your sick ass on over to the corpsmen? They're up already, and you sure as hell could use some help."

"Okay," Mitch choked out. "Where is it?"

The friendly soldier pointed the way, but he saw Mitch wasn't tracking very well. So he took Mitch by the arm and steered him right up to the entrance of the aid station. There he handed him off directly to the medics. Mitch was pretty well out of it when they took him in.

The corpsmen spent the biggest part of the morning going over him. First they satisfied themselves that his concussion was better. Then they bathed and debrided all of the raw surfaces of his face. Mitch flinched every time they tugged his torn skin, clenching his teeth to keep from cursing. Punishing injections of antibiotics followed. Mitch gasped with each jab, and each grimace hurt his face even more. The whole episode was one big, interminable torture contest.

Mitch left the aid station and started walking back to his tent. He had just turned the first corner when he nearly ran right into Colonel Strong himself.

"I'm sorry, sir!" Mitch blurted out. "I didn't see you!"

"I'm surprised that you could see anything, Rice," the colonel said, looking at Mitch's fresh dressings.

"Yes, sir. Your medics did a pretty good job. I should be ready to go back to work in a couple of days."

"Watch it, marine!" Strong caught Mitch as he tripped over some unseen debris. "Come on, son, let's get you back to your bunk before you fall down."

Mitch surrendered and accepted the colonel's help. His head was starting to spin again, and he struggled desperately to stay upright. Strong took Mitch by the shoulder and pulled him along back to the bivouac. There the colonel helped Mitch back into his cot.

"I'm okay, colonel. Really I am," Mitch choked.

"Well maybe you are and maybe you aren't," Strong countered. "Stay down until I get the corpsmen up here to check you out."

Mitch tried to nod.

"Just one more thing, Rice," the colonel said as he turned to leave.

"Yes, sir?"

"You won't be going back to AnHoa for a while. Your skipper has let me have you on a sort of detached duty status. So take enough time to get back on track, and do what the medics say. You don't have any place to go. We'll talk about things later."

"Yes, sir."

The colonel left for the aid station, leaving Mitch alone for a few minutes. Lying there, he wondered just what in hell he had gotten himself into. He wished Dave Tooks were still alive to help him figure it all out.

Mitch stayed down for the next two hours while the medics rechecked him. It was enough time for his head to stop spinning and for his vision to clear. It was also enough time for him to see that the colonel's compound was a busy place. Jeeps, trucks, and helicopters came and went at a furious pace. He was glad he was temporarily out of the traffic pattern, and since he was starting to feel better, he took the time to check his pack and rifle. By two o'clock he was good enough to stand a shower and by mid-afternoon, he could handle food. It appeared he would live after all.

After eating, Mitch went over to the compound's armorer. He had to check on Tooks's bolt gun.

"Yes, goddamn it! Your bolt gun's safe and sound! I've got it locked up in here!" snarled a veteran sergeant, the place's lord and master. "This might not be your almighty Marine Corps, but I still know how to clean a rifle!"

Mitch drew back a little.

"What did you do with that thing? Use it as it club? It was dirty as sin. I thought you marines took better care of your weapons than that."

Mitch sized up the armorer. "Marines fight for a living, gunny. The guy who shot that piece died using it. So back off and don't give me any shit about it being dirty! Your own goddamn colonel took it from me before I could clean it!"

The old army sergeant saw that Mitch wouldn't be intimidated. "Aw, hell! Here, take the damn thing and check it out yourself! Army snipers are weird about their long rifles too. But, so far, none of them have ever complained about my work! Here!"

Mitch took Tooks's rifle and checked it over thoroughly. The sergeant had done a good job. "Thanks, sergeant," Mitch said, handing the rifle back. "I just had to be sure that Tooks's baby was okay."

"That's Dave Tooks's rifle? He's the one who bought it?"

Mitch shrugged an acknowledgment.

"Ah hell, marine! This place's the shits! I'm sorry." The armorer shook his head. "Tooks was my friend. He was almost ready to go home. Damn it all to hell!"

"Yeah, I know," Mitch said. There wasn't much more he could say.

"Sarge, would you check out the scope mounts on my M14?" Mitch asked after the awkward silence. "It saw a lot of hard use the other night. I have to know that everything is still tight and up to specs."

The old sergeant took Mitch's rifle. "Sure, marine. I'll check it out. Leave your night scope too. I'll clean its lenses and check the batteries. If you were with Tooks, I owe you that much."

Mitch was appreciative and gave the armorer all his sniper gear.

"Do you have anything to carry while I work on this?" the grizzled armorer asked as he gathered up Mitch's weapons. "A man without a piece around here is just asking to get wiped."

"I still have my. 45. It saved my hide the other night, and there isn't too much that can go wrong with it. It's right here." Mitch patted the big pistol that rested on his hip.

"Can you shoot it?"

"Yeah, sarge, I'm pretty good with it. The Corps expects all of us to be pretty good with whatever we shoot."

"Good!" snapped the old man. "Come back after supper. I'll have all your babies ready to go. Try to stay out of trouble in the meantime. That *hawg leg* of yours is better than spittin', but you have to be a lot closer to Charlie than you're used to."

Mitch grinned a little. "Sarge, I think I've learned a little about being up close and personal with Charlie." Mitch patted his bandaged head.

"And you wonder why we call you fuckin' marines "jarheads?" The armorer almost smiled. "Get out of here before I forget my manners!"

Mitch stepped back outside, still resting his right hand on his big service automatic. It was a comforting touch. As he walked in the hot sun, he remembered another comforting touch… Sarah Thornton's.

"Hey, marine! You need a ride somewhere?" shouted the driver of an outgoing jeep.

"Yeah!" Mitch shouted right back, not even thinking. "Can you take me to the orphanage? I'm supposed to eat supper there!"

"Which orphanage, marine? There must be six or seven in the city."

Mitch suddenly realized he didn't even know the name of the place. "Yesterday I met an American girl from Missouri who works at an orphanage with a bunch of French nuns. The girl's a friend of Colonel Strong. He's the one who introduced me to her."

The driver, an army corporal, looked over at his passenger, a Special Forces captain.

"What the hell are you waiting for, corporal?" the captain snapped. "If our beloved colonel thinks enough of this jarhead to introduce him to Sister Sarah, then I think we'd best give him a ride!"

Mitch climbed aboard, and the jeep took off across the Perfume River Bridge.

Hue was an ancient city, full of temples and palaces. Most of its present structures had been built in the nineteenth century by an occupying Chinese warlord who wanted to honor his patron in Beijing. It was full of small streets that were just wide enough for foot and animal traffic. Some of the city had been modernized by the colonial French, and those areas were almost Parisian. But most of it was still as it had been left by the Chinese—intricate, beautiful, and congested.

The city had always been a seat of government so sprawling neighborhoods filled in the small spaces that separated one temple from another. The city had almost no industry. Most of the more than a million residents were historically dedicated to the servicing of bureaucracy. The whole city was centered around a huge, old fort. Mitch used that landmark to keep his bearings as the jeep careened through the crowded alleys.

"How did you meet Mother Marie, marine?" asked the Green Beret captain.

Mitch didn't answer at first. He was still trying to memorize the route, but after a moment, the captain's question registered. "I'm sorry, sir. This is a big place. A guy could get lost here real easy."

"Yeah, I know. Have Mother Marie draw you a map home. She knows all the best routes."

Mitch thanked him for the advice and then answered the original question. "Sir, I just got here a couple of days ago. My partner and I had been up country, just a little outside of AnHoa. We tangled with Charlie there, and when it was all over, Colonel Strong had us picked up and brought us here. I was a little banged up, and I don't remember even seeing Mother Marie. But…" Mitch suddenly felt a little sheepish. "But I do remember Sarah Thornton. She said I could come over here tonight for supper. That's about all I remember."

"Private, was your partner Dave Tooks?"

Mitch hesitated for a second. "Yes, sir. I was his spotter."

"I'm sorry about your friend, marine. He was a good man. We worked together a few times in the past," the captain said. "That was quite a fire fight there at Delta Company. We heard about it from several quarters. It sounds like Charlie was pretty serious about wiping the place out."

"I guess so, sir. But the base's big guns and the gun ship with all the Gattling guns took care of things."

The jeep pulled up in front of the orphanage. It was a fairly large place, having previously been a school for children of French government workers. The grounds held a small convent, a chapel, and a main building that now served as a dormitory for all of the orphans. A large, stone wall surrounded the whole complex. It was a place that would have been much more at home in France than Vietnam.

"Rumor has it that it was a sniper, not "Puff", that saved Delta Company's ass," the captain said. "Any truth to that?"

"Sir, I bet rumors fly around here all the time," Mitch answered simply.

"Yeah, they do," the captain agreed. "But tell me, marine. Where's Tooks's bolt gun now?"

Mitch answered slowly. "I guess it's mine now, sir. Sergeant Allison has it in the armory."

"That's what I thought. What's your name, marine?"

"Mitchell Rice, sir."

"Well, Private Mitchell Rice, the next time I need a Marine scout, I'll give you a call." The officer looked up at the orphanage's door where a peasant with a wagon full of vegetables was just leaving. "This is the orphanage Sarah Thornton calls home. This time don't miss Mother Marie. She's quite a case."

Mitch got out of the jeep. "I won't, sir. Thanks for the ride."

The captain returned Mitch's salute and motioned for his driver to move on. Moments later he spoke to the driver. "Corporal, remember that name, Mitchell Rice. If he has Tooks's bolt gun and Colonel Strong has already introduced him to Sarah Thornton, then he must be the sniper that headquarters says shot up two NVA companies all by himself. He's the kind of guy we just might need some day."

The driver nodded agreement. Cambodia required people with special skills.

A young, fairly plain-looking nun opened the door to Mitch's knock. Her English was heavily flavored with her native French, but Mitch could understand her.

"May I help you?" she asked.

"Yes, sister, I hope so," Mitch said. "I'm Mitchell Rice. Yesterday I met a girl named Sarah Thornton. She said I could come by and see her. She does work here, doesn't she?"

A mature sounding voice came from behind the young nun. "Who's at the door, Sister Danielle?"

The young nun turned slightly. "Mother, it's the young marine from Colonel Strong's that Sarah told us about."

"Well, let him in, sister. It's Christmas, and we should share our blessings with all of our friends."

Mitch hesitated as Sister Danielle opened the door to him. Just beyond it was a courtyard that held a lot of Vietnamese kids. Most of them looked a little Caucasian, and Mitch realized they were the leftovers of the French and American occupations. That made them all outcasts. The kids were excited and streamed toward a double door on the side of the main building.

"Please come in, Private Rice. You're just in time for our evening meal," the old nun said. "My name is Sister Marie Edwina. I'm the mother superior here."

"Ah…" Mitch stammered.

"Don't be shy, private. Sarah told us all about you, and we're happy to have you come and visit. She's inside the refectory. You can sit with her and her children. Having you here will make Christmas more fun."

Mother Marie had a look of gentle but certain authority about her. Mitch decided not to take her on. She reminded him of several nuns from his past all rolled up into one, and that made her a very formidable figure indeed.

"Thank you, Mother. What's for supper?"

"I'm afraid it won't be all that unique for you, private, but the children love your American food. Colonel Strong has supplied us with quite a feast of your field rations. The drab wrappers don't look like Christmas, but the colonel was able to trade all of the cigarettes that come with the meals for some more colorfully packaged food and a large number of toys. The children are so excited."

Mitch saw that Mother Marie seemed excited too. "They're just like children everywhere. They all love to open packages on Christmas Day," she said.

Mitch entered the large dining hall and saw a sea of small faces looking at him. He suddenly felt huge even though he wasn't quite six-foot tall. Some two hundred children sat at ten or twelve long tables.

A nun sat at the end of each table. To his left, just two tables over, sat Sarah. She caught his eye and smiled.

"Private Rice has accepted your invitation, Sarah," Mother Marie said. Sarah stood up, still smiling at Mitch, and Mother Marie continued. "Private, are you the young marine who threw up all over our ever-watchful colonel?"

Mitch squirmed even though the old nun had a twinkle in her eye. "Yes, Mother, but I'm trying to forget that."

"Is that a sign of pride or wisdom, private?"

"I don't know, Mother. I really don't remember too much about any of it. I…"

Mitch was floundering, but Sarah came to his rescue and walked up to take him in.

"How's your head today, Mitch? Did the medics get you all checked out?"

"Yeah. I don't plan to throw up on anyone today. I don't even need all of the bandages any more. I'm pretty sure they'll let me get back to work in a couple of days."

Mitch tried to stand at ease, but he was fidgeting. He didn't know what to do with his hands. He felt like he was too big for the place, and he knew all of the children were still staring at him.

"Go and sit with Sarah, private," Mother Marie said. "We trust we will get the chance to know you better soon."

"Yes, come on and sit down," Sarah said softly to him, pulling him along. She pointed to the opposite end of her table.

As Mitch got settled, Mother Marie walked quietly to the front of the room. All eyes turned to her. She smiled, and the children grew very quiet. Little, wrapped packages of field rations along with brightly packaged candy bars and small toys sat in front of them, but not one child reached out. The mother superior stood still, holding the moment, and then began an easy flow of Vietnamese. It was time for her story.

For the next twenty minutes every child in the place was fixed on the old woman. Her distinctive voice rose and fell with a gentle rhythm. Mitch didn't really understand Vietnamese, but somehow he knew what she was saying. It was the Christmas story.

The story of the Christ child's birth was universal. Part of the way through the tale, Mitch caught Sarah staring at him. He wondered if he was doing something wrong, but her blush reassured him. He smiled at her and then looked away. For some reason, he felt warm inside too, and it was a nice feeling.

Sarah smiled back self-consciously. Not even Mitch's bruised face could hide his obvious pleasure at her attention, and she liked that. She didn't care if the nuns and children saw her or not. But, as it happened, no one saw their exchange.

With a long breath, Mother Marie finished her story. The children looked at her with great anticipation, but they didn't move. Mother Marie bowed her head, and all the children did the same. Together, they all made the sign of the cross and said grace. Moments later, when the little prayer was finished, Mother Marie smiled and nodded. That was all the children needed. They tore into the wrapped food as if there was no tomorrow. The party had begun.

For a while Mitch got lost in the children's pleasure. The rations, mostly stews, canned fruits, and puddings, were just like Christmas presents to them. They smiled, giggled, and threw the drab olive wrappers everywhere while they hoarded the candy bars and toys like gold. It was quite a sight, and it went on for almost thirty minutes. When it was over, Mother Marie resumed command and led them all in a final grace. The children murmured the prayer through chocolate-smeared lips. Mr. Hershey himself would have been proud of all the smiles.

After the dismissal Mitch watched the main group of children file out of the dining hall. One or two kids from each table stayed behind and gathered the debris from the meal. Sarah was in charge of the clean up detail, and Mitch joined her.

"That was quite a party," he said. "Thanks for inviting me."

"We're all glad you came, Mitch. It meant a lot to the children that you were here to share their meal. Mother Marie told them that you were like one of the wise men who brought gifts to the Christ child. They love the idea that the Savior was once small like them." She paused. "Their lives on the streets are really pretty awful. We try to care for as many of them as we can."

"I think this was the best Christmas I've ever had," Mitch said, helping her gather up the trash. "You know, until you mentioned it yesterday, I had forgotten that today was Christmas."

"I have to watch the children outside in the courtyard now," Sarah answered, smiling at his statement. "The sisters have to go to evening vespers."

Mitch smiled self-consciously. "I guess it really wasn't that long ago that I was going to evening vespers myself."

Sarah gave him a puzzled look, but then she understood. "Oh, yeah… the seminary."

"Uh-huh, we had evening prayers there too."

"Do you want to go to chapel with the sisters? They would welcome you."

Mitch's face clouded a little. "Sarah, I'm not sure I belong in a chapel anymore. I guess I'd rather stay here with you and watch the kids."

Sarah caught the sudden darkening of his gaze and frowned at it. Motioning for him to follow, she took him out to the courtyard together where the children were busy at their evening play. She and Mitch had nearly half an hour to talk before Mother Marie returned. The children didn't interrupt them even once.

"Well, Private Rice, have you and our Sarah had a chance to visit?" Mother Marie asked, returning from the chapel.

"Yes, Mother," Sarah answered quickly, not giving Mitch a chance to speak. "Mitch was catching me up on things back home. He's only been in Vietnam for a few weeks."

Mother Marie looked at Mitch, surprised. "If you are that newly arrived here and Colonel Strong already has need of you, you must be a very special soldier indeed, Private Rice."

"Na… nah, I'm just another marine, Mother. That's all." He looked at his wristwatch. "I guess I should be heading back. It's about a thirty-minute walk, isn't it?"

"Yes, it is," Mother Marie said. "Do you know the way?"

"I think so. I paid pretty close attention on the way over here."

"Sarah, why don't you draw Mitchell a map anyway? Our city can be confusing even to those who think they know their way. Then, when he has time, he can use it to find his way back to us." She made sure she had Mitch's eye. "The invitation is real, Mitchell. You are always welcome here."

The ROK guard at the Perfume River Bridge saw Mitch coming. He immediately called for his superior, a lieutenant named Baick, and soon both men were frowning in Mitch's face. Mitch realized he hadn't bothered to check out when he had left earlier that day, and it had been very stupid. He was about to pay the price.

"Did you enjoy the orphanage, private?" the lieutenant began.

"Yes, sir. Those people there are very special."

Mitch knew he was in for it, but he couldn't tell just how angry the stern-faced Korean officer really was. Mitch wondered how the man knew he had been at the orphanage.

"Yes, private, they are special, and we would like to see that they stay that way." He paused to make sure he had Mitch's full attention. "Now listen to me very carefully while I explain, as you Americans say, the lay of the land."

For the next several minutes, Mitch got a tongue- lashing on the status of the orphanage, the nuns, Sarah Thornton, the compound where he stood, and the risks of Hue itself. Mitch learned that Mother Marie and her nuns were remnants of the old French occupation. When the Vietnamese had thrown off the French shackles, the nuns had been exempted from any reprisals because they were known to be holy people who cared only for the half-breed children no one else wanted. The nuns had no government loyalties, and that included the North Vietnamese, the puppet regime in the south, and even Colonel Strong. It was the nuns' absolute neutrality that guaranteed their protection. The lieutenant told Mitch that, though the colonel was very attached to the nuns, his command had to appear very non-involved with them. It was a matter of survival.

"Now, private, do you have any questions?"

Mitch took a breath before answering. "Sir, I understand about the nuns. They're all French. But what about the American girl? How's she protected?"

"Private, as long as the mother superior vouches for her, she's protected. But realize that if Sister Sarah screws up and involves the orphanage too much with us, she endangers the whole group."

"Does that mean the orphanage is off limits, sir?"

"No, private. It's more like the orphanage isn't even there. There's nothing to be off limits from. It doesn't exist for us. Do you understand now?"

"Yes, sir," Mitch answered, but he really didn't understand at all.

Mitch's confusion lasted well into the night. Sleep wouldn't come, and he was lost in the tangled web of the events of the last couple of days. He knew Colonel Strong had wanted the photos he and Dave had taken at Delta Company. That whole episode seemed clear, but that had somehow led to the apparent secret relationship between the colonel and Mother Marie and her orphanage.

Mitch wasn't sure why the colonel had made him privy to that relationship when the risks of discovery seemed so great. The colonel himself had introduced Mitch to Sarah, and some of the colonel's own people had taken him to the orphanage. It seemed common knowledge that it had been the colonel himself who was supplying the goods for the children's Christmas party. So was the colonel's connection to the orphanage secret or not? Did the colonel want Mitch to be friendly with Sarah and Mother Marie? If so, why? What could Mitch do that would justify risking the whole orphanage?

And then there was Sarah. Mitch realized she was a little older than he was, but the years didn't seem to matter. They had a lot in common—their backgrounds, their personalities, and even their idealism. Even Mother Marie paired them together. Sarah stirred something inside him that made him feel excited and uncomfortable all at the same time. He didn't know what name to give this new feeling, but he did know he didn't want anything to happen to her.

His confusion worsened as the night dragged on. If his actions were putting Sarah and the orphanage in danger, should he try to go back there like he wanted? The dilemma tortured him most of the night. Near morning, sleep finally intervened. It came and pressed down on him like a great weight, crushing away his consciousness. Trapped under the weight, Mitch once more was fair game for the nightmares. Serial montages of combat and death played behind his eyes the rest of the night. It was a never-ending story.

"Private, how's your head this morning?" Colonel Strong asked.

Mitch snapped to attention. He was just returning to his tent after going to the latrine. He hadn't heard the colonel's approach. "Just fine, sir."

"Good. Come with me. We need to walk."

Mitch fell in beside the colonel. They seemed to be walking back to the colonel's command bunker.

"Did you enjoy last evening at the orphanage?"

"Yes, sir. I did. But I didn't know I wasn't supposed to go there. I'm sorry if I fouled anything up, sir."

"You didn't foul anything up, marine. I wanted you to meet all those remarkable women. What did you think of them?"

Mitch hesitated. He wasn't used to officers asking about his personal feelings. Mitch saw that the colonel's question was real, however, so he answered slowly. "Sir, they were something else. Most of those little kids there are half-breeds. I know the locals here would rather see them all dead. Those nuns have a lot of guts, bucking the system that way."

"What did you think of Sarah?"

Mitch felt his face warming, but he answered clearly. "I liked her a lot, sir. I don't think I've ever met anyone quite like her before... I..."

"You... what, private?"

"I'm scared for her, sir," Mitch answered. "I can't believe that Charlie'll leave her alone if this place ever heats up."

"You're right, Rice. Sarah's very exposed." Strong went on. "What about Mother Marie?"

"Sir, I don't know just what to say about her," Mitch said a little sheepishly. "With Mother Marie, maybe it's Charlie who should be scared."

Strong chuckled. "Rice, have you ever heard of the French Jesuit named Teilhard de Chardin?"

Mitch stared back at the colonel. "Yes, sir. I think he was a philosopher or a theologian or something. I know he had something to do with the Vatican Council the Catholic Church had three or four years ago. I had to read a lot of his stuff in high school. Is he connected to all of this?"

"Actually, he was an anthropologist." Strong had a funny look about him. "I keep forgetting about your stint in the seminary, Rice. Maybe that will make the rest of this easier."

Mitch suddenly felt very uncomfortable. How did the colonel know about the seminary?

"Rice, before World War II, our Mother Marie Edwina was a fairly famous anthropologist herself. She worked with Chardin and even traveled with him on his expeditions in China."

Mitch was surprised. "Sir, how did she end up here? I think Chardin was a pretty big deal until he disagreed with the big authorities in Rome. Did Mother Marie get in trouble with him?"

Strong looked at him a little quizzically.

"No, sir..." Mitch stumbled. "I didn't mean *'that'* kind of trouble.

Strong laughed. "Rice, you're an innocent! What are you doing here?"

Mitch shrugged, completely off balance from the colonel's response. He didn't know how to answer.

The colonel continued. "Her trouble was nothing like that, son. On one of her trips with Chardin into China, back in the 1930s, she ran into something that changed her. She gave up all of the pomp and circumstance of her position at the big university in Paris and decided she "wanted to do something of value" with her life. At least that's the way she described it to me. She somehow figured all the little orphans around here were more important than all the stuff she was doing in Paris. She's been here ever since. She hid children from the Japanese all through the war and has been protecting them ever since. She has quite a history around here. The locals consider her sort of a saint."

"Does that include Charlie?"

Strong frowned. "That's the problem, Rice. Probably not. Charlie figures all of Mother Marie's little half-breed orphans are just products of the decadent West. Charlie wants them all dead. Mother Marie won't go away so Charlie will probably take a shot at her whenever the time seems right." Strong saw Mitch's face darken. "Private, I've told you all this because the day's coming when I'll need your help protecting them. Come on. There's someone over here I want you to meet."

The colonel started walking again, and Mitch followed. They approached a small bunker that was just a few yards from Strong's own command post. An American dressed in unmarked khakis stood there, waiting for them.

"Private Rice, this is James Underhill. He has some equipment that I want you to become familiar with." Mitch and Underhill exchanged glances. "Can you have him ready in two days, Jim?"

"Colonel, if he's as good as you say he is, I'll have him ready tonight."

Strong nodded and turned to leave. "Rice, learn all he can teach you. Mother Marie, Sarah, and all the children are going to need you very soon."

Mitch and Underhill watched the colonel leave. After a moment, Underhill picked up the conversation where Strong had left it. He told Mitch he was a former mechanical engineer who had become frustrated with the usual chain of command of the military industrial complex. His specialty was small arms development, and he had left a big company a few years ago to start his own little manufacturing facility in the plains of northern Texas. There he had hand-made special weapons for different branches of the government. He made them so well that the government decided that it couldn't live without them. As Vietnam heated up, his marvelous little implements of destruction came into such demand that he moved his whole shop to Okinawa to be closer to the action. Now he was almost the sole supplier of special applications weapons for the whole SOG.

Mitch soaked up all that Underhill volunteered. Mitch wasn't sure just how he figured into all of it, but he got an indication when the engineer started asking about his shooting skills and knowledge of ballistics. Mitch answered the questions as best he could, and Underhill seemed satisfied with his responses. After several minutes, Underhill reached down into the bunker and took out an aluminum gun case. It was similar to the one that had held Mitch's first Remington 700 sniper rifle in training. Underhhill handed the case to Mitch.

"What do you think of this, private?"

Mitch stared down into the foam-lined interior of the case. It was shorter than the one he'd had at Pendleton, but it still held a Remington 700. But this one was different. It was a take-down rifle, and it came in three sections. The first one extended from the butt stock to the front action ring. The second section was the barrel and fore end. The barrel was just twelve inches long. The third section was a foot-long tube that snapped onto the front of the barrel. It was a silencer.

"Can I pick it up, sir?"

"Sure. That's why we're here."

Mitch picked up the action and looked at the bolt. "This bolt face is too big for any standard military cartridge that I know of."

He picked up the rifle's detachable magazine and the short barrel. "This has to be at least a. 45 caliber, and the whole thing's suppressible."

Next came the rifle's special telescopic sight. "Whatever it is that this thing shoots, it must have a trajectory like a mortar. The adjustments on this scope show the drop at 100 meters to be at least two feet. Is the round this thing shoots subsonic?"

"Yep, it is," Underhill answered. "What do you think it's for?"

Mitch paused. "Sir, if I had a concealable, silenced. 45 caliber rifle that could drop a bunch of big bullets on a target in a hurry without making a sound, I'd say I'd have a murder waiting to happen. This thing's an assassin's rifle."

Underhill nodded. "Do you think you could shoot it?"

Mitch shifted his weight from one leg to the other as he held the assembled rifle. He realized he was at the threshold of a whole, different world. This new rifle was a huge leap beyond his coveted bolt gun. It was still a rifle, but it was something that would take killing one step farther than Mitch had ever gone. He felt like running away, but Colonel Strong had said Mother Marie and Sarah would soon need him. So after a long, labored pause, he made his decision.

"Sure. I'd just have to practice with it some to get the handle on its trajectory. What's it shoot?"

Underhill reached into the bunker again and pulled out a nondescript box of ammo that held some really big bullets. "Don't worry, Rice. These fit within the guidelines of the Geneva Convention. But you're right. They make less noise than a baby's burp. Let's go see if you can shoot as well as you can talk."

Later that night Underhill reported back to Colonel Strong. "You were right about the kid, colonel. He can shoot the eyelashes off a gnat at four hundred meters. He has the fastest hands I've ever seen, and on top of all that, he's gotta have some sort of automatic range finder built into his head. He just pulls down on the target and fires—no hesitations and no misses. I've never seen anyone like him before. I ran him all the way out to 400 meters. Out there, the slugs have almost six feet of drop. He was still hitting a four-inch bull nine times out of ten. I think you have your man."

"He's completely checked out on the rifle then?"

"I can't teach him anything more about the rifle, colonel. At this point, he knows it better than I do. He's the best rapid-fire rifle shot I've ever seen, and that even includes Dave Tooks. I guess now it's just a question as to whether he'll do what you want or not."

Strong held out his hand to the engineer. "Thanks, Jim. You've done your usual great job. Where's the rifle now?"

"Right here, colonel. I have seven more just like it to deliver. And then I'm off for my beloved, little Okinawa. This one's all yours. Good luck with it… whatever it's for."

"Thanks, Jim. Safe trip."

The next day Mitch once again found himself standing in front of the colonel in the command bunker.

"Rice, Mr. Underhill was very impressed with your marksmanship. He doesn't impress too easily."

Mitch stood quietly, waiting for the colonel's next parry.

"You realize by now that I want to recruit you for a job that's out of the ordinary, don't you?"

"I guess that's about the way I got it figured, sir."

Strong eyes bore right through Mitch. "Rice, if you had the day off, what would you do?"

Mitch blinked. He felt off balance again. "Sir, if I could do whatever I wanted, I guess I'd go over to the orphanage."

"Does life make more sense to you there, Mitch?" It was the first time Strong had used Mitch's first name.

"Yes sir. It does. It's about the only place around here where things make any sense at all."

Strong stiffened, but he went on anyway. "Then maybe you should take the day off and go over there. While you're there, think through things very carefully. Tomorrow, I'm going to ask you to do something that's very risky. If you agree to do it, it may cost you your life. But if you pull it off, you'll save a lot of lives, including Mother Marie's and Sarah's."

Mitch stood still, weighing every word.

"Rice, realize this," the colonel continued. "I neither overstate nor understate my assignments. And I won't lie. Dave Tooks knew this. Something big is in the wind around here. If I can insert you into the right place at the right time with the right equipment, and if you're motivated to succeed, you might be able to stop the whole damn thing. A lot of people need you, son."

Mitch shifted his weight.

"Get out of here, private. Take the rest of the day off, and think it over. Go wherever you have to go to make sense out of what I've said. If that's Mother Marie's, then go there. Report to me at 0500 tomorrow."

It was washday at the orphanage, and Sarah was elbow-deep in soapy water. In the months since she had come to live with Mother Marie she had washed more dirty clothes than she had seen in her whole her life. Mother Marie seemed to think clean clothes made one more presentable to the Almighty, and some two hundred children of various ages and ten nuns generated a lot of laundry living in a tropical climate. So Sarah washed clothes by the ton. She had just begun to attack a large basket of bedclothes when she looked up and saw Sister Danielle.

"Sarah, Mother wants to talk to you. Here, I'll take your place."

"She's upset with me over Private Rice, isn't she, Dannie?"

"I don't know, Sarah. She knows the private is someone special. We were all taken with him."

"Yeah, me too," Sarah said quietly. "But he worries me. He has a different soul from the rest of the Special Forces types we always see. Mitch feels everything he does. And he already has had to do so much. I don't know how much of him will be left if he stays here for very long."

Danielle looked at her friend. "I think you're looking at this marine through eyes that are a little different than mine, Sarah. I think this man has a great deal more steel in his soul than you want to admit. I think that as long as he believes in what he's doing, he'll be fine." Danielle smiled and went on. "Now, go to Mother before she puts us both on permanent laundry duty."

"But I'm *already* on permanent laundry duty!" Sarah quipped.

"I know, but I'm not," Dannie answered. "If you're too tardy in arriving, Mother might put me right back in here. The kitchen is so much cooler than here, what with the ovens and cooking all those vegetables we've been able to get lately. I don't want to lose an easy job because of you." She winked at Sarah. "And besides, Mitchell Rice is with her."

"What!" Sarah gasped. She threw off her wet apron and tossed it at Danielle. "Where are they?"

"In the chapel. They've been there for quite a while." Danielle dropped the smile. "Listen well when you get there, my friend. I think they have something important to tell you."

Mitch had arrived at the orphanage about an hour and a half before Danielle relieved Sarah in the laundry. Upon his arrival, he had spied

Mother Marie as she was putting some flowers at the foot of a statue of the Virgin Mary at the orphanage's gate.

"Hello, Mitchell Rice."

"Hello, Mother." He frowned, puzzled. "Mother, am I a problem being here like this? Is it dangerous for you to talk to me? I don't want that."

She chuckled.

"Do I look that ridiculous?"

"No. Just needlessly burdened and worried. The colonel has spoken to you, hasn't he?"

"Yes. He didn't explain too much to me, but, from what he did say, I'm not sure if I'm your curse or your salvation."

"Oh, certainly I think the latter, Mitchell." Her simple smile touched something inside him.

"Mother, can I talk to you?"

"Of course you can. But why don't we go into the chapel? I think we'd both be more comfortable in the Lord's special presence."

"I'm not so sure, Mother, but if you say so… sure, in the chapel."

The two walked through the courtyard on their way to the chapel. Children were everywhere. They were all playing and appeared happy. One little girl came right up to Mitch and held out her arms to him.

"We're pretty free with hugs around here, Mitchell. Sometimes they're the most important things we have to give."

Mitch gathered up the little girl and gave her a big squeeze. As he put her back down, he reached into a baggy pocket on the side of his field pants. Almost by magic he produced a chocolate bar and slipped it into her fingers. She took it with both hands and held it for dear life.

"So, Mitchell, do you think the way to a girl's heart is through her stomach?"

Mitch grinned sheepishly. "I don't know very much about little girls' hearts, Mother, but my grandmother always said that chocolate was soothing. She said that talk about politics, religion, or family matters should happen only over a cup of hot chocolate." He turned back to Mother Marie. "She always thought the world would be better off if everyone had more chocolate."

Mother Marie nodded. "I think your grandmother must have had a special wisdom, Mitchell. But come quickly now into the chapel before the rest of the children see what you have done and mob us."

For the next hour, Mother Marie asked Mitch questions about his past and answered his questions about hers.

Mitch learned that the sisters always lived on the edge, always at the mercy of the politicians and soldiers controlling the land. Somehow those men had always chosen to ignore the sisters as long as they concentrated on the countless orphans that overran the streets.

More recently, however, the political winds had begun to change. The communists held no love for the mixed race orphans or for the nuns who cared for them. For the communists, the easiest answer was extermination. Charlie wanted both Mother Marie and her children dead.

The Vietcong and the NVA were known to be infiltrating Hue from the countryside. Several incidents had already been reported where Europeans in the city had been killed, and Mother Marie realized it was only a matter of time before the North came for her and for her children. After the farmers from whom she normally bought food for the orphanage were scared off, Mother Marie had sought out Colonel Strong and had made her case.

The colonel hadn't shared her fears at first, but she persisted and soon the colonel, using his South Korean men disguised as peasants, had started quietly supplying her with food and clothing. After more atrocities, he helped her piece together a kind of underground adoption agency. Already about three hundred children had been slipped out of the city to safer homes in the country. Just two hundred children remained.

Mitch listened carefully as Mother Marie told her story. It dawned on him that the colonel had also managed to put together a whole network of native peoples who appreciated him. All the colonel had to do was listen, and he had the most sophisticated intelligence gathering apparatus ever invented. Finally Mitch could take it no longer.

"Mother, don't you realize the colonel is using you to gather information about Charlie?" he blurted out.

She simply nodded. "Of course, Mitchell. We all know it. And we all know that it makes us even more of a target for the Vietcong." She smiled sadly. "But Mitchell, we are already targets anyway. This time we have been forced to choose sides. They want to kill our children." Her face hardened. "Mitchell, the VC must not have their way!"

Mitch was stunned by her sudden revelation. He realized this gentle, sainted woman was also at war. She was just as much a soldier as he was.

Mother Marie's gentle smile returned. "Don't you realize that you too are just a tool in all of this?"

Mitch was quiet for a second before answering. Somehow he had to show her the same part of his own soul as she had just shown him of hers. He wasn't sure he was ready for such honesty.

"Yes, Mother. I know that I'm a soldier. I guess you are too." His face darkened. "But after that, we're different. You're doing all this to save lives. I'm just here to kill." He looked at her, quietly desperate, knowing she saw his naked self. He knew what was there was almost too ugly to show anyone, so he turned away from her.

Mother Marie saw his pain and slid closer to him on the chapel pew. She knew an orphan when she saw one.

"Mother, I'm really not too scared of dying," he whispered. "There really aren't too many people who depend on me. My family would miss me, but they understand that soldiers sometimes die. If my number comes up, it won't be too bad."

She saw he couldn't cope with his abandonment. He started to cry.

"Mother, how do you know if what you're fighting for is really worth it? I've only been in combat zones here for about a month. I don't know how many people I've killed so far, but it's a bunch. That includes at least one little girl who wasn't much older than that one out there who wanted the hug. They all had a lot more reasons to live than I do. I know they all had families, and now they're all dead. They're dead because I killed them!"

A tear ran down his cheek.

"And for what? As far as I can tell, all I did was make a lot more orphans."

Another tear fell.

"Why am I here, Mother? I see their faces all the time! I can't stand it!"

She took him in her arms, and the floodgates opened. She felt him shaking all the way down to his core, and she pulled him in closer. She didn't want him to drown in his own despair.

Mitch wept for several minutes. She let his remorse flow out, and, after a while, his shaking stopped. She reached down and lifted his chin.

"Now listen to me, Mitchell Rice. I must tell you something about yourself."

Mitch strained to see her through his swollen eyes.

"Yes, you are a soldier. That makes you a special breed of creation. Most people seek to survive and to prosper. Soldiers don't. They are the ones who are willing to die so that everyone else can live their dreams." She touched his hand. "You see, you are willing to give away the very thing that everyone else is trying so hard to preserve. That makes the two of us more alike than you'll ever know."

Mitch wiped his eyes.

"Mitchell, the problem is that you don't seem to realize that you aren't fighting for an arbitrary government. You're fighting for people, for the people that God Himself has given you as your charges. You fought for David Tooks at Delta Company, not for anyone else. Yes, he died. But you still saved his life. The honor and purpose he lived for still lives because you picked up his rifle. Here, you'll fight for other people. That includes me, Sarah, and the children. That makes you our guardian, Mitchell. When you fight, remember *our* faces, not those in your nightmares. The dead have already forgiven you anyway."

She saw that Mitch was bewildered by her words. She had to make him understand.

"Think of it this way then." Quiet desperation suddenly filled her voice. "God has formed the world according to His Own pleasure. In it, He has made wondrous food chains. At the head of each food chain is a predator that is beyond attack from all except for the smallest in its world. Realize, Mitchell, that our God isn't squeamish. He made the predators, the prey, and the microbes all together, and they're all good. The dinosaurs of the past, the sharks of the sea, the tigers that roam the jungles here… they are all good."

She touched him again.

"And God has even made a few human predators. They too belong in His creation, and He uses them to protect His world. You, Mitchell Rice, are one of these."

She squeezed his hand. She had to make him see what she was saying.

"Hold onto this, Mitchell! Don't lose your purpose in despair! Trust your instincts! Stop trying to die! Take what you have in your hand and fight for it!"

Mitch's face was still dark.

"Mitchell, who's in your hands right now?"

He focused on her, trying to understand.

"No, Mitchell! Don't think! Just answer me! Who's in your hands right now?"

"You are!" he blurted out.

"That's right! And I'm the reason you'll go on and do whatever else you have to do. You see, I'm one of those whose life you must save, just like you saved Dave Tooks's. You must save Sarah and the children too. Only God knows how many others there will be before your time is over."

Mitch turned away.

"Don't worry about the world, Mitchell." She pulled his face back to hers. "It is what it is. God has put us in it so that we might go through it to reach some other place. Hold your ground! Don't run away from your purpose!"

She smiled as she saw his face soften.

"Yes, Mitchell, the world is full of violence and conflict, and you were created for it."

She took his other hand.

"But realize that you were also born one of God's special warriors, and He does not make mistakes. You are one of His *awesome ones*! He realized that He would need a mighty warrior when He created you. It is yours to rule here! In this whole, war-torn place, you are the final warrior!"

She pulled back to catch her breath. She felt her own tears. Much of what she had just said was like a two- edged sword, and her soul was hanging just as ragged and bare as was Mitch's.

"Mitchell, I have my demons too. All these children are in my hands, and I see they are in great peril! Colonel Strong and you are the only way I can see to protect them. I must protect them! They are *my* charges! Somehow I *must* protect them!"

She wilted, exhausted by her admission.

"And I also want to pass on the purpose of my life, Mitchell, just like Dave Tooks did. I want you to pick it up like you did his. I want my life to have meant something when it's over."

Mitch reached out, touching her tears.

"I'm here, Mother."

The impact of his simple statement ran all the way to the foundation of her soul.

"So you do see! You do see that we're all connected!"

"Mother, I see, but I'm not sure I really understand."

She squeezed his shoulder and slowly nodded. "Understanding will come in God's good time, Mitchell. Don't rush Him. Until then, protect those who are in your hands. We are your purpose!"

There was a noise behind them. They turned to see Sarah standing at the back of the chapel. She had been there for quite a while. She too was crying.

"Come here, daughter." Mother Marie motioned to her. "I think, for a while, we all need to be in each others' arms."

Chapter Four

The specially modified Cobra ran hard and low. It was an ominous-looking helicopter, almost a bird of prey. Mitch had never seen anything like it before. It was painted with a special, non-reflective black paint that made it blend into the night sky, and its engine was so muffled that it made less noise than a gentle breeze. The craft had already cleared the Cambodian border and was quickly approaching the landing zone. Mitch was one of the three men inside it.

"How you doin' back there, Rice?" It was Cooper, the mission's handler. He rode in the copilot's seat in the elongated cabin of the secretly modified attack craft.

"I'm fine," Mitch answered flatly from his place in the small cargo bay. "How long until we reach the LZ?"

"About ten minutes. Anything on your mind?"

"Yeah, there is, Coop. I've been thinking about my pick up."

"You mean 'your extraction'?"

"Yeah, my ticket home," Mitch growled. "You know, Coop, I'm really getting tired of all of this jargon."

"What's on your mind, Riceman?" chimed in Schmitty, the pilot. He knew that the arrogant and cold Cooper was not Mitch's favorite person. "Ignore the egghead."

"Well, like I said, I've been thinking," Mitch said again. "Why don't you guys make the pick-up point that small mountain to the west of the target zone?"

"But that's twenty kliks farther inside this god- forsaken country, Riceman," Schmitty answered. "Why in hell would you want to go there?"

"Because, Schmitty, that's the last direction the VC down there would think I'd go when this thing is over."

Schmitty and Cooper traded stares. Mitch's idea wasn't part of the mission profile.

"And I think that instead of coming each night on the fifth, sixth, and seventh days, just come on the seventh," Mitch continued.

"Riceman, you're nuts!" Schmitty snapped. "We're supposed to haul your ass out of here ASAP when you're finished. That's not friendly country down there!"

"I understand that," Mitch said. His voice held a sharp edge. "But just listen for a minute. If I go east like we planned, I'll probably be walking right into the arms of some VC patrol. Charlie's everywhere down there. I'm betting there won't be nearly as many of them to the west. As long as you guys don't come too early and tip my hand, I'll be better off going west."

Schmitty turned back to Cooper. "What about it, Coop?"

"Hell, I don't know. Maybe Rice has a point. After the hit, Charley will bust his butt to find the shooter."

"That's right," Mitch went on. "Besides I don't think I can get to the top of that hill before the seventh night. If you two are there two or three nights in a row before I get there, you'll just be making all of us an easy target. Is that what you want?"

"Hell, no!" Schmitty snorted. "I don't want my pretty backside shot full of holes!"

"And besides, the colonel will kill you if you let anyone ventilate this secret little bird he's let us borrow," Cooper added.

"Yeah! No shit!" Schmitty admitted, shaking his head. "You sure about this, Riceman? Because Coop and I will come to get you in broad daylight, if that's what it takes."

"Schmitty, I know you probably would… even if the colonel says not to," Mitch said, his voice distant. "Yeah, I'm sure. You just be over that hill at 0200 seven nights from now. I'll hit you with three shorts and one long from my black light, and then one of you can come down on this winch and pull me out. Okay?"

The two men looked at each other again. "Are you really sure that's the way you want it, Rice?" Cooper asked. "A week out here alone is a long time."

"Look, Coop. We both know that if I'm relatively intact, I should be able to make it to the hill by the seventh night. If I'm early, I'll just wait. If I'm not intact enough to get there, then I won't be coming home. I know I can't be captured. If I'm hit too bad to move… well, you've already told me that I'll have to take one of these cyanide-laced sleeping pills."

"Goddamn it, Riceman! Did this jerk give you those friggin' things?" Schmitty demanded.

"Yeah, I got them," Mitch said. His voice was really distant now. "So you guys make damn sure you're on station over that hill at 0200 a week from now. I don't plan to die out here."

"Can't argue with that," Schmitty snorted.

"So three shorts and one long?" Mitch asked.

"Yeah, that's right, Riceman. Three shorts and one long," Schmitty echoed. "Just don't disappoint me. I've got money riding that you'll come out of this thing alive."

Mitch threw a glance up to the nose of the craft. "That's great. So that's why you're so interested in my welfare. What kind of odds did you get on me?"

"Damn good ones, Riceman! Two hundred to one! You stay alive, and I'm a rich man! Hell! I'll even give you half the pot! How's that for an extra incentive?"

"That's really great," Mitch mumbled. "Here I am with my ass in this sling…" Mitch was getting into the harness that would take him to the jungle's floor. "… and you're making like this is some kind of football pool."

"Two minutes to the LZ, Rice," Cooper said.

"Schmitty?" Mitch said more loudly.

"Yeah, Mitch?"

"Ah… ah nothing. Just get home in one piece so you can come back and get me."

"Well hell, marine," Schmitty drawled. "Me and Coop… we're just Air America. We're just here to please. You just keep your head down and your ass covered. And we'll be right there on schedule to take you home."

"One minute to the LZ," Cooper said, keeping the countdown going.

"Okay, Coop! Are you coming back here to help me, or do I have to run this damn thing myself?" Mitch snapped back.

"Cool it, Rice. I'm here." Cooper tapped Mitch on the shoulder. "Damn! You're a deadly looking bastard! With all that black you're wearing, you almost look like you're Charlie! Shit! You even have on Charlie's sneakers! Whose idea was that?"

"Mine. I thought that was the idea was that I was supposed to a ghost," Mitch said, "someone who was never here. Who wants a bunch of Marine Corps boot prints all over the place, telling the whole world who's really been here?"

Cooper shook his head a little as he pushed Mitch out of the loading door. "I'll file that one away for future reference, Rice! Give them hell down there!"

"LZ!" yelled Schmitty. "Out the door, Riceman! We'll see you in seven days! Good hunting!"

"Right! Seven days!" Mitch yelled back, and then he disappeared into the top layer of the dark, triple canopy jungle. It swallowed him whole.

The Cobra spun on its axis and headed off to the northeast just at the treetops. Its course was full of turns and erratic maneuvers. No discernible path was left to suggest to any NVA radar screen that a drop had been made.

"Do you think he can really pull this off, Coop?" Schmitty asked as he jockeyed the silent helicopter all over the sky.

"Hell if I know!" Cooper muttered, hanging on for dear life.

"Are we getting that desperate, boss man? Now we're sending in nineteen-year-old lone rangers on suicide missions?"

Cooper recognized Schmitty's suddenly serious tone. It was something he didn't hear that often. "We've been doing this kind of thing for years, Schmitty. You know that. The mission profile gives someone like Rice the best chance of killing those NVA generals and coming out in one piece."

"Yeah, right." Schmitty's tone had become cynical. It dripped with bitterness.

Both men knew they were still over Cambodia. There were so many NVA troops in the jungle underneath them that it had been deemed impossible to get any kind of sizable strike force on the ground undetected. Headquarters knew that if the NVA picked up anything unusual, several high ranking NVA generals meeting at a secret bunker complex would just disappear. So what many men couldn't do, one man had to.

"Coop, isn't this kid pretty green to put out on a line like this?"

"Maybe," Cooper answered. "But Strong usually knows his operatives pretty well, and he handpicked this guy. And besides, Rice has Dave Tooks's rifle. That pretty much says it all, doesn't it?"

Schmitty was quiet at that. There was really no way to argue with Cooper's last statement. Tooks was a legend, and he had personally chosen Rice to be his heir. Schmitty shook his head. It was going to be a long week.

Mitch hit the ground running. He needed to get away from the LZ as quickly as possible. He sprinted about one hundred meters north, stopped, and then just melted into the night.

Mitch heard the sounds of the jungle all around him. Only the sound of his own breathing spoke of any human presence. He rested in the shadows. Stealth was everything on this trip. He knew the area was full of NVA, booby traps, and land mines, and if that wasn't enough, the jungle itself was full of a lot of unfriendly critters—everything from mosquitoes to tigers. So no matter where Mitch stood, he was someone's prey.

As Mitch caught his breath, the reality of his situation sank in. He was completely alone in a sweltering jungle that was trying to kill him. The hard realization chilled him so severely that even his clenched teeth started to chatter.

Some twenty kilometers from Mitch was a large complex of underground bunkers left over from the Japanese. The complex now housed a large contingent of NVA. Recently, some really important NVA generals had been seen there. Headquarters had gotten wind of a North Vietnamese-inspired offensive, and these generals, the leaders of the planned attack, had been slated for extinction.

Unfortunately, wanting these men dead and making it so were two entirely different things. Headquarters had discarded plan after plan until it was finally left with just Colonel Strong's suggestion to send in a silent scout team.

Tooks was supposed to have been here with Mitch, but he had bought it at Delta Company. There just hadn't been time to find another qualified sniper. The NVA generals just wouldn't be on site that long, and their deaths might well affect the outcome of the whole war. So Colonel Strong gambled and decided to go with just Mitch. Mitch had to go in, do the hit, and get out without ever being seen. There was no allowance for failure or capture. Mitch was an arrow that would either hit its target or fall dead at the end of its flight. It was all or nothing.

Mitch clamped his jaws together and ground his teeth to control his shakes. Consequently, he almost didn't hear the brush of clothing on limbs thirty meters to his right. People were hunting him. They were so close that Mitch could actually smell them. Instinctively Mitch squeezed the handles of both of his close-combat weapons, his silenced pistol and his fighting knife. Mitch squeezed so hard that even his own cold sweat refused to drip. Lost somewhere between a panic-stricken catatonia and the tension of an over-stretched spring, he watched as six NVA passed by just three feet away. Not one of them had a clue he was there.

It was quite a while after that before Mitch could think straight again. It was even longer before he could start walking.

When his panic finally subsided enough, he forced himself to review his orders. With each forced step, he replayed Colonel Strong's words. Mitch remembered he could only move in the gray light of early morning and late evening. Moving in the darkness when he couldn't see booby traps would be suicide. Moving during daylight when he could be seen would be even worse. So he only had about four hours a day to walk, and he had to make the entire twenty kilometers in three days. If the colonel was right, that was just enough time for him to catch the generals on the fourth day, the last day they were supposed to be at the bunker complex.

Mitch made himself keep walking. If his strike was successful, he would have just three days to cover another twenty kilometers to reach his mountain top extraction point.

In all this Mitch carried no radio and was completely on his own. He knew no one would miss him if he didn't come home. His obituary had already been written, and it would be published if he wasn't home within a week. It would say that he had died a long way from this Cambodian trail on which he currently walked, and no one would ever know where to look for his body. In truth, Mitch was already a ghost. Only his rifle was real.

That first night Mitch covered about five kilometers. He had to dodge three campsites of sleeping NVA regulars. Their posted lookouts never had a hint of his passage. When daylight came, he was nestled under the roots of a large tree. He stayed there for the whole day and watched some two hundred uniformed soldiers pass by. Those troops likewise had no inkling of his presence. He watched them carefully, memorizing their steps so he could avoid hidden land mines. It cost him precious sleep to learn where the unforgiving tripwires were, but it was a price he was willing to pay. But even so, by dusk he was completely exhausted.

The second evening Mitch inched along the edges of foot trails. He encountered several more encampments of NVA, but he was able to skirt around them without incident. The effort, however, gradually pushed his already frayed nerves past the breaking point. His heart became a trip hammer, each beat shaking his whole body.

Mitch was moving around yet another NVA campsite, the sixth or seventh he'd come across. Struggling to control his shakes, he concentrated on every step almost to the point of tunnel vision. Sweat drenched his every thread and burned his eyes. Mosquitoes out for their evening feeding fogged his face so badly he almost choked. They were so loud that Mitch was certain their incessant buzzing would give him away. The whining joined with the beating of his heart and filled his head so completely that he looked right past an obvious tripwire. Luckily, he was moving so slowly that his gentle brush against the wire didn't set off any explosives or alarms. The NVA had no idea he was there, but blast or no blast, the wire still did its work.

The touch of the wire was worse than that of any high-voltage power line. It jerked Mitch straight up in an instant convulsion and silenced the whole jungle. Mitch was suddenly a dead man. Just yards away a whole platoon of NVA regulars ate their rice rations. Mitch knew all they had to do was stop chewing, and they would hear his very blood racing through his veins. He tried to pull back silently from the wire, but it was too much. The wire stayed tight and jerked out the last fiber of his courage. In the next second Mitch broke and ran like a frightened animal, leaving his tattered soul strangled on the wire.

The startled NVA sentries never saw Mitch. They heard him crashing through the brush, but he made so much noise that they thought he was a startled wild animal. Wild water buffalo were known to be in the jungle, and the sentries assumed that was what they were hearing. Consequently, they neither shot nor came looking. Who wanted to mess with an angry buffalo?

Mitch ran as far and as fast as he could. He was far down the trail when a tree root caught his foot and sent him sprawling. He lay there in the mud for quite a while as wave after wave of panic and despair washed over him. Exhaustion and shame overwhelmed him. He shook with silent sobs, but no one was there to hear him crying. His isolation, his utter aloneness, bore through him like a tent stake pinning him to the ground. He was finished.

Mitch just lay in the muck, completely lost. It didn't matter whether his eyes were open or closed. All he could see was the decapitated girl, her dead, accusing stare framed by a collage of nameless Vietnamese faces he had destroyed at Delta Company. He tried to shake off the silent stares of judgment and regain his focus, but there was no mercy. Sinking deeper in the mud, Mitch slipped farther and farther into the horror and insanity that surrounded him.

After about twenty minutes the mind-killing visions let up. Mitch struggled to his feet. It didn't matter whether he was sane or not. He had to go on.

Mitch's black-clothed body responded, but his heart was gone, strangled by the tripwire and smashed by the flashbacks. He knew he had to find a safe place to wait out the rest of the night. He had to find a place where he could regain what the wire had taken from him.

Mitch was on a game trail. In front of him was a barely perceptible fork in the path. He was starting to step onto the more-traveled route when he suddenly realized he was not alone. The hair on the back of his neck stood straight up. He neither heard nor saw a thing, but *another's* presence overwhelmed him. Mitch tried to make his feet move, but they wouldn't respond. Instinctively, he reached back behind him with his right hand. There, at less than an arm's length, just above the level of his waist, he touched the final face of fear.

Mitch's fingers felt the *other* move at his touch. The face was large, more than a foot across, furry, and ringed with stiff whiskers. A large, coarse tongue reached out and abraded Mitch's fingertips. Then it surrounded his hand, almost forming a loop, and drew Mitch's whole hand into a huge, gaping mouth. As Mitch's hand was engulfed, he felt canines nearly four inches long, all with long, serrated edges on their back borders. The great cat, holding Mitch like a captured rat, gave off a guttural growl that ripped through Mitch's skin like a skinning knife. Terror gutted Mitch right where he stood, dismembering him from his very soul.

The guillotine-like mouth closed down on his arm, and Mitch collapsed. His life was forfeit. All that remained was the tiger's deep-throated purring. It was a sound that drowned out even the beating of Mitch's heart.

When Mitch woke up, he was sprawled alone on the muddy, less-traveled jungle path. All around him were the marks of the great tiger's paws. Mitch felt fluid running off his face. Wiping it clear with his strangely undamaged hand, he tasted not his own blood but rather the saliva left by the tiger's tongue. The greatest of all predators had taken Mitch, consumed him totally, and yet somehow had still left him whole. Mitch clutched at his still-damp face and traced the pattern of the cat's paws. Somehow he was still alive.

Inside his head, Mitch heard a gentle laughing female voice. The voice echoed distinctly that one great predator had just paid its respects to another. And that laughing voice, soothing and familiar, was suddenly enough. It told him Mitch he really wasn't alone. It told him he could find himself again if he only looked. It told him the mission was just and doable if he would just get up and go do it. It took several minutes, but the voice stayed with Mitch, repeating the message over and over again until Mitch finally recovered his soul.

Just a few yards away, hidden in the darkness, sat a huge Royal Bengal tiger. The great animal shifted on its haunches as Mitch resumed his long walk. Mitch had no idea the great cat was there, but the great animal saw Mitch clearly. It watched Mitch inch his way westward, down the tiger's own secret, less-traveled path. It seemed comfortable with Mitch's company. After all, they *were* brothers.

The bunkers Mitch sought were dug into the side of a small Cambodian mountain. They were an important installation, and the

North Vietnamese had expended a lot of time and energy to make the whole place as bomb and attack proof as possible.

Both B-52's and F-111's had already visited the site several times, but they'd had little effect. Their bombs had cleared away a lot of the jungle around the complex and filled the ground with gaping craters, but that was all.

One of those bomb craters was Mitch's goal. This particular hole, some sixty feet across, was about three hundred meters from the entrances that Mitch needed to watch. The result of two thousand pounds of misguided explosive, it offered Mitch a clear view of all of the complex's underground entrances. It was exactly where he needed to be to make the shots he had come for. The only catch was that the whole crater was full of land mines, all of them etched with Mitch's name.

At about about 0200 hours, Mitch finished working his way around an encampment of fifty or sixty NVA. He parted some of the underbrush and could just make out the buried bunkers in the moonless night. The crater was right in front of him.

Mitch entered the depression very carefully, every movement deliberate. He had already made several long probes of bamboo, and he used them like fingers to feel underground for the hidden explosives.

Over the next two hours Mitch read the crater like a blind man reading Braille. Every hesitant, delicate thrust of the bamboo told him of the sudden death just inches below.

Mitch found mine after mine. Some were only a foot apart and several were hooked in sequence for simultaneous explosion. He surrounded every man-killer with small stubs of bamboo so that he gradually marked a trail that was both his way into and out of the pit. After nearly two hours, he finally reached a slightly deeper depression near the opposite rim, the place that would be his fire station.

The eastern sky was just beginning to lighten slightly when Mitch settled on his final spot. Working carefully but as quickly as he dared, he arranged the little depression so he could lie fairly comfortably. Finally satisfied, he pulled a fine netting over his whole miniature emplacement. The netting, woven full of local grasses, allowed Mitch both ventilation and cover. When he fixed its edges down and crawled under it, it was as if the bomb crater had taken him for its own. He was part of the landscape, someone buried alive.

Mitch didn't sleep that third day. He lay in the middle of the minefield and carefully scanned the bunker with his binoculars, the special Remington now ready. The day was long and hot, and Mitch's sweat made the mud under him slick.

The jungle's mosquitoes and crawling insects zeroed in on him and swarmed under his camouflaged cover. Their buzzing was maddening. As the tropical sun burned down with its smothering heat, the whole day turned into one huge, unforgiving sauna. Blinded by sweat and nearly choking on the bug-filled air, Mitch endured, numbed by a pain that pounded inside his head, a pain of a conscience that suddenly wasn't sure of itself.

For nearly the whole day the agony won Mitch nothing. The big NVA brass made themselves scarce, and by early evening, Mitch began to fear that they had already departed. But suddenly, just as the evening shadows began to form, everything changed.

Mitch was watching the biggest of the complex's underground entrances. With no signs of duress, he had figured that the generals would come and go by the easiest routes. After all, brass was brass no matter which side it was on.

Just as the tropical sun touched the tops of the western hills, Mitch saw a flurry of activity. Several men came out whom Mitch recognized as being captains or higher in rank. In the middle of the group were three older men who wore no insignia. They walked with obvious authority, and their clothes were of much better fit than anyone else's. Mitch had found his targets.

With almost no motion, Mitch shifted from his binoculars to his rifle. In the next two seconds, the weapon coughed almost silently three quick times. That was all it took to make Mitch an assassin.

The heavy bullets Mitch turned loose fell on the unsuspecting generals as quick, silent, instant death. The first round took the oldest general in the forehead. The next round tore away the second one's neck. And the third ripped open the last one's chest. The generals died standing next to each other, torn apart by the falling sky. They had no idea what killed them.

The confusion that followed was complete. No one heard the subsonic bullets as they fell from the sky, and no one heard the silent reports of Mitch's rifle. It took long seconds for the junior officers to recognize what had happened, and it took several more seconds for them to drag their dead leaders back to cover.

As the survivors scrambled in panic, Mitch went over the next part of his plan one more time. He knew the NVA wouldn't be able to easily figure his angle of attack, and the bottom of their own minefield wouldn't be a place they would think to search for him. His job now was just to sink deeper into his pit.

Mitch took down his Remington and stored it quickly, his hands moving almost automatically. He had rehearsed his post-shooting drill to the point of mindless perfection, but not having to think about his movements was a mistake.

In all of his previous combat, Mitch had always shot out of self-defense. This was the first time he had actually hunted down and executed unsuspecting men. Before he had always been just another combatant struggling to survive. This time he was a killer, and his victims had no chance at all.

The impact of what he had done shook Mitch to his very soul. He tried to concentrate on the situation around him, but he couldn't hold his focus. All he could see were the three men he had just killed. He saw their last looks and felt his own conscience being pulled down into a deep quagmire.

This new pit was a dark, cold place, one that Mitch had visited before. He had forgotten his previous encounter with hell, but now with his eyes wide open, he returned to another killing time, this one long buried in his past.

Mitch was suddenly eleven years old again. He was on his grandparent's little farm, squirrel hunting on an Indian summer afternoon. He had just had a big tongue-lashing from his father over chores that hadn't been done, and he was still boiling mad, his mood just as fiery as the brilliant, autumn colors of the Midwestern hardwood forest.

Once more Mitch soaked in the scene's beauty just as he had done all those years before. But just as it had happened then, it happened again. The beauty couldn't extinguish his anger. In an instant Mitch felt the autumn's beauty slip away, replaced by a cold, gray, evil *presence* that was everywhere. The *presence* took away the colors of the trees and chilled the sun. Mitch felt his soul leave his body, and he watched again in horror as the *presence* once more took control of every square inch of his body.

Eight years ago Mitch had watched his little. 22 rifle turn around in his hands and take aim on his own forehead. Now that rifle was his silenced Walther. Now, just as it had happened before, Mitch watched his dispossessed fingers draw back the weapon's hammer and reach for the trigger.

As an eleven-year-old, Mitch had found enough strength to deny the suicidal impulse. But this time he had no such strength. His eyes stared into the pistol's muzzle, dilated beyond full. The pistol filled his whole vision, and the explosion that followed shattered his brain.

One of the NVA patrols that Mitch had bypassed the night before had been near when Mitch had made his three shots, and it had been quickly deployed in the confusion that followed. One of the patrol had thought he had seen something move down in the shell crater where Mitch was and had cut loose with his AK47.

The sudden burst had set off three connected land mines simultaneously. Flying shrapnel had filled the air, killing the young soldier and three of his fellows where they stood. The shock wave of the blast had ripped into Mitch's depression, tearing away part of his camouflaged netting and knocking him senseless. Mitch had dropped his unfired pistol into the mud. After that, there was only darkness.

A long period of unconsciousness followed before Mitch's eyes gradually filled with light once more. He heard angry Vietnamese voices all around him. The men were gathering up their dead and wounded and were not interested in searching farther into the shell crater. They soon departed, leaving Mitch alone to regain the use of his limbs. He was deathly cold, drenched completely with his own sweat, and barely alive. Somehow, he had once more escaped death at his own hands.

The price of Mitch's ransom, however, had been high. It took him the rest of the night to regain control of himself. Consequently, he was forced to spend yet another day in the pit. Motorized and foot traffic were everywhere, and Mitch dared not move. The NVA were abandoning the compromised complex, and everyone and everything were being moved out. Hiding in his hole, Mitch didn't know where all the men were going, but wherever it was, he knew it would be without their leaders.

By mid-afternoon, the patrols that searched for Mitch were called in. The NVA hunting him had been shooting their own when they ran into each other in the jungle. Forgotten land mines and booby traps were also taking their toll. By nightfall, the cost of continuing the search for the "ghost rifle" was just too high. The whole jungle was in chaos.

By evening Mitch, hiding in his depression, had accounted for more casualties than a whole company of battle-hardened marines. The whole western command of the North Vietnamese army was compromised. Mitch had been hiding in his bomb crater the whole day long, but his "ghost" had walked through the jungle, making it its own. And it had killed and maimed with every step it had taken.

So, in the end, it had all come true. What whole flights of B-52's and F-111's couldn't do, one sniper had done. The generals were dead and the bunker complex abandoned. All that was left was for Mitch to cover some twenty kilometers in two days. He was almost home.

"Hey, Coop! There he is! Three shorts and one long!" Schmitty hollered into his headset.

"Yeah, I saw the black light too! Get over him!"

"Hot damn, I'm rich!" Schmitty whistled.

"How much money did you put on Rice's nose, anyway?" Cooper asked as he activated the chopper's winch.

"Just a 'C note'."

"And what kind of odds did you get?"

"Two hundred to one, like I said. I wanted higher but couldn't get it."

"You blood-thirsty, money-hungry, son of a bitch!"

"Down, boy, down!" Schmitty answered. "Be respectful. I'm rich."

Cooper relented a little, working the winch's controls. "Okay, wise guy, but remember. Half of it goes to Rice. I heard you say so."

Schmitty jerked back. "You can't make me do that! That was just bullshit talk!"

"You watch me, you sorry mother! I'm going down to get him, and you had better be ready to give him his money when I come back! Then we're all getting the hell out of this fuckin' place!"

Schmitty made an obscene gesture at Cooper, but then he smiled and pointed at the winch. "You're right. Go get him."

Schmitty steadied his controls while Cooper dropped into the jungle. No one had made Schmitty open his fool mouth about his bet. That had been his own doing. So now he would just think of the $10,000 he would give Mitch as a business expense. He grinned to himself… come to think of it, that $10,000 probably was the best investment he'd ever made.

Mitch was right there, waiting on the jungle floor when Cooper slid down out of the trees.

"Riceman, you smell awful!"

"Hell, Cooper! You smell plenty good enough to me!" Mitch answered. "And I don't even like you."

"Keep your distance, marine, or I'll leave you right here!"

Mitch hooked himself onto the winch line beside Cooper. "Hey! This is Air America, isn't it?"

Cooper just shook his head. "Yeah, this is still Air America, Riceman. We still aim to please."

"Then lets get the hell out of here! I've had all of this shit hole I want!"

Cooper gave Mitch a thumbs-up and started the winch. The flight home had begun.

It was very early in the morning of January 16 when Schmitty and Cooper landed their secret helicopter on the pad outside Colonel Strong's bunker. The colonel was there to meet them.

"Good flight, Cooper?" Strong asked.

"Yes sir. It was a real milk run. We skirted a long ways south like you suggested and actually approached the pickup point from the west. Rice was right there flashing his UV light just as pretty as you please. I brought him up on the lift, and we made the run home without even one round coming our way."

"Is he okay?"

"As far as I can tell, sir, he's just fine. He smells awful and looks leaner, but I guess he actually pulled it off. Charlie never laid eyes on him."

"Excellent! Get him cleaned up, and get some food into him. Then bring him to my office. I want to debrief him myself."

"Yes sir."

"Ah… Cooper?"

"Yes sir?"

"You and Schmitty did a good job."

"Any time, colonel. Like Schmitty says, we're Air America. We aim to please."

About an hour later Mitch again stood in front of Colonel Wilson Strong. Mitch should have been too tired to feel nervous, but he was up-tight anyway. Strong saw that and tried to put him at ease.

"Relax, Rice. Just sit down and tell me as best you can what happened this last week."

Mitch sat down and took the next hour to recount his experiences. He spoke in a bare bones manner with no particular elaboration. He was brutally honest about everything that had happened, even about the times when he'd nearly given up on the mission. Strong didn't seem taken aback by anything Mitch said. When Mitch had finished, Strong asked if there was anything else.

"Well, yes, sir, there is," Mitch admitted. "Did I get what I was sent after?"

Strong's battle-hardened face broke into a smile. "Hell yes, Rice. You got exactly what you were sent after. You took out one third of the supreme command structure of the North Vietnamese army. You even got General Truong, and we didn't even have a recent picture of him. He was General Giap's best tactician."

"Your intelligence must be pretty good for you to know all that already, sir."

"Yeah, it's pretty good, Rice. Actually, one of your friends is one of our best sources."

Mitch cocked his head to one side.

"We'll come back to that later," Strong said. "Now tell me how you knew to take out Truong."

Mitch just shrugged. "Colonel, I just figured to whom everyone was kowtowing and made my shots accordingly. Besides, those three didn't dress like normal officers. Their clothes were too nice. I just took out everyone who was well-dressed."

Strong snorted and shook his head. "I guess that's about as good an answer as any." He offered Mitch his hand. "Son, you did a great job. I'm glad you made it home."

Mitch took Strong's hand. "Thanks, colonel. I'm glad I made it too."

The colonel seemed to enjoy the moment, but then his smile slipped. "Mitch, there's one more thing you need to know. You did such good a job out there that the Vietcong's offering a huge reward to anyone who can tell them who the "ghost rifle" is. They want your head, son. They're never going to forget what you've done to them."

"Sir, I won't tell anyone if you won't."

Strong's smile returned. He usually didn't smile in debriefings. "No sweat, marine. The "ghost rifle" never was. Nothing you've said here has ever happened. In fact, you've spent most of the last three weeks recovering from your facial wounds. Your medical record shows that you actually had quite a nasty facial infection. You almost didn't make it."

Strong's smile continued. "Both Sarah Thornton and Mother Marie have been by to ask about you several times, but you were riding it out in an isolation unit on one of the hospital ships out in the Gulf. In fact, you just got back this morning. Welcome home, Corporal Rice."

"Thank you, sir," Mitch answered as he shook Strong's hand. "But what do you mean 'corporal'?"

"That's what I said, Rice," Strong answered. "All my operatives are at least sergeants, but your Marine Corps command structure won't let me give you that big of a promotion. So I guess you're the lowest ranking field operative I've ever had. I'm sorry the pay isn't better."

"Don't worry about it, sir. If marines were supposed to have money, the Corps would give it to us. I…" Mitch silenced himself in mid-sentence.

"Is there something else, Rice?"

"Yes, sir, I guess there is. Thanks to Air America, I have $10,000 to dispose of. Do you think you could get the money to a certain orphanage for me without anyone knowing about it?" Mitch extended his hand. He had a wad of one hundred dollar bills in it.

Strong recoiled a little. "Where'd you get that?"

"Schmitty had a little bet going as to whether I'd get back or not, sir. I guess we won."

The colonel shook his head and took the money. "Rice, you're unreal. Sure, I'll see that Mother Marie gets the money. Right now she could really use it."

"Thank you, sir."

"Get the hell out of here, marine. Find your bunk and get some rest. In the morning, report to Lieutenant Baick."

"Yes, sir," Mitch answered, trading salutes with his commander.

"Lieutenant?" Mitch asked the next morning after he had reported in as ordered.

"Yes, corporal? What is it?" replied Lieutenant Baick, one of Colonel Strong's adjutants.

"Sir, would I be out of line if I went over to the orphanage this afternoon?"

"Rice, all passes into the city have been canceled. With the amount of traffic into the city, we're pretty sure that a large number of NVA are already there. It wouldn't be safe for you on the streets, and it certainly isn't safe for Mother Marie if she is seen in your company."

"Oh…" Mitch's face fell. He turned to go. "Thank you anyway, sir."

"Wait a minute, corporal," Baick said. "I think you should go to church this afternoon."

"Excuse me, sir?"

"Look, Rice. I know that you're Catholic, and just down the road is a cathedral. It's Sunday, and since the church isn't inside the city, the colonel hasn't put it on the off-limits list yet." The lieutenant had a funny look on his face. "So why don't you go to church? I think that you'll find it very uplifting."

"Ah… thanks, lieutenant," Mitch replied. He tried to read Baick's inscrutable expression, but he couldn't make any sense of it.

"Good, corporal. Get going. You can still make the late service."

It was early afternoon when Mitch entered the ornate, white church. He figured all the Masses would be over, but the lieutenant had been right. A service was just starting.

The Mass was in a mixture of French and Vietnamese. Mitch couldn't speak either language, but the message of the ceremony was familiar and universal. He knelt down in the last pew at the back of the church and soaked it in.

Way up at the front of the pews sat a group of nuns and several small Vietnamese children. Their backs were to Mitch, and he didn't focus on them. His focus was on the altar.

A lot had happened since Mitch had last sat in a church pew, and he found he no longer had words to pray. So he just knelt quietly, focused on the altar, and blocked off the rest of the world. Somehow it was enough to make him feel peaceful. He hadn't felt that way for a long time.

Mitch's spell was suddenly broken by a tug on his sleeve. He looked down and saw a familiar little face. It was the same little girl to whom he had given the chocolate at the orphanage, and she was holding out her arms to him again. Mitch looked around. The Mass had been over for a while, and he hadn't even realized it. Behind the little girl stood all of the nuns from the orphanage. Mother Marie was there, and so was Sarah. They were all smiling at him as he gathered up the little girl.

"Welcome home, Corporal Rice," Mother Marie said.

Mitch couldn't find his voice.

"What's wrong, Mitch? Did you leave your tongue on the hospital ship?"

It was Sarah.

"Ah… ah…" Mitch stammered.

"Don't pester the corporal, Sarah. I'm sure he has been quite busy since he was last with us. Why don't you visit with him while we finish with the children?" Mother Marie smiled her special smile for him and then gathered up all of the children.

Mitch started to put the little girl down, but she stretched upwards and gave him a kiss on his cheek. The gesture surprised him, and his whole face turned crimson.

"Mitchell Rice, I do believe you're blushing!" Sarah said.

"I guess I'm just surprised to be seeing all of you," he mumbled, trying to recover. "I asked the lieutenant if I could come to see you at the orphanage, but he said that all passes into town had been canceled. It was his idea that I come here. He didn't mention anything about seeing you."

"Baick knows a lot more than he lets on," Sarah answered. "We're here delivering the last of the children to the families who are going to care for them."

Mitch was stunned. "You mean all the children have been adopted?"

"In a manner of speaking… yeah, I guess that's about right," Sarah said. "A certain unnamed American colonel has furnished each child with a dowry of greenback American dollars. Mother Marie has been screening foster parents for some time now, and the colonel's money was all it took to let the families take them in. She feels pretty good about where all of the children have been placed."

Mitch was on a roller coaster. Things were happening too fast. "So where does this leave all of you?"

"Mitch," Sarah answered, "Mother Marie is sending all of the sisters home. She's really worried about what's happening here. Just before we came here, she got word from Colonel Strong that he has come up with even more money. Everyone is going home to France. The colonel says there is a big VC build up in the city, and the whole countryside is about to blow up. So nearly everyone is leaving tonight."

Mitch caught her words. "What do you mean 'nearly everyone'? Who's staying?"

Sarah dropped her voice. "Well… I guess Mother Marie, Sister Danielle, and I are staying behind for now."

"What?" Mitch erupted. "That's crazy! Why aren't you going?"

Sarah looked at Mitch. His eyes seemed to shoot out red sparks. "Mother Marie said we had to keep some sort of presence at the orphanage, or it would seem suspicious and jeopardize the children. The rules of the order say that at least two sisters have to be together at all times so Sister Danielle, being the youngest and the strongest, said she would be the one to stay. Mother didn't fight her over it."

Sarah hesitated again.

"So why are you staying?" Mitch demanded.

"I don't belong to the order, Mitch." She was almost pouting. "They can't order me around. I would feel like a coward leaving them at a time like this. Everyone has tried to make me go, but I won't until this whole thing is over. I won't!"

She saw Mitch wasn't buying her explanation, and her pout turned angry. "Don't you dare give me that kind of look! I know damn good and well that you weren't on any hospital ship for the last two weeks! You have been on some sort of spy mission for Colonel Strong to god-knows-where! Only God Himself knows how you managed to come back in one piece! So don't you look at me with those red eyes of yours! Mine can get just as hot as yours! If you can do what you want with your life, risking it for some worthless politicians, then I can put my life on the line for someone who means something!" Her eyes had their own fire.

"Someone like Mother Marie?" asked Mitch, refusing to wilt under her outburst.

"Don't try to talk me into going, Mitchell Rice! I won't go!"

Mitch stood his ground. He had a knowing look about him. "I wouldn't think of trying to talk you into anything, Sarah. In fact, I'm grateful that you'll be around to help keep Mother Marie from turning herself into some sort of martyr." He smiled slightly at her. "But, shouldn't you lower your voice a little? After all, we're still in church."

Sarah looked around. No one seemed to be looking at them. Suddenly, it was all more than she could take, and she melted.

"Oh Mitch! I'm scared shitless! Everything's coming undone!" She started to cry. The veneer of her courage had just worn through.

Mitch took her into his arms and just held her. After a few moments, she stopped sobbing, dried her eyes on his shoulder, and drew back.

"I still won't go without her, Mitch!" It was an oath. "I won't!"

Mitch drew her back into his arms. "I know, Sarah," he whispered into her hair. "I won't go without her either."

Chapter Five

Tet eve began quietly enough, but Wilson Strong's stomach ached with a growing uneasiness. Three months ago Dave Tooks had captured documents that said this would be the time of a big communist offensive. Strong had pushed hard to have headquarters take Tooks's information seriously, but everyone from General Westmoreland on down had decided such a plan was too ambitious. They concluded that the documents were phony and wrote the whole idea off as just a big propaganda trick. Strong had been nearly insubordinate over the decision, but it didn't matter. Tooks's captured documents had been discarded.

Strong had refused to buy into the party line and had prepared his command as best he could for the attack that he knew was coming. His little base was armed to the hilt, and his ROKs were psyched for the worst. He'd even gotten all of the orphans and nearly all of the nuns out of harm's way. Only Mother Marie herself, along with Sister Danielle and Sarah, remained. Strong had tried his best to get the old nun to leave her mission, but she refused to give up the idea of covering for her children. Neither Danielle nor Sarah would leave her. It hurt him deeply, but there was nothing more he could do. The attack was coming. There was no more time.

Strong's intelligence suggested that perhaps two North Vietnamese divisions were poised right outside the city, ready for a single, monstrous thrust. There were already a huge number of Vietcong were inside the city. Just the previous day Lieutenant Baick had nearly been killed at the north end of the Perfume River Bridge when a grenade exploded under his jeep. The lieutenant had to leave the crippled vehicle and retreat home with all guns blazing. It had been close.

It was now nearly 1900 hours. Strong was in his command bunker when Lieutenant Baick came in. Baick, who had calmly stared death in the face just the day before, was fidgeting and stammering. His uneasiness immediately alerted Strong.

"Lieutenant, what's the problem?"

Baick gulped and then blurted out. "Sir, I have a problem with Corporal Rice."

"What kind of problem?"

Mitch Rice had been a real find. The kid wasn't as experienced as Dave Tooks, but he was the best pure shooter Strong had ever seen. The foray into Cambodia had the makings of another battlefield legend. Tonight Rice had to be on track. His nighttime shooting was an edge that the colonel had to have. Everyone's survival was at stake. And besides, Strong grudgingly had to admit to himself, he had feelings for the young marine and that was something that Wilson Strong just didn't allow himself. He had to know what had Baick so shook up.

"Sir, the corporal wants to go into the city to get the mother superior and the other two women. I don't think I can stop him unless I put him under arrest."

Strong caught Baick's eye and saw panic. "That's crazy, lieutenant! You know better than anyone here what it's like inside the city. He wouldn't get ten steps! He's just one man! All he'd do is get himself killed!"

"Begging the colonel's pardon, sir. Just a few days ago that same one man did more damage to the enemy's high command than anything else we've done during this entire war."

Strong's stomach cramped hard. He wasn't use to his ever-faithful executive officer taking issue with him.

"Sir," Baick went on, "I know Rice would be invaluable here if the attack comes, but tonight he's... I don't know... different. He paces, back and forth, drawing and sheathing his knife like a cat baring his claws. If he doesn't go..." The lieutenant lowered his voice. "Don't take this wrong, colonel, but tonight Corporal Rice is going to kill something. Let it be the VC."

Baick's last statement bristled the hair on the back of Strong's neck. "Explain yourself, lieutenant! You think the corporal's a threat to us?"

"I'm sorry, sir. I'm not accusing the corporal of anything crazy, but it's just that... tonight, sir, he's a tiger."

Strong felt his gut seize.

"Sir, it's his eyes. Tonight he's not like us.

Tonight he's walking death."

Strong's stomach went way past cramping. All that remained was a hollow numbness. Baick was one of the coolest operators Strong had ever seen. Yet here the lieutenant stood, caving in to downright superstition. The colonel shuddered. The hell of it all was that Strong knew that Baick was right.

"Sir, Corporal Rice is right outside. He's already in his blacks. He's a shadow that will kill anything in his path. Let him go, colonel. He's the only chance the sisters have." Baick was past hesitating. "Colonel, it *is* the right thing to do!"

"I know, Yang. I feel the same debt of honor and affection for the sisters that you feel."

Baick started to speak, but Strong silenced him with a toss of his hand. A few long moments passed. "Do you really think he could get to them, Yang?"

"Sir, tonight Corporal Rice is more than a "ghost rifle. He's..." Baick stopped.

"He's what, lieutenant?"

"Colonel, when I was a little boy, my grandmother told me a story of a great tiger, a beast with eyes of fire and claws of steel. The tiger killed everyone who looked on it. The story scared me to death."

"That was a Korean boogey-man story, lieutenant."

"I guess so, sir. But that's what Corporal Rice is tonight. His eyes *really* are burning! Let him go, colonel. He's all fire inside. Tonight, he really is that tiger!"

Strong saw that Baick's face was beyond fear or superstition. It was in absolute awe. He saw that Rice had overcome him, a consummate professional, without ever landing a blow, and somehow the impact of it all had taken Baick all the way back to his childhood fears. The colonel knew an omen when he saw one.

"He's outside, lieutenant?"

"Right outside, sir."

"Well, bring him in then. I want to hear how he intends to pull this off."

Thirty minutes later Lieutenant Baick and a small contingent drove across the Perfume River Bridge. Presumably, he and his ROK's were checking on the South Vietnamese forces that were guarding the bridge. Once the jeep reached the north bank a shadow slipped out of the rear of the vehicle and disappeared into the city. Baick looked at his watch. It was 2040 hours. Mitch's race against the clock and a ferocious, vengeful enemy had begun.

Mitch was dressed completely in black and was even more heavily armed than he had been in the Cambodian jungle. Moving in the shadows of the city's alleys, he was as invisible as wind-driven smoke. His pace was swift but careful, and his mind was as focused and deadly as the weapons he carried. Tonight he knew who he was, and the dark angel inside him hesitated no more. He had sworn to Sarah he wouldn't leave either her or Mother Marie alone. He would live and die, if need be, by that oath.

As he walked through Hue's back alleys, a metamorphosis took place. All his life Mitch had been looking for a cause to die for. On this night, in the alleys of Hue on the eve of Tet, he had found that purpose. Mitch was no longer a confused nineteen-year-old marine. Rather, his soul saw its reflection clearly. He was *both* a predator and a guardian! He *would* reach the orphanage! Mother Marie, Sister Dannie, and Sarah were both his trusts and his witnesses! The great battle of Hue had begun.

Mitch stopped outside the orphanage and listened carefully as he stood quietly in the shadows. The scene was much too silent, and he was afraid he was already too late. The word was out that any Westerners found in Hue would be dealt with very harshly by the invading North Vietnamese, and that edict especially included any Western women.

The door to the courtyard was slightly ajar. Mitch moved to its side, still hidden by the darkness. He heard an odd sound inside. He couldn't quite identify it, but it sounded like his old bicycle spokes clicking against a playing card. Whatever it was, it didn't belong.

Mitch backed up slowly along the wall of the courtyard until he found a place where he could get a handhold. Pulling himself upwards, he scaled the wall and carefully peered over into the interior. To his left he saw what was making the sound, a reel of detonator cord.

A Vietcong was busy unreeling the wire. Tracing the wire, Mitch saw satchel charge after satchel charge set up along the wall of the orphanage. The wires ran into the buildings that had once housed all of the children. It was obvious that Charlie was going to make a political statement with the destruction of the orphanage even if the children were gone. The three women were nowhere to be seen.

Looking around, Mitch counted at least five VC setting the charges. Farther to the left, he saw the lights burning in the chapel. No wires ran in there yet. If Mother Marie could have picked a place to make her last stand, the chapel would have been it.

Without making a sound, Mitch lowered himself into the courtyard. Drawing his fighting knife, he slipped up behind the busy Vietcong. Like a tiger killing a deer, he jerked the man's head forward and plunged the blade into the back of his neck right where the spine joined his skull. The man died silently before he could even spasm, pithed like a lab animal.

Mitch sheathed the knife and moved to the dormitory. He now held his silenced Walther. From the children's old sleeping quarters, the pistol's quiet cough couldn't be heard in the chapel, and Mitch used it like an executioner. Five more Vietcong died.

In the chapel, Mother Marie was almost numb with the pain. She was bound hand and foot, a long pole running behind her back through the crooks of her elbows. One of her captors pushed her down hard onto her knees and yanked back on her short hair so she had to stare straight ahead.

Mother Marie saw a barbaric scene. Sarah was stripped naked, bent forward over the epistle side of the chapel's small altar. Their captors had lashed her hands and feet with nylon cords to the altar's supports. One of the VC had already dropped his pants and was coming up behind her, laughing, eager to start the rape.

The leader of the group suddenly ordered Sarah's assailant to wait. The leader drew a machete from its sheath, and then exposed his own taunt self. He would be the first to violate Sarah.

"I know you understand what I'm saying, you wrinkled bitch!" he screamed at Mother Marie in French. "You're too old to rape so you'll just have to watch me fuck your American bitch with these!" He shook his big member and his cold blade at her. "After we're all finished with her, I'm going to chop off her tits and split her open, starting with her worthless cunt! Then I'm going to cram a grenade up her worthless, white ass!" He laughed. "You'll watch her explode into a bloody pulp just before this precious building of yours blows apart and crushes you!"

He took a big swing and smashed Mother Marie's face with the machete's handle. She fell backwards, but he caught her by her hair and jerked her back upright before she could hit the floor.

"Watch, old woman! Watch what I do to your daughter!"

Mother Marie started crying. She saw the Vietcong leader come up behind Sarah, tense and full in his purpose. Mother Marie was too desperate to even protest. She didn't care for herself, but she was beyond desperation for Sarah. The Vietcong officer grabbed Sarah's exposed buttocks and started his first thrust. Mother Marie, seeing that her prayers weren't going to be answered, despaired. And with that, hell opened up before her.

But the Vietcong leader never finished his thrust. He suddenly stumbled backwards and fell over. His face still held a cruel, demonic smile, but his narrowed eyes had opened wide with sudden astonishment. He had a small hole in his forehead. The machete fell from his hand and rattled on the floor.

From behind her, Mother Marie heard two almost simultaneous grunts of similar surprise from the two men who held her. She turned and saw them fall aside just like their leader. Each had his own hole is his forehead.

The whole scene turned surreal. Mother Marie was there, but she wasn't really within herself. Time had no more meaning than did the fleeting shadow that flew across the rear of the chapel. Two more Vietcong seemed to lose interest in life and fell oddly askew. From the corner of her eye, she caught view of Sister Danielle bucking against the last captor. Mother Marie heard Danielle scream, and then her trance was shattered by the sudden roar of an AK47. She saw Danielle roll away from the Vietcong and heard the sharp cracks of a smaller caliber, higher velocity weapon. The AK fell silent as it bounced on the chapel floor.

For the next few seconds, the world seemed to be strangely dark. Then Mother Marie felt strong hands lift her. She turned slightly and for a split second glimpsed the darkened face of the archangel of death. She gasped and blinked, and then she saw that her *dark angel* was Mitchell Rice.

"Mitchell!" she whispered sharply. "Go and help Sarah! Make sure she's all right!"

Mitch went to the altar. Drawing his knife, he cut Sarah's bonds. She was too terrified to even breathe. Lifting her off the altar, Mitch held her close while he wrapped the altar cloth over her exposed body.

Almost with a mother's touch, Mitch freed the cords. "It's okay, Sarah. I got them all. Dannie and Mother Marie are okay too." He put her down carefully. "Here, rest a minute. I have to untie Dannie. She bought me the time I needed to make the last shot."

Sister Danielle was crying silently but was very much aware. She gasped as Mitch cut free her bonds, stunned by the pain of her returning circulation.

"I know it hurts, Dannie. But you saved us all when you knocked that last VC off target. You did good."

For the next few seconds, Mitch's and Sister Danielle's gazes joined, and they saw deeply into each other.

Mitch saw the fear and felt the paralyzing, searing agony of a woman who had been on the brink of destruction. It was a despair that tore his heart from his soul.

Likewise, Danielle saw the mixture of hate, fear, and purpose that was consuming everything that was Mitch. She reached out to his face, but a horrible heat made her pull back. She could see him. She could see his whole soul. But she couldn't touch him. He was in hell.

"Dannie, can you help Sarah? She needs a sister's touch. I'll go help Mother Marie. We have to get out of here right now, before any more VC come."

Mitch freed Mother Marie and gave her back the torn habit that had been ripped from her. It took a few seconds, but, as she put on the garment, she returned to her old self. Somehow she found another habit, and she and Danielle slipped it over Sarah's still trembling, shocked form.

"It's all right now, Sarah," Danielle whispered into Sarah's ear. "Mitchell Rice is here, and he's going to take us to Colonel Strong."

Gradually, Sarah's eyes cleared and began to focus. "What's this, Dannie? You know I can't wear your habit. It doesn't belong…"

"Hush, child!" commanded Mother Marie. "If ever we held a sister, it is now! We are all of the same cloth!"

With that all three women held each other in a healing embrace.

Mitch turned away from them in respect. He knew they needed a few more moments of privacy and rest. The walk back to the river was going to be hard.

It was 2300 hours on the eve of Tet. The commander of the local Vietcong contingent was going crazy. It was his job to establish a corridor of attack through the southern portion of Hue to the Perfume River. In about an hour, an entire division of North Vietnamese regulars were supposed to enter the city. The commander intended to ensure they could walk right up to the river without any worry of the defending South Vietnamese ARVN.

The incompetent southern troops and their American overlords were to be contained at the bridge, and he had set up scores of sniper stations, machine gun nests, and hundreds of land mines to do just that. Not even the American tanks were to be a threat.

The first part of the evening had been easy. The South Vietnamese either didn't believe an attack was coming or were too trusting of the American's supporting firepower to believe they were at risk. Consequently, they offered no obstacles to the Vietcong. The commander, a long time Hue resident, bypassed and flanked them with ease.

Hue, once the capital of Vietnam, was a beautiful and unique city, a wonderful mix of Asia and Europe. The Vietcong commander felt that the city's character and the civilian population it still held would prevent the Americans from unleashing their fearsome artillery and deadly, dragon gunships. Any counterattack they might mount would have to be a building by building effort, and he knew the Americans couldn't sustain such a thing.

Hue would be the beginning of the Americans' end. They would be driven into the sea, drowned along with their southern puppets.

The commander had also been assigned the honor of ridding the central portion of the city of any Westerners or Westerner sympathizers. It had been his people that had taken control of Mother Marie's orphanage earlier that evening. The commander's superiors were especially anxious that the French nuns be made examples of. The population had to recognize that any warm feelings for the West would result in merciless reprisals. Besides, there were many rumors that somehow the nuns had managed to slip a great deal of intelligence to the Americans.

Consequently, the orphanage was to be utterly destroyed. In fact, the retribution was so important that the commander did the unexpected and followed up on the orphanage mission himself. And that was where the craziness began.

There were no words to express the shock the commander felt when he entered the orphanage's courtyard. He saw that not only were the buildings still intact but also that all his explosives had been neutralized. His attacking force, all of whom were proven combat veterans, were dead. They were dead not by strength of battle, but rather by simple execution. All but two had single bullet holes in their foreheads. One of these last two had a neat stitch of bullet holes across his chest, and the other had been nearly decapitated by some wild animal's vicious bite.

The commander felt cold, angry vomit in his throat. But the worse was still before him. Not *one* child or nun was anywhere in the place. Somehow, his men had been powerless to resist an enemy they could actually see, and nuns and children had been set free to disappear into the very air of the night. The commander wasn't sure if he was more scared of the orphanage's powerful protectors or of his own soon-to-be furious superiors. Both could eat his soul. The curse of his own doom was right before him.

The commander was still trying to figure out the mystery of the orphanage when several of his scouts reported back to him. It seemed that some sort of skirmish had been going on in the streets for over an hour. The scouts said machine gun nests were somehow blowing up by themselves. Experienced snipers, five of them in fact, had been found dead at their posts. Each one had been executed by single knife strokes to the head or neck.

The commander reeled inside. It was almost as if the demon of the orphanage was loose on the streets, and his force was fast becoming its plaything.

The commander tried to hide his confusion by tearing and cursing his way through his maps. As he did so, it suddenly hit him. The opponent that so plagued him was making a straight run for the Perfume River Bridge. The commander swore a bitter oath that this "demon" would never reach his American friends.

Mitch was tired. He had driven the three women as hard as he could to get them to Colonel Strong. The obstacles had been formidable. He had lost track of how many men he had killed and of the number of emplacements he had taken. He did know, however, that his silenced pistol was long since empty and that his grenades were all gone. He was now down to just his M16 and his faithful fighting knife. He hated to use the M-16 because its unique report would tell the world where he was, and his knife was dulling, having sliced through too many bones.

Five or six hundred meters ahead lay the bridge. Mitch knew that Colonel Strong would be there waiting as he promised, but they still had a third of a mile to go.

He turned to Mother Marie. "Mother, the bridge is just a little ways up there. Colonel Strong is there. You three will be safe once we reach him."

The old nun caught Mitch's eye and smiled at him. "Corporal, we have already been safe for a long time now. Where could we have been more secure than in the hands of our own guardian angel?"

Mitch couldn't believe her. Exasperated, he turned to Sarah and Dannie. "Sometimes she's just plain nuts! I'm no angel!"

"I don't think you have any idea who you really are, corporal," Sister Danielle said simply. "Sometimes a person is blind to his own light. Only other people can see it."

Mitch shook his head violently as though he was trying to throw off some great weight.

"But it really doesn't matter," Danielle went on. "The result will be the same. God will save us all."

Sarah smiled at Mitch. "It's okay, Mitch. It doesn't hurt to have God on your side." She looked out over the last row of buildings that blocked them from the bridge. "Are there more VC up there?"

"Sure," Mitch answered. He was quiet for a second. "Do you remember all those Claymore mines we saw on the side of the streets back there?"

"Uh-huh."

"Well, if you look under those carts up there, you'll see a bunch more. Everything here is mined to the gills! We'll have to grow wings to get through it all! Damn!"

Sarah let him curse and then asked quietly. "So what's the plan, Mitch?"

Mitch shrugged wearily. "We don't have the time for me to take on all that's up there, and my ammo is just about all gone anyway. So let's make a little detour around through that alley over there. That's the way I came into the city. It smells of dead fish, but it leads to a little path that goes down to the river. If we're real lucky and the real guardian angels of this place…." He stared firmly at both Mother Marie and Sister Danielle. "…. are still with us, it won't be mined yet. Maybe we can crawl our way home."

"It's a good plan, Mitchell," Mother Marie said. "We are all accustomed to spending a great deal of time on our knees. That short crawl should be easy. No one will see us. Our habits are nearly as black as your uniform. The darkness will be our friend."

Mitch squared his shoulders. "Sarah, are you and Dannie ready to go or do you need a little more time to catch your breath?"

The two younger women looked at each other and then back at Mitch. "Just show us the way, Mitch," Sarah said. "We're as ready as we'll ever be."

With that Mitch nodded and turned toward the alley.

The first one hundred meters or so were easy. The four just kept in the darkness of the street and stayed hidden. The last part of the alley, however, was blocked by a fire burning in an old fuel barrel. That light was the last barrier that held them in the city.

"Mother, you stay here with Sarah and Dannie while I go check out that fire up there. It wasn't here when I came in."

Mitch was about twenty-five meters from the barrel as he spoke. He inched forward another ten more meters and came somewhat into the light. Instantly, an AK47 ripped the air, catching him with its full blast.

The first two slugs hit Mitch, catching the frame of the empty pistol that was tucked into his waist. The third and fourth had better aim. They caught him in his lower right belly, tore through his muscles, ripped open his intestines, and blew a huge hole out his back.

Mitch was thrown backward two or three meters by the force of the multiple impacts. His air was crushed out of him, and his eyes dilated full with the sudden, ripping pain. He landed in the alley with a sickening thud.

The AK continued to roar. Its bullets chewed up the street all around Mitch. He could see the muzzle flash just twenty meters away. Mitch couldn't breathe and couldn't stand, but it didn't matter. He slipped his M16's fire control to full auto and brought it up. The M16 lit up the alley with fire brighter even than the fire in the fuel drum. Mitch caught the Vietcong commander full in the chest, and the AK fell silent.

The next seconds were suspended in the time warp that comes with sudden battle. Mitch felt himself slipping away. He struggled to regain his feet, but his legs denied him. His belly was on fire, and he couldn't breathe. He fell back down and sprawled in the alley, his consciousness slipping away in sudden agony.

Just as he was about to go out, he felt a familiar hand touch his. It was Mother Marie's. Her voice was strange, labored and distant.

"Mitchell, my life and all its purposes are now in your hands! They will always be there!"

She coughed and blood ran from her mouth.

"Remember, Mitchell! Look for things that last! Find things to live for, not to die for!"

She coughed again, and blood streamed from her nose.

"Remember me, Mitchell!" she gasped.

Through his pain, Mitch crawled to her and gathered her into his arms. She sighed deeply, coughed one last time, and died.

"*Noooo*!" Sarah screamed.

She had seen Mitch go down in the hail of rifle fire. Several of the bullets had bounced around her, and she had to watch in horror as one of them tore through Mother Marie's chest. Sarah had tried to reach her, but Dannie had kept her from diving into the fire. Sarah tried again just as Mitch's shots found their mark. She came up to Mother Marie just as she sighed her last, nestled in Mitch's arms.

"*Noooo*!" Sarah screamed again.

Behind Sarah, from the larger street they had just left moments before, four figures came at them at a dead run. It was the rest of the Vietcong unit.

The four had been supposed to stop Mitch's little band on the bigger street but had not seen their black-clad figures glide by. Only the commander, aided by the fire, had been able to make Mitch's band out. He had positioned himself as a final stopper, and he had been successful. But it had cost him his life.

The men yelled for their commander as they came at full tilt, spraying rifle fire everywhere. Sarah reached down and picked up Mitch's M16. She had never held one before and didn't know what all its switches meant. She just held the rifle awkwardly on its side and pointed it at the charging Vietcong.

"*You bastards*!" she screamed.

Sarah's scream was a death curse. The rifle's selector was still on full auto. She yanked the trigger, and the rifle ripped the night, burning away the very air. The rifle's own recoil pulled its muzzle transversely across the Vietcongs' paths. It caught them all in mid stride, dropping them dead right beside their leader, all of them frozen in a hail of fire.

The next several minutes were a complete blur in Sarah's later memory. She remembered dragging Mitch's unconscious form down the rest of the alley. Dannie did the same with Mother Marie.

Behind them, the whole world blew up as American mortars, Vietcong machine gunfire, and hidden land mines all thundered together.

Sarah, stunned and deafened by the battle's roar, stumbled and fell. When she looked up, she saw Colonel Strong coming, lunging through the killing fire. It was the last thing she remembered.

Colonel Strong and his ROKs pulled them all across the Perfume River Bridge at 2355 hours. Five minutes later, history would record the beginning of the great battle of Hue. History was several hours late.

Chapter Six

The stench of death in the central African jungle was awful. Jacob Wade could smell it long before he was even close to the quarantine lines, the place where he would have to seal his isolation suit. He cursed quietly. He wasn't sure which was worse, dying a quick death from a strange tropical plague or dying a slow death, melting down inside the bio-protective rubber suit. Maybe his estranged wife Marilyn had been right. There had to be a better way for a research microbiologist to make a living.

The rain forest of the Congo was a long way away from Berkeley, California. Jacob Wade, an up-and-coming virologist, had, not that long ago, called that university home. He had left its hallowed, technology-filled corridors to take his present position as a researcher for the Department of Defense.

Wade loved the bright lights of the academic world, having been raised in it since childhood by his college professor parents. Only the siren song of the Defense Department's offer, one packed full of limitless facilities and cutting-edge technology, had been enough to pull him away from it. However, now as the quarantine line came into view, Wade found he was having some second thoughts about his choice.

The quarantine lines stood right in front of him. Beyond them was a whole native village of some two hundred rotting human corpses, both adult and child, who had fallen prey, just four days ago, to some horrible disease bred by the jungle.

Wade felt his sphincters tighten as he closed up his suit. He hated being locked inside its steaming interior, but when faced with the specter of a plague-ridden death, he knew there was no real choice. His arrogance and brilliance might buy him a lot of slack in the normal world, but here, with a mindless, killing virus on the loose, there was no room for error.

Wade walked on and entered the dead African village. Corpses were strewn everywhere, already horribly decayed. By the amount of tissue damage he saw on each victim, it almost looked as if each villager had simply exploded, turned inside out by some horrendous internal pressure. It was like nothing Wade had ever seen before. Not even the photographs of the last bubonic plague victims in Bangladesh had shown anything like all this. If only whatever had caused all this devastation could be isolated and saved, all of Wade's sweating and cursing would be worth it. Perfect, killing viruses were far more precious than gold, and finding that kind of treasure was what his job was all about.

That first day in the African jungle quickly grew into a whole week. Wade, a near genius who had long ago had visions of genetically engineering away all sorts of diseases, worked tirelessly. He categorized autopsy after autopsy, analyzed specimen after specimen, and collected sample after sample. But, even with the most sophisticated equipment in the world (all of which the government had airlifted to him), the end of the week saw him no closer to the answer of the dead village than he had been at the start.

"Professor Wade?"

"Yeah…what do you want now, Amos?" Wade answered one of his field assistants, annoyed by the interruption.

Amos Bruce bristled. He hated his boss's selfish egotism. Genius or not, Amos swore this would be the last time he would work for the little demigod.

"Maybe you should look at this one, doc. This woman was pregnant. She has a dead twelve-week-old fetus inside, and the kid hasn't decayed at all."

Wade dropped the glass slide he was studying like it was a hot iron. "Goddamn it! Get out of my way!" he shouted viciously as he ran to the dead mother.

Every victim Wade had examined up to that point had deteriorated almost to the point of being unrecognizable. A fresh, undamaged fetus whose syncitial chorionic membrane was still intact was totally unexpected. Maybe, Wade thought, this new killer was like the syphilis of old, unable to penetrate the placental barrier of a first trimester pregnancy. It was a question he had to answer.

"Get me tissue cultures of this whole membrane!" Wade ordered. "Then let's try for some electron micrographs!" His hands flew over the little body. "At last we have some decent tissue to work with!"

"Right, doc! I'm already on it!"

Wade hawked his assistant's handiwork as the man lifted the little unmarked fetus out of its exploded uterine home.

"No! Don't do it that way! Don't let the umbilical cord touch the outside of the uterus!"

"Watch it, doc!" Amos hollered back, but it was too late. Wade had already torn his isolation glove on the clamp Amos had placed on the fetus's minuscule umbilical cord. In doing so, Wade rammed the sharp-tipped instrument right into the palm of his hand.

"Oh shit, doc! What've you done?"

Wade looked in horror at the clamp as it dangled in the torn fabric of his glove. His response was the wordless recognition of his own soon-to-be horrific death. He was too shocked to even react.

Eight hours later, Wade was airborne, winging his way westward over the Atlantic, locked inside an isolation chamber that was strapped into the cargo bay of an unmarked Air Force transport. The precious fetus that had signed his death warrant was locked inside its own isolation chamber right next to him.

"Oh God, Marilyn!" Wade prayed as he thought of his wife at home in Utah. "Oh God! I'm sorry! You were right all along! I should never have been here!"

The plane ride was worse than the worst nightmare Jacob Wade had ever had. His hand, punctured, neither bled nor swelled. But his mind, trapped in the isolation chamber, ran all over itself, swamped by thought-killing panic and remorse.

"I'm sorry, Marilyn!" he wept. "If I get through this, I promise I'll chuck it all and come home! I *will* be the husband you deserve!" Wade was so scared that he was bargaining with a god he really didn't even believe in.

Just ten days before, Wade and his wife had a horrible fight. Marilyn, a clinical psychologist, had somehow realized what kind of assignment the Defense Department was giving her husband. She had seen right into his dark purpose even though he hadn't said a word to her about it. She knew her husband's pride and ambition too well and had forced him into a showdown. Either he left his forbidden agendas behind or else she and Katie, their little four-year-old daughter, were history.

Ten days ago Wade had made his choice. Now, those same ten days later, that choice had turned him into a walking dead man. No matter how hard he cried there were no tears that could wash away what he had done. Each shuddering sob brought him one breath closer to the moment when his body would start falling apart, exploding from the inside out, another victim of this new thing called "Ebola."

Fate, however, like truth and fiction, sometimes held both gentler and stranger visions than could be expected. Jacob Wade did not contract Ebola. The fluids he had rammed into his own hand had been only fetal fluids, not those of the dead mother. The protective barrier at the base of the little baby's placenta had not allowed the infant to become infected. The little one had died only of asphyxia as its mother had convulsed her way into oblivion. That same placenta saved Jacob Wade's life.

It was also this same placenta that gave Jacob Wade the key to his future. Buried on its underneath side were several little pockets where the killing virus had been held in stasis, intact. Over the following weeks in a secret underground research lab in Nevada, Wade and his coworkers successfully isolated the wondrous killing machine. In the end, Professor Jacob Wade had gone from being a dead man to becoming the hottest property in the whole biological armamentarium of the U. S. government.

Normally, all this success and notoriety would have put Wade into seventh heaven, but the time in the isolation chamber had done something to him. After he finished isolating the Ebola virus, he went no farther. He remembered some of the promises he had made while strapped inside the isolation chamber. Consequently, the day quickly dawned where the once arrogant professor left the secret underground lab complex and again sought out the woman and child he had left behind.

It took some time, but in the end, Wade managed to maneuver his way to a place where he could both win back his family and re-stake his claim to the academic world. He left the Defense Department a free man and returned to the university life, collecting Marilyn and Katie along the way.

All of this -- the sparing of his life, the return of his family, and the promise of his professional future -- should have been enough for the adventure of a lifetime. Wade started with good enough intentions as he re-charted his life, but as the months went on, separated as he was from the Defense Department, he felt like he was tied to a chafing post. His ambitions just weren't satisfied by what he had in his hands at the university. He tried to do the right things, but all too often it came to him that he was just riding along, hitchhiking on the coattails of a twelve-week-old fetus. He wanted much more than that.

Chapter Seven

Mitch stood, transfixed by the streaks of green and red light that flew by him. Fire, death, explosions, and suffering were all around him. The ground beneath him was bloody, and his own right side burned ferociously. He tried to stay upright, but the pain was too great, and he fell back down into the fire-torn street.

Mitch reached out, quivering in the bloody dust, and found a hand beside him. It was warm and strong, and it pulled him up when he couldn't stand on his own. He looked at its owner and saw a woman he should have known. Her chest was bloodied, but she stood straight and tall, a warrior queen locked in a great battle.

"Mother?" he asked.

"Yes, my son?" The woman's eyes were full of fire.

"Mother! Let me help!"

Her eyes burned brighter. "My son, this is not yet your time! This battle is mine, not yours! You must go!"

"No! I can't leave you!" Mitch screamed.

The woman pushed him away with a strong hand that was turning cold.

"Go, my son! It is not yet time for you to meet your brother!"

The green streaks and red flashes came closer.

"Go! Go now!"

The woman's hands were almost ice, but Mitch couldn't resist them as they flung him aside.

"Remember me, my son! Remember me on the last day of fire!"

Mitch slipped down into a dark place, safe from the fire and pain that had almost claimed him, defeated and crushed by a loss he could not bear.

"Mother..." he cried. But he couldn't remember her name.

"Hey, Mitch! Wake up! You gotta stop this shit!"

Mitch stirred, mumbling something unintelligible as he saw a light at the other side of his darkness.

"Come on, man! The war's over! Wake up! No one's shooting at you here!"

Mitch picked his head up, lifting it off the calculus book that had been his pillow. Al, his roommate, was long suffering, but it was 2:00 a. m. Mitch had been asleep, collapsed on top of his textbook, for over an hour.

"Ah, damn! I've done it again," Mitch muttered. "I'm sorry, Al. I just dozed off."

"Dozed off ? Hell! You flat died! That was the worst nightmare I've ever seen! I've been trying to wake you up for half an hour! I was just about to hit you with a bucket of ice water!"

Al walked away from Mitch's offending desk light.

"Shit, Mitch, I don't know! You can't sleep because of all of these nightmares, and you can't study because you're too damn exhausted from not sleeping! Maybe I should just hit you in the head and put you out of your misery! Maybe then you wouldn't dream, and you could just soak in the math while you were unconscious! Hell! We could call it "nocturnal osmosis"!"

Mitch didn't take offense at the obvious cynicism. He probably deserved it. Al, a junior and a brother of a Vietnam MIA, had put up with a lot. Mitch flipped off the desk lamp and crawled under his covers. He hoped he would be able to go back to sleep.

It was early October, 1968. Mitch was not quite a fourth of the way through his first college semester at the University of Missouri/ Rolla, a really serious technical university nestled in the Ozarks. But the way things were going, he wasn't sure he would see a second.

The school had tried nearly two years ago to recruit him after he had graduated from high school. It had even offered him a juicy scholarship on the strength of his ACT scores.

Mitch had been flattered then, but that was a time when his life had a whole different agenda. Consequently, he had gone against everyone's advice, ignored the scholarship offers, and enlisted in the Marine Corps.

That was almost two years ago, and this was now. Now Mitch was out of the Corps on a medical discharge and was lucky even to have been admitted. Wounded Vietnam vets were a-dime-a-dozen and not considered prime scholastic candidates.

Mitch flipped off the desk light and crawled deeper under the covers, exhausted and haunted by the visions he had just seen. Like his covers, defeat and failure encased him. His despair was slowly extinguishing him.

For weeks nothing had been right. Mitch's powers of concentration, once his strongest suit, were shot, and his classes --especially calculus -- were eating him alive. His body, once faithfully strong and easily ignored, ached from fatigue and weakness. The summer had been long, but not long enough for him to completely recover from the evisceration of Tet. And beyond that, his soul was torn in half, ripped apart by a conscience that wouldn't let go of war's horrors.

Mitch's eyes grew heavy as streaks of math equations again flew by. His last thought, just as sleep finally brought him down, was that maybe the registrar's office had been right. Maybe he had no business being here at all.

The last month had been miserable. Mitch had faithfully gone to class every day, but it was all wasted effort. He was so tired from his sleepless nights that, more often than not, he nodded off in the middle of his lectures. When he did stay awake, he usually had trouble hearing what the professors were saying. His ears still rang with the echoes of battle, and, in place of blackboard diagrams, his eyes still focused on the grizzly sights of battle.

At night, those same bloody visions exploded into full-fledged terrors. All the scenes of AnHoa, Cambodia, and Hue came together, pillorying him to his past defeats, flailing him with his failures.

Tonight was no different than any of the others he had endured in recent days. He tossed and turned, sliding in and out of an uneasy sleep.

The evening's second dream, a sort of macabre kaleidoscope, was of the aftermath of Tet.

First there was Colonel Strong pulling him across the Perfume River Bridge while the whole world exploded around them.

Then there was the hospital ship in the Gulf of Tonkin with its endless days of surgery and post-op abdominal drains that vented his peritonitis to the outside world.

The hospital ship became a hospital in Guam where he groped at a colostomy that took away his pride.

Finally, Guam changed to the V. A. hospital in San Francisco where an experimental protocol of intravenous elemental feedings finally saved his life.

With each repeated step of the journey, all the remembered suffering shook Mitch ferociously, jarring his whole frame. He was just a rabbit caught in the jaws of a nightmarish wolf, and the creature was tearing him apart.

"Oh, goddamn it, Mitch! Wake up!" It was Al again. "You just *gotta* stop this shit! Come on! Wake up! You're doing it again!"

Mitch rolled over. Al was shaking his shoulder. It was a little before 7:00 a. m.

"Mitch, you gotta see someone about all this crap! I don't care if it's a shrink, a priest, or a goddamn bartender! But see someone! You're going nuts, and you're taking me along with you! This total lack of sleep is killing both of us!"

Mitch sat up and swung his legs off the bunk. He held his throbbing head in both hands.

"If you won't see a shrink, then at least go talk to your academic advisor," Al pleaded. "He can help you set up some tutoring."

Al was already dressed and was heading out to his first class.

"Some of the guys over at the TKE house are doing it, and they actually passed the last calc test."

Mitch groaned.

"Look, Mitch. I know you're a hell of a lot smarter than those beer-drinking frat rats. If they can break through the math curve, you can too. Talk to your advisor. Let him help you."

Mitch didn't even look at his friend. His head throbbed too much.

"I'm serious, Mitch! If you don't do something to change all of this, I'm going to move out! I won't let your shit take me down too! I've had it!"

Mitch knew Al was right. They'd had this conversation a couple times before.

"Okay, Al. You win. I'll try to talk to Dr. Fulton today."

"Good! It's about time!" Al turned to go. "But,

Mitch…"

"Yeah?"

"This time, do it, man. I'm not kidding any more about moving out. I want you to do better, but I won't blow my chances if you don't get that way. Get some help so we both can start sleeping. Okay?"

Mitch shrugged, surrendering. "Yeah… okay. I will today."

Mitch's scholastic advisor was one Sherman Fulton, Ph. D. Dr. Fulton was the chairman of the physics department. Mitch wasn't sure just how he had rated having the head of the department as his advisor. In fact, he really wished he had someone less intimidating for the role. Nevertheless, that's the way it was.

"Mitchell Rice?" It was Dr. Fulton's secretary. "Dr. Fulton can see you now."

Mitch got up and entered the professor's inner office.

"Well, Mitch, how can I help you?" Dr. Fulton asked.

Mitch started to stutter, but he caught himself. Steeling himself and pulling his shoulders square, he answered slowly. "Dr. Fulton, I need help. I'm having a real hard time getting my feet on the ground here. Calc is killing me, and I just can't seem to pull myself together." He took a quiet breath. "Sir, I've never flunked anything in my life, but I'm flunking *big time now*."

"Yes, I see that," the professor said. He was holding Mitch's test grades.

Dr. Fulton focused on Mitch. He had already reviewed the file that included both Mitch's high school transcript, SAT and ACT scores, and an abbreviated military record. It was obvious to the professor that Mitchell Rice was a very capable young man. It was also obvious that there were a lot of holes in the records, so many that Fulton was having a hard time measuring Mitch.

"Mitch, how much math did you really have in high school? I guess I don't know exactly what they taught you in this seminary."

Mitch answered slowly. "I think I had pretty good courses in algebra and geometry, Dr. Fulton. But I guess trig was a little light. No one figured anyone at St. Tom's was ever going to be a scientist. They put more emphasis there on the humanities than on anything else."

"Well, that might explain some of your trouble then." Fulton picked up Mitch's folder again. "It looks like you didn't even have a math course at all in your senior year there. Is that right?"

"Yes sir. That's right," Mitch admitted flatly.

Fulton was a little puzzled. "Son, how did you end up here and who set you up in our accelerated program? You obviously need college algebra and trig before you tackle calculus. I know you can do this stuff, but you need a better foundation to build on."

Mitch hesitated. "Dr. Fulton, I think it was you who signed off on my schedule when I enrolled."

Fulton looked surprised. Thumbing back through the registrar's forms he saw that Mitch was right. Fulton himself had signed off on Mitch's course choices. Or rather one of Fulton's grad students had, one who had been doing that chore for the department chairman. Still, the responsibility was Fulton's.

"You're right, son. I did approve all this. I'm sorry. I guess you slipped by me."

Mitch just sat there, not sure what was coming.

Fulton put the folder down again. "Mitch, how long have you been out of Vietnam?"

"I left there around the first of February, sir. Right after Tet."

"So what happened from February until you got here in September? You're record seems to be missing a lot of pages."

Mitch turned and looked out of the office's windows. "I guess most of the time I was in various VA hospitals, sir. I got a little torn up over there, and the medics were trying to patch me up."

Mitch's simple answer ran through the professor like a knife. Fulton realized that a really big foul up had happened here. This Mitchell Rice was barely out of the rice paddies, barely over whatever wounds he had received there, and no one in the registrar's office had even bothered to put that information in the file. If they had, Fulton, a veteran of Korea, would have picked up on the situation long before now. This kid was still recovering from a war. No matter what his IQ and ACT scores were, he should have had time to heal before tackling the rigors of Fulton's accelerated physics curriculum. Something had to be done.

"Can you tell me anything about Vietnam, son? Your military record looks like Swiss cheese. All it says is that you were a scout… that you were on detached duty…. and that you won *two* Silver stars and *two* purple hearts!" Fulton gasped. "Damn! Is this right? You were over there only about three months?"

"Yes, sir. I guess that's right. I wasn't there very long. And I guess I can't say very much more than what's there. Most of my record is classified."

"Classified or suppressed?"

Mitch shrugged. "Take your pick, sir. Is there a difference?"

Dr. Fulton pushed back a little in his desk chair. This wasn't right. This young man was in trouble, and he didn't deserve it. The semester was already far progressed, and somehow Fulton had to find a way to fix this mess.

"You just relax, Mitch. Go on back out to my secretary. She'll get you something to drink. Then take a walk. I need to make some phone calls. Come back late this afternoon, and I'll see what I can have ready for you. Okay?"

Mitch acknowledged his professor's suggestion and slipped out. When he returned around 4:00 p. m. , Fulton greeted him with a large poster board that held Mitch's whole schedule. The professor had laid out all of Mitch's classes, and he had added whole blocks of time dedicated to tutoring sessions that he said Mitch had to attend. It looked like Fulton had recruited about half of the department's grad students to act as Mitch's personal mentors.

"It's okay, son," Fulton explained. "All these guys want to keep me on their sides. I'm the department chairman, and I control all the grants that fund their research projects. They all owe me."

He grinned a little malevolently.

"They'll be *happy* to help you."

Dr. Fulton had organized Mitch's whole life, the poster board detailing nearly every step of every day. It was a structure that Mitch could grab hold of, and in the days and weeks that followed, he followed it to the letter. Tutors came and went in abundance, and Mitch surrendered to their prompting. Slowly, the semester got better.

While Mitch struggled to get his academics together, he also strained to get his body back on track. In high school he had been a pretty accomplished athlete, both in track and in basketball. In the Corps, he certainly had been no shrinking violet. Consequently, once the books started to improve, he began to frequent the gym and to run again. The exercise time was even on Dr. Fulton's schedule.

Mitch's workouts were hard. His body complained constantly, hurting in some place new nearly every day. But somehow it all helped. Mitch's mind cleared, and he starting sleeping better. The horrible nightmares still came on a lot of nights, but the daytime flashbacks almost disappeared.

Gradually, he established a rhythm. He ate, drank, slept, studied, and exercised nearly every day, and with the new cadence, he got better. It was in the middle of this healing process that Mitch met Jacob Wade.

Jacob Beel Wade, Ph. D. was brand new in his position as the head of the chemistry department's new biochem section. He had been on the job only for about three months. UMR had never offered biochemistry before, and Wade, frightened by his near disaster in the Congo and shaken by his almost failed marriage, had taken the position as a chance for a fresh start. Somehow he had to leave both Berkeley and the Defense Department behind.

Wade quickly learned after his arrival in Missouri that UMR was a far cry from Berkeley. In that liberal California university, he had been recognized as a "wunderkind" as he had completed his Ph. D. work. Here in Rolla, Wade was looked on as just someone else to compete for the university's research grants. And so far, he hadn't won too many battles for the bucks.

Wade's little lab and office weren't even in the main chemistry building. Rather, he was relegated to the "barracks," as the temporary buildings were called. There he struggled to win students and recognition for his brand of chemistry. It was pretty frustrating, and frustration was never something Jacob Wade could tolerate for very long.

Marilyn Wade, however, was happier than she had been in years.

She had been devastated when Jacob scrapped their marriage, choosing his career over her and little Katie. She had chided herself for the self-pity she felt during the first years of her marriage to Jacob. She had known from the beginning that, at best, he was just agnostic, a man bound to no real moral standards. But she had married him anyway, and rather it was her stubbornness or her pride, she had wanted her marriage to survive. When Jacob returned from Africa a frightened, almost deranged, man, she had swallowed her pride and agreed to try it again. It had taken a huge effort and a lot of humility, but she was ultimately rewarded. She, Jacob, and Katie got their second chance.

At UMR Marilyn was offered a position in the school's academic enrichment program as a career counselor. She was getting to use a lot of her psychological training in the position, and she found it wonderfully stimulating. Even Katie seemed to be doing better in first grade than her previous, tantrum-filled, kindergarten year had predicted.

So when it was all totaled up, the whole Wade family was doing better than anyone had expected.

On this particular day, Jacob had finished early and taken himself down to the handball courts to pick up a couple of matches with the students. The games were fun, and when they were over, Wade moved to the weight room to finish his workout with some time on the slant board. Marilyn seemed to like the recent loss of his "love handles," and he liked her renewed responsiveness.

Wade slipped into the weight room but saw the slant board was already occupied. He was winded from handball and wasn't under any particular time pressure. So he waited.

The young man on the slant board was really putting himself through it. His efforts exposed his abdomen, and the scars there spoke of a recent surgical hell. Wade recognized the scars for what they were, and his curiosity was piqued.

"Hi," Wade introduced himself.

Mitch had just finished his routine and was disengaging himself from the board's footrest.

"I'm Jacob Wade. I'm one of the teachers here." Wade offered Mitch his hand. "Have we met before? You look familiar."

"I don't think so, sir," Mitch answered slowly. His belly muscles were burning, but he tried to be courteous. "What's your department?"

"I'm in the chemistry department," Wade returned. "Are you taking any chemistry courses this term?"

Mitch nodded yes.

"Maybe I've seen you there in the building then."

Mitch didn't know what to say. With all the attention he had been getting from professors and grad students lately, he could scarcely remember his own name, let alone all of theirs. But he didn't remember ever seeing this Professor Wade before.

"Yeah, that's probably so," Mitch said. "But I guess I don't remember seeing you there, sir. What section do you teach?"

Wade laughed a little. "I teach biochemistry. I'm the section head."

"I'm sorry, sir. I'm just a freshman," Mitch apologized. "I'm so green I didn't even know we had a biochemistry department."

Wade smiled a wry sort of grin. "That's okay. A lot of other people don't know I'm here either. This is the first semester biochemistry's been offered. Right now the only students I have are humanities students who are looking for an easy science to fill out their transcripts."

"Boy, I bet they're getting a rude awakening," Mitch replied. "Biochemistry's pretty heavy stuff."

Wade liked the youngster's reply. It was nice to be recognized by a more serious student. It was enough to make Wade press on.

"Do you like your major thus far, Mr....?"

"I'm sorry, professor. I'm forgetting my manners. I'm Mitch Rice. I'm a physics major."

"Good to meet you, Mitch Rice. Don't worry. I'm sure I wouldn't remember much of anything either if I had just finished the workout that you've just put in."

Mitch shrugged.

"Do you work out like that a lot?"

"Lately I have been," Mitch answered. "I didn't at the start of the semester, but things are going better now, and I have a little more time."

"Good." Wade grinned. "Maybe we'll see more of each other then. I'm trying to get back into shape too."

Mitch gave a courteous reply as he picked up his sweats, and the two made their parting comments.

Wade made a mental note to check on this Mitchell Rice. He liked him. He was the kind of student Wade wanted in his classes. And besides, all those scars were fresh. Wade liked little mysteries, and there seemed to be one here. Marilyn would have to use her connections to funnel him the answers he wanted. As much as he liked mysteries, he liked solutions more.

Chapter Eight

Sarah was busy with her new life in the nation's capital. She was now the assistant to the personal secretary of Senator Seward Simons, the powerful senior senator from Missouri.

After leaving Vietnam, Sarah's father-- a long time player in Missouri politics-- had helped her land a position as an administrative intern in the senator's office. In just months she had risen from that humble start to her present position. She wasn't Senator Simons's 'girl Friday', but she was "Friday's Friday."

Helen Adams was the senator's "boss lady." She ran his office like a finely tuned instrument, and no one challenged her authority, not even the senator himself. Mrs. Adams had recognized Sarah's talents quickly and had put her on the fast track for advancement. That decision was about to bear fruit.

The buzzword around Washington was the "Vietnamization of the war." The idea was for the South Vietnamese army, the ARVN, to take over the lion's share of the actual combat responsibilities of the war while the Americans reverted back to an actual advisors' role.

The senator had begun discussions with a group of officials from the Thieu regime who were in Washington to begin work on the whole deal. Obviously, in the wake of the recent Tet offensive where the South Vietnamese military performed so poorly, such discussions were fraught with difficulties.

The discussions had barely started when Senator Simons realized the language barrier was going to be a problem. He knew what he and his American colleagues were saying, but somehow the translated replies from the South Vietnamese officials were not exactly appropriate. Statements were misinterpreted, innuendos missed, and social sensibilities bruised. It was a mess.

Helen Adams came out of the conference room, and Sarah was waiting for her with a stack of documents the conference was supposed to go over. Mrs. Adams's face was not a pretty picture.

"Is something wrong, Mrs. Adams?"

"Yes, Sarah, something is *very* wrong in there. Senator Simons is trying very hard to be courteous to our South Vietnamese guests, but all they've said is that they wished they had some *cobra venom* to share with him!" She was seething. "I thought the senator was going to lose it, being insulted like that! I don't know how he was able to keep his composure! Why, they even smiled when they said it!"

Sarah hesitated for a moment, and the pause caught Mrs. Adams's attention.

"Sarah? You look like you want to tell me something."

Sarah started slowly. "Ma'am, you know that not too long ago I was in Vietnam myself?"

"Yes, I remember that."

"Well, ma'am, I was there long enough to learn the language pretty well, and I learned some of the customs."

"Yes?"

"Well, you see, Mrs. Adams, cobra venom is a drink that is shared only with a friend-in-arms. You drink it when you and your friend are trying to size each other up for friendly purposes. Sharing it is actually quite an honor."

Sarah saw confusion in Mrs. Adams's face.

"You see, ma'am, the drink is kind of like an instantaneous, but short -acting drunk. Your host has to share it with you, and he'll end up drunk, just like you. It takes only a few minutes for the liver to process the poison, but it's still a neurotoxin."

Sarah saw Mrs. Adams processing the new information.

"It's really pretty incapacitating stuff. You would want to share it only with someone whom you really trust."

"Oh, my God! I've never been briefed on such a thing! The senator's in real trouble in there!"

She dropped the folder back into Sarah's arms and turned to go back into the conference room. But, after taking just one step, Mrs. Adams seemed to think better of it.

"Sarah, I know you're inexperienced, and I know you're not rated as a linguist, but would you come with me back into the room? I think you could help our translator in there. The senator needs to have a better understanding what's really being said."

Senator Simons was grateful that his "boss lady" interrupted the strained silence that hung over the conference table. Her story about the cobra venom seemed preposterous, but Helen had never steered him wrong before. Consequently, he nodded for Sarah to go ahead.

For the next twenty minutes, Simons listened to Sarah orchestrate a steady dialogue with his South Vietnamese peers. He didn't understand what was being said, but he quickly realized things were improving. Faces began to soften and even an occasional smile surfaced.

After a few minutes, the head South Vietnamese negotiator came around the table and approached the senator. The Asian diplomat held out his hand and spoke in slow, careful English.

"Senator, it seems we have a good starting point for our discussions after all. We both have had a friend in Hue." He looked back at Sarah. "Any sister of Mother Marie's is our friend and sister too."

Senator Simons smiled back at his newfound friend and took his hand. From there the conference was off and running.

"Helen?" Simons asked later that day at a break in the talks, "Did you know that our Miss Thornton worked at an orphanage in Hue with a Benedictine nun who was a sort of sainted legend?"

"Yes, senator. Today I've made a point to learn as much as I could about our Sarah. She seems to have quite a dossier."

Senator Simons responded with a puzzled look.

"It seems," Mrs. Adams continued, "that Sarah is also a bit of a legend in the locale. The Catholic population there think of her as a young saint, a sort of Joan of Arc, who was brought to them by an almost deified old nun named Mother Edwina Marie. Even the Buddhist population there hold them both in high regard."

The senator looked uncomfortable.

"Senator, did you know very much about Sarah before you hired her?"

"No, I guess not. Her father and I go back a long way in Missouri politics. So when he asked if I could get her a job, I was obligated to find her a place. Why do you ask? Is there something wrong?"

"No, senator, I'd say that Sarah Thornton would be a true asset to anyone's staff. In college she qualified for a Rhodes scholarship. She didn't take it for some reason and went into high school teaching instead. After that she spent a lot of time in Vietnam. She knows the country's customs intimately, speaks the language as a native, and even has proven that she can be pretty handy with an M16. I think her acquisition was very astute."

"Sometimes it's better to be lucky than smart, Helen," Simons said sheepishly. "It was a very lucky stroke having her here today. The whole negotiating process was about to go down the tubes."

"Yes, I saw that." Helen Adams chuckled one of her infrequent little laughs. "You know senator, I would've liked to have seen you all sipping cobra venom. According to Sarah, it's a kind of truth serum."

She chuckled again.

"Wouldn't that have been something—a bunch of snakes made to tell the truth by their own poison."

Simons winced visibly, but he had the good sense to keep his mouth shut. Being a pragmatist, he had long ago realized that having a bunch of women running his life had both its good and bad points. Sometimes the price for all the organization and efficiency was a big dose of humility—his, that was. So he just smiled and endured the insult. It wasn't the first time she had put him in his place.

That day's effort ensured that Sarah would continue to rise quickly in the senator's organization. Soon she was working independently as one of the senator's project directors. It was there that she and Wilson Strong crossed paths again.

Colonel Strong's compound outside of Hue was never overrun by the NVA during the Tet offensive. Neither was the bridge over the Perfume River destroyed. Strong and his ROK troops held their ground ferociously until reinforcements came, and then their position became the starting point for the counterattack that won back Hue.

Early in the conflict, the colonel learned that the two thousand or so Europeans that lived in Hue at the start of Tet all suffered the same atrocious deaths Sarah, Mother Marie, and Sister Danielle had nearly endured in the chapel. Strong took command of the American counter-offensive and fell on the enemy like a great guillotine. He and his ROK's killed everything they touched. Whether it was vengeance for the two thousand deaths or vengeance for just one, no one knew.

In the days that followed, the supposedly impossible house-to-house conflict the colonel oversaw gutted nearly two divisions of General Giap's finest. Over fifteen thousand North Vietnamese soldiers died at Strong's hands.

He wasn't able to bring Mother Marie back, but his counter-attack was so fierce that it succeeded in enshrining her memory. In life, she had been Hue's very soul. By Wilson Strong's bloody efforts, in death, Mother Marie became its patroness.

While Wilson Strong tore the soul out of the NVA on a grand scale, he also was cared for the smaller details.

Mitch was spirited off the mainland and started on the road to recovery that ultimately saw him granted a medical discharge at the rank of sergeant, the winner of two Silver Stars and two Purple Hearts.

Sister Danielle flew back to France with Mother Marie's remains, and Sarah was safely escorted stateside to be reunited and reconciled with her father.

The aftermath of Tet, however, held very dark months for the colonel.

Strong's sense of honor and duty were far out of sync with those of his superiors. The colonel was too professional to accept their monumental incompetency, and he wasn't afraid to confront even General Westmoreland himself with the truth.

None of it should have been very good for Strong's career, but the tales of his battlefield prowess had mushroomed to such mythical proportions that no one on the command staff could dare confront him.

So what couldn't be accomplished with a usual court martial and disciplinary action was accomplished with duplicity and deceit. The colonel became the object of an elaborate scheme that saw him get both his general's star and a quick transfer out of Vietnam.

The dogs of war persisted and had their day. They got rid of Wilson Strong, and, as they did so, they took away even the honor of his new star. Their day lasted seven more years, and in the end, that day proved to be as dark as night.

And that was how the now General Strong came to the point where he was about to enter Senator Seward Simon's conference room. Inside sat his new boss, CIA Director David Helsey, who was going to give him his new assignment.

"Will Strong! How the hell are you?" greeted the enthusiastic Senator Simons. "I think you already know Dave Helsey, right?"

"Yes, sir. The director and I go back together all the way to West Point," Strong answered. He offered his hand to his old nemesis. "Hello, David."

"Good to see that you're still in one piece, Will. I'm glad we were able to get you out of Vietnam before you self-destructed completely." Helsey was only half-smiling. "You took that Tet stuff much too personally."

A quiet but firm clearing of a feminine throat interrupted. All three men, Strong, Helsey, and Simons, turned toward the sound. It was Sarah.

"Tet was a very personal time, Mr. Director," she said. Her gaze was chilling in its disdain. "Very personal. Too bad you couldn't have been there."

"Hello, Sarah," Strong said, noting Helsey's sudden consternation. Tet had left its mark on her. She was obviously a long way from the girl he had known there.

"Do you two know each other?" Helsey demanded, wanting a pint of the upstart girl's blood.

"The general and I share quite a bit of history, Mr. Director," Sarah answered, ignoring his angry stare. Wilson Strong was her target now, and her stare froze him in his tracks. The room around her was her home turf, and she was proving that she could rule here with all the harshness of a woman scorned.

"General, I never really had a chance to *thank* you for all that you did for us at the orphanage." Her voice was edged with something sharper than bitterness. "In fact, it took me quite a while to realize just exactly *what* you had done."

Simons shrugged. All this served him right, letting women dominate him. "Let's see if we can all put our hurt feelings aside for a while, shall we?" he ordered. "It's time to begin the briefing."

"Yes, sir," Sarah replied with an instant, cool professionalism. "Of course."

The briefing that followed was a revelation, a scary revelation.

Gen. Strong learned that he was being given a new posting in CIA headquarters itself. Sarah, and those that followed her, explained that his assignment was to monitor security problems associated with the peculiar kind of terrorism that the Middle East was breeding. It didn't take Strong long to realize that the quagmire of Vietnam was nothing when compared to the jumbled mess of oil, nationalism, and fanaticism that festered in the Middle East. In fact, he realized his new assignment would leave him a lot more exposed and vulnerable than he had ever been in Southeast Asia. There he had at least understood the combat. Here, he didn't understand a thing.

When the briefing was over, Simons walked out with Strong. "Sorry about the way that started, Will. I thought you and Sarah Thornton were friends."

"It's okay, senator. Sarah and I probably have a few things to work out from our time together in Hue."

Turning to Sarah who was several feet behind them Strong stopped and asked, "Sarah, can we talk sometime?"

Sarah didn't even break her stride.

"Certainly, general."

She was colder than ice.

"Even after all this time, I'd still like to hear your side of Tet."

She passed him without even pausing.

"It's just too bad that Mother Marie can't be here to what you have to say. I think she would be interested in knowing what's the current price tag for your loyalty. What is it? A general's star?"

"Sarah!" Senator Simmons demanded.

He started to say more, but Sarah kept right on walking, leaving both him and General Strong wallowing in her wake. For her, the battle of Hue still raged.

Chapter Nine

A cold, January wind brushed Mitch's hair with a promise of snow. The first semester had just ended, and Mitch was holding the computer printout of his grades. He was oblivious to the cold and sat down on a bench outside the physics buildings to read the paper's contents for probably the fiftieth time. All he could see were three As and two Bs, and one of the Bs was in calculus.

Mitch chilled as he stared at the paper. He wasn't sure if it was the cold or his disbelief that numbed him. The grade in calc had to be there only by the skin of his teeth, but it was there. It was a pretty sight.

"Hi, Mitch. What do you have there? Your epitaph?"

It was Dr. Fulton. He knew what Mitch was reading, and the man's smile was nearly a yard wide.

"You did it, didn't you? You pulled out of one of the worst starter's slumps in history and nailed it! Congratulations!"

Mitch jumped up from the bench. "I was just about to come looking for you, sir." He couldn't contain his smile. "Yeah, things have worked out really great, thanks to you and about half the grad students in the department." Mitch shook his head still in disbelief. "How can I thank you, sir?"

"I think you just did, Mitch," the department chairman said. "And besides, you're the one who did it anyway. Tutoring can only do so much. Learning happens on the inside, and that paper proves you can beat this place after all."

Mitch's smile widened. He had worked his tail off, and it felt good to have won a big one.

"Come on into the office, Mitch. We can talk there. It's cold out here."

Once inside, Dr. Fulton started to offer Mitch a cup of coffee but then remembered Mitch didn't drink the stuff.

"How did you ever managed to burn all that midnight oil studying without coffee? Coffee is a required part of every college curriculum."

Mitch shrugged. "I guess no one ever told me that, sir. Besides, after all the effort everyone had put in me, I was too scared of blowing it to sleep very much anyway."

Fulton slipped around behind his desk which was littered with paper. It might be the semester break, but a department chairman's work was never done.

"So what else is on your mind, Mitch? I think there's something else going on behind those steely gray eyes of yours."

Fulton saw that Mitch was happy, but there was still something else there. He waved Mitch to a chair.

"I don't want to take too much of your time, Dr. Fulton, but there are a couple of questions I'd like to ask you."

"Sure," Fulton replied. "Shoot."

Mitch gathered himself. "Sir, I guess the main question is just *why*. Why did you do all this for me?"

Mitch made sure he had the professor's eye.

"I know the school offers tutoring services for all of its freshmen, but no one I've talked to had the kind of help that you set up for me." Mitch's look probed deeply. "Why did you do it?"

Fulton saw that Mitch was serious, grateful certainly, but still insistent for an explanation. The professor settled back into his chair.

"Would it be enough if I just told you that it looks bad when on a department's scorecard when a student with an IQ like yours flunks out?"

Mitch didn't budge. "Dr. Fulton, we both know that you have all kinds of students whose IQ scores blow me off the map."

Fulton found himself squirming. "Yeah, but IQ tests aren't everything, Mitch." He saw Mitch wasn't buying his pat answer. "Look, Mitch. You've already said thanks. That's enough."

"If you say so, sir. But it just seems to me that you went way above and beyond the call to pull my backside out of the fire."

It was Fulton's turn to shrug. "Is an explanation that important to you?"

"Yes, I guess it is."

Fulton took a big breath. "Well, Mitch, I suppose it goes something like this. You really are bright, brighter than you give yourself credit for. But your start here was a snafu. You should have never been given the course schedule you had. I'm your scholastic advisor. I screwed up by letting the grad students cover for me during the registration period. That means that I was responsible for your horrible start. I had to try to make up for it."

"Dr. Fulton, most of the other full professors have their grad students take care of the undergrads, just like you did. I know. I checked it out."

Fulton realized Mitch wasn't going to let him off the hook.

"Mitch, I only know a little of what you went through in Vietnam. Most of your military record is blacked out, but I know that they don't give Silver Stars away. And you have *two* of them. That means that not that many months ago you went way beyond what would normally be expected to pull someone else out of a big hurt. And you must have done it at least twice. And, since you have a medical discharge from the Corps, you must have taken some big hits doing it. I guess I just wanted you to have a better chance here than you started with. That's all."

Fulton wanted to stop, but the pressure of Mitch's gaze told him he had to go on.

"Sure, Mitch. The teacher in me wanted you to do the best you could. Even though I seem to spend most of my time competing for research grants, I'm still a teacher at heart." Fulton took long breath. "And I also know a little of what it's like to be lost when a war's over. A long time ago, someone helped me when I got out of Korea. I guess I saw that this was a time when I could do the same for you. It just seemed like the right thing to do. Call it an old debt or whatever you want, but it *was* the right thing to do."

Mitch was quiet, soaking it all in. He felt like he'd had this conversation before.

"You see, honor cuts both ways, Mitch. It doesn't always cost. Sometimes you have to accept what others choose to give you. It's like a chain that connects us all. Someday you'll do something like this for someone else. That's what it's all about."

Mitch got up from his chair. His face looked a little different as he came over to Fulton and offered his hand.

"I think I'm beginning to understand, sir. Thank you. Thank you for everything."

Fulton took Mitch's hand and returned his squeeze. "Are you going to be around some over the break?"

Mitch nodded.

"Well, come back later in the week, and we'll talk more. But right now, I have some work to do, and you should go have a beer or do whatever you do to let off steam. You deserve it."

Mitch said he would and let himself out. He guessed that sometimes things just worked out.

Over the rest of the short break and off and on over the course of the next semester, Mitch and Dr. Fulton had several more talks. The professor liked Mitch's company, and Mitch loved their exchanges. They talked about all sorts of subjects, everything from quantum mechanics (one of Fulton's main interests) to politics and religion. Anything was fair game.

One day, about half way through the term, Mitch opened a whole new Pandora's box. They were walking together back from a guest lecture where a special presentation had been given by a couple of Nobel laureates. The subject of the presentation had been quantum mechanics and its proposed application to cold fusion.

"Dr. Fulton," he asked out of the blue. "Do I have what it takes to be a physicist?"

The question caught Fulton flatfooted.

"Sure, Mitch. You're one of those characters who can do whatever he wants," Fulton saw the clouds on Mitch's face. "What's on your mind, son? I know that look of yours."

Mitch walked on besides his professor, staring down the hall. "I enjoyed the presentation tonight."

"Okay?"

"No, I mean it! All that discussion you had in there about clean, unlimited electricity is the stuff that dreams are made of."

"So what's the problem? That could be your future."

"Maybe," Mitch said slowly. "But isn't it more likely, if I keep doing what I'm doing now, that I'll probably end up building weapons for the government? Isn't that what most physicists do these days?"

Fulton stopped. He started to take up Mitch's challenge, but then he thought better of it. In a lot of ways, Mitch was right. He had to admit that most of his time was spent doing the bidding of the government or at least that of the companies that really owned the government. He really had very little freedom to follow his own inclinations. His pet projects on clean energy had long languished unfinished as the time requirements of his position tied him down.

Fulton turned to face Mitch. "Mitch, your life doesn't have to be like mine. Physics is a huge field. A lot of physicists do very little for Uncle Sam. You can set your life up any way you want."

Mitch looked away. "I guess I'll ask it this way then, sir. Do you think I have what it takes to be happy as a physicist?"

"Mitch, I don't know the answer to that. That's one you'll have to find for yourself."

Fulton could see Mitch was a long way off.

"Mitch, why did you come here to start with? You picked this major. No one forced it on you. What did you expect?"

Mitch came back from wherever he had just been. "I've been thinking a lot about that lately, sir. I had a hard time getting focused after Tet. The VA hospitals gave me lots of time to think, but I just couldn't get it together. After a while there, I just decided to pick the hardest thing I could think of and try it. Physics seemed like as good a way of starting as any."

"Okay. That sounds fair. So what now?" Fulton asked.

"That's just it. I don't know. My course work is going all right so far this term. I feel more like my old self. Shoot, even my running is getting better. But I don't know where I'm going, and it's really bugging me."

"Okay, Mitch, come to my office tomorrow after classes. I'll see what I can do. I don't think your problem is all that unusual. I bet we can work something out."

About a week later, Mitch was seated in a testing cubicle in the psychology department. Dr. Fulton had been true to his word. The day after their conversation in the hallway, he had pulled out a small note he had received the previous term. The note was from a clinical psychologist who worked for the university. In it, she inquired about the status of one Mitchell Rice. Fulton discovered the note's author, a Dr. Marilyn Wade, was married to the university's other Dr. Wade (the new biochemist over at the chemistry department). Somehow one or both of them had stumbled across Mitch and taken an interest in him. Fulton had made a mental note of it.

After the hallway conversation with Mitch, Fulton had finally returned the lady psychologist's call. Since then he'd had three or four conversations with her about Mitch. In the last one she agreed to give Mitch a vocational aptitude analysis.

And that was how Mitch had come to his present point, toiling diligently over page after page of questions for which there were no particularly right answers. It was a long test. Mitch just hoped it would be one of those times when the questions would reveal more truth than the answers.

A week later Mitch was again in the psych department. This time he was in Dr. Wade's office, seated directly across from her. She had her nose buried in his test scores.

Marilyn Wade was amazed by the results in front of her. The department's personality trait batteries were usually a morass of mediocrity, but not this one.

"Mr. Rice? It's Mitchell, right?"

"Yes, ma'am." He was completely alert.

"Well, Mitchell, you understood when you took this test that there were no right or wrong answers and that this was not any sort of achievement test, right?"

"Yes, that's what I was told."

She went on. "This test is just a composite of a large group of personality traits that seem to be held in common by successful professionals who are already in the working world. Whether a person scores high or low in a given category doesn't necessarily mean that he'll be a success or a failure in that profession. The scores just represent which personality traits he holds in common with these professionals."

"You mean," Mitch answered, "that these scores *might* indicate where I could fit in. But no promises, right?"

"Yes, that pretty much says it," she said. "Well, let me start by telling you that these tests usually put the majority of people somewhere in the middle of most categories. But in your case, there are some really striking results."

Mitch waited. He felt like a large ax was about to fall.

"Let me begin by telling you where the test says you definitely don't fit." She took a short breath. "Mitch, you have scored one of lowest scores ever recorded for any sort of business aptitude." She smiled a little. "You really don't value money very much, do you?"

Mitch was on edge. "I guess I don't dislike money or what it can buy, ma'am. But I guess I don't want anything to own me *again*. It's too easy for money to own those who have it. I don't like that."

The psychologist in Marilyn Wade caught the "again" portion of Mitch's reply, but she went on without asking questions.

"You're a physics major, right?"

"Yes."

"Well, aside from the absent-minded professor portion of the equation where you scored high, you've scored in the neutral range regarding shared personality traits with successful physicists."

"So maybe I could get along, but I might not really be lit up by a life of rubbing elbows with the real geniuses?"

"Something like that," she answered, burying her nose back into his report. "You know, this really is something! The scores that relate you to hard physical scientists are the only middle of the road scores you have. All the rest are more or less in the negative column, except for three professions. There you've blown the lid off the scale for shared characteristics. I've never seen one of these tests go this way before."

"Does that mean that the test is invalid?" Mitch asked.

"You listen to the answers, and then you tell me yourself if it's valid or not."

Marilyn Wade looked straight at Mitch and read off the results.

"According to this, you could fit right in with the mind-set of a religious minister."

Mitch's face fell. "I have already tried that."

"And it didn't work?"

"Well, no, it didn't. There seemed to be too much politics and money involved. It turned me off."

"Okay. You've made really high scores for a career as a professional military man."

Mitch's faced fell another notch. "I've tried that too."

"No good?"

Mitch squirmed uncomfortably but then squared his shoulders. "The discipline of the military fit with me just fine, Dr. Wade. But…" Mitch seemed stuck. He didn't want to tell this stranger about his recurring dreams of combat and the gallery of ghosts he knew so well. Lately, his dreams had been worse, and he could only sleep if he thoroughly exhausted himself with running the day before.

"You were in Vietnam, right?" she asked.

Mitch nodded while she made a note for future reference.

"Don't despair. I've saved the highest score for last." She caught Mitch's eye. "Have you ever thought about being a medical doctor?"

"Medicine? Me… a doctor?" Mitch suddenly felt as though a huge light bulb had flashed on in his otherwise dark world. His right hand tingled… no, it actually vibrated right where Mother Marie had touched him just before she died. He suddenly remembered her words about shared purposes, preserved honor, and things that had true value.

Marilyn Wade watched Mitch's face as it made what seemed to be a long journey.

"I guess you've never thought about medicine before. Right?"

"No, ma'am. I haven't."

A long pause followed as she watched Mitch make some sort of transition. If she hadn't seen Mitch's initial look of enlightenment, she would have been worried.

"Dr. Wade, if I scored high in all three categories, there must be a connection. I don't see it."

Marilyn Wade glanced back to the summary sheets.

"There's one common thread that ties these three professions together." She looked up at Mitch. "In today's world, these are the three professions where people actually value other people more than they value themselves." She smiled. "That's why these jobs are called "vocations." Ministers, the truly dedicated military, and doctors are the people who will spend themselves for others." She still was smiling. "It seems that you have already invested heavily in this set of values, Mitch. Maybe you should consider finishing what you've already started."

"I never thought of being a doctor before," Mitch muttered, still numb.

"Well, if your expression is any indication, maybe you should think of it now."

Mitch's gaze finally came all the way back from whatever far-away places he had just seen.

"I don't know, Dr. Wade. Medicine?"

"It's just a suggestion, Mitch."

Mitch got up.

"Well, I'll think about it, Dr. Wade. Thanks."

As he went to the door, she called out. "Come back anytime you like, Mitch. We could talk more about medicine… or anything else that might be on your mind."

"Okay. Thanks for the invite, Dr. Wade. I just might, later. But right now, I feel like I want to go running. Is that all right?"

She laughed. "Sure, Mitch. Get out of here! We can talk later."

She felt very warm inside. Her Jacob loved his answers more than the mysteries. But for her, it was the surprises that were the best of all.

Chapter Ten

"Hello, General," the voice over the phone said.

"Sarah! I didn't expect you to call back this soon," General Strong answered in his most upbeat voice. "The secretary at your office said that you would be out most of the day doing the senator's errands."

"General, even civilians jump a little when a general speaks. Erin found me over at the Library of Congress and gave me your message. What can I help you with?" Her voice sounded cold. "Is this personal or business?"

Strong took a breath. "Personal, Sarah… in fact, very personal."

Her silence gave him no quarter at all, so he went on. "I wasn't very satisfied with our meeting the other day in your boss's place. I said then I'd call you, and so I have. Can we get together? We need to talk."

"I think that's what I said the other day. What do you have in mind?"

Strong suggested supper at a nice but modest Washington restaurant. Sarah knew of the place and agreed. Four hours later he was helping her with her chair.

"Thanks for coming, Sarah." He felt stiff and awkward. Their last episode at the senator's office had really gotten under his skin. Sarah's opinion of him meant far more to him than he wanted to admit.

The Sarah in front of him was not the same girl he had known in Vietnam. Then she had been a frumpy, uncertain, but stubborn whelp who needed a father figure. Now Sarah seemed taller and was obviously a lot more accomplished. She had already proven she was now a woman who could go toe-to-toe with anyone she chose. She *almost* intimidated him.

Sarah took the initiative. "How can I help you, general? I know you always have so little time. What piece of information would you like from me today?"

Strong winced under the sudden attack. Any parental-like advantage he'd once had over her had long since disappeared.

"Sarah, why are you so angry with me?"

Her eyes spoke louder than her voice. She had been very angry with him for a very long time.

"Angry? No. Actually I'm more puzzled than angry," she answered. "For a long time now I've wondered how someone like you, someone who professed to have a sort of honor, could use up and kill so many innocent people just to make points with his superiors."

She paused, but only to load up for another volley.

"You see, I'm confused. Ever since Tet I've wondered just what Mother Marie and the rest of us did to deserve what you did to us. If it hadn't been for Mitch, we would've all been raped and mutilated right there in our own chapel."

She paused again and then went for the killing shot.

"Can you explain any of that, general? Should I be angry? Or should I just be vomiting out of disgust?"

Strong sat back in his chair and started to speak. But before he could get a word out, they were interrupted by a waiter. She had drawn blood even before the water glasses were filled.

"Sarah," he began after the man had left. "I'm sorry that we lost Mother Marie. She was probably the most remarkable woman I've ever known. I…"

Sarah cut him off with an angry look and picked up her menu, blocking his view of her.

Strong flushed red. He was not used to being treated in this manner. His famous stoicism, that self-control that had been part of his myth ever since West Point, cracked. He reached up and jerked down her menu.

"Okay, Sarah! I know you're not a little girl anymore! You don't look like one, and you sure aren't acting like one! Just what do you want?"

She flared right back at him. "I want to know *why*, Wilson! I want to know *why* you used us—me, Mother Marie, Mitch, all of us -- to gather your goddamn intelligence! You're the one who compromised the orphanage's neutrality! You're the one who caused the VC to come after us! You're the one who killed Mother Marie!" Her voice cracked. "I trusted you, Wilson!" She was barely whispering. "I even thought I loved you!"

Strong saw the waiter returning and waved him away. Part of him wanted to be gentle, but a bigger part wanted her blood. So he went for her jugular.

"Sarah, I guess I had hoped we could visit civilly and then work our way into this subject bit by bit. But I see that's not the way it's going to be. You attacked me the first moment you saw me in the senator's office, and it's no different now. So if that's the way you want it, you got it!" He paused, but she didn't move.

"Sarah, who did you think I was? Your father?" His eyes had their own fire. "Well, I'm not! My name is Wilson Strong, and I'm a soldier!"

He saw her wilt ever so slightly, and he pressed on.

"A soldier, by definition, is someone who fights other peoples' battles! A soldier dies so that they might live! He makes that his duty!"

He thought he saw his words hitting home.

"Sarah, I've never been a killer." His voice softened. "In Hue my duty was to save as many lives as I could. That meant saving my command. For a while that seemed like more than I could do. Westmoreland and his flunkies were more interested in body counts than in honor. I was caught between the NVA and my own superiors."

He looked at her. She was listening.

"So, given that, one day this old sainted nun shows up and begs me to help her save the half-breed orphans in her pitiful little orphanage. She said she knew that her days were numbered and that the NVA would exterminate her children just because they were half-breeds."

He reached out and touched her hand.

"Sarah, it was Mother Marie's idea to funnel information about Charlie from the orphanage to me. She said I could use that information to save both my command and her kids. I told her she was crazy, but she wouldn't back down."

Strong's eyes pleaded with Sarah, probing for a way to break through her anger.

"And her information was good! In fact, it was the best damn intelligence I ever collected! It saved a lot of lives! All of the children got out to the countryside in one piece! All of the nuns made it out too, all except Mother Marie! And even she could've made it if she would've just left when I asked her to!"

He shook his head with a sudden, quiet violence and looked away.

"Sarah, I knew Charlie was coming for you and that it was going to be bad. But it wasn't my fault! I'd have gotten you out, if you would've just left her! But you wouldn't!"

His voice now vibrated with a quiet fury.

"Your death would've been on her head, not mine! She was the one who was willing to have you all die so that the children could have a better chance! She was the one who was willing to use up those she loved for the duty she was bound to! It wasn't me!"

He stopped as if to catch his breath. When he spoke again, his voice echoed sadness.

"Sarah, Mother Marie was the greatest soldier I have ever known. I couldn't even hold a candle next to her."

His voice became desperate.

"Don't go on trying to hang this guilt trip on me! I tried to stop her because I couldn't stand the thought of losing you! But she stopped me cold! She was willing to sacrifice both you and Sister Dannie to cover for the children! I wasn't that faithful! If it has been left to me, I would have abandoned my post to come for you!" He was shaking. "But she left me no choice but to hold my position!"

Strong saw Sarah's shoulders stoop.

"I envy her, Sarah! She was the truest warrior I've ever known! She died an honorable soldier's death!" He stopped, almost sobbing. "Sarah, don't desecrate what she did with your anger!"

Strong stopped. He had said all he knew to say. He had nothing left to peel away whatever layers of anger and righteousness Sarah still had left. Whatever happened now was up to her.

It had taken Strong a long time to put together what he had just said. He had learned of duty from his father who had faithfully cared for his mother from the day she had stroked giving birth to Wilson. That care had lasted fifteen years until she finally died. Strong had witnessed duty in action all through his childhood. It was a lesson he never forgot.

Later, in his second year at West Point when his father died, Strong had vowed never to marry. Nothing would get in the way of his duty -- not family, not anything. And he had lived his whole life that way, dedicated to his duty just as strongly as any cleric who ever breathed. Mother Marie had seen that dedication and had realized that she was his sister-in-the-cloth even though he didn't even acknowledge the God she worshiped. Strong hated losing her, but he was jealous of the way she died. Such honor was hers! Sarah had to see that.

Sarah surrendered with a big, shuddering breath.

"Mitch said nearly everything that you just said months ago. I couldn't accept it then." A tear rolled down her cheek. "I guess I have to accept it now." She cried quietly into her napkin.

Strong got up from his chair and went to the one next to her. He said nothing. He just took her in his arms with a powerful but gentle hug. He felt her shoulders shake, and something inside himself responded to her. It was their first real touch.

After a while, Sarah pulled back. "I'm sorry, Wilson. I wanted to hate you for her death." She was completely exposed. "I just couldn't believe she could do it --sacrificing both me and Dannie! I couldn't blame her, so I had to blame you!"

Strong reached inside himself again trying to find the gentleness Sarah needed. "But you're just like her, Sarah!" he said. "You were willing to die with her rather than to get out when you could have! You saw your *duty* just like she saw hers, and you did it even though it nearly killed you! I loved you for that then, and I still do now. I know Mother Marie was proud to call you her sister!"

Sarah felt herself pulled back into his strong grasp. Somehow his embrace made her remember the healing embrace she had shared with Mother Marie and Dannie after Mitch had cut her free from the chapel's altar. The shame she felt now was connected to the terror and shame she had felt then. She had been stripped of everything then, and now her soul was just as naked. Somehow she felt her general's touch repairing her now just as Mother Marie's had then. She settled into his arms, grateful to finally be there.

"But I was so scared, Wilson! On the altar... I thought I had lost myself forever! I couldn't think of Mother Marie or Dannie! I was just too scared! All I could hear was that man laughing as he started to rape me! I'm so ashamed!"

Strong took a long breath. "Sarah, I feel just like you do. I couldn't come to save you. I wanted to, but I couldn't. I could only send Mitch. Or rather, all I could really do was to get out of his way."

He picked up her chin.

"Sarah, there was no way that anyone was going to keep Mitch from coming for the three of you that night.

It should have been me, running that awful gauntlet with you, but it was Mitch. It should have been me that got all shot up, but it was Mitch. But that was the only way you could be saved. I couldn't send a force for you, and I couldn't leave my post. All I could do was send Mitch. He was my only hope. I'll never be able to repay him for bringing you home."

Sarah wiped her eyes. "Mitch said that you two were sort of brothers. I didn't understand what he meant until just now." She stroked Strong's weathered face. "I'm lucky to have you both."

She moved her face upward, and somehow he understood. The kiss that followed sealed their forgiveness. Whatever the future held, they were connected again. It was something each of them could hold on to.

Chapter Eleven

The fall term of 1970 and the spring term of 1971 were good times for Mitch. Everything surged forward in those months like a fast-paced but friendly race.

Time had wrought a lot of changes. The most obvious one of which was that Mitch had found his stride in his studies. All of the work Dr. Fulton's grad students had put into him had borne fruit. He had learned the mathematician's mindset, and the first and most universal language no longer stymied him. In fact, its utter logic became a sort of haven for him. He had spent the summer in classes to get a head start on the coming fall term, and the effort brought him to a place where now, beyond the numbers and equations, he could sometimes see glimpses of an intelligence, a being that was bigger than anything he had ever imagined before. He felt like a baby just learning to talk, but he liked finding his voice.

Equally important, Mitch had come to some sort of peace with himself. Dr. Fulton's interest in him continued, and the two struck up a friendship. That personal touch was something Mitch needed.

Marilyn Wade was also there. Mitch saw her sporadically, and she had taught him some relaxation skills that helped him conquer some of his night terrors and flashbacks.

Marilyn never got very far into his past, though she knew it was there. She was a good psychologist and realized Mitch's progress was more important than her professional voyeurism. So she didn't force his confidence. Though sometimes, she did catch herself speculating about whatever it was Mitch had hidden inside, and sometimes she shared those thoughts with Jacob. But that was just married couple talk. Mostly she contented herself with watching Mitch become a more settled individual. He was still an enigma who'd almost certainly had a violent past. But at least for now he had learned how to put that violence aside.

Jacob Wade was continually caught by his wife's comments on Mitchell Rice. He and Mitch still ran into each other in the gym, but Mitch was pretty tight-lipped about anything in his past. Wade wanted to know how Mitch had gotten all those scars, but he had contented himself with the fragments Marilyn gave him. He was still searching for recognition for his fledgling little biochem section, and that was a lot more important than any curiosity he had about any one student.

Throughout the previous year, Marilyn had suggested to Wade that he start a pre-med program at UMR. The university didn't have such a curriculum, and she was convinced that his little one-man show could really become a lot more visible if he just offered one. After her encounter with Mitch, she had screened several other students who also seemed to have some aptitude for the healing arts. Jacob's biochemistry would be a way for them to begin their new courses.

Consequently, with Marilyn beckoning, Wade sought out Dr. Fulton and several other department chairmen and made his case. Medicine needed good scientists and engineers the same as other technical fields did. The other chairmen agreed, and Jacob Wade's new program came to be. In the days and months that followed, enough students had responded to give him some of the notoriety he sought. Mitch was one of them.

Along with his academic progress, Mitch used the second year to recapture his health. He continued his exercise program and gradually won back some of his strength. In the fall he had tried out for the cross-country team. He hadn't really made the team, but the coach had let him run and train with the team anyway. By the spring, he had improved enough to make the track team on his own merits. True, he didn't win any races, but he placed once or twice in some minor meets when the coach put him in as an extra in the mile. It wasn't spectacular, but he made progress.

So when it was all summed up, Mitch's sophomore year at UMR was a good one. So good, in fact, that Mitch chose to stay in school again that second summer. He realized he really did like the academic life.

That summer Dr. Fulton had a little project for Mitch to work on regarding Fulton's ideas about cold fusion. A lot of it was over Mitch's head, but it gave him a chance to keep up on his math courses.

The summer days at Rolla were easier than the frenetic-paced fall and spring terms, and Mitch managed to use the extra time to continue his quiet training for the mile. He had transitioned from using his running as anesthetic to having it become actual recreation. He loved the sense of freedom running gave him, and he ran a lot. It was almost like flying.

Mitch was not the only one at UMR that summer who saw real progress in his or her life. Marilyn Wade was also having a banner season. It was early July. The summer's mid-term break used the July 4 holiday, and she and Jacob and Katie were going on another wonderful float trip down one of the crystal clear little streams they had learned about since coming to the Ozarks. She had been looking forward to the break for weeks.

The past year had been good for her and Jacob. With his connections to the Defense Department on hold, she had won back his attentions and her marriage. The Ozark hills had softened his arrogance and selfishness, and she had rediscovered the passionate learner she had originally fallen in love with.

And that was why she was hurrying so fast down State Street on this particularly warm summer day. She had just made a wonderful discovery she had to share. She was pregnant. Jacob's little lab in the temporary building complex was just a few blocks from the doctor's office so she was hurrying to take her news to him. She knew he didn't have a clue as to what was going on, and she intended to play it to the hilt. She felt very much like a newlywed again. It was so amazing what a difference a year could make.

Jacob Wade was busy in his little lab. He missed the high tech research facilities the Defense Department had allowed him. Now he scarcely could do little more than prepare tissue cultures for the little bit of research he still attempted.

When Wade left the Department of Defense, he'd been heavily involved in the development of artificial viruses that could be programmed to perform different functions. He'd once had visions of being able to cure diabetes by developing a virus that would repair the disease's genetic miscoding. The defense department had, of course, been more interested in viruses that could be used as weapons.

In the end, Wade had been content with the notoriety his science gave him, not caring to what purpose his genius was being used. Had Marilyn not forced their marriage to the breaking point, he would have still been in his old underground lab giving his little creations all the attention they deserved.

As it was, he was now reduced to manual labor, cleaning all his micro pore filters by hand. He hated being a backwoods researcher, but he knew he would have hated being divorced like his parents even more. So he endured and kept cleaning his filters.

The micro-pore filters were used to harvest viruses from tissue cultures. Their cleaning required him to use an alkaline solution of cyanide. The solution was very poisonous. He hated using it, but nothing else worked as well. Consequently, he used it very cautiously, always keeping sodium thiosulfate and amyl nitrite ampules in the lab as antidotes should the unthinkable happen. Additionally, he worked carefully under exhaust hoods with non-porous work gloves to make doubly sure there would be no such awful surprises. And beyond all that, he always made sure he kept the alkaline solution of the cyanide away from any acids. Mixing the two would cause the formation of gaseous cyanide that would be quickly fatal. Wade may not have been a happy researcher in his current position, but he was a careful one.

"Jacob?"

Wade's head jerked upward. He had not heard Marilyn enter the lab.

"Marilyn, what in blazes are you doing in here? Can't you read that sign on the door that says there's dangerous material in here?"

"Oh, you grump!" she pouted. "What are you doing? Using that horrible cyanide again?"

"Yes, dear." He knew she hated being called "dear," and he added a note of condescension for good measure. "That's right. Poor college professors have to get back to basics if they want to do any research, and this place doesn't offer many of the amenities that my former employer did."

A few months before, his caustic answer would have hurt Marilyn's feelings. But today nothing was going to lessen her spirits. She came up behind him.

"Jacob?"

Wade paused in his washing routine at the odd tone in her voice. "What's going on, Marilyn? What's wrong?"

She gave a little laugh. "Would you please take those gloves off and make wild, passionate love to me?"

"What?" Her coy expression threw him way off balance. "What did you say?"

"No one else will come in here with that sign you have on the door. I've always had a fantasy that I would tell my husband of his soon-to-be-arriving son while we were locked in each other's arms." She was smiling with all the innocence and guile of a woman whose passion would not be denied.

"What?" Wade gasped again, stupefied as he watched her slip out of her blouse and shorts, revealing her tan-lines underneath.

She came right up to him. "Jacob, our baby's in here," she said, pulling his hands out of his heavy gloves and tossing them aside. "It'*s* a boy. I know it is."

With single-minded purposefulness, she pulled his hands onto her bare skin, opened his belt buckle, and slid her hands inside so she could stroke him in her special way. The next twenty minutes saw her orchestrate a seduction that covered the lab floor and Jacob's desktop. Neither her fantasy nor her passion fell short.

Mitch was busy winding down the first half of the summer term. As he was leaving the computer center and walking back to the dorm, his path came close to Professor Wade's lab. So he decided to stop and say hi. On the lab door he saw a sign in big, red letters warning that dangerous chemicals were being used on the inside.

"Cyanide," Mitch said to himself. "He's cleaning his filters again."

Wade had let Mitch help with this tedious, dangerous task several times during the spring term. It was a job that Mitch didn't enjoy, but he didn't mind helping out when he could. Dr. Wade could sometimes be a jerk, but Mitch had seen he also had a likable streak. One just had to wade through ten miles of ego swamp to get to it.

Likable jerk or not, Wade had carefully instructed Mitch in cyanide precautions and had familiarized Mitch with the filter cleaning procedure. Wade had been surprised that Mitch already knew the basics of cyanide poisoning. When he had asked about Mitch's apparent knowledge, Mitch had just replied that it was something he had to pick up before he could take a walk through a certain jungle not that long ago. Wade had been both shocked and pleased by Mitch's revelation. In fact, Wade had been so pleased that he asked no more questions.

Mitch turned to leave Wade's lab. He had not knocked on the door because he didn't want to disturb the professor. But as he turned, he heard a heavy thumping sound from inside. Something heavy had fallen, and the sound of broken glass followed almost immediately.

Recognition flashed behind Mitch's eyes. He whirled around and yanked on the door. It gave way, and he immediately smelled the sweet, sickening, almond-like smell of cyanide gas. Taking a big breath of fresher air, he plunged into the metal building knowing he would find the worst inside.

Mitch saw both the professor and his wife on the floor which was covered with broken glass. On one of the work counters was one of Wade's heavy lab gloves. It looked like it had been tossed there and had knocked over a bottle of sulfuric acid. The acid was covering the counter top and ran down to where a small metal bowl sat. It was the pan Wade had used to weigh the sodium cyanide crystals to make his cleaning solution. The concentrated acid had not taken very long to eat through the thin metal of the balance pan, and once through, it had immediately begun to generate the poison gas from the crystals.

Mitch, still holding his breath, lunged to the safety cabinet where the antidotes were kept. Grabbing a handful of the amyl nitrite ampules and two IV bags of sodium thiosulfate, he raced back to the two downed victims. He couldn't tell if Mrs. Wade was breathing or not, but Professor Wade was still gasping. He crushed two ampules under each of their noses. Fighting hard not to take a breath, Mitch next grabbed both Professor Wade and Mrs. Wade by back of their shirt collars. He was dragging them towards the door when his lungs betrayed him. The air he sucked in was sickening with the sweet poison it held.

No sooner had he tasted the cyanide than Mitch felt Marilyn Wade's thin blouse join in the betrayal. It tore free in his hand, causing him to lurch to one side with the sudden loss of balance. Reeling, Mitch crashed into a different work counter that held several beakers of Professor Wade's newest tissue cultures. The beakers shattered as Mitch crashed onto them. Glass shards cut his arms, instantly inoculating him with whatever Professor Wade was growing.

Spinning from the tainted air he had inhaled, Mitch ignored the cuts and threw Mrs. Wade over his shoulders in a fireman's carry. From there he could just barely grab the professor by his belt. Luckily, neither one was an overly large person, and Mitch was able to lurch his way outdoors with them even though his chest was being crushed by the effects of the cyanide.

Two or three other students were walking down the sidewalk that left the computer center, and Mitch screamed at them.

"Get help! There's been a lab accident!"

Mitch left the professor and his wife lying side by side, took another big breath, and plunged back into the lab. He had to get the IV solutions and plug them into their veins if they were going have any chance at all.

The next several minutes were a blur. Mitch did successfully retrieve the antidotes, and he did get the IV started on the professor. But later he couldn't remember if he had been able to get the needle into Mrs. Wade or not. He had absorbed enough of the poison that both his chest and head throbbed mercilessly. Whether or not those moments of confusion were enough to seal Marilyn Wade's fate or whether she was already dead was something Mitch would never know. When the paramedics arrived a few minutes later, he and Professor Wade were still salvageable. Mrs. Wade was not.

Mitch had no recollection of the next few hours. When he woke, he was in an ICU bed in Phelps County Hospital. His head throbbed mercilessly and his chest ached from the near-fatal cyanide exposure. His arms, covered in thick bandages and full of stitches, burned fiercely too. The wrecked lab's broken glass and spilled chemicals had done their work.

"Did Mrs. Wade and the professor make it?" he croaked.

An ICU nurse who was standing near him turned. "Good. You're coming around."

The woman's voice sounded far, far away, but her words still touched something vital inside him.

"What about Mrs. Wade and the professor? Did they make it?" he whispered again.

The effort made his head spin. He had to swallow hard to keep from vomiting.

"The professor should be all right. He probably didn't get much more of an exposure than you did," the nurse answered.

"And Mrs. Wade?"

The nurse just gave him a sad look and said nothing.

"Oh, God!" Mitch muttered, trying to raise his restrained, bandaged hands to his face. His whole body started to shake.

"You did all you could, son," the nurse comforted, taking his right hand. "You nearly died yourself trying to save them. It was an awful accident."

Mitch shook harder as he tried to turn away. Tears were starting to run down his face, overflowing the gauze there. It seemed as though a great darkness had come back to claim him and that this time there would be no escape.

During the same time that Mitch was trying to piece himself back together, Jacob Wade was coming apart at the seams. He couldn't bear losing Marilyn, and he couldn't face the fact that the accident was his fault.

So in those desperate, clouded hours, Jacob Wade's mind constructed a story, a delusion that would rule both the rest of his life and that of an unspeakable host of others. In it he hallucinated that a vengeful government had descended upon him and took its due for his abandoning his previous weapons' research work. His plummeting mental state constructed a group of shadowy assassins whom he made responsible for his wife's death, and he named them the CIA. As he lay in his hospital bed, his guilt-ridden mind plunged over the sharp ledge of paranoia and fell into insanity.

Mitch was able to visit Wade the next day, but the brilliant egocentric professor he had once known just wasn't there. Mitch watched with a broken heart as the professor turned away from him to face a blank hospital wall. The turning away was, Mitch realized, a somber gesture. Their friendship was just as dead as was Mrs. Wade. Vietnam, the Marine Corps, Rolla, this hospital… . it was always the same. Death followed Mitch like his own shadow.

Two days later, Mitch had recovered enough from the cyanide to get out of the hospital. His recovery, however, was short. The very next day he had to be readmitted. For some strange reason, Mitch had suddenly contracted a case of the *mumps*. He'd had this illness when he had been ten years old, but something about the accident had caused it to return. Mitch's lymph nodes became swollen everywhere, and his parotid glands in his neck grew huge. Worst of all, the mumps settled into his testicles, causing them to swell mercilessly with what the doctors said was a severe orchitis.

There was no good explanation of how the mumps virus had reactivated inside Mitch. The university's doctor thought it might have something to do with his immune system being adversely affected by the cyanide.

Happily, the illness lasted only a few days, and Mitch quickly recovered. But that was still long enough for Mitch to become the object of an intensive medical scrutiny.

Several doctors who had once been Professor Wade's colleagues in the Department of Defense arrived on the scene and tested Mitch from head to toe. All of his body fluids were sampled. A bone marrow biopsy was taken along with liver and skin specimens, and a number of cultures were drawn.

Mitch never knew exactly what all these studies finally revealed, but it didn't matter. As the swelling abated, the episode was quickly forgotten. Only Marilyn Wade's face, now another sad ghost who haunted his nights, remained.

Chapter Twelve

Wilson Strong was seated behind his desk at Langley, CIA's headquarters in Washington, D. C. He was still an army general, but these days he mostly wore a civilian business suit in place of his uniform. Now he was in charge of a large group of intelligence analysts. His field days were pretty much a thing of the past. However, this didn't mean that his job wasn't demanding. In fact, it was *very* demanding. The workload was huge, his men and women dedicated, and the work definitely needed. But it was sterile work. Strong missed the contact with the actual combat troops. Their spirits were the only things that gave conflict any honor.

Strong had not wanted to leave Vietnam in the months after Tet, but it had become obvious that he was on a collision course with his superiors. Those above him were not going to be replaced, and the strategy of the war was not going to be changed. So something had to give. Wilson Strong was too much of a legend to be denigrated and too much of an honorable warrior to be left in Vietnam where he could cause trouble. Consequently, powers in Washington had intervened, and Senator Simons, the powerful senior senator from Missouri, had been made the point man. Strong had not liked what the senator had told him, but in the end, the senator had his way. Strong was forced out of Vietnam and relocated into his present position. That was over a year ago—a long year full of labor and very little honor.

Rumors had been flying throughout the intelligence community for weeks that something big was up. The Olympic Games in Munich were just three or four months away, and the whole world's attention would be focused on the event. It was a stage full of bright lights--a wonderful platform that could show off any purpose or cause resting on it.

The security challenges for the event were almost insurmountable. Happily, Strong was not really responsible for the Game's security, but he was supposed to maintain an overview of possible terrorist scenarios. To that end, he had a whole multitude of skilled workers-- both in house and in the field-- several satellites, whole banks of computers, and a considerable amount of funding. When Strong had taken the job, he had been told that his resources would be abundant. That, at least, had been true.

In modern times, the Olympic Games had evolved into a political showpiece. True, the games had moments when human effort did transcend the various national party lines. The 1960 Rome Games had demonstrated that when an Ethiopian marathon runner had lifted the whole world beyond itself with each of his barefooted strides. But for the most part, the ethics of the individual athlete had long since been bought off by the military-like training programs of the Eastern Block and by the greedy, bonus-baby propositions of the West's media circuses.

Now, on top of the traditional East/West competition, the Games' publicity provided a prime-time opportunity for the disenchanted and disenfranchised of the world to gain a moment of brilliant exposure for their respective causes. It was Wilson Strong's job to oversee the denial of such an opportunity to any who sought it.

Strong's morning briefing was set to begin shortly. The previous evening's efforts were summarized in the computer printouts on his desk. He was pushing his way through this heavy pile of paper when he came upon a highlighted section that contained an updated list of American citizens of note who had travel plans for the Munich sports festival. Anyone the computer could connect in any way to national interests was listed by name, type of travel, accommodations, and area of concern. Mostly listed were politicians, business leaders, and ranking military personnel.

Strong was speed-reading through this highlighted section when his eyes caught a name that rang a vague alarm. Jacob Beel Wade, Ph. D.

The computer listed Wade as a college professor who had been formerly a researcher of some note for the Department of Defense. All the printout said was that the man had been once deeply involved in sensitive biological studies, and the security clearance the professor still possessed enforced the fact that the man had once been very, very deep into the workings of the defense establishment. In fact, he was still listed as being on staff at Fort Detrick, the Army's long-time bioweapons research center.

That bothered Strong, but there was something else, something vague and half-remembered that made him even more uncomfortable.

"Sherry, please come in here," Strong spoke to his secretary through his intercom.

"Yes sir."

"Sherry," Strong said as she entered his inner office, "you were my predecessor's girl Friday, weren't you?"

"Yes, general. You know I was." She frowned slightly. She had served several of Strong's predecessors in her nearly thirty years of service. She wasn't sure where the general was going with his question.

"Don't worry, Sherry. I'm quite happy with you. In fact, if you hadn't been with me over these last several months, I'm sure I would've bungled any of several different assignments."

Sherry seemed to relax a bit. She had come to know this general was a demanding boss.

"Now I want to use your brain again, if you'll let me."

"Certainly, general. How can I help you?"

"Sherry, does the name Jacob Wade mean anything to you?"

She hesitated. "Maybe… General, can I use your computer terminal for a moment?"

Strong motioned to her to come around his desk. "Here. It's all yours."

Sherry's fingertips flew over the keys as she entered several different codes. The small monitor screen on Strong's desk blinked repetitively and then settled down.

"Here he is, general. He's a microbiologist. His file is too deeply buried by security clearances for me to get into it, but I do remember there was some sort of biological accident about a year ago that killed his wife and almost killed him. He was lucky some college student was around who knew quite a lot about cyanide poisoning. The student saved his life."

She paused at the strange look she saw on Strong's face.

"Later, there was something about him blaming us for the whole episode. It got a little ugly for a while. Command didn't know what to do with him."

Strong's face, surprised a moment before, had turned into a blank wall. "Thank you, Sherry. I'll take it from here."

"Any time, general." She turned to leave. "Remember, sir, morning briefing will begin in about fifteen minutes."

Strong nodded to his boss lady, and then he keyed in his special codes. The screen blinked again and then came alive with Wade's biography. Born in 1934 in Provo, Utah, the man was the younger of two children. His undergrad years had been at Brigham Young where he had finished *summa cum laude* with a B. S. in microbiology. His M. S. and his Ph. D. were from Berkeley in biochemistry--areas of interest: recombinant RNA synthesis, retrovirus applications.

The screen continued with Wade's listed publications. All were papers about virology, immunology, and related viral mutation mechanisms.

"Pretty heady stuff," Strong thought.

Then the general saw that the professor vanished from the academic world.

"That's when the Defense Department boys put him underground," Strong muttered.

The next several years of record were blank. Even Strong's own codes were inadequate to open the files on whatever the professor had done in the desert. The general would have to get different codes to open those years.

Strong scrolled on and saw that in 1969 Wade had left the Department of Defense without prejudice and taken a position as a section chairman of biochemistry at the University of Missouri-Rolla. The screen indicated personal, religious, and marital reasons for his leaving his Defense Department post.

"Apparently," Strong thought, "the young professor came upon something out there under the sand that was so big even he couldn't swallow it." He hesitated. "Whatever it was, the Defense Department must have decided that it had to have it… and they couldn't afford to alienate him."

The CRT in front of Strong changed its picture. Some months ago, the young, superstar virologist had nearly died in a lab accident. His wife did die. And the capable, college student who saved the day? None other than Mitchell Rice.

Strong pushed back from his desk. For a split second, he was again in Hue. His closed eyes were again full with the smoke and fire that hemmed in Mitch, Sarah, Sister Danielle, and Mother Marie. He blinked, and all of Tet replayed itself. He remembered it had been his own men who had trained Mitch in the finer points of cyanide poisoning.

"Well, at least some good finally came from those damn pills," he whispered.

Strong continued his reverie. Mitch was right in front of him. The kid had been deadly effective in everything the general had ever asked of him, but Strong had realized early on that Mitch would not do well in the moral cesspool Vietnam had become. Strong was glad he had been able to maneuver Mitch out of the Marine Corps. Mitch was too good to be used up there in the jungle, and it was a way Strong could repay some of what he owed Mitch for bringing Sarah home.

Strong rubbed his forehead. He and Sarah had come a long way over the last year. She was still working for Senator Simons, but they had been seeing so much of each other that she had been forced to submit to a level five security clearance review. The CIA had to know everything about its generals, and Sarah was becoming more and more a part of his life.

Sarah had really changed from her shy, uncertain ways of 1968. Tet and its aftermath had molded her into a force to be reckoned with. She and the general had already agreed that she would be his next "Friday" when Sherry retired. It only made sense because she was already, more often than not, his "Saturday" and "Sunday" anyway.

Strong returned his focus to his monitor screen. The Jacob Wade story was growing clear. Some strange fate had placed Mitch in the man's path. Mitch had done what he had to do, but he had paid dearly for the effort. Both the cyanide and an odd infection of Wade's manufacture had heavily marked him.

Strong read the whole investigative report as it scrolled by on his screen. Wade had suffered some sort of mental breakdown and had accused the CIA of being responsible for the accident. That wasn't true, but whatever the professor had in his little lab had been potent enough to bring the full weight of the agency down on the scene afterwards.

The aftermath of the accident was buried just as deep as Wade's old underground lab in Nevada. All that Strong could see from the records was that Mitch had survived without apparent permanent damage and that several tissue and genetic studies were still continuing on samples that the agency had taken from Mitch's body.

"Goddamn it!" Strong cursed. "The virus boys have turned Mitch into walking, living experiment!"

It was enough to turn the general's stomach. Strong realized he should have been angrier that Wade hadn't been punished for his treason, but he was more fed up with the system itself, a system that had lost all sense of morality. The only saving grace to the whole affair, he realized, was that Mitch had survived.

The report concluded by saying Professor Wade had taken an indefinite sabbatical from the university and had entered a special rehabilitation program that the Defense Department maintained for its wayward "*wunderkind*." The whole affair sucked.

Mitch's fate was sealed by his bone marrow. Something genetic had been found there. And whatever that "something" was, it was significant enough for Mitch to have been classified as someone who required perpetual observation. In effect, Mitch would be a living, breathing experiment in bio-warfare for the rest of his life. The virus boys had turned Mitch's bone marrow into an everlasting tissue culture for *in vitro* experiment, and Mitch would always be an object of *in vivo* observation. And he was never to be told a thing about it.

Strong shook his head. Maybe it would have been better if Mitch had never left Vietnam. At least there, Mitch would have had some idea who the bad guys really were. Now he had already become a victim, and he didn't even know it.

For the rest of the day Strong was distracted and bothered. He felt the same battlefield sense of impending doom that had haunted him in Hue. By late afternoon the feeling had gotten so bad that he found himself requesting a late appointment with his old adversary, David Helsey who was still the director of the CIA.

"Wilson, good to see you. How can I help you?" Helsey asked as he held out his hand.

The director was obviously a victim of a day of hassle, but he was still trying to be friendly. Strong knew the act was taking a significant effort as the two men's past history was far from amicable.

"David, I have a problem with the Munich Olympic security situation," Strong answered, getting right to the point.

"What kind of problem?"

"You know my crew has been over-viewing all the incoming tourist travel information connected to the Games. Right in the middle of all this, I've run into a couple of names that I can't put down."

"Who are they?"

"Well, one is a former Marine scout/sniper. He was the kid who was my ace in the hole during Tet."

"Is that the kid who pulled those nuns out of the orphanage?"

"Yes. He's also the one who took out those NVA generals in Cambodia."

"Oh yeah, I remember him. The iceman assassin who had a heart. He's a problem now?"

"No. He's not. But somehow he has gotten mixed up with a high-grade biological weapons researcher who has security clearances so deep that even I can't easily get into his file." Strong paused to be sure Helsey was giving him his full attention. "My kid pulled this virologist out of a cyanide-filled research lab, and they both lived to tell about it."

"Okay?"

"The problem, David, is that this virologist laid the blame for the accident on our doorstep. That accident killed his wife."

Helsey's eyebrows went up. "Did we do it?"

"You know we didn't. We were as clean as the driven snow. But this guy -- his name is Jacob Wade -- isn't entirely stable. He thinks we did, and he's pretty adamant about it. I've found out that he's going to Munich as a spectator and that there's no provision for any observation or protection for him while he's there."

"Okay. So what's the problem? Just arrange for someone to be attached to him."

Strong shifted his weight in the chair as he faced Helsey. "David, I'm pretty sure that this guy is so spooked by his past that if he even sniffs our presence, he will bolt like a scared jack rabbit. I don't know where he would end up, but I suspect he's carrying enough biological weapons info in his head to make him a prize for any of our international competitors."

"This situation's really gotten you bugged, hasn't it?"

"Yes, it does," Strong answered. "My gut is cramping worse than it did before Tet. I'm extremely uncomfortable having this guy run around Germany free as a bird, but I'm not quite sure what we should do about it. Apparently, he's still quite a valuable commodity for us, or else I'm sure we would have already *fixed* him. Right?"

Helsey turned away at Strong's last remark, feeling its intended sarcasm. He was quite familiar with the name Jacob Wade. Wilson was right to feel uneasy.

"Wilson, I'll have to take this up with some of our other people. Thanks for bringing it all to my attention."

Strong realized he was being dismissed. The sudden snub left him with a tight jaw and a wrinkled forehead.

"Wilson, I trust your instincts, and I will call you later," Helsey answered.

Strong's stared right through his old adversary.

"Look, Will, I really will call you. I know we've crossed swords enough in the past, but this Wade deal is something I just can't talk about now. Trust me. You and I are much better off working together on this than we are fighting each other. I *will* call."

Strong's jaw was still tight. "David, the past is the past. I'm more than willing to get on with the present if you are."

Helsey nodded. "Sounds good. Now get out of here. I'll call when I have something for you."

Strong left Helsey's office, ruminating on what had just transpired. He and Helsey went all the way back to West Point and to Korea after that. They usually held different positions about nearly everything that had subsequently filled the Cold War era. So far, Helsey had proven to be the better politician, but Strong had by far been the better field officer. For tonight, Strong hoped his old rival had taken him seriously. Somehow, Strong's old battlefield feeling told him the stakes here were about as high as they could possibly get.

The confusion of Strong's late afternoon encounter didn't last long. The following morning, he was busy working at his desk. The CRT was humming, and he was deep in thought.

"General Strong?" It was Sherry's voice slipping through the intercom. "I'm sorry to disturb you, but Director Helsey is on line two."

Strong turned his attention away from his computer. "Thank you, Sherry. I have it." He picked up the phone, he said, "Good morning, David. This is Wilson."

Helsey's abrasive voice returned the greeting and then pressed on. Strong listened attentively, and after a while, he answered. "Sure I'm available for lunch. Your place or mine?"

"Mine," was the reply. "Come on up around 1300 hours."

Strong said okay and put down the receiver. Maybe he had done some good last night after all.

Lunch proved to be Chinese carry-in. Strong chose cashew chicken.

"Wilson, I want you to know that I have taken last night's conversation very seriously. This Professor Wade is truly an interesting character. The fact that his name has been un-flagged to this point has already caused more than a few heads to roll."

Strong paused, his mouth full of lunch. The two men's eyes met.

"I really don't know what to say about this, Will. This Wade was into some research out there in that underground lab in Nevada that was really important. He left the Defense Department in good standing, but you're right, his personality is prone to depression. He had some family problems before the accident, and his wife's death may well have left him in a pretty precarious position. It would have been easy for him to transfer his guilt to us."

Helsey turned away from Strong, and he started to pace about the office. Strong had never known Helsey to be a pacer and realized that the truth must be a pretty uncomfortable proposition. Professor Wade had to be *really* important.

After a few laps around the office, Helsey went on.

"Outside of his area of expertise, Wade's not well known. His work was so secret that he was not able to publish anything for some time. That compromised him in the outside world. My psych people think his taking a position at an engineering school was either an act of rebellion or of penitence. His wife's death, which probably was his own fault, may well have been enough to push him over the edge."

"Just what exactly does this guy have that makes him so valuable, David? I've never known you to be so considerate."

"Wilson, can your sarcasm! I have never liked it!"

Strong met Helsey's gaze and said nothing, but the man hadn't yet heard Strong's last word.

"Look," Helsey continued. "You know that I am not well-versed in biological weaponry, but this guy is so far ahead of all of the rest of our people in the fine art of developing noxious little artificial viruses that the whole biological community seems to look at him like he's a god."

"And that's why we want him back in those labs. We want him doing his thing with enthusiasm, right?" Strong asked.

"Exactly." Helsey seemed glad that Strong understood. "We have to finesse this thing. Wade's a genuine genius. We have to protect him while he regains his balance. We *have* to bring him back into the fold."

Helsey seemed to be challenging Strong.

"Will, earn your pay. Give me some options."

Helsey returned to his desk chair.

"I have to live within conventional parameters. Wade's now just a private citizen. He can travel wherever he wishes, but he still must be protected."

Helsey leveled his gaze at Strong.

"What can you do for me, Will? I'm sure you had a plan before you set foot in here last night. What is it?"

Strong was quiet for a moment. His thoughts were a long way away.

"David, once before and not really all that long ago, I was in a similar position. I very much wanted to protect someone who was not really a 'player'. I was frustrated. No one was cooperating, and the situation was deteriorating at a rapid pace."

"So what happened?"

"Well, in plain English, the skies opened, and down came a guardian angel. He was a pretty beaten up marine sniper whose partner had just been killed. This kid sailed into Hue on a chopper with both a concussion and a developing reputation for being one of the most remarkable rifle shots the Marine Corps ever produced. When he left later on another chopper, his guts were all shot up, but he had pulled off everything that I had asked him. My people were out of harm's way, and I was very much in his debt."

Helsey's face turned upwards in mock disgust.

"I always suspected you played with a stacked deck! But what the hell? Do you still have a connection with the powers above? Can you produce another guardian angel to pull our bacon out of this fire?"

Strong's expression was uninterpretable.

"I don't know many angels, David, but I do know this one. And he may just be willing to help me out again, if I asked just the right way."

Helsey shrugged. "It's your call, Wilson. Give your kid a call. I'll undersign whatever you come up with. Just come up with a plan quick and keep me informed."

The two men shook hands. That made two more or less successful encounters in two days. That was more agreement than they had shared in all of their previous days combined. The world was definitely full of changes.

Shortly after that, Strong pulled out of the CIA's parking lot and started his drive downtown. He had to find Sarah and convince her to help him. If he did, then maybe he could put this Jacob Wade deal to rest.

"This is crazy," he thought as he drove. "Sarah, I need you here, not on the other side of town. Where the hell are you?"

Chapter Thirteen

Spring was far along, and, even though it was just morning, the day was already hot. Mitch's spring term had just ended, and he had the summer before him. He stepped onto the cinder track that surrounded UMR's football field, this time maybe for the last time. He stared down the straightaway and saw the past year. It had been an eventful one.

Last fall, after the Dr. Wade affair, Mitch had switched his major from physics to chemistry. It wasn't that he had been less enthused with physics -- a science that had allowed let him see a little of the mind of God. But Mrs. Wade's suggestions about him considering medicine as a way of life had struck home. Consequently, he had dedicated the whole year to making a run for medical school. Dr. Fulton, true friend that he was, had come through, and even though Mitch really wasn't one of his students any more, the physicist had done all he could to help Mitch with his new goal. Remarkably, everything had come together. Mitch had been accepted by every med school he had applied to, and with each acceptance, Mitch and Dr. Fulton shared another steak dinner. It had been a time to remember.

"Remember, last summer in my lab, Mitch?" Fulton had asked at their last meal together. "You know, the time when you popped out that statement about math being the first written word of God?"

Mitch had his mouth full of baked potato, but he had nodded yes.

"Well, that's the kind of insight that genius is made of. Son, you may be going on your way with your medicine, but don't forget what you've learned here. Math is God's first 'written word', and physics is His 'music'. One day you may want to come back to them. Reading God's Own thoughts and listening to Him conduct His Own personal symphony are both pretty amazing experiences. Remember that."

Mitch had said that he would, and the two parted as two men who had become more than friends.

The memory faded, and Mitch looked at the cinders under his feet. His last track season had been hard. All of his class work had hampered his training, and he had not really lived up to his personal expectations. Maybe that was why he was out here now. He still had something to prove to himself, and this was his last chance.

Mitch gathered himself at the starting line and started to run. His stride felt good. There was no pain anywhere. So it was easy to let the beast out.

The first mile passed in easy fashion, and Mitch wasn't even winded. He followed with a half mile of farleks, 330 yards pushing and llO yards gliding, and was thoroughly warmed up. He then allowed himself fifteen minutes or so to completely recover from the interval work. Finally he was ready.

Mitch stepped up to the starting line he had come to know so well over the last two years. "Well, I guess it's time," he whispered. Taking a long breath, he cleared his stopwatch, and then like a long spring unwinding, he took off.

"Pace!" he muttered inside his head. "Establish pace!"

Each stride for the first 220 generated more acceleration. The rhythm was easy. The stopwatch read 0:27 seconds at the half-lap mark. The next 220 yards glided by almost without notice. Mitch felt the flow of the run, arms and legs pulling at the track and the air rushing by, and it was good. At the quarter, the watch read 0:53 seconds.

"I wonder if this is too fast," he thought, but it was time to hold nothing back. So he didn't.

The second quarter was a near repeat of the first. Mitch's body continued in its self-contained cadence. The air continued to slide by, and sweat continued to pour. He had entered the "zone," that place where existence was condensed only to the effort of the run. By the half-mile mark, the stopwatch read l:55. 2.

Mitch came out of the trance on the next back turn. The pace was beginning to hurt, but he knew he couldn't let up. This was his *last* race, and he strained to go even faster. By 1100 yards, the clock read 2:22. 7.

A half lap later the strain was replaced by real pain. The clock read 2:52. 4 at the bell lap, but Mitch could tell the odds had switched into the timepiece's favor. His lungs were on fire, and he was suddenly in agony. In front of him, at the start of the front turn, loomed the "wall," a barrier of hypoxia that Mitch had never conquered before.

At this point Mitch's oxygen debt was dulling his mind, and his legs were screaming for air. Mitch ignored the pain and kept pumping his arms, demanding that his legs follow. All of his muscles were on fire, but they obeyed. And Mitch kept flying.

He was almost to the backstretch when the "wall" fell away. His peripheral circulation almost instantly rearranged itself, and suddenly he felt pulsing blood where just seconds before there had been none. The pain was gone, and his brain was suddenly crystal clear with a focused euphoria. All of his life seemed to come down to the next three hundred yards, and it was a simple purpose he could embrace.

At this level, Mitch was reaching beyond himself. He was in a state of adrenaline-induced otherness, burning bright with a terminal flame. The next two hundred yards gave Mitch a little glimpse of another world. He was literally soaring down the back straight, his feet barely touching the ground. The normal world was left behind. Only the last 110 yards remained.

It was halfway through the last turn that reality returned. Instantly his euphoria became a ferocious agony. The air around him became as inferno, searing his lungs closed and racking him senseless. He kept running, but each stride brought pain that was worse than anything he had ever felt anywhere, even in Hue. His vision blurred, and his brain melted. But he kept running anyway. All he had left was his heart, but it understood. He *had* to finish! He *would not* quit! His legs *had* to keep working!

And they did. Seconds later, with all of his senses way past overload, Mitch forced himself across the final line, choking the stopwatch as he did.

Over the next several yards Mitch faltered badly, stumbling all over the cinders. His eyes wouldn't focus, and his legs turned to rubber. Breathing was impossible. Everything was on fire, and his heart screamed in protest. But he kept running. His momentum had not yet expended itself, and his agony was not yet over.

Several yards and an eternity later, sanity began to re-assert itself. By the first turn Mitch was able to slow to a walk. For a moment he was better, but then his abdominal muscles started cramping. A severe nausea followed. By the time he had just passed the far side of the high-jump pit, his frail humanity had completely reasserted itself with retching ferocity. From the sublime heights of but a few seconds before, Mitch fell to his knees, lost in the hypoxic depths where he all could do was vomit.

The next several minutes were anything but dignified. Gradually, however, the retching passed. Mitch's gasping slowed, and his pain-racked frame slumped, quivering with severe exhaustion. He realized he would probably live.

"Hey, marine! That was some kind of show," spoke a distant but familiar voice. "That was better than the Wide World of Sports."

Mitch was still winded, but he forced himself to focus. "Sarah? Where'd you come from?"

"From over there." She laughed, pointing behind her at the morning shadows of the stadium. "You're just as crazy now as you were four years ago. What was your time anyway?"

Mitch looked down at the watch. It read 3:54. 2. He gave her the watch. Sarah didn't say anything at first, but after a moment she asked. "Isn't the world record for the mile something like 3:51?"

"Something like that."

She looked up from the watch. "Oh, Mitch! Why aren't you running in the Olympics?"

Mitch just shrugged. "Because I'm not good enough. That's why."

"Don't they run the 1500 meters in international competition?"

"Yeah."

"I saw how hard the last 100 yards were! You may well have just set a world record for 1500 meters right here! You belong in Munich!"

Mitch just stood there.

"Oh, Mitch! This is just another time when you're going to wonder for the rest of your life what might have been!"

Mitch stood up straight. "Sarah, cool your jets. The guys who'll run and win at the Olympics can run three or four runs like this one back-to-back. I'm dead after just one. I couldn't have gotten much past the first time trial."

He paused. "You're a little right, though. I needed this run to prove something to myself."

He paused again. "I *did* have a good run left in me after all, and it felt good."

He grinned. "And you know what? It feels even better knowing that you were here to see me do it!"

"You dumb jarhead! You poor, dumb jarhead!" Sarah muttered.

"Hey! I love you too, sweetheart!" Mitch growled, trying to look threatening. "What are you doing here? You're supposed to be in D. C."

"Oh, I came home to see my folks, and I thought I'd come see you while I was here."

"Sarah, you were never a very good liar."

"That's the truth, Mitch! I *did* want to see you…

even though you almost always scare the hell out of me every time we're together."

"Sarah, how can you be scared of some fool running around a cinder track, chasing himself until he ends up throwing up?"

"Mitch," she said, her voice suddenly quivering, "the thing that scares me the most is not knowing what will happen if you ever realize just who you are. Just then, on the track, were you running toward or away from something?"

"Hey, Miss Red Cross worker, will you shut up and give me a hug?"

She saw him coming and ducked to one side. "No way, *Jose*!" she squealed. "You smell too bad!"

Her efforts were a sham. Mitch caught her easily, and she surrendered to his embrace eagerly. His arms, as they had always been, were a safe haven for her. She was home again.

Later, at a brunch, the two friends caught up on each other's lives. He told her of his last few months and of how med school had come his way. She told him of her life in Washington and of her work for the senator.

Politics was proving to be much more involved than she had ever thought possible. Sarah admitted she was having trouble with the lack of black-and-white that existed there. Gray was never her color.

Her admission made Mitch chuckle, but she didn't join him. Instead, she almost frowned. For a minute, Mitch didn't understand. But after she had taken several big breaths, he did. What followed was her description of her developing relationship with General Strong. Her description went on for a long time.

Mitch did his best to listen. Sometimes he let his eyes meet hers; sometimes he looked away. Certainly, Sarah's time with the general preceded what he'd had with her. And it was pretty easy to see their time in D. C. would have given their relationship the chance to grow. All Mitch ever really had with Sarah was Vietnam and their letters since then. His head understood all this, but his heart didn't. It could only understand what it had felt when she had been in his arms.

When she had finished, he sat in silence for several long seconds. He felt her gaze searching him, pleading for the right combination of words. And he understood… it has been his to bring her home… his to keep her safe. But that was all. She had chosen the general, and now it was time for him to give her his blessing.

Taking a long breath, he slowly answered. "I'm really happy for you, lady… if that's what you want." He tried his best to smile. "But I'm not sure that old war dog deserves you."

Sarah broke eye contact with him and turned away. It wasn't the reaction he expected.

"Mitch," she said, "Wilson asked me to come here today." She hesitated for a long second. There was guilt… or maybe a look of betrayal on her face. "There's a mission, Mitch, and he needs you again."

The sudden changing of the tides stopped Mitch cold. "What?" he whispered, not believing what he had just heard.

"I said Wilson needs you, Mitch." She had tears in her eyes. "He asked me to find you and to tell you that he needs a 'guardian angel' again."

Her tears started to fall. "Something bad is happening, Mitch! Something almost as bad as that last night in Hue! I told him it wasn't fair… not to you or to me! But he said it was that bad, Mitch!"

She looked back to him sadly. "That's why I'm really here today. I'm Wilson's messenger. I'm sorry I couldn't think of a better way to tell you." It was Mitch's turn to look away. "You're right," he answered. "This isn't fair. It isn't fair at all."

He turned back to her. "I thought all this was about you and the general… or about you and me. What do you mean…he needs me again? What the hell is going on?" Mitch's eyes were snapping with red sparks. "And why isn't he here to do his own dirty work? This is wrong!"

Sarah wilted. "I told him that's what you'd say. But he said the situation was bad enough that he had to send me… "the first team." He said he knew you could easily say "no" to him… but you couldn't to me. He said you'd understand when I told you this: "There are times when there's only one man who can make the difference." Her voice was choking back her tears. "And this is a time when duty is more important than your hurt feelings, his pride, or… my love." That's what he said I should say to you."

Sarah saw the fire in Mitch's eyes go out. In its place she saw a great, gray, cold emptiness that she knew her heart could never warm again.

"You really do love him, don't you, Sarah?" Mitch asked simply.

"Yeah… I guess I do," she answered. "Or else I wouldn't have come."

In the next instant she saw the emptiness in Mitch's eyes fill in with several figures. She was there. So was the general. Likewise, she caught glimpses of Dannie, Mother Marie, and a whole host of Vietnamese children. It seemed Mitch was making a choice… or maybe, the thought hit her, he was just remembering a choice he had already made years before.

"And I guess I do too," he said quietly. "Tell me what this is all about."

The next day found Mitch in the back seat of an F4 taxiing down the runway at Whiteman Air Force Base. Washington, D. C. was just a few hours away. The pilot asked about his comfort and then left Mitch alone with his thoughts. Mitch was still lost in those thoughts when the plane came down just outside of the capital at Andrews.

"Thanks for the flight, captain," Mitch said as he deplaned. "I've never been in an F4 before. That was quite a trip."

"She's a good bird, sir," the pilot said as he shook Mitch's hand. "I think that car over there by the hanger is for you. Good luck, sir."

"Thanks, captain, but I was never a "sir." The most I ever really was… was a corporal."

Mitch walked over to the car. A familiar large wedge-shaped figure got out of the back seat. It was Wilson Strong.

"Hello, Mitch. How was the flight?"

"Uneventful, sir, but it was a lot more exciting than a commercial flight."

"Good," Strong said, offering Mitch his hand. "Come on. Let's get in the car."

The two settled into the back seat of the limo. There was a glass panel separating them from the driver. The compartment was obviously soundproof.

"Sarah couldn't tell you very much because I didn't give her very much. I knew whatever I did give her, she would immediately spill to you. She's worthless at keeping secrets from those she loves."

"She loves you too, general."

"I know, Mitch. We are both lucky men to have her on our side."

"Yes sir. We are."

Strong looked out of the car window as the vehicle navigated traffic.

"Mitch, how is your German?"

"Excuse me, general?"

"Well, let me put it another way. How would you like to go the Olympics?"

"General, you're nuts!" Mitch snapped back, suddenly exasperated. "What's all this stuff about me going to the Olympics? Not even the president himself has enough pull to get me on that team! Even if he could, what would I do there? Play tiddlywinks? My times aren't good enough! Besides, I have a starting date for medical school around that time anyway!"

Strong stayed calm. "I didn't say you would be competing, Mitch, even though Sarah thinks you should. I figured you would go as part of the training staff. It's true you would be a little late starting your class work at MU, but you've coped with slow starts before. You could do it again."

Mitch gave up any attempt of waiting Strong out. "What exactly do you want me to do, general? What's so god-awful important that you've had to arrange all of this?"

"Mitch, this is a lot different than it was in Hue. Then I could give you orders. Now I can only make requests. Don't get me wrong... I don't have any regrets of the past. Everything you did in Vietnam was right. And everything I did after Tet to get you home was right too... it's just wasn't enough."

Strong grimaced a little with the last sentence, but he kept right on going.

"The fact is that you had no business staying in the Marine Corps. You would have developed a significant ability for alienating commanders. You never respected the chain of command enough. You'll be a lot better off being a doctor."

Mitch was silent for a moment. "If you really feel that way, general, what can be in Munich that's worth you pulling me away from med school... and your using Sarah the way you did to get me here?"

Strong looked away from Mitch. "Mitch, what have you heard lately from Professor Wade?"

"Jacob Wade? My old microbiology professor?"

"Yes."

"Sir, I haven't seen him or heard from him in months, not since the day after... the accident."

"I know all about that," Strong said quietly. "The professor hasn't been the same since. That has become a great worry for those of us who are supposed to be on the lookout for loose ends." Strong was looking out of the car window. "You see, Mitch, your old professor was and still is quite a whiz kid. He knows more about recombinant RNA synthesis and retrovirus manufacture than any man in the western world. And he also appears to be the victim of his own exaggerated conscience."

Strong took a minute for all that to soak in.

"Mitch, you know, don't you, that the cyanide was the result of either Wade's or his wife's own doing. It may have been an accident, or it may have been intentional; we really don't know. But I'm absolutely sure that no one from any branch of the CIA was even within a hundred miles of Rolla, Missouri when the whole thing happened."

Mitch listened carefully to his old commander words. "General, I know that Wade was spouting a lot of stuff about the CIA being behind the accident, but I just figured it was the result of cyanide. I know I was pretty messed up for several days afterwards."

Mitch shrugged and turned away.

"Like I said, I haven't seen him for quite a while. Is he still standing by his story? Blaming the CIA at all?"

"Yes."

"Does that make him a 'loose cannon'?"

"We're not sure, Mitch. We do know that, at present, he's a resource that we can't afford to lose. We know that he really isn't attached to us in any official way, and we also know that we don't want to aggravate his sense of paranoia. In short, we need a way to watch him, to protect him, to contain him, and we need to do it without him realizing that we're doing it."

Mitch kept looking out the car window. He didn't reply right away.

"General, do you think I'm the guy who can do all that?"

Mitch felt the general's stare pulling him around.

"Mitch, you're not 'company'. The professor already knows that you'll go to the extremes to protect him. He knows that you were a runner and that you're going to med school, so it wouldn't be too hard to swallow seeing you in Munich as part of the training staff. And I know that you're one of the most reliable field men I've ever had. Yes, I believe that you are the best man—maybe the only man, for this job."

Mitch took the next step slowly. "General, just how far would this concept of containment go? Would I truly just be protecting him, or would I be the one who would have to eliminate him if things got messed up? General, I don't want any more killing."

It was General Strong's turn to be silent, but it was just a short pause.

"Mitch, we aren't even sure that anything's going to happen in Munich. If anything does, we aren't sure that it would even involve Wade. We don't want him dead. If we did, he'd already be gone. You have to know that. We really want him protected and brought *home* in one piece."

Mitch caught Strong's strange emphasis of the word *home*.

"General, I was around you in Hue long enough to know that you don't waste your resources. You must be pretty nervous about Munich, or you wouldn't have whisked me here in the back seat of an F4. And…"

Mitch stopped for a second.

"Damn! Something *bad* is coming down in Munich, isn't it? If it wasn't, you wouldn't be asking me to postpone med school!"

Mitch's eyes flared bright, and the general's unchanging expression told him more than words ever could.

"I guess I understand," Mitch said, after a long silence. "Something really bad is likely to come down over there, and you want me to protect him at all costs. But if all else fails, you don't want him in unfriendly hands. Right?"

Strong nodded. "You always could think on your feet, Mitch. That's why you could always stay ahead of the chain of command. And that's what I need now. And more than anything else, I need to know that if something does come down, the man on the scene will play that final trump card only if it's absolutely necessary. I was able to trust you before with that kind of responsibility. I think I still can. If there is *any* was Jacob Wade can be brought home, that's what we have to have. But there isn't…"

Mitch let the general's last statement find its measured depth. Inside, he felt familiar winds of war beginning to blow again. It was a scorching wind that he had hoped he would never feel again. Somehow, he knew it would soon be a fiery gale. Slowly, he nodded his head.

"General, I'm not a stupid nineteen-year-old kid anymore. And I've had about all the killing I can stand. But I guess you are still my general. Sarah loves you, and no matter what else has happened, I still trust you. So if you really need me… if whatever it is that Jacob Wade has is really *that* important… Yeah, I'll go. God help me… I'll go."

Chapter Fourteen

Munich was a beautiful city, even when it wasn't decked out in its international best. Mitch arrived two weeks before the Olympiad began. He had spent most of the summer preparing for this. General Strong always insisted that his agents be completely prepared for their missions, and Mitch had been no exception. The whole summer had been spent at "spy school."

The *school* was not something that was permanently stationed anywhere. For Mitch's purpose, the whole training course had been set up at Fort Leonard Wood which was just twenty miles or so from Rolla.

The summer had seen Mitch ingest large doses of surveillance techniques along with a lot of hand-to-hand combat drills and small arms practice. He also spent a lot of time improving his threadbare German and practicing high- speed pursuit driving. He had even made six parachute jumps. In short, the school was rigorous and Mitch's preparation was thorough.

It had taken a genuine act of faith on Mitch's part to trust that General Strong had enough pull to insure his late admission to med school. But since Senator Simons, the Missouri senator, was the general's friend and Sarah's boss, Mitch figured that the problem was as well covered as it could be. So as soon as he got to Munich, he set out right away to familiarize himself with the city. He didn't even allow himself to think that his medical school class had already been in session for over a week.

It hadn't taken Mitch long to realize that maps were fine, but they just didn't cut it when it came to giving someone an actual feel for the geography. That kind of familiarity was essential if Mitch was to have any kind of chance to shadow Professor Wade unnoticed. Consequently, Mitch spent a lot of time in his first week in Munich just driving his issued late model BMW around the city and the surrounding countryside.

General Strong's crew had learned Wade was going to stay at the Isis Hotel. The Isis was an older building, but it carried an honest two-star rating. That meant it was comfortable, but not plush. Wade was already confirmed into a single room on the second floor. Mitch checked into a room on the first floor that was very close to the path Wade would be taking in his comings and goings.

The plan was to monitor the professor at night via a simple but effective set of electronic "bugs" that would be installed in his room a few days before his arrival. A panel truck would be on station outside the hotel to listen to whatever the "bugs" picked up.

It was Mitch's job to be the primary legman. He would follow Wade wherever he went. Mitch had been allowed to keep his normal appearance. The psych people at Langley felt the professor would be less threatened if he saw Mitch than he would be if he discovered he was being followed by a stranger. Mitch, however, was still supposed to try very hard not to be seen.

When Mitch landed in Munich, he was met by an army major named Mallory. Mallory just waved his hands, and all of Mitch's luggage magically passed through customs. In those two suitcases were Mitch's special weapons, all of their accouterments, his ever faithful. 45, and the lightweight Kevlar vest Strong had ordered him always to wear. The addition of that last item had spoken louder than words that this assignment was almost certainly a lot more than just an ordinary surveillance jaunt.

Jacob Wade arrived in Munich two days before the Games began. He was alone, just as advertised. He was also totally unaware of Mitch's presence.

Wade attended the opening day festivities just like the rest of the myriad of spectators that filled the city. Over the next five days, he rose each day to the tune of an alarm clock, ate quickly, and took a bus to the events he wanted to see. He seemed to favor the aquatic events almost exclusively, and that made Mitch's job easier since Wade was stationary while watching the swimming events. Each night it was the same restaurant, the Hoffbrau Haus, located just down the street from the hotel.

The Jacob Wade Mitch followed was a far cry from the flamboyant man Mitch remembered. Wade's face, once animated, was now nearly without expression. He was solitary and seemed to shun the very crowds he got lost in. It struck Mitch that anger had taken the man's soul. Mitch felt like he was shadowing a stranger, almost a ghost of someone he had once known. If it all hadn't been so boring, it would have been scary.

It was in the early morning of September 5 when the game changed dramatically. Mitch was awakened by the jangling of his bedside the phone. As he lunged for the noise, his eyes glanced at the clock beside the phone. It said 5:15.

"Rice, this is Mallory! Strong was right! Arabic-speaking terrorists have taken over the Israeli dorm in the Olympic village! There have been deaths, lots of them! Damn it! We weren't ready for this! "

Mitch's sleep fogged brain was beginning to click rapidly. "What's my assignment now, major?"

"Your assignment's the same that it's always been, Rice! Just keep track of Wade! It's just that now you'll have to do it by yourself. I'm going to have to pull your support people to help in the Olympic village. Just keep Wade in sight. It should be pretty easy. He's not going anywhere. I'll be in touch as soon as the situation allows."

"Okay, major. Good luck."

"Thanks, Rice, but I think we're going to need a lot more than luck. The press is everywhere, and these terrorists are ruthless when they have an audience."

At exactly 8:00 a. m. Professor Wade left the hotel. This time, however, was different. Wade walked right past the usual bus stop. Mitch followed him for nearly thirty minutes as he walked a curiously circuitous route that brought them right back to the front of the Isis. There Wade paused.

Suddenly, from the street, Mitch saw a blur of motion. Two men, one light in complexion and the other dark, hustled Wade from the sidewalk and into the back seat of a late model Mercedes.

And just like that, the Mercedes pulled away and Mitch lost Jacob Wade.

Mitch knew he was in deep trouble. He sprinted down the sidewalk, dodging the heavy pedestrian traffic until he reached his BMW. It was parked out of the way on a side street. He slid behind the wheel, and started the engine just in time to see the Mercedes turn at the corner and go out of sight.

"Goddamn it!" Mitch cursed. He flung the roadster down an alley that ran behind the hotel in a desperate attempt to catch the big car. Luck was on his side because when he surfaced on the other end of the alley, he saw the Mercedes moving down the street to his left. Mitch jerked the gearshift down and pulled in behind the kidnappers' car. It was anyone's guess as to whether or not they had seen him.

The BMW was equipped with a two-way radio. Mitch hadn't really needed it up to that point, but this was the time.

"Watchman Control, this is Watchman!" he said into the mike.

There was only static.

"Watchman Control, this is Watchman!" he said again and again, but each time there was only static.

"Switch to tach two, you idiot!" he snarled to himself, remembering his summer of training. "Watchman Control, this is Watchman! Come in!" But still there was only static.

The Mercedes was now heading for the autobahn and was picking up speed. Mitch had to really concentrate to keep pace and still not be obvious.

"Watchman Control, this is Watchman! Get off you fat asses and answer me! This whole thing is blowing up right in my face!"

Again, for an instant, there was just the static, but then a voice came back. "Watchman, this is Control Backup. Control's in transition. What's your status?"

Mitch should have realized that the control van might be off line while Mallory was repositioning it closer to the Olympic village. He tried to settle down.

"Okay, Backup. This is Watchman. I'm rolling east on Winterstrasse, following a slate gray Mercedes. Its license plate is AGK 817. Three adult males have kidnapped my target. I wasn't able to stop them. They were too goddamn fast. But I'm on their tail, and so far I don't think they know I'm here."

"Hold one, Watchman."

Mitch continued to trail the gray Mercedes as he listened to the dead static on his radio. The wait went on forever. The Mercedes pulled farther out of Munich and entered the autobahn. Finally, after nearly fifteen minutes, the radio came back to life.

"Rice, this is Mallory. Stay on tach two. We think tach one's no longer secure. What the hell's happened?"

"Mallory, they grabbed him right under my nose and put in him the back seat of a Mercedes! I saw two adult males, and one more is driving. Right now I'm doing about 150 kph on E533. We're heading south. Munsing is just ahead. They still don't know I'm tailing them."

"Rice, we're all in deep shit! We're at least forty-five minutes from your present location! Keep tailing them, and we'll try to free up a unit to cover you as soon as we can! Israeli blood is knee-deep in the Olympic village! It's a real mess! Do the best you can, and keep me updated as to your location!"

"Roger, Mallory! But don't waste any time! I think those guys in front of me are pretty serious characters, and I'm just a lone ranger out here!"

To himself, Mitch muttered, "Goddamn you, Wilson Strong! Goddamn you! You got me here all by my lonesome just like you did before! Why the hell did I let you do this to me again? Goddamn you!"

The Mercedes continued on the autobahn for about another twenty kilometers and then left the highway. Mitch relayed their location to Mallory. It was obvious they were getting steadily farther and farther away from Mallory and his control people.

Near the Starnbarger Sea, the Mercedes turned onto a secondary road and slowed considerably. The surrounding terrain was uneven, and some of it was even swampy. Mitch let the Mercedes pull ahead. He had to in order to keep from being spotted. As a result, Mitch lost sight of the gray car for long minutes at a time. After several such lapses, he realized that he had lost it completely.

"Son of a bitch!" He grabbed his mike. "Watchman Control, this is Watch… Oh, to hell with it! Mallory get on this miserable thing and talk to me! I've lost Wade in the swamps down here by this damn lake!"

The radio squelched loudly and then cracked to life.

"Rice, this is Mallory! You gotta calm down! We're up to our necks with PLO types here! You're all we have out there! So get your shit together! I can't free anyone up to back you up! You're it! Backtrack and find them!"

"I'm already doing that, major! You just get my friggin' back-up out here! This is going to turn into a shooting war any minute now!"

Mitch was angry and frustrated. He knew he was losing. Backtracking was dangerous and made him an obvious target. The bad guys were holding all of the cards.

"Goddamn you, Strong! Where's my friggin' backup?"

Cursing steadily, Mitch continued to backtrack. After covering about a quarter of a mile at a snail's pace, he noticed a small dirt road he had missed before. It held fresh tire marks. That had to be where Wade had been taken.

"Mallory, how close are you?" Mitch keyed into the mike, ignoring all radio protocol.

"Rice, have you reestablished contact?"

"Yeah! And I'm going to have to leave the car and walk from here! I gotta know how long I have to hold before you can get here!"

The radio was silent for a long second. "Honest answer, Mitch... about thirty minutes."

"That's too damn long!"

Mitch, soaking wet with sweat, started to shake violently. Mind-killing fear overtook him, freezing his very thoughts. It was Cambodia all over again.

"Tell Strong I'll do the best I can! I don't know what'll be left when you get here, but get here! Rice, out!"

Mitch slipped out of the BMW quietly. He quickly checked his. 45 and then pulled binoculars and a specially prepared M-16 from its compartment in the trunk. The rifle was similar to the CAR he had carried in Hue, but this one was in a heavier caliber and had a silencer in place of a flash suppressor. Cradling it, Mitch moved out slowly down the tree-covered slope that bordered a grassy glade.

It took Mitch about 300 meters to catch sight of the Mercedes. The car was parked at the edge of the open field. Mitch slid in behind some large rocks and took in the whole scene.

Three hundred meters or so away stood Professor Wade and the three men. With his binoculars Mitch could see them easily. One, apparently the leader, was the blondish man Mitch had glimpsed outside of the hotel. He was carrying on an easy conversation with the other two kidnappers. Mitch couldn't make out what they were saying, but he could see that they were laughing. The professor was slightly off to one side and seemed nervous.

Mitch carefully surveyed the range and figured the range to be actually 280 meters. He put down his binoculars, switched to his rifle, and waited.

For about five minutes, nothing happened. Mitch noticed that the three kidnappers were paying very little attention to the professor. That didn't seem right.

"They're waiting for something," Mitch whispered. And then he heard the sound of rotor blades… and it wasn't a Huey.

No sooner had Mitch heard the helicopter than he saw the threesome brighten and start to slap each other's backs.

"Well, that tears it!" Mitch swore. "Here comes the pickup!"

It really was just like Cambodia all over again. Mitch was totally isolated, stuck on the tip of a spear, and the next fatal decisions were his alone to make. He did not want to kill again. The sense of *deja vu* almost made him vomit.

The professor still stood off to one side and seemed unaffected by the sound of the approaching helicopter. The other three men continued their celebration. Their mission was just seconds from being over. Mitch quickly resurveyed the ground that separated him from the group. It was broken country, and he figured that, at his best pace, it would take at least sixty seconds to cover the distance. That was too long.

The silenced M-16 came up and steadied itself against is shoulder almost of its own will. The crosshairs of the scope centered on the torso of the blondish leader. The rifle coughed once, shifted to the temple of the first underling and coughed again. The third man, the driver, had a surprised look on his face when the sight picture settled on him. He was still surprised when he died a second later.

Then Mitch was up and running. Wade had turned towards the fallen threesome and didn't see Mitch coming. The helicopter, however, had just cleared the tree line, and it saw Mitch clearly. It hesitated, circled once, and realized its connection was compromised. After that it roared in with all guns blazing.

Mitch threw himself into a ditch and heard slugs ripping the ground all around him. He didn't think; there wasn't time for that. He just reacted. He had seven rounds left in his rifle. In less time than it took to inhale, he sent all seven skyward.

The heavy, full-metal-jacketed slugs had been designed to penetrate mild armor. The aluminum fuselage they punctured offered no such resistance. The hydraulic lines, fuel tanks, and turbine blades behind the aluminum skin were easy prey. The helicopter died mid-flight in a flash of exploding gas. All of its occupants were cremated before the wreckage hit the ground some fifty meters from Mitch.

It took a few seconds for Mitch to see a clear path through the fire that suddenly surrounded him, but as soon as he did, he took off for the professor. Mitch wasn't sure if there was any more gas that could explode, and he wanted Wade out of there.

Wade saw Mitch coming through the fire. He waited until Mitch was close, and then he drew a pistol from his coat. In a slow motion instant, he leveled the weapon right at Mitch's chest.

"You bastard!" Wade screamed as he emptied the whole clip as Mitch's flying form.

"No, professor! I'm not…"

Mitch tried to dodge the professor's fire, but one of the slugs took him right in the pit of his stomach, slamming him backwards.

"You bastard!" Wade was still screaming as he ran up to Mitch. "You goddamn bastard!"

Mitch tried to speak, but his air was gone. The Kevlar vest he wore had held, but Mitch's diaphragm was spasmed.

Wade slowed and started cursing, his voice cold and almost possessed. "Rice, I'm going to kill you and send your sorry soul straight to hell! Then I'm going to make your CIA and the whole fuckin' world pay like it has never paid before!"

He brought the pistol up and aimed it right at Mitch's head.

Mitch knew his rifle was empty so he went for his. 45. Wade froze when he saw the big government auto staring him in the face, and that was all the time Mitch needed. The ever-reliable. 45 found Wade's right shoulder and spun him around and down. The professor's nine-millimeter auto fell to the ground still cocked.

Mitch struggled to his feet. He could breathe a little now. He was bruised, but that was all.

"Damn it, professor!" Mitch cursed as he picked up the bleeding man. "I'm here to help you, not hurt you! Now we have to get out of here before another fuel tank blows!"

Mitch had Wade on his shoulder and was running hard when the last fuel cell went. The blast knocked both of them to the ground and singed their backsides. But a moment later, Mitch was up and running again. The heat was unbearable.

It was a long run, but Mitch made it to the protection of the boulders that bordered the glade. There he gently put Wade down.

"Rice, I knew it was you who killed my Marilyn! You and your damn government! Now finish the job they sent you to do, or by God Himself, I'll make you wish you had never been born!"

The professor's threat slammed into Mitch like a sledgehammer. It was all suddenly very clear. This had not been a kidnapping! It had been a carefully planned defection! Probably the conflict now ongoing at the Israeli compound was just a diversion for all of this!

Mitch was processing this last thought when he heard the sound of a second helicopter. He looked for his M16 and saw it lying at the edge of the dead helicopter's fireball. He had to have it if he was going to have any sort of chance against another helicopter. So, not even thinking about the flames, he plunged back into the inferno.

The air was white hot, and Mitch couldn't breathe. His eyebrows curled from the heat, and his skin scorched. But he reached the rifle. Pulling it from the charred ground, he slammed in a second clip, threw it to his shoulder, and found Major Mallory framed by his crosshairs.

And almost as suddenly as it had begun, the battle was over. Mitch dropped the rifle to his side. The inferno still raged, and Wade still whimpered, but it was over. Mitch walked out of the fire untouched.

The Huey landed, and Mallory jumped out. "Hell, Rice! You scared the shit out of me! What were you going to do? Shoot us down too? Can't you idiot marines tell who's on your side?"

Mitch smiled a little through his scorched lips. "You're still alive, aren't you, major?"

"Ah shit, Rice!" Mallory muttered. "Just shut up and let my men secure this fuckin' place!"

"Anything you say, major." Mitch was suddenly very tired and very sore.

Over the remainder of that day, Mitch was debriefed three different times.

The first was by Major Mallory's crew. That session wasn't too bad since Mitch already knew them, and being military, they all spoke the same language.

The second debriefing was by the U. S. State Department. Those people were already stressed to the max with the ongoing crisis in the Olympic Village, and they came across to Mitch like *he* was the terrorist, not the men he had just killed.

The interview was long and adversarial. As it progressed, Mitch wistfully thought several times of reaching for the. 45 he still carried in the small of his back. He couldn't understand how Sarah put up with these egocentric fools. These "diplomats" were no more than expatriated politicians. No wonder the world was in the shape it was in.

The third interview was with the German police. After all, Mitch had shot down an unidentified helicopter, killed five men, and wounded another on their soil. Considering all of that, they were most courteous and professional. In fact, at the end of the interview, the officer in charge, a man named Wolfe, apologized to Mitch that he had been left in a position where he had been forced to take such definitive action.

"We try hard to keep these foreign terrorists under control, Herr Rice, but sometimes we fail. Thank you for ridding us of these vermin."

When Mitch finally looked up it was nearly 4:30. He was tired and his bruised abdomen ached. He tried to stretch but the bruise hampered him.

"Well, since you can't seem to dodge trouble, I'm glad that at least, you've learned to obey orders."

Mitch looked to his right. It was General Strong.

"Did the Kevlar vest earn its keep?"

"Yes, sir. It did. I wish I could've had one in Hue."

"I wish you could have had one there too, son."

Strong motioned for Mitch to walk with him, and Mitch fell into place besides him. The two walked around the blackened countryside where the burned helicopter was now being loaded onto a covered transport for removal.

"Tell me about it, Mitch. What really happened here?"

Mitch looked at Strong. "General, I've been over this three times already with the guys you sicced on me. I don't think I can add anything to what I've already said."

"Just tell me this then, Mitch. Was Wade really defecting, or was he just out of his head when he said all that garbage about bringing vengeance down on all of us?"

"General, I can only guess what's going on inside Wade's head. I know he threatened dire things on me and on the whole world for our collected sins. Maybe he's just a nut case. But the way he said it and the way those three kidnappers were lounging around… I don't think this was a real kidnapping. I think it was a planned defection. Maybe even the PLO stuff in town was a diversion… I don't know." Mitch looked straight at the general. "But I do know that Wade's really gone over the edge. General, I wouldn't trust him with my salt shaker, let alone any biological weaponry."

Strong walked on in silence. Finally, he spoke.

"Thanks, Mitch. I'll take everything you've told me under careful consideration. Whatever becomes of Dr. Jacob Wade, I'll do my best to see that it all comes out right."

Mitch heard what Strong was saying. Inside, Mitch wished he could really believe that the world would always be safe from Jacob Wade. The professor was really no more than a victim himself, but his insanity made him a true villain.

"Has the professor done all right with his surgery?" Mitch asked.

Wade had been airlifted out quickly after Mallory arrived and had been taken directly to a hospital to repair the. 45 caliber hole Mitch had put in his shoulder.

"The word is that you hit nothing irreparable," Strong answered. "He'll be laid up for a few weeks, but his arm and lung should be okay."

"That's good. I came here to protect him, not to shoot him. I don't want him to be a cripple."

"Rice, you *are* nuts," Strong muttered. "For all I know, we'd all be better off if you had planted the son of a bitch. I don't know whether to thank you or cuss you."

Strong held out his hand to Mitch.

"So I guess I choose to thank you. You did a hell of a job!"

Mitch took his hand.

"You're welcome, sir. But I'm going to hold you to your word about my still getting into this fall's medical school class. I don't want any more of this shit."

The general started to smile.

"I'll get you into your med school, Mitch. But wouldn't you rather reconsider your career choice? You're really a pretty handy guy to have around."

"I'll take that as a compliment, general. But we both know that if I stayed with you one day you would ask me to do something that I'd have to say no to, and then where would we be? You've already said that I know how to alienate commanders, and I won't tolerate you abusing Sarah again the way you did to get me here this time."

Strong didn't speak, and so Mitch answered for him.

"I'll tell you where we'd be, general. You'd be in trouble with the people you answer to, and I'd be all used up, dead, on the run, or maybe just as crazy as Professor Wade. That's not the way I want us to end up."

"You're right, Mitch. That's not what I want for us either."

"Then it's med school, right?"

"Yeah, it's med school. When can you be ready to go home?"

"Right now, general! Right now!"

A little later General Strong watched his young protégé walk off with Major Mallory. Mitch had a military flight to catch. It would deposit him back at Whiteman Air Force Base in Knob Noster, Missouri. From there med school was just an hour away.

Strong knew this goodbye was different from the one in Hue. Then, Mitch had still been his minion. Now, Mitch was more his equal. The trials of fire that Mitch had endured had left him stronger. No one would ever again be able to order him to do anything he didn't really believe in. Strong knew it probably would be best if Mitch went on with a life that kept him far away from the machinations of the government… a government that was losing both itself and the people it was supposed to serve. The maelstrom of the political world did not have the honor Mitch required. And for that matter, Wilson Strong recognized he no longer had that kind of honor either.

Strong shook his head in self-reproach. Mitch was too simple for the world, or maybe too pure. Strong really didn't know which. He just hoped Mitch could hide in medicine and be happy there much as his old friend Mother Marie had been happy in her orphanage. They really were very much alike, he thought feeling a tingle of jealousy. They were almost mother and son.

Interlude

(*Excerpt from the commencement speech given by Major General Wilson G. Strong, at West Point, 1996*)

"What does the word 'royalty' mean? To the American mind the word conjures up visions of pomp, circumstance, privilege, and, sometimes, unbridled license. At its best, the word speaks of golden grandeur and purple majesty. At its worst, the word is nearly synonymous with dark abuse and mind-searing depravity. Consequently, 'royalty' is a word of great paradox and even greater ambiguity.

"There is, however, a different way to understand the concept of 'royalty'. This different view sees 'royalty' as being the condition of greatest freedom whereby a person is simultaneously responsible both for himself and for those around him. In this context, the word is closely connected to the ideas of self-sacrifice, nobility, and true heroism.

"Of the two descriptions, I favor the latter. I favor it because when an individual embraces that which is loving, brave, and selfless, the very act transforms the individual. The act stimulates a kind of metamorphosis. It is a moment when a person becomes more than the sum total of his or her individual parts. And it is this kind of change that is necessary if a person is to become the master of his or her own destiny.

"On this, the day of your graduation and commissioning, it is my prayer that all of you will experience this kind of change, a change that will transform you into the princes and princesses that you were meant to be. I wish this day to be the day of your coronations."

PART TWO:

PURIFICATION

REFRAIN

(*Excerpt from* The Book of the Archangel Uriel, *date and author unknown)*

"My name is Michael. I am one of the ancient ones. I have been with you since before the beginning. Now that the end is near, it is finally time for you to hear my voice.

"For those of you who will listen and learn, do so that you may survive what is to come.

"For those of you who will scoff and make light of my words, prepare for the unthinkable. Your fate is already written.

"Now listen to the story that I will tell."

Chapter Fifteen

John Fredericks looked out over the one hundred and fifteen or so faces that made up the first-year med school class of the University of Missouri-Columbia. Classes had been in session for almost a month, and there were already student casualties. Two more students had dropped out the previous Friday. The first batch of exams were just a couple of weeks away, and Fredericks, demanding professor that he was, was pushing himself to present a "true, heartfelt challenge," as Dean Means put it, to the students in front of him.

Today, however, was something a little different. Over the weekend the dean had, in a somewhat unprecedented manner, admitted a new student to fill a slot left by one of the fallen. Never before in Fredericks's memory had this been done so far into the fall term. Fredericks looked to see if he could spy the newcomer's face while everyone was still milling around.

Fredericks had already seen the file of this newcomer. His name was Mitchell Rice. He was an ex-marine, a wounded and decorated veteran of the rice paddies of Vietnam. The file had told Fredericks of Mitch's stellar course at UMC's sister campus, the University of Missouri-Rolla. There he had run his way through both the physics and chemistry departments, drawing high praise from nearly all of his professors. UMR was known to be a superior technical school, known for engineering and hard sciences, but very few, if any, physicians had ever come from its halls. So, in Frederick's mind, Mitch was suspect.

Scanning the crowd for a new face, Fredericks rolled over and over the dean's meager explanation for Mitch's last minute admission. Rice apparently had been involved in the just finished, tragic Munich Olympic Games, but that didn't impress Fredericks. He hated damnable, jock, surgeon-types, and he really hated anything to do with Vietnam. A passionate antiwar activist, he still bore scars from a beating Mayor Daily's Chicago police gave him at the 1968 Democratic Convention. In Fredericks' view, gung-ho military types didn't belong in medicine, and he was incensed that Dr. Means had let such a character into his class.

"Well, Mr. Rice, you may be in this class, but that doesn't mean you will stay here," Fredericks whispered to himself as he organized his lecture.

He didn't have the reputation for being one of the toughest young professors in the med school for nothing, and he intended to make his reputation felt by this Mitchell Rice right from the start.

Today's lecture was to be a bit of a treat for the fledgling M-1's. Fredericks always did a very thorough job on abdominal anatomy, but today there would be a guest lecturer. The eminent Charles A. Golden, M. D. , chief of the department of surgery, would be here to make his annual cameo appearance to the first-year class. Golden always had a good time with the freshman men and women, frequently at their own expense. (That's why Fredericks tolerated the surgeon's invasion of his space.) Fredericks had it figured that Mitchell Rice was going to have an interesting first day in class.

"Good morning, doctors," Fredericks began. "Today's presentation is going to be special. Dr. Golden is going to help with our review of the abdomen by sharing some case presentations with us. I *know* we will all do our best to show him what we've learned."

Several eyes turned skyward. Fredericks' comments meant that questions would be asked of the students from the podium. It wasn't good to be without the right answer when Dr. Fredericks called on you, and with the chief of surgery looking on, the stakes were even higher.

The first case was that of a middle-aged male with an apparent history of a stomach ulcer. Several students were asked about the supporting circulation and anatomic obstacles that a treating surgeon might encounter upon entering this patient's abdomen. The crux of the case, however, was the stomach's lymphatic drainage pattern. As the case study unfolded, Dr. Fredericks built a case of stomach cancer rather than one of a simple peptic ulcer. A bright, young woman named Mary Aspers had the right answers when she was called upon. Dr. Golden smiled openly at the good start.

The second case was one of the surgery chairman's perennial favorites, the penetrating, high-velocity gunshot wound.

The wound was described as a penetration some six to eight centimeters to the left of the umbilicus with the exit wound straight through the back.

"Dr. Peters, what organs are likely to be involved in this injury?" Dr. Fredericks asked.

Bob Peters was a studious, bespectacled son of a prominent St. Louis surgeon.

"Dr. Fredericks, the location of this wound indicates that, after the skin and subcutaneous fat, the external obliques would be damaged. The wound is too low for rib involvement. Small intestine and the descending colon would probably be penetrated." Peters paused. "The wound is a bit lateral, but there is a chance that the left ureter would be involved."

Peters was obviously pleased with himself for thinking of the ureter. Fredericks smiled his approval back, reinforcing that young Peters had solved the riddle of the case.

"Dr. Peters, isn't it?" said the so far silent Dr. Golden.

"Yes sir."

"What else is likely to be involved here?"

Peters hesitated. He knew he had taken the torso in good cross section and had listed all the appropriate organs. After a long silence, he finally answered.

"Well, Dr. Golden, it seems… I guess the left kidney might be damaged if it was positioned a bit lower than usual. Then the renal artery, renal vein, and even the adrenal gland and its supporting vasculature might be involved."

"Very good, Dr. Peters," replied Dr. Golden. "What else is likely to need our surgical attention?"

Bob Peters's face fell. He had thought he had nailed the case. He looked defeated.

"That's all right, Dr. Peters. You did very well," Dr. Golden said. "Does anyone else here have an inkling of what I am looking for?"

No hands went up.

"Okay, if there are no takers, let me see who's next on the role. Dr. Rice, do you want to take a shot at this one?" Dr. Golden chuckled at his own little play on words.

Mitch stood up. Fredericks was surprised and pleased. Dr. Golden was obviously in a bloodthirsty mood and had remembered Frederick's suggestion to call on Rice. Fredericks smiled at the prospect of seeing the upstart ex-marine being put in his place.

"Where's Dr. Rice?" asked Dr. Golden who had not seen Mitch stand up from his seat at the side of the lecture hall.

"Over here, Dr. Golden," Mitch answered.

"I'm happy to make your acquaintance, Dr. Rice. This is your first day here, isn't it?"

"Yes sir. It is."

"Well, welcome. And relax. I just wanted to get your attention. I know you'll have to play catch-up in here for a while so we'll let you off the hook this time. But be ready the next time I call on you."

Turning back to the rest of the class, Golden said again. "Come now, let's not be bashful. Who'll give it a try?"

Only one hand went up. It was Mitch's.

Dr. Golden didn't see Mitch, but he did see the surprise on John Frederick's face. He followed the anatomy professor's gaze right back to Mitch.

"Yes, Dr. Rice?"

"Sir, I believe that you'd want to pay attention to this patient's spleen," Mitch said quietly.

Dr. Golden focused intently on Mitch. "Why that organ, Dr. Rice?"

"Well, sir, this was advertised as a high-velocity bullet wound. High velocity bullets set up hydrostatic shock waves as they pass through flesh. They also sometimes tumble in their passage through a body so that their pathway through a victim is not always a straight line. The spleen, while it's higher in the abdomen, would probably be torn up and bleeding into the retroperitoneum. A surgeon could miss a hemorrhage there if he wasn't careful."

Dr. Golden was silent for a second, but then he smiled broadly. "You know, Dr. Rice, it's not considered healthy around here to scoop the chief of surgery, especially right on his own home turf. Your answers and your explanation are entirely correct."

Golden was still smiling, but John Fredericks was not. He had relished the thought of the former marine standing there embarrassed. Having Mitch stand toe-to-toe with Dr. Golden was beyond belief.

Golden went on. "Tell me, Dr. Rice, how do you know that much about bullet wounds? Do you have some hidden medical background?"

"I've just spent some time around VA hospitals, sir."

"Oh, I see. Were you a medic or a surgical technician there?"

Mitch answered slowly. "No, sir. I was just a patient."

Everyone's eyes, including John Fredericks's and Dr. Golden's, widened.

"Thank you, Dr. Rice," Dr. Golden said, his voice slow but even. "Thank you both for your answers and for a demonstration of what can be learned if one just listens. I trust the rest of your class will take this demonstration to heart."

The lecture ground on for another thirty minutes. It closed with Dr. Golden giving a pep talk to the whole class on the importance of a good anatomic foundation for all future medical endeavors. The whole room clapped in agreement, and Dr. Fredericks voiced his thanks to the department chairman.

No one looked Mitch's way, but everyone knew he was there.

Mitch's start in medical school may have been impressive, but his course didn't continue that way. The late start proved to be a severe handicap, something much worse than even the slow start he had suffered at UMR. The whole remainder of that first semester was a nightmare.

Unlike college, here no one was interested in helping him catch up. Most medical students were of a cutthroat, competitive breed, and the professors seemed anxious for competitive attrition to thin the ranks. As a result, Mitch was pretty much on his own. Happily, his mind was a lot more balanced than it had been in 1969, but it took all he had just to survive. He made it to the second year only by spending the summer in remedial anatomy classes. It seemed that, in the end, Dr. Fredericks had the best of it after all.

Mitch's second year should have been a great improvement over his first, but it wasn't. The first year had taken everything Mitch had, and he never broke through the barrier his late start caused. All of his classmates held him at arm's length, and, as the M-2 year started, this isolation was really beginning to wear him down.

In medical school, competition and one-ups-man-ship, not teamwork and friendship, were the rules of the land. Image and perception were everything. Had Mitch not remembered some of his conversations with Marilyn Wade and before that, with Mother Marie, he would have gladly chucked the whole place and run back to his beloved math. It seemed unbelievable to him that soon-to-be healers could be so cruel.

As he slipped deeper and deeper into a depression, he felt even the Marine Corps had more heart than this place. He was angry most of the time, and only his sheer stubbornness kept him going.

"What's with this Rice character?" Dean Means asked Dr. Holtz, the dean of students.

"I don't know, John. He should be tearing up the place, but he's just buried in the middle of the pack."

"I know. Dr. Golden was asking about him the other day at the admissions committee meeting. I hadn't looked at Rice's file for a while, and Chuck pointed out to me that Rice entered here with the highest MCAT science scores of anyone in his class."

"I didn't know that."

"Yeah. I didn't either. It was pretty embarrassing being scooped by the chief of surgery. Chuck was pretty upset, and he's not someone I want to butt heads with."

"What did Golden want? Why's he interested in this kid?"

"I'm not sure if it's Rice he's interested in, or if he's trying to figure a way to make a run on our pathology department's hold on the dean's office," Means answered.

At that time, all of the med school's deans were pathologists, and they controlled all of the school's policies and money. It was a position of power they didn't want to lose.

"So what do you want me to do, John?"

"I asked Chuck if he'd like to have Rice on the admissions committee. We still have a place open for a med student there, don't we?"

"Yeah, I think so."

"Good. Do it. Maybe that will keep the surgery department off our backs for a while. Golden seemed to like the idea. He said this place needed some new blood and that people like Rice needed more recognition."

"What? That's doesn't sound like "Gengis Khan Golden." You gotta be right! He's coming after us." Holtz shook his head like a boxer who had just taken a left cross. "I'll go ahead and put Rice on the committee. We still hold enough votes there to control admissions anyway. Shoot, it might even work out that having Rice there might actually hurt whatever plans Golden has. This Rice character is supposed to be pretty unconventional. Golden might live to regret taking this kid's side."

"Who knows?" Means answered. "Just fix the committee appointment and keep an eye on things."

Holtz nodded agreement--anything to keep the other clinical departments out of the dean's office.

The admission committee was responsible for the composition of each freshman med school class. It was a big and important job. Everyone on the committee, including the two appointed med students, was expected to carry his or her own weight and had an equal vote.

Over the next several weeks Mitch fulfilled his role faithfully, but it wasn't easy work. He frequently found himself at odds with the more senior committee members, and the discussions were often pretty heated.

Mitch always seemed to favor potential students who appeared to be more interested in clinical medicine than in research. That didn't win him any friends in the dean's office, but it did take some pressure off Dr. Golden who prior to Mitch's appointment, had pretty much been a solo objector to the path department's slide-specimen vision of medicine.

Mitch did win an occasional argument, but the victories were few and far between. And the losses showed him more of medicine's clay feet than he cared to see. One meeting in particular, made this very clear.

It was early December. The admissions committee was deep into the interview season. Some of the slots for the next year had been filled, but most were still open. The day's planned admissions committee meeting was rescheduled from its usual evening time to an early afternoon time. That pretty much left Mitch and Dr. Golden out of the mix because Mitch had classes and Dr. Golden had scheduled surgeries. That was unfortunate because at this particular meeting, two visiting federal officials were to make a special presentation about the possibility of additional federal funding for the next year's class. The whole dean's office would be in attendance.

It was 2:00 in the afternoon, and Mitch was in the middle of his microbiology lab. He knew the special meeting had been already going on for half an hour, but he was stuck. It was sudden death to cut classes, labs especially.

"Dr. Rice, come over here would you?" It was Dr. Ellison, Mitch's micro professor. "Dr. Golden called my office a little while ago. He said the two of you needed to be at some meeting downstairs in the dean's office."

"That's right, sir, but the meeting's going on right now, right in the middle of classes."

"Well, Dr. Golden's tied up too. He's in the middle of some big vascular case. So he asked me to free you up."

Golden and Ellison were long time friends.

"So get out of here. I'll help you make up this lab later. One of you needs to be there. Something big is going on down there."

Mitch caught the look Dr. Ellison gave him and threw off his lab coat.

"Thanks, Dr. Ellison. I'll get back as soon as I can."

Ellison waved him on, and Mitch took off jogging down the hall.

A couple minutes later, Mitch slipped into the back of the conference room in the dean's office. No one seemed to notice his arrival.

"Thank you for your presentation, Dr. Means," one of the two federal officials said, taking the podium. "We in Washington are very much aware of the doctor shortage in rural America. That's why we're here."

Mitch thought the man had too big of a smile. He reminded Mitch of some of the pimps he had seen in Saigon.

"My proposal today is pretty simple. We know of your financial constraints here, running this school, but we in Washington want more doctors. So here's the deal. If you'll increase the size of next year's freshman class from the current one hundred and twenty to two hundred, we'll guarantee a federal subsidy of $15,000 per student for the whole class. That's $3,000,000 for you to use any way you see fit. And we'll keep doing it every year you meet that enrollment quota. That's it. No strings attached."

Mitch heard the whole room fall dead silent. Dollar signs were flashing across everyone's face. Dean Means had been trying for years to find more money to fund more research programs at UMC. Medical research meant prestige and national recognition. Three million dollars a year could buy a lot of recognition.

"That's right, Dr. Means. No strings attached. You know the business of running a medical school a lot better than we do in Washington. We'll give you the extra money and get out of your way. That amount, along with all of the extra tuition, should help a lot." The federal official's smile got even bigger. "We want more doctors, Dr. Means. Just give them to us."

Mitch saw the wheels turning in Dr. Means's head. It seemed like Christmas had come a couple of weeks early. It sounded almost too good to be true. Mitch sat back in his folding chair and watched the rest of the meeting turn into a fiscal feeding frenzy. Every professor wanted a piece of the huge windfall for his own pet project, and the two guys from Washington seemed to have a big enough checkbook to satisfy everyone. It really was Christmas.

"What can we say, Mr. Dillon?" Dean Means said as he returned to the front of the room. "With this kind of governmental support, I think I can guarantee that you'll... that is, the state of Missouri will get the extra doctors it needs. Thank you."

"It's our pleasure, Dr. Means. After all, everyone in Washington wants just what you want anyway. Just give us the doctors."

The meeting broke up with all of the deans and professors basking in the glow of newfound riches. They each spoke individually to the two men from Washington, and then they streamed out of the conference room, already spending their portions of the jackpot. The two federal officials were the last men in the room save for Mitch whom they didn't see.

"Those poor, dumb, sons of bitches! They don't have a clue, do they, Sam?" the younger man said to Mr. Dillon.

"Nah, all they can see are dollar signs," Dillon replied. "They..." He stopped as his eye caught sight of Mitch at the back of the room.

He cleared his throat. "Who are you, son? This was a special meeting just for the school's admission committee. You don't belong here."

"I'm a member of this committee, Mr. Dillon. I may only be a student, but I have a full committee vote." Mitch wasn't smiling. "Am I one of the 'sons of bitches'?"

The younger man turned to his superior. His hand had just been caught in the cookie jar. Dillon just stared at Mitch, taking measure of the damage already done.

"So, you don't trust Greeks bearing gifts, Dr.…?"

"It's Rice, Mr. Dillon, Mitch Rice." Mitch approached from the back of the room. "I know enough to know that the government never turns loose of its agendas. And it sure as hell doesn't give money away."

"Well then, that makes you the smartest one here, son," Dillon said, waving aside the concerned look of his junior partner. "Here, sit down for a minute. I'm tired of talking to fools anyway."

Mitch took the offered chair as Dillon took another.

"You must be a pretty bright kid, to be a full, voting member of the admissions committee, but you're still a kid. That means no one will pay you much attention." Dillon lit a cigarette. "I'm going to do something I don't usually do. I'm going to let my hair down and tell you what's this all about. No one will believe you anyway, and you're smart enough and young enough maybe to use this information to help yourself. Sometimes intelligence needs to be rewarded for its own sake."

Mitch sat quietly. The color drained from his face leaving only the shadows of battles not yet forgotten.

"Your dean and his cronies will do just what we've agreed to. They'll increase the size of your med school classes, and they'll take the money and run. They'll keep doing it year after year until they think the money is theirs automatically.

"Sure, a lot more doctors will be graduated. The problem is that they won't be primary care docs. They won't be because your medical school doesn't give any kudos to primary care docs. It only rewards researchers and specialists. So that's the kind of docs it'll produce."

Dillon took a long drag off his cigarette.

"More and more specialists, each one thinking he should be paid more and more for knowing more about less. It'll be great! These guys won't practice in the needy areas. They'll move to the big cities where the hospitals will build and then overbuild to accommodate them. The price of medicine will go up and up. After a while it'll go so high that medicine will fall from its sacred perch and lose the trust of the common man. The rural areas still won't be taken care of, and the urban areas won't trust the 'mercenaries' who run their clinics and hospitals."

Mr. Dillon flicked some ash away.

"It'll take a while, but by the end of the century, medicine will be right where we want it. No one will believe in it anymore, and it will be easy for the government and big business to move in and take it over. The end result will be that the socialized rationing of medicine will take over just in time, right before the baby boomers get old."

He took another long drag.

"The public won't know what happened, and for that matter, neither will medicine. A new order will be in place, and those we can't afford to care for will be left out. We'll save the system."

Mitch drew up in his chair. "Population control at its best? Is that what you're selling, Mr. Dillon? It's almost a program of not-so-passive euthanasia, isn't it?"

The older man snuffed out his smoke. "Damn, you don't miss a thing, do you!" He laughed. "Maybe someday I'll regret telling you what I just did." He chuckled again. "But I doubt it! All you doc types are so blinded by your own egos that you can't see anything else. This'll be a done deal before any of you realize what's happened. By then, it'll be too late. Medicine will be ours!"

Something inside Mitch snapped. He got up out of his chair. The younger man saw Mitch's eyes glowing with a horrible red fire. Only death and destruction were there. He grabbed Dillon's shoulder as Mitch came on.

"Mr. Dillon? Excuse me, Dean Means would like to speak… ."

The dean's secretary, who had just returned to the conference room, couldn't help hesitating. She wasn't sure just what she had just walked into. The two feds were drawing back from Mitch as he slowed his menacing approach.

"… some more with you. And I think he'd like to take you to dinner, if you're free."

She still hesitated. Mitch looked really threatening, and he was scaring her.

"Am I interrupting something?" she asked.

"Nothing important, darling," Mr. Dillon said hastily as he bent over to pick up his briefcase. "Let's go see Dean Means!" He hurried to catch up to his younger companion who already was beating a hasty retreat to the door.

"The next time I get crazy and try to explain anything to anyone," he said as they bumped shoulders going through the door at the same time, "you shut me up! That kid in there is nuts! I thought he was going to turn me into hamburger!"

"No kidding!" the younger man answered. "Did you see his eyes? I didn't think animals like him still walked the planet!"

"Yeah, there are still a few dinosaurs out there!" Dillon replied. "I got too cocky and just about blew it! I won't make that mistake again!"

Later that evening Mitch related all of the meeting to Dr. Golden. The surgeon didn't seem all that surprised by anything Mitch said.

"This has been coming for quite a while, Mitch. The battle lines have been drawn up for years." He smiled a little. "I'm just sorry I wasn't there to help you with those two. It would've been fun."

Mitch shrugged. He still had a cold fury inside him, just like he had had at the Delta firebase.

"Don't worry, Mitch. One battle doesn't make up a whole war," Dr. Golden said. "We're both in this thing for the duration. We'll have our chance later."

The year ground on mercilessly. Class work was heavy, and the conflicts on the admissions committee continued. The more Mitch saw of academic medicine, the more discouraged he became. By late winter his nightmares had returned. The sleep disruption they brought pulled him down even farther. As the second semester ground on, med school was definitely getting the best of him.

Mitch's roommate that year was a fellow named Matt Anders. Anders was a grad student in agricultural chemistry, and Mitch roomed with him in the grad students' dorm. Mitch hadn't been able to find any fellow med students who wanted to live with him, so he had just taken the luck of the draw in university housing. Matt had been a good draw.

The first half of the year had seen Mitch and Matt do pretty well together, but after Mitch's violent nightmares returned, things in the dorm room got a little rugged. By February, Mitch stopped apologizing for them, and by March Matt started sleeping in other peoples' rooms. Mitch's nightly tortured groans and hypnotic convulsions had become unbearable.

In place of complaining, however, the ag-chemist sought out a campus minister, who was himself a Vietnam vet. The minister told Matt about post-trauma syndromes and explained that there was little that anyone could do for Mitch until Mitch himself sought some help.

Mitch was stubborn, but he had learned something from his college years. He sought out the help of a couple of psychologists at the med center, but they were nothing like Marilyn Wade. After a while, going to them was more of a burden than a help. So Mitch just slipped farther and farther into the dark abyss that ate his soul. He was dying.

It was nearly the end of April. Matt had managed to finish his work in the library a bit earlier than expected and had gone back to the room to get some extra sack time. Mitch would not come in from his study cubicle in the med school for quite a while, and Matt had settled down for some peaceful snoring.

Mitch found Matt that way when he came in at 1:00 a. m. Mitch slipped into the bunk as quietly as he could and, moments later, was sleeping the sleep of the dead.

A couple of hours passed, and Mitch's level of consciousness rose about half a notch above *rigor mortis*. It was there that the ghosts usually came. Tonight was to be worse than usual.

It started the same way it always did. Once more Mitch was slammed down onto the streets of Hue by a horrible, exploding pain in his side. Once more he reached out for Mother Marie's hand, felt her touch, and then felt her fingers go cold.

Instantly, the scene changed and Mitch's ears filled with the tortured screams of all the men whose final moments had been etched by his cross hairs. He watched their faces explode all over his crosshairs, over and over again.

The scene changed again, and Mitch saw the decapitated girl lying on the side of the road. Her bodiless head was still crying silently for itself, still wordlessly naming him as her executioner.

By this time, Mitch was neither asleep nor awake. He seemed to be in some sort of trance-like state where he was aware of Matt's sleeping form and yet was still sweating out all those eternal hours he spent under the gillie cloth in the mined shell crater in Cambodia. His soul was in the jungle, but his mind was in his dorm room. The schism was ripping him apart. It was as if Mitch was impaled on a spit. It turned him over and over, roasting him over the fire of his conscience, and the fire was merciless.

Suddenly, Mitch's trance of torture was interrupted by a voice. Mitch turned to the dorm room's door that was now somehow open. There, framed by the hall light, was a figure of a man. The man was dressed in what seemed to be a robe.

Mitch heard his name called out again. The man came to him, held out his arms, and cradled Mitch much like a father cradles his infant child. In that instant, the fires torturing Mitch went out. For a very long time, Mitch rested in the arms of this stranger. It was the finest rest Mitch had ever known.

Morning came, and Mitch turned over in his bunk. The alarm was turned off. He had slept through his first two classes. He should have been upset about missing the lectures, but he only felt refreshed.

The visions of the night, both the good and the bad, were burned into his memory. But the pain that had always been there was now replaced by a kind of peaceful feeling. It was as if someone had actually pulled him out of the darkness, and now he was in the daylight. And it felt good.

Mitch was still marveling at the transformation in his dreams when Matt returned from his early classes.

"Hey, man, are you okay?" Matt asked.

"Yeah. I think I am… finally."

"Well, it's about time," Matt said. "Those nightmares of yours were just about to get the best of me. Shoot, last night you even had me dreaming."

"What do you mean?"

"Oh, I don't know exactly how to describe it." Matt hesitated. "Last night I felt like I woke up to someone calling your name. Some guy was here. He was kind of tall and dressed in some sort of robe. He was standing there in the doorway at first, but then he came over to you and just hugged you. You calmed right down from whatever was tearing you up, and he just held you for a really long time. After a while, you finally went to sleep. Then this guy got up to leave. He turned toward me as he was leaving, and I somehow had the feeling that everything would be okay."

Mitch felt as if a great warmth had just washed over every fiber of his being.

"That's some kind of weird dream, huh?"

Mitch nodded.

"I hope you're really over those nightmares, Mitch. It's just been too weird around here for too long."

"Yeah, it has been a pretty strange trip," Mitch muttered. "Maybe things will settle down now. It's past time."

He was speaking more to himself than to his roommate. He still felt the warmth of the embrace that had held him for most of the night. His constant, familiar pain inside was gone.

Chapter Sixteen

Nicki Belton was just coming on duty in 4-East. She was a staff nurse at the VA hospital in Columbia, Missouri. Wing 4-East was an internal medicine ward, and that made it the stomping grounds of the university's internal medicine department. She had been a nurse on the unit for over a year. During that time Nicki had seen any number of med students and residents come and go. Today another fresh rotation of med students would hit the decks. This changing of the guard, however, would be a little different because this new crew was *really* brand new… brand new third-year students who had yet to touch their first patients. The whole ward was braced for the newcomers' arrival.

Freddie Myles was a twenty-seven-year-old Vietnam vet. He had been a patient of 4-East for nearly four months battling a severe mixed collagen vascular disease that was probably the result of Agent Orange exposure. His immune system had turned against his own body and was trying to destroy both his kidneys and his heart, as well as most of his joints.

Freddie and Nicki had first crossed paths in the outpatient clinic and then had connected more permanently once he hit the floor. They, along with Freddie's wife Sally and his two little girls, had forged a sort of a special bond by which they all tried to endure both Freddie's disease and the arcane nature of academic medicine. It was an effort that sometimes took everything they had.

This new bunch of med students would be the third batch that Freddie'd had, but it was the first time the med students in the rotation would be truly new. It was enough to make a strong man tremble.

"Good morning, Fred. It's reveille."

"Oh… hi, Nicki," Freddie groaned.

Of late it had been really hard for him to keep his spirits up. His illness was wearing him down, and even the aggressive chemotherapy wasn't turning the tide. Fred hated all that was happening to him. He despised the periodic times of isolation, feared the recurrent vomiting, and was almost panicky of late whenever the lab came for more of his blood. Today was his day for another bone marrow sampling, and that was about as bad as it could get.

"So what's on tap for today, Miss Nursey?" he asked with obviously phony courage.

Nicki decided to play along with him. They had done this before.

"Well, after the little bone marrow test that Dr. Nickels has planned for you, the day's real challenge will begin."

Freddie caught her tone and flashed a questioning glance. "What can top the exquisite pleasure of Dr. Nickels driving a railroad spike through my hip?"

"Have you forgotten already, Fred? Today's the day we get to meet the new batch of third-year med students."

"Oh, God! I had forgotten! That's worse than the bone marrow! That means another whole crew who'll want to use me as a training dummy for all of their fumble-fingered attempts at doctoring!" Fred paused. "And this crew will *really* be brand new, won't they?"

"Yeah, Fred. Green as grass."

Somehow the specter of all those failed IV's, messed up bloodlettings, and fouled up catheter placements did take his mind off the bone marrow test. A few moments later he didn't even complain about Nicki's driving as she wheeled him down to the treatment room.

"Who are these rookies, Nicki?" he asked while they were still in the hall.

"The floor has drawn four guys, Fred. One is named Mark Gustin; another is Phil Chambert; the third is Bill Lawson; and the fourth is a guy named Mitchell Rice."

"No women this time?"

"That's right, Fred," she said, almost teasing. "No new bods to distract you. You'll just have to be content with me."

He smiled at her. Nicki, tallish and blonde, was no bad looker, and she was a heck of a good nurse. As the door to the procedure room opened, he took her hand. He was glad she was there with him.

Mitch's first several days on 4-East were pretty challenging.

Morning rounds started early, and the med students had to start even earlier to memorize the fresh lab results on all their assigned patients. Woe be it to any student who didn't have the most current answers when the resident staff asked for the new lab values, and it was almost a death knell if the student messed up in front of an attending physician.

It may have sounded harsh, but that's what rounds were all about—confrontational, in-your-face education in its most refined form, and it was as old as medical education itself. It cost everyone a lot of anguish, but that's the way the system worked.

Each morning's rounds were followed by a full schedule of the various diagnostic and therapeutic procedures that made up modern medicine. Everyone was involved, all according to his or her position in the pecking order. Bone marrow biopsies, thoracenteses, various IV and central line placements, arterial blood gas samplings, spinal taps, nasogastric tube placements, sigmoidoscopies, Foley catheter insertions, and bladder taps all had to be learned. The motto was "see one, do one, teach one." That's how it all worked. Patients got care, and neophyte physicians were trained.

The house staff's afternoons were spent in outpatient clinics. There the med students either worked with the residents, or else they spent long hours working up the ward's new admissions. Evening rounds followed, and then the night was set aside for all the studying and reading that had to be done to prepare for the next morning's rounds.

The night was set aside, that is, unless it was the night the student was *on call.*

Call was a special time. For the students on the fourth floor, it came every fourth night, and it was a time when sleep was scarce. All the procedures that didn't get done during the day had to be done at night.

New IV's, catheter placements, and any nighttime blood work were part of a normal evening's work as were any leftover ward admissions or transfers to the ICUs.

Finally, *call* included the Code Blues, the pivotal and, many times, climactic moments of the patients' lives that every *call* student had to attend. These last events were always life-and-death experiences, and each time tempered another little piece of each student's soul, always leaving him or her either stronger or harder.

And that was what *call* was all about, a time of forced independent responsibility and action that either made or broke each med student's mettle. It was a conditioning process unlike anything else found in professional education—education by mortal trial and error, the first "practice of medicine."

All of this made the medical ward seem like a harsh and uncaring place, but it really wasn't. The ward's workloads were heavy because the patients' needs were great. The patients had to be cared for… that came first. And new doctors had to be trained… that also came first. So everyone tried hard, and somehow it all worked out. And everyone who came there was different when he or she left, changed by the dynamic symbiosis of healing, dying, and learning.

At the top of the ward's chain of command was the floor nurse. She was the true queen of the place, its ultimate ruler and truest guardian. The deified attending physician would come and go, but the nurse lived with the patients all the time. More often than not, it was her instincts and experiences that really dictated policy when it came to each patient's treatment. Residents and med students quickly picked up on that fact. They did, that is, if they wanted to survive very long.

The nurses likewise made it their business to quickly size up the new physicians-in-training. The lives of the patients depended upon the reliability and untried skills of the neophytes, and the nurses had to know who could do what. It wasn't that the nurses wanted to haze a student—a good student was a tremendous asset to the floor. The nurses just had to figure out quickly who was good and who wasn't. Lives were in the balance.

Mitch fell into the pace of the rotation fairly easily. He had already been through several different kinds of "boot camps," and he reverted to that mindset almost automatically. However, he realized up front what was happening, and in contrast to most of his peers, he remained a little detached from the emotion of the educational fray. He had already been in more life-and-death situations than the rest of his class combined. This gave him a maturity they didn't have and made him different. It was that separateness, that strength that Nicki Belton first noticed.

Dr. Tim Sullins was chief resident of the VA's medical service. He was an aggressive Ivy Leaguer who had opted for this Midwestern med school so that he could be under the tutelage of one Dr. Nathan Harris, a famed oncologist who called Mizzou home.

Mitch had met Dr. Harris during his admissions committee days, and he had not always seen eye-to-eye with the abrasive, brilliant man. Sullins was a lot like his boss, super-smart and almost a bully, and his status was an extra burden to everyone on the floor. It was Dr. Sullins who was responsible for the actual protocol of immunosuppressants that made up Freddie Miles' therapy.

Freddie's treatment centered around two drugs. One was methotrexate, and the other was cortisone. Both dampened his immune system, and since that was the system that was steadily killing him, both drugs were being thrown into Fred in large amounts.

The drugs weakened Fred dramatically. He had all kinds of yeast infections which affected most of his body orifices. He also had a lot of abdominal cramping and diarrhea, and he was almost always on the brink of congestive heart failure. It was this heart trouble that had been his biggest problem of late.

Tim Sullins, along with the rheumatology fellows, believed it was the small vessel occlusive nature of Freddie's mixed collagen vascular disease that was wreaking havoc on Freddie's heart. So they proceeded on with their medicines with ever-increasing fervor. However, some of the house staff and the floor nurses, including Nicki, had real reservations. They thought the medicines themselves might be the culprits. Whichever the case, the fact remained that Freddie was slowly dying.

Mitch hadn't been on the floor for very long before Nicki realized he was more of a listener than he was a talker. That in itself was a bit unusual for a medical student. It was during one of his listening times that he overheard Nicki talking to her floor supervisor about Freddie's drug protocol. Both Nicki and the supervisor had a lot of questions about the correctness of Fred's therapies, especially the amount of cortisone being used.

Nicki learned later that Mitch spent the next two nights booking it hard in the medical library. On the third morning, as she stood in the background, she witness Mitch and Dr. Sullins have their first real confrontation.

"Dr. Rice, how much fluid did you tap off Mr. Miles's chest yesterday when you did the thoracentesis?"

"About a thousand cc, Dr. Sullins."

"Well, I guess we'll have to proceed with the chest tube then. Dr. Allison, write a consult to surgery for it."

Rachael Allison was the intern who was ultimately responsible for Freddie's daily care.

"Yes sir," she replied.

"Excuse me, Dr. Sullins," Mitch said.

"Yes, Rice?"

"Sir, I don't think Mr. Miles wants the chest tube."

Sullins stared at Mitch. "Is that right?" He continued his stare. "What do you think Mr. Miles wants then?"

Mitch didn't shrink and returned Sullins's gaze levelly. "I think Mr. Miles wants the time he has left to be time he can spend with his family."

"That's what we all want, Rice." Sullins turned to Rachael. "Explain it to him after rounds, Allison, and then get the tube placed."

Mitch's eyes pulled Dr. Sullins's attention back to him. It was obvious that Mitch wouldn't be put off.

"What else do you want, Rice?"

"Dr. Sullins, I'd appreciate it if you could explain the rationale of the chest tube placement to me. I don't really understand what you're trying to accomplish with it, and I know that Fred is scared to death of it."

Sullins gather himself for the attack. The man wasn't accustomed to med students questioning his orders, and Mitch's stubborn insistence was an affront to his authority.

"Okay, Rice. This one time I'll make an exception for you. So listen up while I explain." There was a real edge in his voice. "Every time we put a needle into Mr. Miles' chest we take a chance of puncturing his lung and giving him a pneumothorax. Once the chest tube is in place, the pneumo won't be a possibility. With no chance for a collapsed lung, we'll be able to use the tube to continually pump his chest dry. He'll breathe easier, and he'll feel better." Sullins was actually growling. "Do you understand now, Rice?"

Nicki saw that Mitch hadn't even flinched.

"Sir," he said, "why don't we keep the fluid from accumulating in the first place? The chest tube will hurt all the time. We'll have to load Fred full of morphine, and then he won't be able to think straight. Visiting with his family will be out of the picture. On top of that, he won't cough with the tube in because that'll make it hurt even more. With his immune system as suppressed as it is, he'll probably catch pneumonia. Then where will we be?"

"Dr. Sullins," Rachael Allison interrupted. "I'll take care of the chest tube, and I'll explain the rest to Rice."

Allison gave Mitch a look that told him to shut up. The look Nicki saw Mitch give her back was something Nicki had never seen before. His eyes seemed to be actually glowing. Nicki realized he was not about to back down. She didn't know Mitch knew exactly what he was talking about because he himself had endured several chest tubes after Tet.

"Dr. Sullins, I understand that Mr. Miles can't breathe with his pleural space full of fluid, but why aren't we looking at the other possible causes for his heart failure?"

Dr. Sullins had just about had it with Mitch. "Explain yourself, Rice! You've gotten in this far; you might as well go all the way!"

Nicki watched as Mitch dug in further.

"Dr. Sullins, one group thinks that Mr. Mile's heart failure is secondary to his connective tissue disease. Another group thinks that it's his methotrexate."

"That's right, Rice!" Sullins interrupted. "That's why we're here! Chemotherapy usually makes patients ill! It's our job to manage our patients so that they get through the treatment's side effects and go on and get well! It's all called clinical judgment! That's what you're supposed to be learning here!"

"I understand all that, Dr. Sullins."

"Then what's your beef, Rice?" Sullins asked. He was exasperated.

"Dr. Sullins, why isn't anyone thinking about the cortisone? I'm sure that if we changed Mr. Mile's high dose cortisone for a steroid that doesn't cause all that sodium retention, his heart wouldn't be failing. With less sodium his vascular fluid volume would be less, and he wouldn't accumulate so much fluid in his chest. Then we might not need the chest tube or the thoracenteses at all, and the essentials of his treatment would go on the same as always."

"Rice!" Sullins exploded, "I've been more than patient with you, but enough is enough! We're using cortisone because that's the way the protocol's written, and that's that!"

"With all due respect, Dr. Sullins," Mitch answered icily, "I read the protocol last night. Mr. Mile's protocol isn't an Institute of Health protocol. What he's getting is a home-brewed protocol that's experimental. I don't understand why a different corticosteroid can't be substituted that might make it easier on his heart."

"That's it, Rice!" Sullins snarled viciously. "Dr. Allison, get your student to keep his mouth shut, or I'll see to it that you both are working night shifts in the morgue 'til hell freezes over!"

Sullins turned on his heel and started down the hall.

"We've been here long enough! Let's move on to the next patient! Dr. Allison, you should also explain to your student that he should talk a lot less and listen a lot more! His success here depends on it!"

Sullins continued on down the hall. Nicki heard Mark Gustin, one of the other M-3's on the rotation, whisper into Mitch's ear.

"Oh shit, Rice! You'll be hard-pressed to live through this rotation now, let alone pass it! Here, stand behind me so that Sullins won't have as much of a chance to tee off on you again."

"Thanks, Mark, but I'll take my own heat. It's the least I can do for Fred."

Mark looked at Mitch and almost choked.

"Oh shit and double shit, Rice! Get that look off your face! You scare the hell out of me when you look like that!"

Nicki was also looking at Mitch's face. It scared the hell out of her too.

Later that day Tim Sullins was sitting in on the morbidity and mortality conference. He was about to contribute his opinion on a surgical case when his beeper went off.

"Dr. Sullins, 2801, please. 2801 for Dr. Harris."

All eyes turned towards the chief resident.

"Excuse me, guys. I guess the chief wants me for something."

A few minutes later, Sullins entered Dr. Harris's office. Mitch was already there.

"Dr. Sullins, I trust you remember Dr. Rice?" Dr. Harris said.

"Yes, Dr. Harris. I know *Mr.* Rice quite well." There was no charity in his voice.

"Tim, I'm going to cut right to the chase," Harris said. "First, you should consider much more seriously Rice's ideas about using a corticosteroid with less sodium retaining effect in place of the cortisone you're using on this Mr. Miles. Then, I think you should see to it personally that Dr. Rice is much better versed in the chain of command that exists around here. I can't tolerate having my chief residents scooped by third-year med students. It makes us all look bad."

Harris had both Mitch's and Sullins's eyes.

"Now, you two get out of here and fix your problems somewhere else! Do you each get my drift?"

Both Mitch and Sullins said yes and turned to go, but Harris stopped Mitch.

"Rice, you've already established a reputation around here for being independent and unconventional. Don't make too many enemies. You may need friendly recommendations one day when you're trying to get into a residency."

"Thank you, sir," Mitch said, almost sounding detached. "I appreciate your advice."

Harris shrugged. He had realized during the previous year in the admissions committee that this med student was of a different cut. He wasn't sure throwbacks like Mitch really belonged in med school, but here he was anyway. So he waved Mitch away.

A few moments later, Dr. Harris stepped out of his inner office and walked over to his secretary.

"Sue, get me the personnel file on that M-3 who just left here. His name is Mitchell Rice."

"Of course, Dr. Harris."

Harris strode back into his office. "That kid has more brass than the navy," he muttered to himself. "He isn't scared of Sullins, and he sure as hell has never been scared of me!" Slowly he started to smile.

"Score: Med Student 1, Chief Resident 0. Look out, Tim Sullins. This kid might well eat your lunch yet."

"I'm sorry, Dr. Harris. What was that?" Sue asked.

"Oh, I'm sorry, Sue. I'm just talking to myself. I guess this Mitchell Rice reminds me of me, and that's kind of scary."

"I'm sure it is, sir," Sue answered.

She was trying not to smile. For sure she was going to enjoy being a little mouse, peeking at the file later to see just what Dr. Harris actually put in it.

"Hey, Miles, you're looking better!" chirped Nicki Belton.

"Hey, Belton! Where have you been?"

"Oh, I've been on vacation, lying out in the sun down at the lake," she answered. "Freddie, you really do look a lot better. What's happened?"

"Oh, the docs changed my medicines. I haven't had to have my chest tapped in more than a week. Shoot, even the sores in my mouth and on my backside are nearly gone."

"That's great, Fred! I bet your girls are really happy."

"Yeah, we're all celebrating." He was grinning. "There's even been some talk about me going home."

Nicki patted him on the shoulder and went on with her work. She had already heard several versions of Mitch's duel with Dr. Sullins. Hospitals were real gossip mills, and this last episode in Mitch's med school career was being embellished almost to the point of a "David and Goliath" saga.

Nicki already knew enough about Mitch to know that he was a Vietnam combat veteran. She knew quite a bit about Vietnam because all three of her brothers had been there. In fact, her youngest brother, Tommy, had just gotten back six months ago.

From what her brothers had told her about the place, this little flap between Mitch and Tim Sullins didn't even compare to what was happening over there. But she had enjoyed it anyway. Hearing the arrogant chief resident had been brought down to Earth was sweet. And, for some reason, it was even sweeter that it had been Mitch who had done it.

It was noon when Nicki crossed paths with one of her friends, Jane Chapel. Jane was another floor nurse on the internal medicine wards, and she was anxious to hear about Nicki's vacation.

"Well, tell me about the lake. Did you come back with any tan lines?" Jane quipped.

"Jane, you're awful!" Nicki retorted, blushing as she did so. "I'm not even back one day and already your mind's back in the gutter! You darn well know this vacation was with my family!" She made a face at Jane. "I was with my brothers and parents, you creep!"

"What, no eligible men?" Jane teased. "I thought for sure that several of the guys around here would've been down there, beating your folks' doors down. Two weeks without you should've been more than they could stand!"

Nicki dated a lot and enjoyed her popularity, but Jane teased her a lot because she never let anything get too serious.

"You know, Nicki," Jane went on, being her usual nosy self, "this Mitchell Rice character is interesting. He seems to have lots of layers."

Nicki looked up from her lunch, feigning irritation.

"Well, just think of it," Jane continued. "He seems like a quiet, almost shy third-year med student on the surface. Then that layer comes off, and underneath it is a chief resident slayer. Then, if you listen to what people say, that layer comes off and under it there's a real live combat hero fresh from the jungles of Vietnam."

Nicki's expression softened a little. She remembered something her brother Tommy had said to her just last week. He had just finished his fourth beer and was getting a little morbid.

"Vietnam," he had said, "is a place where a man's soul gets ripped apart. The pieces left over are what makes a man either a hero or a coward."

Nicki had made such a scene after his comment that Tommy stopped drinking for the rest of the trip. She always hated it when he got depressed, and the beer was bringing him down.

She continued her reflection, ignoring Jane's questioning stare. If what Tommy had said was true, then maybe this Mitchell Rice wasn't made up of layers at all but rather just a bunch of broken pieces. The thought made her sad.

"Earth to Belton! Earth to Belton! Are you in there, Nicki?" Jane chirped.

Nicki came out of her silence blasting. "Chapel, you're incorrigible! What would your husband say if he heard you carrying on like this about Rice?"

"Oh, Jack's a pretty secure type, sweetie. He knows I'm his one and only."

"Good!" Nicki said as she reached for her soup. "Just be sure you remember that!"

"Get over it, Belton. I know I'm married," Jane countered. "But you're not."

"And that's the way I intend for it to be for quite a while, Janie, old friend!"

Jane made an awful face at Nicki and then started chewing on her sandwich. Later, after she had washed down several bites with her iced tea, she started again.

"Nicki, Freddie Miles thinks Rice was a Marine scout in Vietnam. Freddie says those guys were really bad actors. He knew a couple of them when he was over there."

"So?"

"So nothing, I guess." She paused. "It's just the way Fred talked about them. Did you know the Marine scouts were snipers? All they did over there was kill people. Isn't it kind of spooky knowing that this Mitch Rice is maybe a killer?"

"My brother, Tommy, was a Marine, Jane," Nicki answered icily. "I think all those guys over there did a lot more dying than they did killing. I don't know if Tommy will ever get over it." Nicki wasn't smiling. "I don't think we'll ever really know what all they've gone through."

"You're probably right," Jane said, a little humbled. "But it doesn't hurt to ask some questions."

Nicki looked up at her friend. "What's the deal, Jane? Why all this interest in Mitch Rice? He's just another med student."

"Old friend, Mitchell Rice is *nothing* at all like any med student I've ever met." She made another face at Nicki. "You're so dense! If you weren't, you'd have already realized that this Mitchell Rice deserves a little extra investigation."

Nicki made an ugly gesture at Jane, but she had already come to that same conclusion two weeks before.

The next four weeks were pretty intense for Mitch. The workload was heavy, and his celebrity status quickly faded away. Rachael Allison worked the heck out of him, and the days and nights blended together, one running right into the next. Rachael and Mitch liked each other, but after his run in with Dr. Sullins, Rachael made every effort to keep him on a very short leash. It wasn't good for her career to be in charge of a med student who bagged chief residents as a hobby. So she really tried to work Mitch to the point of silence.

The twenty-eighth day of August was Mitch's last night on call as an internal medicine M-3. The evening began with the usual run of assorted late-day lab tests, but Mitch sailed right through them. No one disturbed his supper, and, after the meal he took his leave of Rachael, presumably to head for the medical library. En route, however, he stopped by Freddie Miles's room.

"Hi, Fred. I got the word that you're getting out of here."

Fred looked over his supper tray at Mitch. "That's right, doc. Tomorrow Sally and the girls are picking me up. I'm gone!"

"Way to go, Fred! You've paid enough dues here. I..."

Freddie had just given Mitch a look that cut him off. He pushed his bedside table back and got up out of his bed. He came over to Mitch and held out his hand.

"Thanks for coming by tonight, doc. Both Dr. Allison and the nurses have told me what you did for me... getting my medicines changed and all. I don't know what to say except thanks."

Mitch took Fred's hand. "I'm glad I could help, Fred. I'm glad you're better."

"Me too, doc. Me too."

Fred squeezed Mitch's hand hard and then turned to sit back down on his bed. He still was weak.

"You were in Vietnam, weren't you, doc?"

Mitch nodded yes as he helped Fred settle onto the bed.

"Well, doc, I won't ask what you did over there, but people talk. Scuttlebutt says that you were into some pretty heavy stuff."

Mitch just shrugged.

"Well, I'm glad you survived whatever you had to do over there. If you hadn't, I'd be dead. It means everything to me that I'm going to have more time with my family. I just wanted you to know that."

Mitch squeezed Fred's shoulder. "I wish you the best, Fred. You deserve it."

"Thanks, doc. Thanks for everything."

"Code blue; Four east; room 4227! Code blue; Four east; room 4227!" the Code blue beeper went off.

It was 2:00 a. m. Mitch jumped out of his bunk and hit the floor running. 4227 was Freddie Miles's room.

Mitch caught up to Rachael Allison in the hall just outside Fred's room. They were the first of the Code blue team in. Nicki Belton was already there, doing mouth-to- mouth resuscitation, and Jane Chapel was right behind them, pulling the crash cart in.

"Does he have a pulse, Belton?" Rachael asked.

"No, Dr. Allison, none at all."

"Get the paddles, Mitch! Hit him with a full charge."

Jane handed the defibrillator paddles to Mitch. "Three hundred and twenty watt-seconds, Mitch."

Mitch took the defibrillator and went right to Freddie's chest. Three jolts later, he pulled back.

"Pulse?" he asked.

"No, Dr. Rice. No pulse," Jane answered.

She had just snapped on the monitor leads and was trying hard to get an IV started.

"Get me an endotracheal tube and some help, Belton!" Rachael snapped. "Mitch, pump his chest! Chapel, push an amp of epinephrine as soon as you get that IV started!"

Mitch pushed hard on Freddie's chest while Rachael and Nicki established a better airway.

"Where's that IV, Jane?"

"I'm having trouble hitting one, Dr. Allison! His veins are all shot!"

"Here, let me try," Mitch said. "I've drawn blood on Fred lots of times."

"Go for it!" Rachael said. "Nicki, do the chest compressions!"

"He's in V-fib, Dr. Allison," Jane said, looking at the heart monitor. "Should we shock him again?"

Rachael hesitated. "No. We've done that already. We need the IV and epinephrine." She looked down at Mitch who was at Freddie's upper left arm. "Mitch…"

"There! I got it!" Mitch almost shouted. "Give me the epi!"

The next minute was almost suspended in time. Mitch pushed the adrenaline in. Nicki pumped Freddie's chest, and Rachael Allison squeezed the Ambu bag, pushing oxygen into Fred's lungs.

"What's the rhythm now?" Rachael asked.

"Still fib, Dr. Allison," Jane answered.

"Give me the paddles!" Rachael ordered. "Clear!"

Three more full voltage shocks jerked Freddie's gray frame.

"Still fib… no, he's in standstill!" Jane said.

"What do we do now, Mitch?" Rachael asked.

This was a final exam the likes of which Mitch had never taken before.

"Push another amp of epi and add an amp of bicarb!" Mitch answered. "Then, if he's still in standstill, push an amp of atropine!"

"That's right!" Rachael agreed. "Mitch, spell Nicki on Freddie's chest! Jane, push the meds just like Dr. Rice said!"

"What's going on in here?" It was Dr. Nickels. He was the senior resident on call.

"It's Miles, Bob," Rachael responded. "Belton found him in v-fib when she was making her rounds. We've been working on him now for about fifteen minutes. He's gone from v-fib to standstill."

"What are his pupils doing?" Nickels asked.

Rachael flashed a penlight into Freddie's face and then looked up, defeated, "Damn! Fixed and dilated!"

"Well, looks like we've just about done it all, people," Dr. Nickels announced. "Does anyone have any other ideas?"

Mitch was still pumping Freddie's chest. Sweat was beading on his brow. He couldn't believe what was happening. "He was going home tomorrow," Mitch muttered.

"What was that, Rice?" Dr. Nickels asked.

"What about intracardiac epinephrine, Dr. Nickels?" Mitch answered.

Dr. Nickels looked at Rachael. She shrugged.

"Okay, Rice. That's part of the drill."

Nickels pulled the six-inch long needle out of the crash cart drawer and gave it to Mitch.

"Here, Rice. It was your idea."

It was a big syringe.

"Have you ever poked someone's heart before?"

Nicki was still squeezing the Ambu bag. She saw Mitch turn pale as he took the long needle.

"Rice?"

"Yes, I have," Mitch said slowly, his voice husky.

"Help him anyway, Rachael. He needs to know how to do this," Dr. Nickels said.

Rachael went over to Mitch, but Mitch waved her back.

"It's okay, Rach! I can do this! It's the only chance Fred's got!"

"That's right, Mitch. It is."

Mitch felt for the correct space between Freddie's left ribs. He glanced at Nicki so she would stop squeezing the Ambu bag. He hesitated for half a second, but then smoothly pushed three inches of the long needle right into Fred's chest. Bright red blood popped into the syringe as he did so. Mitch pushed the whole syringe-worth of adrenaline right into Freddie's heart and quickly eased the needle out.

"Good job, Rice!" Dr. Nickels said. "Now pump him a few times, and we'll see if it's going to work."

Mitch did just what he was told, and then they all waited.

"Rhythm?" Nickels asked.

Jane stared at the monitor screen, trying to will it to do something. "It's still standstill, Dr. Nickels."

"Rachael?" Nickels asked.

"I guess that's it, everybody." She pulled back from Freddie's side, falling in besides Dr. Nickels. "Freddie's gone."

Mitch fell back from Freddie's chest. He picked up the long intracardiac needle and just held it. He didn't say a thing.

"You all did a good job," Rachael comforted. "Freddie's time was up."

Nicki and Jane looked at each other, and then they looked at Mitch. He was just standing there, holding the long needle almost like it was a knife. They didn't know how to describe it. It was like he was looking a thousand yards away with eyes that were full of fire and shadows.

"You okay, Dr. Rice?" Jane asked.

Mitch said nothing. He just pulled back. His eyes were full of things no one else could see.

Chapter Seventeen

It was the first day of October, and Mitch was a month into his second clinical rotation, surgery. He was still in the VA and had only moved one floor, from the fourth to the fifth, to start the new block.

Surgery was another demanding rotation, maybe even more so than internal medicine, but Mitch had already established his pace and was moving on with the program. The only real difference between medicine and surgery was that the time spent in medicine doing all of the diagnostic procedures was now pretty much replaced by long hours assisting and holding retractors in the operating rooms. The rest of the workload and roundsmanship were pretty much the same.

In the weeks since Freddie Miles' death Mitch had scarcely stepped foot back onto the fourth floor. He tried to keep himself totally focused on his current rotation, just as he had with the rest of medical school, but memories of the fourth floor kept cropping up anyway. Even when he tried to ignore them, the people and events of the previous two months were always close to the surface. Mitch thought a lot about Freddie Miles (the day after Freddie's death had been tough, especially facing Freddie's wife), but mostly he found he was thinking of someone else, someone a lot more disconcerting… Nicki Belton.

Mitch had worked with Nicki a lot during the two months he had spent on 4-East. Freddie had been the focus that brought them together at first, but as Mitch's rotation continued, he had found a lot more to talk to her about. Somehow he hadn't felt so solitary when he was around her. Now that he didn't see her, it was harder being alone.

A quiet chime announced the elevator's arrival, and its doors slid open.

"Hi, Mitch. Where have you been hiding yourself?"

It was Nicki.

"Oh... hi, Nicki. You surprised me," Mitch fumbled. "I didn't expect to see anyone on the elevator at this time of night." It was 1:00 a. m. He was on surgery call and wasn't getting any sleep.

"Yeah, I'm doing nights this week," she said, not noticing his uneasiness. "I hate it."

"I thought you were finished rotating your shifts."

"No, I'm still just like everyone else," she smiled. "I see your call nights are still busy."

"Oh, tonight hasn't been too bad. Not really," Mitch answered. "I think the ICU is settled down for the rest of the night. I was just heading back to the call room."

"That's good."

The look on her face made Mitch feel funny, almost like he needed to say something more. The elevator stopped.

"Well, here's 4-East," Mitch said as the elevator stopped. "Your home-sweet-home."

Nicki moved to get off the elevator. "Yeah," she answered. "Don't forget us down here. Call sometime."

"Sure," Mitch hesitated. "I... Nicki?"

She stopped in the elevator's doorway, her face a question mark.

"Nicki, I miss seeing you," he said slowly. "Could I talk you into going out for a meal Saturday?" His face felt warm. "That is, if you don't have other plans?"

Her smile dropped, her question mark replaced by a small frown. "Mitch, I'd like that a lot, but..." She hesitated. "But I already have a date. I'm sorry."

Mitch bit back his disappointment. "Oh, that's okay. It's pretty late to be asking anyway. Maybe we could work out something some other time?"

"Sure!" Her smile came back. "I'd like that!"

"Good. I'll call you later."

The door closed and continued on to the second floor where Mitch's call room was.

"Boy, that was smooth!" he chided himself as he slipped into the call room.

He was pretty certain Nicki Belton had her pick of any number of guys.

"You idiot!"

He rapped himself on the forehead.

"You don't even have her phone number!"

The next morning Nicki gave Jane her report for the day shift. She also told her about Mitch's invitation.

"Nicki Belton! You're crazy!" Jane actually yelled at her. "You mean he actually asked you out, and you said no! I can't believe it!"

Nicki, already wilted, shrank even more under Jane's fire.

"Jane, I really *do* have dates this weekend! I just can't break them!"

"Why the heck not? Who is it, that second-year pediatric resident?"

Nicki nodded.

"Dump the jerk! He's not worth your time!"

Nicki started to argue.

"Don't get righteous with me, Nicki Belton! I remember what you've said about this guy. "Kind of a flake," I think was the quote!"

Nicki settled back down. "Yeah, I know… but how can I break a date for no good reason?"

Jane shook her head.

"Sweetie! *This* is Mitchell Rice! You've been talking about him more or less nonstop for weeks! Now he's actually paid you some attention, and you said no!"

She threw her eyes toward the ceiling.

"Unbelievable!"

She leveled her eyes back onto Nicki.

"He won't ask again, Nicki. He's not that kind of guy."

Nicki's face fell.

"You don't think so?"

"Wake up, Nicki! This is Mitch Rice! The 'iceman!' That's what his classmates call him! He won't ask again!"

Nicki felt her face getting hot.

"Jane! Stop it! That's not right! You were there when Freddie died! You know as well as I do that Mitch isn't cold! We almost had to carry him out of that room!" Her eyes snapped. "And we *did* have to pry that intracardiac needle out of his hand! I think part of Mitch died in that room along with Freddie!"

Jane retreated a little.

"I know, Nicki. You're right about that night. But that was then, and this is now. When someone like Mitch opens up a little, you have to step right in. Otherwise, he closes right back down."

Nicki's eyes fell again. She knew Jane was right.

Jane reached out and grabbed Nicki's arm.

"Do something about this, Nicki! You've dated more guys in the last two years than I can count. No one has ever lit you up like Mitch."

"You're right." Nicki looked miserable. "What can I do?"

"Girl! Wake up! The ball's in your court! Get rid of that other guy! Lie, cheat, tell the truth! I don't care! Just dump him!" She still had Nicki's arm. "Then tonight you trot right up to the fifth floor and humble yourself! Tell him you're free after all!"

Nicki gave Jane a helpless look.

"Look, Nicki, just once *do* what I'm telling you!" Jane demanded. "Get this date!"

And that was why, hours later, Nicki found herself standing outside the med students' chart room on the fifth floor.

"Nicki?"

She turned, surprised. It was Mitch. He had come up behind her.

"What are you doing up here? Doesn't your shift start soon?"

She started to answer, but was interrupted by Mary Aspers, one of the few classmates Mitch seemed connected to.

"Go ahead, Mitch… ask her. I'm tired of hearing you talk about it."

"Ask me what?" Nicki asked.

Mitch looked really sheepish.

"Thanks a lot, Mary."

"Well, ask her then. You've been worthless all day long." Mary had a funny grin. "And I'm tired of covering for you. That's what you usually end up doing for me."

"Ask me what?" Nicki asked again, a little exasperated.

Mitch turned to her and took a breath. "I guess I was just hoping you'd reconsider about this weekend, that's all."

Nicki tried to be coy for a second, but she couldn't pull it off.

"This weekend… I… oh, heck! That's why I'm here, Mitch. I was hoping the invitation was still open."

Mitch's sudden smile lit up the hall.

"Great!"

He looked almost like a kid at Christmas.

"Sure, it's still open! When can I pick you up?"

"About six?" Nicki answered.

She was stunned. This had been too easy.

"Great!" Mitch said again.

It seemed to Nicki that Mitch was actually glowing.

"Saturday," he said with a big smile, "about six sounds great!"

Nicki had to bite her lip to keep from giggling. Mitch's silly grin was contagious.

Mary Aspers turned to leave, shaking her head. She tried not to laugh at what she had just witnessed, but it was almost more than she could do. What she had just witnessed could have been a scene right out of some 1950's Saturday matinee. She chuckled silently. Whatever it was, it sure had been fun seeing the "iceman" melt.

Chapter Eighteen

Sarah Thornton settled into her seat on the 737. She was off again. Short trips, long trips, stateside jaunts, or international forays—the last two years had been a veritable roller-coaster ride. Of late, she had probably logged more air miles than most airline pilots.

The plane taxied down the runway, and she reviewed the previous twenty-four months. First, as a trouble shooter for Senator Simons's various senate committees, and then for the bigger portion of that time, as General Wilson Strong's personal secretary, she had become a jet-setting problem solver. She was a long way from the unhappy elementary school teacher she had once been.

General Strong was now a deputy director of the CIA, and she (depending on one's point of view) was either his dragon lady-watchdog or his softer alter ego. In either case, her dossier was now nicknamed "Princess," and she played the parts well.

As the plane lifted off, Sarah's thoughts flew back over all that had happened. Senatorial politics, international projects and intrigues, and, finally actual espionage had all fallen to her lot. It had been a wild trip.

She looked out the window and watched the clouds slip by. Happily, this trip was not business. She was just Missouri- bound, going home to see her folks. She wasn't needed at the week-long command course Wilson gave at the War College each year, and she needed a break.

Wilson had gladly given her the time. She'd had enough of D. C. for a while, and he had shooed her home.

Sarah's move from the senator's office to the CIA had been an amazing thing. Sherrie, the general's first secretary, had reached her thirty-year mark about six months after the general and Sarah had come back together. Those had been an important six months. Sarah had needed them to find a final resting place for her emotions about Mother Marie's death. That first night in the restaurant, she had accepted the general's explanation of what had happened in Hue. She knew Wilson was right. But it had taken longer for her soul to finally find peace with it.

Those six months had also been good for her and Wilson in a lot of other ways. During that time they discovered how to make a place in their lives for each other. They began almost as strangers, each worlds apart and joined only by a tragic past. From there they first came to understand who the other was. Then they each learned to forgive the other for what had happened. After that, wonderful days and evenings had followed where they showed each other special little parts of Washington and the nearby Chesapeake. Those simple meetings soon led them to much deeper truths, and, as the months worn on those deeper truths had evolved into a wonderful new mystery. In the end, they were no longer strangers.

In those days Sarah had come to see her general in ways she had never imagined before. She discovered he had a soft, almost innocent, place inside of him… a place that even he didn't know very well. They entered that place together, and the whole world blossomed. Even though they had nothing formal (the system frowned on boss/secretary liaisons), they had become one. Later when their relationship had become obvious, not even Director Helsey and all of his CIA stooges had enough power to separate them.

Consequently, they hammered out a solution. Wilson was still the general, but Sarah became his truest executive officer, his "princess." Together, they became the most potent one-two punch in the CIA. No one in Washington took them lightly.

As the plane continued westward, Sarah remembered the morning just past when she had handed Wilson his briefs for the War College lectures.

"Wilson," she said, using their private tones, "here are your notes, all typed up."

She handed him a large stack of paper.

"The introduction you have in there about the three different kinds of soldiers is good, maybe as good as anything you've ever written."

Strong looked at her with a small squint. He had caught the tone of her voice and knew she had something more to say.

"Good," he had answered. "So what's wrong?"

"You haven't told the whole story."

"What do you mean?"

"You didn't name the fourth kind of soldier, Wilson. You named the first three, but not the fourth."

He wrinkled his forehead.

"Don't give me that look! You know exactly what I'm talking about!" Sarah chided. "You're the fourth soldier! You're the commander, the guy who manipulates and uses the other three." She stared right through him. "You know, Wilson, sometimes I can still hate you for Hue and Mother Marie and…"

"And for Mitch?" he finished for her. "Are we going to start this all over again?"

"No, we're not." She took a big breath. "You know I understand now why you did what you did. It was all about duty. That's why I'm here too. But sometimes it seems too sad, using up the best people we have."

"Sarah, we've already been all through this. Duty is more important than personal feelings. Mitch understood that. We have to be willing to give our very best, even the people we value the most. Otherwise, it's guaranteed that we'll lose the whole ballgame."

"I'm not arguing, Wilson. But I don't think I'll every stop hating that we have to do it."

She had been in one of her reflective moods, and the general had already learned that he would just have to let her run down.

"How can we always be so sure that the cause is worth such sacrifice?"

Sarah knew Wilson felt the edge of bitterness in her voice.

"I guess it would be easier if I could just see some good coming from all of it. Most times I just don't." Sarah paused. "Look at this Professor Wade deal. Mitch saved him in Munich, nearly got killed any number of times doing it, and…" She swung her eyes back to him. "… and for what? Wade was actually defecting and was a traitor! Mitch should have killed him on the spot!"

Strong remained silent, waiting for the next volley she had already loaded up.

"You know I'm right, Wilson! Wade's a traitor! He should be shot or, at least put away forever! But is that what's happened? No! First, we fixed his shoulder. Then we put him in 'psychological rehabilitation,' whatever that is. Then we worked him out of his university and put him right back into the Defense Department labs, first at Fort Detrich and then out in Nevada."

"You saw that brief?" Strong had asked, aghast.

"You bet I saw it! Whatever else I may or may not be, I'm still your secretary. That damn security clearance you gave me lets me see everything that you see."

She made a threatening face at him.

"What's the sense of all this, Wilson? What kind of horror is Wade building out there in Nevada? Wouldn't it have been better for Mitch to have just planted him there in Germany?"

She paused, running a little out of steam.

"I love you, Wilson, but sometimes I just don't understand."

"You know I tried to stop all that from the very start, Sarah," Strong answered wearily. "You, of all people, should know how much time and effort I've invested trying to put that jerk in jail. But I don't always have last say on what happens around here. You know that."

"Yeah, I do. But since when has that ever stopped us?"

She had a look of true malevolence about her.

"We have to figure some way to get the bastard!"

"Oh, God! I've created a monster!" Strong groaned, surrendering.

"And don't you forget it!"

She suddenly softened and came around his desk to plant a kiss on the top of his head.

"You just be sure you impress upon all those command-types at Fort McNair just how awful a responsibility it really is to order men and women around. Make them see what *duty* really is."

Strong waited, knowing her finale was coming.

"Wilson, make them see that duty must serve the truth. Make them see that's the only way duty can be honorable."

With that Strong took her into his arms.

"I *have* created a monster," he said gently. "Sometimes you even scare me."

Then he kissed her, but not on the top of her head.

Sarah could still feel his touch now, many hours later. When she had pulled back from his embrace, all of her rancor had left.

"I love you too, Wilson. Just make those young pups see the truth. Okay?"

"Okay," he had said.

Then he had kissed her again. The glow it had given her still warmed her.

Sarah looked at the farm fields below her. She was really looking forward to being home. It had been months since she had last seen her folks.

Sarah's dad was still a little uncomfortable with her. That hadn't changed. He had opposed her leaving Simons's office and didn't like her working for the CIA. But he did like Wilson Strong and didn't ask too many questions. He and Sarah were still living by the truce they had made after she had returned from Vietnam.

Sarah's mother, on the other hand, didn't have to ask any questions. That hadn't changed either; she had always seemed to know Sarah better than Sarah knew herself. It had been enough for her mom that Sarah had come home from Vietnam in one piece. Now to know that Sarah was in love and happier than she had ever been in her life was all a wonderful gift. She and Sarah were closer now than they had ever been.

Sarah was also anxious to make a side trip from Cape Girardeau to Columbia. She was supposed to make the drive over there later in the week. She was looking forward to meeting the nurse Mitch had written her about. This Nicki Belton sounded pretty interesting.

Nicki was pretty used up. She had just come off a series of double shifts. A few weeks ago she'd started filling in odd shifts on the psych floor in addition to he normal shifts on the medical floor. Jane Chapel had said she was crazy, but Nicki didn't care. Mitch was proving to be too hard a nut to crack.

She and Mitch had dated all summer and fall. They'd had wonderful times, everything from sun-drenched float trips down crystal clear Ozark streams to quiet, peaceful evening walks in the parks. On the streams, Nicki had been as outrageous she could tastefully be, clad only in the little hot-pink, come-on bikini that Jane Chapel had helped her pick out. And in the parks and later in her apartment, she had been as receptive as her conscience would allow. It should have been wonderfully romantic. But it wasn't… at least, not enough of the time.

The problem was that a lot of the time Mitch just wasn't with her. His body might be, but his mind sure wasn't. More often than not, his thoughts slipped off to some strange, dark land from where she was completely excluded. She hated it. Sure, sometimes Nicki felt she was close to breaking through to Mitch. But then in their next meeting, she had no idea of where she stood. It was driving her nuts. When she felt nuts, she worked. And of late, she had been working a lot.

Nicki had just kicked off her white uniform and slipped into her old terry cloth robe when she heard a knock at the door.

"Oh crap!" she cursed.

She had been delayed leaving the psych floor by an incident between one of the patients, an ex-Green Beret, and one of the psych residents. The two almost had gotten into a fight. Nicki had been forced to separate them and then had to file an incident report about it. It had all taken up too much time, and she was way off schedule.

"Hold on! I'll be right there!" she shouted as she cinched up the robe. "This should be interesting," she mumbled as she went for the door. "Nothing like making a good first impression."

Originally, Nicki had thought Sarah's visit was just meant for Mitch. Mitch had spoken of Sarah lots of times, and Nicki knew she was a special person of his ill-defined past. Of course, Nicki didn't know whether to be respectful or jealous. How was she supposed to compete with a myth?

"I'm coming!" Nicki shouted again, pulling the robe even tighter.

"Nicki?" Sarah asked as Nicki opened the door.

"Yeah, that's me," Nicki said offering her hand. "Are you Sarah?"

Sarah nodded yes and took Nicki's hand.

"I'm sorry, Sarah. I got off work late and haven't had time to change." Nicki tried to smile an honest greeting. "Some stuff happened on the floor, and I'm behind. I'm sorry."

"No sweat," Sarah answered, "I know a lot about screwed up schedules. Should I come back later?"

"No! Of course not! Come on in. You might as well see me in my native state." Nicki smiled a simple, guileless grin and held the door open for her. "*Mi casa, su casa*… that is, it is if you'll overlook the laundry that I haven't had time to put away."

Sarah came in laughing. Nicki saw that Sarah was darker and a little taller than she was. Nicki also felt a radiated sense of confidence and accomplishment that Nicki couldn't come close to. Nicki tried, but she felt pretty intimidated. She wasn't sure if she was being checked out by Mitch's one-time employer, his sister, his mother, or his former lover. It was pretty unnerving.

Sarah must have seen Nicki's uncertainty because she moved immediately to put Nicki at ease.

"Mitch's last letter, as usual, was pretty much off base," Sarah said. "You're even more of a knockout than he said."

"Wh… what?" Nicki stuttered, holding her bathrobe in close.

"Yeah. He said you were one of those people who was so beautiful you didn't have to take yourself too seriously."

Sarah started laughing. To Nicki, the sound was almost a sister's laugh.

"Are you as nervous about this as I am?" Sarah asked.

Nicki started to take a moment to collect her thoughts but changed her mind and just plunged in.

"Nervous? Why should I be nervous? Here I am just in my bathrobe, meeting a mysterious woman of my boyfriend's hazy past who's telling me things I've never heard before. Nervous? No! I'm petrified!"

Sarah dropped her smile. "Didn't Mitch tell you why I was coming?"

"No."

"The bum! He and Wilson are just alike. They both take too much for granted!"

Nicki shrugged. She was still off balance.

"Do you have to get dressed?" Sarah asked.

"I do if I'm ever going to be ready to meet Mitch." Her head was spinning.

"Oh, let Mitch cool his heels for a while!" Sarah snapped. "Sometimes that focused, 'oblivious to the obvious' way of his drives me crazy! Give me your phone and fix us some hot chocolate. I'll tell him we'll be a couple of hours late. You and I need to have some girl talk."

It took only minutes for Nicki to realize Sarah wasn't competition as far as Mitch was concerned. In fact, as they sipped hot chocolate and talked, it dawned on Nicki that she probably *was* meeting a new sister. It was a wonderful experience.

The conversation went on for more than an hour. They were working on their third cups of cocoa when Sarah suddenly lost her smile and said, "Mitch must really be screwing things up pretty royally, right?"

"That's putting it mildly," Nicki admitted. Her defenses were now completely breached. "I just can't seem to get past a certain point with him. I think that I'm getting close, and then he just isn't there."

"Yeah, that sounds like Mitch all right. You're hurting pretty bad, aren't you?"

Nicki suddenly felt a wave of emotion sweep behind her eyes. Sarah's sudden insight seemed to give Nicki a sudden vent for all the confusion Mitch had caused her, and she started crying. Long, hard sobs came up from somewhere deep inside. Sarah came over and held her close.

"How can I help you, Nicki?"

Nicki couldn't answer. She just kept crying, and Sarah just kept holding on, soon crying herself. The tears dissolved any barriers that remained between them.

After a while Nicki felt better. She pulled back and dried her nose.

"Sarah, would you tell me about the two of you?"

"You mean Mitch and me?"

"Uh-huh."

"Well, that's a fair question." Sarah took a breath. "But first things first. Where's your bathroom? All this cocoa is going right through me. My bladder's about to bust!"

"Back there," Nicki said, grimacing too. "I'm in the same shape. So hurry."

"Maybe that's why we're crying!" Sarah suddenly giggled. "That makes a whole lot more sense than crying over Mitch!"

It was silly, but Nicki started giggling too. For some reason she suddenly felt like a she was back at one of her teenage sleepovers with her high school friends. The laughter, however, was almost disastrous. They raced each other for the bathroom and just barely made it.

After that Sarah explained a lot of things to Nicki about the Mitch she knew. She told Nicki all she could about Vietnam, about Hue, Mother Marie, the orphanage, and of all the final moments she and Mitch had shared there. She let Nicki know that many other things had happened in Vietnam and that Mitch had gone far into harm's way for the then Colonel Wilson Strong, the same general for whom Sarah now worked.

Nicki caught the way Sarah's face changed when she mentioned the general.

"Is the general your Mitch?" she asked.

Sarah answered slowly. "Mitch said you were almost psychic... Yeah, Mitch and Wilson are just alike. Both of them have shells nine miles thick and harder than concrete. But, yes, I love Wilson just like you do Mitch."

Sarah started sniffing.

"Oh, heck! Let's not start crying again!" Nicki pleaded. "I don't have enough bathrooms!"

At hearing those simple words Sarah's tears melted to laughter. She could see why Mitch loved this woman. She was wonderful! Now they just had to make Mitch see his own feelings.

Sarah wiped her nose and resumed her story. She told Nicki that some of what Mitch had done for the general was still covered by a blanket of security and couldn't be talked about.

"Oh, great!" Nicki moaned. "I'm in love with a spy!"

"And he's very much in love with you, my dear," Sarah replied. "And he really isn't that much of a spy. He's just a very special guy who sometimes has been asked to risk a great, great deal for a lot of other people. And he has always come through." She took Nicki's hand. "But not without paying some big dues getting it done."

"Nearly everyone around here who knows Mitch is either scared of him or is in awe of him, even his professors," Nicki answered. "But no one sees just how lonely he is."

"But you do, and you can't understand why he clings so hard to his emptiness. Right?"

Nicki just nodded. "How can you know that?"

"I guess anyone who has loved Mitch has had to deal with that question."

Sarah saw the question on Nicki's face.

"I love him too, Nicki, but it's more of a brother-sister thing."

Nicki just kept looking at her.

"You're right. It's not a brother-sister thing at all, but it's not like what I have with Wilson either." Sarah slumped, drawing back into herself. "In Hue, on the eve of Tet, I was in the chapel with Mother Marie. We were all tied up. She had bamboo stakes holding her arms back, and…"

A steady stream of tears slipped down her cheeks, but she wasn't crying.

"And I was tied up on the chapel's altar and was about to be *raped*."

Nicki caught her breath. "Don't go on, Sarah. It sounds too awful."

"Yeah, it is," Sarah answered. "But you need to know this. I was right there, right on the edge of insanity. When, all of a sudden, there was Mitch. He saved me, Nicki!"

Sarah's hands told their own intense story, pointing out terrors Nicki could almost see.

"He saved me,Nicki! He pulled me right off that altar, gave me back my soul, and carried me all the way back to Wilson."

She suddenly put her hands to rest in her lap and dropped her eyes.

"That's how I love him, Nicki! Every day I've had since then, every breath I've taken, I've had because Mitchell Rice was there!" Sarah looked up at Nicki. "How could I not love the man who gave me back my life?"

Nicki reached out to Sarah, sudden understanding written all over her face.

"Sarah, Mitch told me about Tet too. And I know he's here only because it was you who shot a way out of that last alley."

Sarah looked at Nicki, confused.

"Look, Sarah. I've wondered for months now how Mitch loved you… he does, you know." Nicki smiled gently. "I didn't know if you were an old flame, a sister, or what. But now I guess I see that he loves you the same way you love him. You saved him too."

As Nicki spoke, Sarah saw what seemed to be a realization that ran right across Nicki's face.

"So, Sarah, I guess I love you just like your general must love Mitch. It's only because of you that he's here for me."

Sarah cocked her head to the side, feeling a wonderful surprise.

"That makes us family, doesn't it?" Nicki asked simply.

Sarah smiled and wiped her eyes. "Yeah, I guess it does." She wiped her nose. "I like that idea, Nicki. I think I like it a lot!"

Sarah basked in her new discovery for a long second but then pulled back. Suddenly she got up out of her chair and started walking around the small living room. Nicki obviously didn't know what was going on. Sarah seemed to be looking for something. Finally, after two or three laps, she sat back down. She had something else to say.

"Nicki, before she died, Mother Marie told me that she was really scared for Mitch's soul. She said he was too close to the edge in his pride."

"What did she mean by that?"

"She had to explain it to me several times, and a lot of time passed before I really understood," Sarah said. "But it goes something like this. Mitch can't believe that anyone can really love him just for who he is. That's why he keeps people at arm's length most of the time. He feels all this guilt, most of which I don't understand, and he doesn't think he can be forgiven."

Nicki stared hard at Sarah.

"Somehow, Mitch has it in his head that if he pays a big enough price, if he risks enough, that he will finally be able win his own forgiveness. And he won't let anyone love him until he's made himself perfect. Mother Marie said that even included God Himself."

Nicki shook her head. "That's not right, Sarah. God doesn't work that way. No one can really be perfect."

"That's what worried Mother Marie. She said the biggest sin of all was thinking that one could earn his own redemption. She said Mitch was a heretic, and that he didn't even know it."

Nicki just sat there in silence.

"And Mother Marie told me that I wasn't the one who could make Mitch see his mistake."

Sarah paused until Nicki looked over at her.

"But, Nicki, I think that *you* might be just that person."

"I wish that made me feel better," Nicki muttered.

She suddenly looked completely lost again.

"Why do I have to love him so much, Sarah? And why does he fight me so?"

"All I can say, Nicki, is that all big fish fight the hardest right before they come into the net. But I can tell you that Mitch is really hooked hard."

She went over and gave Nicki a hug.

"Now you just have to figure a way to play him. He's the biggest catch you'll ever make."

Chapter Nineteen

Michael Bickerston was a fourth-year surgical resident. He was small of stature but wiry in composition, somewhat sharp of tongue and generally someone who radiated that he was quite comfortable with who he was. He was enjoying the new crop of fourth-year med students. Becuse he was trying hard to be next year's chief surgical resident, the positive interaction with the students was not just fun; it was essential.

The current group of M-4's seemed very willing to work hard, and Bickerston found he enjoyed teaching them nearly as much as he enjoyed surgery itself. Connie, his wife of six years, had started to complain that he spent too much time at the hospital, but his ego really reveled in being the kingpin. Connie would just have to understand that this time of his life would come around just once, and he was having too much of a good time to hold anything back. Chief resident slots never came easy, and Mike Bickerston was willing to pay the price.

"Hey, Rice! That was a good pick up yesterday when you found that prostate cancer on old man Slattery."

"Thanks, Dr. Bickerston. But you said at the start of the rotation that every patient was to get a rectal exam. I was just doing what you told me to do."

Bickerston liked Rice. The guy was quiet, but he was proving to be very capable and didn't seem to rattle too easily. Mike Bickerston was about to find out just how durable Mitch really was. The experience would prove to be quite enough for any fourth-year resident who hoped for a successful career.

Mitch and Bickerston were walking across University Avenue from a noon conference at the Med Center. They were heading to the outpatient surgical clinic at the VA where they were scheduled for the whole afternoon. The conversation had just passed beyond Mr. Slattery's prostate when a dilapidated old Chevy bucked traffic and careened into the circular drive that led up to the VA's main entrance. Mitch and Bickerston plus two student nurses had to jump to get out of the car's way. Bickerston yelled at the driver, but the car blundered right past them.

At the main doors, the car jerked to a halt, and a young nondescript man got out. Mitch saw the man brandished a small automatic pistol. Mitch grabbed Bickerston and the two student nurses, halting their advance. Before much of anything could be said, the young man pointed the weapon at his own chest and pulled the trigger.

For a small second the report of the pistol hushed everything on the hospital lawn. A moment later the two student nurses screamed, and Bickerston, still speechless, felt himself being towed right up to the scene. Except for the screaming, the rest of the VA seemed frozen in time.

"Come on, Dr. Bickerston! This guy needs you!"

Somehow, Mitch's voice carried an authority Bickerston couldn't resist. In seconds they both were at the man's side. Mitch quickly reached down and freed the small pistol from the man's grasp. Bickerston followed suit, bending down. He tore open the man's shirt. There was a small hole ringed with a powder burn just to the left of the man's sternum. Bickerston reached for the man's neck and felt a carotid pulse, but it lasted for only a second and then faded away. The man's eyes started to dilate and his neck veins began to bulge.

"I'm pretty sure he got his heart," Bickerston heard himself say. "He's probably tamponading his heart."

The scene on the lawn quickly became hysterical. The student nurses had arrived and were going berserk. No one from the hospital came forth, but others from the street started to crowd around them. Bickerston felt no pulse and knew the man's life was quickly slipping away. He felt powerless to do anything.

Mitch still held the small pistol. He dropped the magazine out of the pistol's handle and jerked the slide back convulsively. A small golden-colored bullet popped out of the chamber as he did so.

"Dr. Bickerston, this is a. 32 automatic that's loaded with full metal jacket slugs."

"So what, Rice?"

"Well, you're probably right. The little slug has punched a little hole in this guy's heart and it's bleeding into its own pericardial sack. I bet nothing else much is wrong with him."

"What's your point? He's just lost his pulse. A hole in your heart is usually enough to kill you!"

"Don't you see, Dr. Bickerston? Low velocity bullets just penetrate! They don't tear up anything else! If we could open this guy up right now and decompress his pericardium, we might be able to bring him back!"

Bickerston just looked at Mitch. The kid was right.

"What the hell, doc? He's dead already! What do we have to lose?" Mitch challenged.

In that instant, Mike Bickerston couldn't find a rebuttal to Mitch's argument. So he reached over to one of the hysterical student nurses and pulled out a set of new bandage scissors that glistened in her uniform's side pocket. With them, he proceeded to deftly open the man's chest right there on the grass of the VA's lawn. And with that, the whole world came undone.

Bickerston reached into the man's chest, and blood gushed everywhere. Both of the already shaken student nurses fainted dead away, falling right next to the spreading pool of blood. From the front of the hospital, security people and a couple of residents came, yelling and gesturing the whole way. Sirens sounded shrilly from the street where a patrol car that had been chasing the derelict Chevy was finally catching up.

"Shit, Rice! You're right! There's a big hemopericardium in here! It's choking off his pump!"

Mitch, who was poised to do mouth-to-mouth, answered, "Can you nick the bag with those scissors, or do you need something else?"

"Yeah, I think I can just reach it."

A long pause of two or three seconds followed. The troops from both the hospital and from the Med Center were still coming at a dead run.

"I got it!" Bickerston shouted. "Breathe for him, Mitch! I'm going to massage his heart and try to plug the hole in his ventricle with my finger!"

"What the blazes is going on here, Bickerston?" yelled Tim Sullins who had just come out of the VA. He and Bickerston were not friends.

"Shut up, Tim! I have my hand on this guy's heart, and I need to get him into an OR pronto, or all this will be for nothing!"

"Bickerston, of all the grandstand plays I've ever seen this is the worse! You're going down for this one!"

"Dr. Sullins!" Mitch said. There was a clear, cutting cold to his voice that even stopped the police, who were arriving from the rear. "Get a gurney from the ER!

And notify OR of our immediate arrival! Or so help me, I'll gut you myself right where you stand!"

Everything about Mitch radiated sheer menace.

"And I don't give a damn if God himself is watching!"

Bickerston looked up as he continued to squeeze the wounded heart. He saw a look on Mitch's face that came from a place of deep, burning anger. That anger erupted as a focused, killing stare that scorched him and everyone on the grass. It obliterated Tim Sullins.

Sullins couldn't take it. He broke and ran back to the VA's entrance, yelling for ER staff as he went. Bickerston continued to squeeze the dying heart, and Mitch went back to his mouth-to-mouth resuscitation.

"Here, Mitch. Move over and let me tube this guy." It was Rachael Allison. "I have an endotracheal tube and an Ambu bag."

Mitch relinquished his station, and Rachael slipped the plastic tube into the man's larynx.

"Mitch?" It was Bickerston. "My hand is cramping something awful. Can you spell me in here?"

"Yeah, I think so." Mitch moved in next to his resident. Sliding his hand over Bickerston's, he found the heart and adjusted his grip so that he could continue the massage and plug the hole at the same time.

Bickerston felt Mitch's hand take charge and withdrew.

"Good! Keep him going, Mitch, and I'll meet you in the OR! Don't let anyone move your hand until I do it upstairs!"

"Don't worry, Mike," Rachael answered. "I don't think anyone will be crossing Mitch today, but get a move on or all this won't mean a thing!"

"Gotcha, Rach!" And Mike Bickerston was off, sprinting for the OR.

The next twenty or thirty minutes were utter chaos for everyone except for Mitch and Rachael. Their world held only one heart and one Ambu bag. Others started various IVs, placed catheters, and prepared a heart/lung machine. Blood was drawn and transfusions started almost simultaneously. The OR crew prepped the man's chest and draped the field. During all that time, Mitch was still squeezing the heart. It was almost as if Mitch's arm had become another appendage coming off the man's torso.

There was a buzz of a bone saw, the crunch of a rib spreader, and then Mitch heard Dr. Golden. "It's okay, Rice. Dr. Bickerston and I have control now. Pull your hand out and then go wash up. You can scrub with us for the rest of the case. You've earned the chance to see this thing to the end."

Two hours later, it was all over. The wound was repaired. The wounded heart beat on its own, and it appeared that the young man's neuro functions were still relatively normal. Whatever was at the root of his desperate action would yet have a chance to be worked out. All in all, it was the most amazing afternoon that the Harry S. Truman VA Hospital had seen in many a day.

In the days that followed, Mike Bickerston strutted in the glow of the spotlight that his actions deserved. Mitch, in contrast, seemed to almost disappear from view. He still worked daily on the surgical floor, but somehow he dodged all the notoriety that his boss basked in. None of his peers, none of the residents, and none of the nurses said a word to him about any of that day's events. Mitch's barefaced threat to Tim Sullins continued to echo, and no one knew how to deal with the killing edge it had bared. Normal civilized people didn't know how to deal with the killing times that were a part of Mitch's soul. So for a while, the world just walked around him. And for his part, Mitch was content to try to heal by himself.

About two weeks later, Mike Bickerston was asked to present the now-famous case in the monthly morbidity and mortality conference. The fact that he was presenting the case at this conference and not in grand rounds should have been a warning to him, but he felt so good about that day's outcome that his normal alarms weren't working.

When Bickerston entered the room, he immediately saw Dr. Golden, the department chief, was there, but that was always the case. Dr. Harris, the hematology chief, was also there. Bickerston and Dr. Harris were not friends. Dr. Emmitt White was also present. Dr. White was the section chief of neurosurgery and had a reputation for being the most obnoxious physician in the med school. He and Bickerston were definitely not friends. Several other staff surgeons and physicians filled the room along with many residents and students. In fact, the conference room was full. The moderator was Tim Sullins.

Sullins began the conference right on time, and all eyes turned towards the front.

"The first case we'll discuss today is that of a twenty-seven-year-old white male who had sustained a gunshot wound to his chest under somewhat unusual circumstances. Dr. Mike Bickerston, who managed the bulk of the case, will be presenting."

Bickerston took his place at the podium. He felt uneasy but shrugged off the feeling and began his presentation. He went through the case from beginning to end. To his surprise, he was not interrupted even once. That was unusual because this bunch of ego maniacal cutthroats loved to upstage each other. When he had finished, he took a breath and asked, "Are there any questions?"

Dr. White cleared his throat. It had been Dr. White whom Bickerston had preempted for OR space on the day in question. Not in anyone's memory had Dr. White ever been bumped out of his OR… not for anything. He had not been a happy camper when Bickerston had done it.

"Yes, Dr. White?"

"Well, Dr. Bickerston, that certainly was a swashbuckling tale. Tell me, how many gunshot wounds have you had personal experience with?"

Alarms began to go off inside Bickerston's head.

"Sir, as you know, Columbia, Missouri is not necessarily a mecca for gunshot trauma. I guess I have been in on ten or twelve cases so far."

White pressed on. "Would you mind telling me some of the essentials of some of those cases?"

Bickerston squirmed a little. "Just what exactly do you want to know, Dr. White? I'm not really prepared to go over all of them today."

"Just keep it simple, Bickerston. Just tell me what you remember of the sorts of weapons that were involved in your previous cases."

The room was definitely becoming chilly. Bickerston took a breath.

"I believe five or six wounds were from shotguns. Some were to the torso or abdomen. Some were to extremities, probably mostly legs. All, I think, were hunting accidents. A couple more were rifle wounds to the head, a double homicide, by a crazy ex-husband who couldn't abide by his ex dating someone else."

White interrupted. "Have you had any experience with pistol wounds?"

Bickerston looked at Dr. White with an uncomfortable stare that everyone in the conference room saw as a plea for mercy.

"Yes, sir. I do recall three or four such cases."

"Go on then," White said, showing no mercy at all.

"One case occurred when I was a first-year resident. A fellow tried to kill himself by putting a. 45 under his chin and pulling the trigger. He succeeded in blowing his face apart and in tamponading his airway."

"Did he die?"

"No, sir. The ER physician in the man's hometown somehow got in a tracheotomy. All I had to do was to help with the IV cutdowns and central lines. The ENT department handled most of the actual reconstruction."

"I see." White rubbed his chin. "What were your other cases?"

"I don't remember all of them right now, Dr. White."

Bickerston looked around, but no one stepped in to stop the inquisition.

"I know I've been in on two or three shootings that involved the highway patrol. Those were. 357 magnum wounds, mostly to the torso."

"Could you describe at least one of these cases?"

Bickerston cleared his throat. He needed help. This was far different than any M & M conference he had ever attended before. It wasn't a discussion. It was more like a target shoot, and he was the target.

"I do remember one case where a bank robber took a patrolman's bullet to his mid abdomen. The liver was fractured, the pancreas contused, the bowel lacerated, and the right kidney was ruined."

"All from one bullet?"

"Yes, sir."

"Did this fellow make it?"

"He got through the initial surgery, but died later when his pancreas auto-digested his suture lines. He became septic and bled out."

"It sounds like that one bullet really wreaked havoc on that fellow's insides."

"Yes, sir. It was like hamburger when we got inside."

"Was the shot that did all this damage from long or short range?"

"I'm not sure, Dr. White. I guess it was twenty or thirty yards."

Dr. Emmitt White stood up from his chair so everyone in the room could see him.

"Tell me then, Dr. Bickerston, with all of the *wealth* of your experience, some of which actually flies in the face of your recent actions, how did you decide you were justified in pulling such a theatrical stunt as doing a thoracotomy on the lawn of the VA?"

White paused so that his words could bore in deeply.

"The fact that this unfortunate man survived in no way excuses your monumental bad judgment. Qualified ER facilities and more qualified physicians were literally just yards away. Your actions not only jeopardized a man's life, but have also put the whole university on the line for possible liability charges. In fact, you have put our whole institution in peril. Only by the grace of God, have we escaped thus far."

White turned to directly face Bickerston.

"Dr. Bickerston, I have a great criticism for your actions involving this case, and as I have just witnessed your presentation here today, I have come to realize that you lack fundamental professional insight. That, I think, is a fatal flaw for any aspiring surgeon."

The whole room was stunned into silence. Bickerston felt the wind go right out of him. He looked at Tim Sullins and saw a smug, satisfied stare. Bickerston felt not only the chief residency slot, but probably his whole medical future slipping away.

Tim Sullins broke the silence.

"If there is no further discussion, I would recommend that this case be forwarded to the hospital-wide quality assurance committee for further disciplinary action. Additionally, there was a medical student who was involved. It is recommended that the dean's office be notified of this case's status and that appropriate disciplinary action also be taken under the dean's auspices."

Sullins looked around the room. No one said a word.

"May I have a show of hands then?"

The room was dead silent.

"Excuse me, Dr. Sullins."

"Yes? Who's that in the back?"

Mitch walked forward a couple of steps.

"Dr. Sullins, I think your recommendation is off base and downright inappropriate."

Some of Mitch's classmates in the room looked at each other. Mary Aspers, now Mary Peters, scooted a little over to her husband's elbow. "Bob, this time I think Mitch has had it! He'd be better off just keeping his mouth shut! If he keeps talking, he'll get thrown out with Bickerston!"

"Oh, the imminent *Dr.* Rice," Sullins said sarcastically. "What do you think you can really add here?"

Mitch remained standing, not budging an inch. "It appears to me, Dr. Sullins, that the whole crux of this case comes down to the judgments that were made about the severity of this patient's internal injuries and of the need for a speedy intervention."

Mitch walked all the way to the front of the room. He had the same killing look that he'd had that day on the lawn of the VA. Everyone present stopped breathing

"Dr. Bickerston has already explained the physical findings and clinical situation that led him to make the judgment that a pericardial tamponade was present. His judgment was correct. Immediate action was necessary for this patient's survival, and what Dr. Bickerston did was the only thing that saved this patient's life. I think your evaluation of this case is incorrect, and I question your motives in making it."

"Rice, I'm going to be more patient with you than you deserve."

Sullins was trying to act like he was in control, but he was obviously back-pedaling under the pressure of Mitch's frontal attack.

"Maybe you should tell us all, on what exactly you are resting your learned opinion? After you answer that, you can then tell me how you think you have the right to speak at this conference in the first place!"

"Dr. Sullins, you know damn well that I'm the medical student that you've just asked to be given the heave ho. That gives me the right to speak my mind."

Mitch walked right up to the withdrawing Tim Sullins and dropped his voice so only Sullins could hear.

"You started this. I didn't."

"And you think you're going to finish it?"

"That's up to you," Mitch said. His voice cut the air between them.

Mitch turned and faced the whole room. "I thought morbidity and mortality conferences were meant for educational purposes, not for disciplinary actions. This isn't a professional review board, Dr. Sullins. You're out of bounds here."

Mitch saw Dr. Golden nodding and pressed on.

"The real issue here is one's understanding the difference between a low velocity bullet wound and a high velocity one. Dr. Sullins, you and Dr. White seem to be blowing right by that."

Bickerston looked at Mitch who suddenly seemed strangely detached. Standing up to re-engage in the fray, he started to speak.

"Sit down, Dr. Bickerston!" It was Dr. White. "I want to hear this medical student explain himself!" Dr. White turned back to Mitch. "Dr. Rice, just how do you think you're qualified to have an opinion about any kind of gunshot wound?"

Mitch turned slightly so that he fully faced the neurosurgeon.

"Dr. White, this is a medical school. I have always thought that any school was a place where one began to learn. One usually learns by observing and by listening to the knowledge of others."

Mitch saw Dr. Golden sitting impassively.

"Someone once told me that wisdom was the ability to recognize truth when one saw it, irrespective of who was bearing it. Dr. Bickerston understood that and saw the difference between a low velocity and a high velocity wound. He realized that, if the pericardial tamponade could be relieved immediately, the patient might survive. He recognized that little other internal damage was likely to be present. That meant that the risk was outweighed by the potential benefit of his actions."

Dr. White, affronted and stunned by Mitch's lecture, shrugged uncomfortably.

"Well, I'll give you this much, Rice. You don't lack for courage, just common sense. Just who do you think you're talking to?"

Mitch stood his ground, ignoring the last question.

"Dr. White, just how many similar cases would you think one would have to have involved in to have the necessary experience to make good judgments in a case like this?"

White, incredulous at Mitch's persistence, almost stammered. "Several dozen, I think, would suffice."

"Would two hundred such cases be considered enough experience then?"

"Who here has such experience?" White snorted, trying to reassert himself! "Not even Dr. Golden himself has that many cases. Do you, Chuck?"

Dr. Golden cleared his throat. "No, Emmitt, I don't."

There was a small smile on his face.

"Dr. Rice, I believe that you and I have had discussions about gunshot wounds before, haven't we?"

"Yes, sir. We have. I believe we discussed high velocity wounds and their implications on the very first day I began classes here."

"As I recall, you explained your obvious depth of knowledge of such things then by stating that you were a combat veteran and that you yourself had been a victim of such wounds. Is that right?"

"Yes, sir."

"Would you tell me now just how you *really* came to have such knowledge. That first day has always intrigued me. I think it would be good for our discussion today if we all really understood the depth of your knowledge."

Mitch seemed to withdraw into himself a little. He paused and then looked up, straight at the chief of surgery.

"Dr. Golden, in my military career, I was trained as a Marine scout/sniper whose specialty was counter intelligence. I was cleared for classified insertions and was deemed qualified for independent actions. I was good at my work and have a variety of decorations to prove it."

Tim Sullins looked thunderstruck.

"Good God! It's true? You've killed two hundred men?"

Mitch turned and focused directly on Sullins. With the calmness that he had always brought to his trigger finger, he calmly said.

"With surgical precision, sir. Even when I was nineteen I knew what it meant to be a *professional*."

No one in the room moved even an inch. The echoes of Mitch's just-made admission froze them in place. Mitch turned away from Sullins and looked over all the widened eyes and open mouths that were glued to him. Somehow everyone there saw the horror of the killing fields where Mitch had once walked shining in his eyes. What they saw was too horrible to bear. After a long moment of tortuous realization, they all looked away.

A short eternity later, Dr. Golden quietly starting chuckling.

"I think this time I'll have to defer to one of greater experience, Emmitt. If Dr. Bickerston had the good sense to see truth in the advice he was given when the chips were down, then I think that Dr. Bickerston deserves credit for his actions, not criticism. If this was a tribunal, which it is not, I would vote against the recommendations that Dr. Sullins has made."

He looked over the room.

"Are there any others who agree with me?"

The room was a forest of raised hands.

"Good. Enough of this case then. Let's get on to the next one.

Mary Peters whispered into her husband's ear. "Do you think Tim Sullins would like a cup of hemlock about now?"

Bob whispered back to her. "Hari Kari would be better, and I'll be happy to supply the knife."

Mary snuggled into her husband's elbow. "Make it a dull one then. Sullins needs to bleed out real slow."

Chapter Twenty

Nicki and Mitch walked up to the door of Nicki's apartment, enjoying the colorful lights and festive decorations that bedecked the whole complex. It was almost Christmas… Nicki's favorite time of the year.

She and Mitch were coming in from an enjoyable night on the town. They had eaten, talked, and danced, and Nicki had glowed all evening. Mitch, however, hadn't seemed to be with her. Several times throughout the evening Nicki had almost gotten upset at his obvious lapses. For example, it had been halfway through the night before he had commented on her new green party dress. And he never did mention her new hairdo. But it was Christmas so she had decided to hold her temper.

So all evening long Nicki had smiled and laughed and had done more than her share to pump a little Christmas fun into their date. After a while it had seemed that Mitch finally did catch some of the Christmas spirit. But when the evening was over, Nicki wasn't totally sure whether everything was okay or not. Certainly she wasn't feeling the warm glow she had expected to feel. Whatever was eating him, she finally figured, he'd tell her whenever he was ready.

As they approached her door, Nicki tried once more to salvage the rest of the evening.

"You don't have an early day tomorrow, do you, Mitch?"

"No. I guess not."

"Good. Come on in for a while. I don't want the evening to be over yet."

"Well... okay... sure."

Nicki's patience snapped.

"What's with you, Mitch? You haven't been really into the whole evening. Don't you *want* to come in?"

Nicki felt like she was forcing herself on him, and she didn't like it. It wasn't as if he hadn't been in her apartment before. They had been dating now for more than a year and a half, and she,d given him the run of the place. Something big was wrong.

Once they were inside, Nicki went over to her little stereo where her Carpenters album was already on the turntable. Nicki had planned for the duet's easy sounds to help keep the evening warm, but Mitch didn't seem interested. Now both angry and scared, she decided to find out what was really going on.

"Mitch, have I done something wrong?" she demanded.

Mitch sat down on the edge of the couch, looking like he wanted to be somewhere else. It was a long, quiet minute before he answered.

"No, Nicki, you've done nothing wrong."

He looked lost, panicky.

"I guess it's just me."

Nicki began to feel really threatened.

"Then could you explain things a little for me. You don't look anything like the guy I just had a wonderful evening with. What's going on?"

His gaze kept going back to her front door, like he was looking for an escape route.

"I... I... I guess I really just don't know what's wrong, Nicki," he finally half- croaked. "Look, I really do *like* you. I've known that for months now."

"That's good," she answered.

She felt real terror now... the way he said "like." Was this how a break up happened?

"But what?"

"I..." Mitch was really floundering. "I can't remember when I have had a better time than I've had tonight. I guess I just don't want to do anything that would mess it up."

Nicki just looked at him, not believing what she was hearing.

"So how do you think you're going to mess it up?"

Mitch looked truly awful. He was in agony—no longer the mythical figure of his med school legend, no longer the giant killer of chief residents, no longer the already accomplished, compassionate caregiver Nicki had seen in action so many times. In place of all that, Mitch was now a stranger, a schoolboy who apparently wanted to say goodbye and who didn't know how.

Mitch took a long, deep, shuttering breath and started again.

"I never thought I'd ever say what I'm going to say right now."

Nicki caught her breath. The ax was falling, and her heart was on the block. She braced herself for the fatal blow, not believing Mitch was actually doing it.

"Nicki, I don't have anything to offer you. I'm just a used-up mess who doesn't belong anywhere."

She felt a tear run down her cheek.

"I don't think I even know *how* to love someone. I sure as hell can't love myself."

Another tear fell.

Mitch reached into his coat pocket and took something out.

"I'm pretty sure I'll make your life an awful mess. So…"

Two more tears trickled down her cheeks.

He held out his hand to her.

"So here's the deal. I can't live without you. Will you marry me?"

Mitch was holding a medium-size diamond ring. It shone with a clear, blue-white light.

"I… I… I…" It was her turn to stutter.

Mitch turned almost transparent. He was scarcely more than a ghost.

"I'm sorry," he said, totally defeated. "I thought…"

Nicki felt the floodgates inside her starting to let go.

"You thought what, Mitch?"

"I thought… oh, what's the use!" he exploded. "Nicki, I love you! I want you! Will you *please* marry me?"

Nicki tried to speak but couldn't. She was choking in the vacuum left by her suddenly evaporating terror. She could only hear the sound of her heart crying out in relief.

"Yes," she said simply. "I will marry you."

Nicki suddenly found herself lost in Mitch's arms. Her heart which had been beating like a frightened bird just moments before, suddenly surged inside her like a great wave racing toward the shore. She reached up for his face and found his lips.

The kiss that followed was a sweet discovery of a whole new country, of a place full of vulnerability and strength. It was her first real glimpse of the life she and Mitch would lead together. The kiss lasted for a long, long time.

Much later, when they separated a little from another embrace, Nicki realized that she, like Mitch, also had secret places where no one else had ever stepped. She pulled back a little and looked into Mitch's face. She saw every emotion there that she had ever imagined possible. With the amazement of someone who had just stumbled across a great treasure, she nestled back into his arms.

"Mitch," she muttered gently into his chest, "just who exactly are you?"

Nicki felt him squeeze her hard, so hard that she could barely breathe.

"I'm just a man, Nicki. But I'm yours for as long as you'll have me."

She let him pull her in even closer.

"Good!" she whispered. "I figure that'll be just about forever!"

Chapter Twenty-One

"God damn it, Strong! What the hell is this?"

David Helsey was not happy. He held a document Wilson Strong had just handed him. It was a directive from the President of the United States.

"God damn you, Will! You just had to do another one of your damnable end runs, didn't you!"

"David, you weren't listening," Strong answered calmly. "In fact, no one in this whole God-forsaken place was listening. I had to get your attention."

"Get my attention! Why in blazes didn't you just come to me and tell me what was going on? I would have heard you out!"

"We tried that six months ago, David. Remember. I told you it was against everything holy to put Wade back into Nevada. *El Armario* is our most sensitive biolab. You ignored me."

Helsey looked like he was going to explode.

"Sarah gave you everything in Wade's file that we uncovered in his rehab. Did you read her report even once?"

Helsey said nothing. Strong knew the man had to be nearing critical mass.

"Go ahead and blow your lid, David. I flat don't care! You knew Wade was an unstable, traitorous son of a bitch even before Munich! You knew all about his paranoid personality disorder way back then.

And you knew that he hadn't improved, not one iota, in all the months and years since then, even with all the recycling you've put him through in the 'company's' psych ward."

Strong saw Helsey groping for words, but at this point any lies Helsey might spout would just reveal more of the truth. So Strong contented himself to watch his old adversary choke on his own silence. The man's famous poker face dissolved right in front of Strong. The distorted, angry expression that was left spoke more truth than any words.

"You don't really get it, do you, Wilson?" Helsey finally managed.

"Oh I get it just fine, David. Maybe a lot better than you realize."

Helsey sat back in his big desk chair, quickly regaining his composure. For all the bad things that he was, David Helsey was still a professional. Strong watched the man slide back into his robe of righteousness, a judge again governing his courtroom.

"Okay, Will! Okay! If that's the way it's going to be, then get on with it! Tell me what you think you know! I'd like to know just what was so almighty important that you had to put together a 'sting' operation on our own people! You've damn near ruined any credibility this agency will ever have with the White House!"

Strong laughed sarcastically. "That's pretty good, David! I'm glad you put it that way! Credibility and honesty aren't the same things… certainly not here and certainly not in the Oval Office!"

He sat down in a chair facing the director.

"You know as well as I do that the president wasn't going to give me the time of day until I mentioned the *Washington Post*! If he hadn't been running scared of the reporters, he wouldn't have even listened to me!"

Strong felt his sarcasm turning to sadness.

"Hell, once you figure a way to get him out of this Watergate mess, the president will be right back in your corner, and everything will be just as it was before."

Helsey shook his head. He wasn't so sure the political storm Wilson had just spoken of could be so easily repaired. The papers in front of him were presidential orders demanding Jacob Wade be pulled out of the underground biological weapons research lab in Nevada. The professor had been put back into his former defense department position almost a year ago. Helsey remembered that Strong had almost had a seizure over the decision and had vowed to prove it a bad one.

The months and months of psychological rehabilitation the agency had invested in the wayward professor meant nothing to Strong. Helsey had explained from the beginning that the professor's mental state or motives really weren't important. "So long as he's contained and monitored," Helsey had said, "all that really matters is that he continues his work on his retro viruses. There's no place on the planet more contained than *El Armario.* So let's just let him work."

But Wilson Strong hadn't been buying, not then and not now.

"Just explain this to me, Will. Why in hell did you plant an Iraqi national on the ground floor of that underground virus canister? You could have gotten someone killed!"

What the CIA director was referencing was an amazing bit of counter-espionage that Wilson Strong had pulled off. The imposition of a supposed Iraqi agent had given Wade the chance to prove that he was both willing and able to sell every bit of his viral warfare expertise to the highest bidder. Strong had planted the research assistant, a native of Baghdad, in the most sensitive part of *El Armario.*

That assistant, a very resourceful young woman, had managed to convince Wade that the Iraqi, even after the failure in Munich, still wanted Wade's little death viruses. No one in the research facility and no one under Helsey's control had any idea what was happening, and no one realized that the waiting arms on the outside were actually Wilson Strong's… or, rather, Sarah Thornton's, which was the same thing.

Sarah, under Strong's instruction, had recruited, configured, and controlled the Iraqi woman for the effort. Sarah, knowing all of Wade's psychiatric history, had been able to program the young woman with just the right combination of innocence, guile, and apparent blood lust so that Wade had easily accepted her as a true spy of the Iraqi leadership. With Sarah's guidance, the woman had arranged for the actual smuggling of a real viral weapon from Wade's level five security vaults to the outside world.

The accomplishment had totally blown away Director Helsey's validity. His concept of containing a known traitor in a secure area had suddenly been shown to be ridiculously dangerous. Helsey had been completely disgraced. The fact that the security of the country had never really been in question was of no consolation at all to the president. His sanctions were about to force Helsey to call in a lifetime's worth of secret markers just to survive.

"David, I told you that I wouldn't rest until Wade was out of that lab! He's bad, and it was wrong to put him there!" Strong spoke with a controlled rage. "No research facility is secure enough to hold a truly motivated saboteur like Wade. He's a genius, demented as hell, and completely motivated to bring us all down!"

Strong tossed another file on the director's desk.

"Here! It's all in the report that your own psychiatrists put together on him last year! I guess you didn't read this one either! Putting Wade in *El Armario* was like putting a pistol in his hands! You left me no choice but to get him out of there before he could pull the trigger!"

Helsey turned away from his accuser. He knew Strong would give him no quarter. Conventionality, the idea that there was both a right and a wrong, was a characteristic Strong had to the point of weakness.

Under normal circumstances, Wade would have never been able to get his viruses to the outside world. Only Strong's machinations had allowed that, but that still had been enough to make a point with an already beleaguered president whose party needed no more bad publicity. It was enough to get Wade out of *El Armario* and to nearly get Helsey's head chopped off.

Helsey shook his head. It was all a deception he should have seen coming, but he hadn't realized that Strong had learned to play so creatively dirty. It was a lesson he wouldn't forget.

Helsey turned back to Strong. As the director of the CIA, he had enough pull with higher powers to survive this surprise setback. Wade would have to be moved away from his lethal, little killers, at least for a while, but it wouldn't matter. The professor would leave behind more than enough of his genius to let lesser minds finish the work. The government would still get its super plague, and the CIA director would still oversee its use. And Will Strong and his princess would still feel the weight of his retribution. Helsey's face changed to a warm smile. Paybacks were always hell.

Chapter Twenty-Two

Nicki slipped her old Chevy into an open slot in the employee parking lot. The VA hospital was right in front of her and one more evening shift, her fifth in a row, was waiting.

This VA, however, was not in Columbia, Mssouri. Rather, this one was in Iowa City, Iowa. She and Mitch had been Iowans for over a year now. Mitch was doing a family practice residency in Cedar Rapids, and she commuted the thirty miles to Iowa City each day so she could continue working in the VA system.

Today, as the gray sun had barely lit her way down the highway, she wondered why in the world she was still doing all this driving. There were hospitals in Cedar Rapids, and her commuting didn't mesh at all with Mitch's crazy residency schedule. Whenever she pulled long stretches of tough shifts like she had now, she and Mitch became little more than acquaintances who just passed each other in the apartment halls. She hated it.

Nicki started to turn off the car's ignition, but the tape player was playing Roberta Flack. Nicki loved the Roberta's haunting notes and decided just to soak in the beautiful sounds for a little while longer. She was a little ahead of schedule anyway.

The last year had been tough. Work schedules, both hers and Mitch's, had been harder to cope with than she had ever imagined. Mitch had changed her. Before him, she had been an independent, modern girl.

After him, she had become a hopeless romantic who couldn't stand the times they were separated. The real, post-honeymoon world required a lot more self-sacrifice than she was sometimes willing to make.

Nicki closed her eyes and once more saw the church aisle open before her. She again had on her magical white gown.

"I guess it's time, daughter," her dad had said.

She had squeezed his arm, looking out at all the faces that were turned her way. Her mom and brothers had all been there, and right behind them, sat General Strong and Sarah. And there, at the far end of the aisle, had stood Mitch.

"Yeah, Dad. It is."

She heard the huskiness in her dad's voice, but she knew that it wasn't the time to talk. They had already done that.

"Mitch had better be ready to take care of you, Nic. No more government shenanigans with that general friend of his."

Nicki had squeezed her dad's arm again. "I really want him, Dad. He's so much like you it hurts. We'll be just fine, just like you and Mom have been.

Her dad didn't say anything. He had just leaned down and gave her a peck on the cheek. Then he had taken her in hand and started down the aisle… her first walk in a new world, the one she and Mitch were creating.

Nicki heard the replay switch in her eight-track player kick over, and Roberta kept singing.

The wedding that had followed had been a timeless blending of tradition and Eucharist, and she stored the whole ceremony verbatim in the part of her memory where she kept only her greatest treasures.

The reception afterwards had been full of laughter and dancing. First Mitch, then her father and brothers, and then a whole line of family and friends had spun her all around the floor. Finally there had been Wilson Strong.

"Are you too tired for one more time around the floor?" the general had asked her. Mitch had just rescued her from her uncle and was taking her back to the head table.

"No, general. I'd love to dance with you," she had answered. "You've come all the way from Washington, and I've barely had a chance to talk with you."

Mitch gave the general her hand.

"I'll take good care of her, Mitch," Strong had said.

"You darn well better!" Sarah interjected. "Come on, Mitch! You're mine for this one!"

Nicki and the general had glided easily onto the dance floor, leaving Mitch and Sarah trying to disentangle themselves from Mitch's feet. He was an awful dancer.

"Mitch always has had the best luck with women," Strong had begun. "You're truly beautiful, Nicki."

Nicki had blushed in spite of herself but rallied anyway. "And just how many other women have there been, general? Maybe Mitch is holding something out on me?"

Strong had laughed. "Believe me, dear. Mitch has no one in his past even remotely in your league. You're his whole ballgame."

She relaxed. "I know… but it's still nice to hear you say it."

The general had pulled her a little closer as they swayed and flowed with the music.

"General?" Nicki had been watching Mitch and Sarah at the other end of the dance floor. "You know, at first, I thought Sarah was my biggest opponent, but I was wrong."

"What do you mean?"

"You know what I mean. Women always seem to think that other women are their competitors, but Sarah isn't. She wants Mitch and me together as much as I do."

"That's right. She does." Strong had chuckled quietly. "Poor, old Mitch never had a chance. With the two of you pulling him the same direction, he had no chance at all." The general had smiled gently. "Sarah and you are sisters, Nicki."

"I know," Nicki had said again. "And I guess that makes you and me relatives too, doesn't it? We are a lot alike."

The general had held her a little out away from him, surprised at her comment.

"Oh, don't worry," Nicki smiled. "I know we're all on the same side. You and I have something very special in common… Mitch. When it's all said and done, that's something that we'll always be able to hold onto."

The general had gathered her back in. After a long pause, he answered, "I can't argue with that."

"But, general," Nicki went on, "there is one place in all this where you and I are completely different." She stared right into his eyes. "All the missions you sent Mitch on… all those times you were willing to use him up… I'm not like that at all." Her voice held a steel edge that she made sure he couldn't miss. "I won't use him up, general. He's *mine*! I'll love him, care for him, and make him whole!" Feeling a sudden, fierce, possessive fire, she had let her gaze rip right through Strong's tough exterior. "He would have *died* for you any number of times, general. But, for me, he'll *live*!"

Nicki remembered that her voice had slipped into a different place. It was a place she still only vaguely knew, but it was a place where her greatest truth lived.

"I'll *make* him live, general! I'll make him live forever!"

Nicki's words had almost stopped Strong right in the middle of the dance, but he had recovered and had pulled her in tight to his chest.

"Yes, Nicki, I believe you will." His voice was husky. "I think Mitch has finally found his home."

The eight-track in the Chevy's dash was just about to cycle through again, and Nicki realized she was out of time. She got out of her car, took a big breath, and started to walk across the lot to the employee entrance. Working was the pits! Why couldn't she be home with Mitch? She punched at the elevator call button with a quick, violent thrust. She wanted to go home!

Mitch slipped into his call room. It was early evening, and he was beat.

The day's activities on the OB floor had gone at full throttle. He had delivered three free clinic patients, assisted a couple of staff men in their C-sections, and covered the hospital's free OB clinic most of the afternoon. Even his supper had been interrupted by a panicky situation when a third-time mother had precipitously delivered her baby in the public elevator before she could even reach the OB floor.

That last event had actually turned out to be almost comical. The young woman had been beside herself with embarrassment and had dissolved into a torrent of hysterical tears over her new baby's impatience.

Both she and her baby boy were fine, and Mitch had tried valiantly to reassure the flustered mother.

Unfortunately, nothing he could say or do seemed to be right.

One of the seasoned staff OB nurses had tried to help by intervening with a description of another situation some two years earlier when a young mother had delivered right in the lobby, not even reaching the elevators. The nurse's efforts went completely awry, however, and the young mother became even more hysterical.

The situation had almost gotten completely out of control when the woman had finally blubbered out through a wave of tears that, two years previously, "that was me too." Her admission had stunned both the nurse and Mitch into silence.

The newborn little boy, however, had been totally unimpressed with his mother's previous delivery experience and had started squalling bitterly over the chilling change of climate that he had just experienced with his entry into the world. His cries were enough to quickly change his mother's hysteria into honest laughter, and by the time everyone had reached the OB ward, everyone was smiling.

The rest of the early evening had settled down to a state of relative normalcy, and by 10:30 or so, Mitch was all caught up.

"Anything else going on around here?" he asked the OB floor nurses.

"No, Dr. Rice. Everything's quiet," they snickered. "Even our elevator lady has settled down."

"Good," Mitch answered. "I'll be here in the call room reading. Buzz me if you need anything."

"Sure, Dr. Rice. Get some shuteye. We're going to have a quiet night."

Mitch shrugged an acknowledgment. "Okay, girls, but don't jinx us." He really wasn't superstitious, but he had already learned the foolhardiness of challenging fate with rash statements. He grabbed his textbook and slid onto his bunk. There, after a couple hours of reading, some dozing, and lots of wistful thoughts of times better spent with Nicki, he finally fell asleep.

Mitch awoke with a start and lunged for the phone at his bedside. It was 3:00 a. m. "Yes? This is Dr. Rice," he mumbled into the receiver.

"Dr. Rice, would you come out here and check a new admission of Dr. Westus?"

"Sure. I'll be there in a second," Mitch said, becoming more alert.

Alex Westus was an old bull moose of an OBGYN who had little time for family physicians and even less tolerance for residents. Mitch hated dealing with him, but a lot of young, soon-to-be mothers still loved his gruff but caring ways. They still flocked to him just as their mothers had done before them.

Mitch grabbed his lab coat and hustled into the exam room.

"Hello. I'm Dr. Rice. I'm the resident on call." Mitch said as he came up to the young, laboring woman. "What's the story here, Dana?" he asked the nurse who had the chart.

"Dr. Rice, this is Sheila Gray. This is her third baby. She's due. She says labor began about an hour ago, and everything seems to be moving along pretty fast."

It was going to be a night for impatient infants Mitch thought.

"Mrs. Gray, I need to check you so that I can tell Dr. Westus what's going on. Okay?"

The young woman grabbed at Mitch's arm and squeezed it desperately. "Oh, God! Please hurry! This is all wrong! I'm going to die! Save my baby!" She had a look of utter panic on her face. "I'm going to die!"

"No one's going to die here, Sheila," Dana Lewis answered. "Just do what we say, and everything will be fine."

Mitch gently pulled his hand free. "Dana, have her membranes ruptured yet?"

"No!" Sheila Gray screamed. "My bag of waters isn't broken yet! Please hurry! This is all wrong! The pain won't let up! Help me!"

Mitch reached out and touched her abdomen. It was hard as a rock. "Have you had any bleeding?"

"I don't think so!" The young woman was gasping. "Oh, God! It hurts!"

"Dana, what are her fetal heart tones?"

"About 140."

"Mrs. Gray, I need to check your cervix so we can see just how close your baby really is to being born."

He still had his hand on her abdomen, and it was still rigid as a board.

"Oh, God! I'm dying! Save my baby!" Sheila shrieked again. Her eyes were widely dilated, her face covered with sweat.

Mitch moved toward the foot of the exam table and gently began the exam. Scant seconds later he stepped back.

"Let's get her into the delivery room right now, Dana! She's nine centimeters and coming down fast! Get a large bore IV into her right away! I'll get Westus!"

"Right away, doctor!" Dana replied. She had a question on her face.

"I think she's abrupting!" Mitch said as he stepped for the door. "Get lab up here for a stat cross match!"

Sheila Gray's shriek drowned out any reply. There were no words in the intense scream, but its message was clear. A birth and whatever else the fates had in store were both very close. Mitch ran for the phone.

"What's your story, Rice?" growled the sleepy obstetrician.

"Dr. Westus, we're going into the delivery room now with a G3P2 lady of yours named Shiela Gray! She's nine centimeters, vertex, and about to precipitate! I don't like her uterus! It's rigid, and I'm worried her placenta's tearing free!"

"Is she bleeding, Rice?' Westus was still growling.

By his standards, residents always thought the worse and were always overreacting.

"No, sir, but her abdomen is board-tight and won't relax at all! She's screaming her head off and is diaphoretic as hell! Dana Lewis says for you to get your butt down here *right now*!"

That was enough to wake Westus completely up. Mitch knew the man respected the floor nurses far more than he respected the residents. It had been time to play the trump card.

"Okay. I'll be right there!" Westus answered.

"We're trying to start an IV now, Dr. Westus," Mitch pushed on. "What about a cross match of six units?"

"Damn it, Rice! Get the IV, and do a CBC like we always do! Don't do anything else until I get there!"

Mitch slammed the phone down and ran for the delivery room. The screams inside were reaching a crescendo.

"Dana, how are we doing? Dr. Westus is on his way!"

"I don't know, Dr. Rice! The fetal heart tones are 180, and I can't get her IV started! She doesn't have any veins!"

Mitch looked at the young woman and saw that she suddenly looked ashen. "What's her blood pressure?" he demanded.

"One eighty over ninety, but her pulse is over one sixty!" answered Jenny Glass, the other nurse on the unit.

"Great!" Mitch snapped. "She's getting shocky! Let's get that IV started!"

Sheila Gray looked right at Mitch. "I'm dying *now*! Save my baby!" She had no color in her face at all.

"Fetal heart tones just dropped to fifty!" Jenny gasped.

"We don't have time to wait for Dr. Westus, girls! We have to deliver right now!"

Mitch went down to stirrups, throwing on a scrub gown and gloves as he went.

"Keep trying for that IV, Dana! Jenny, call the blood bank and have them send up all that O negative whole blood they drew yesterday for that aorta case! I want it all!"

"Oh, God..." Sheila's scream faded away to silence. She was at the end of her rope.

"Give me a set of Elliot forceps right now!" Mitch snapped. "We're losing them both!"

Just then Alex Westus flew into the room. He must have been sleeping in his scrubs because only three or four minutes had elapsed since Mitch had hung up on him.

"Dr. Westus, she's complete and deliverable!" Mitch snapped. "We've just lost her BP and the fetal heart tones are under forty! We have to get this kid out now!"

"Give me those forceps, Rice! You'll have the baby until the pediatrician gets here! Move!"

Mitch yielded the metal blades to his senior and stepped aside. Less than a minute later he held the limp body of a newborn baby girl in his arms. Running for the newborn isolette, he saw the horror of a completely detached placenta falling out of Sheila Gray's vagina right onto the floor, propelled by a huge gush of blood clots. The abruption had been complete.

Mitch saw that the mother was slipping away, and realized that somehow he had to resuscitate the baby that she had pleaded and spent herself for. Grabbing a laryngoscope, he began a rapid, desperate effort to cheat death of at least the younger of its two victims.

"Where's that IV, Dana? She needs pitocin and volume!" Dr. Westus yelled.

"I'm trying, Dr. Westus! But I can't find any veins!"

"What's her BP now?" Westus asked. He was furiously massaging the hemorrhaging uterus, trying to force it to stop bleeding by the sheer pressure of his grasp. "Fifty by palpation!" Dana yelled back. "I can't count her pulse! It's too fast!"

"Get the anesthesiologist in here!" Westus ordered. "We need a subclavian line now!"

The anesthesiologist on call was in the hospital, but was five or six minutes away at best. That was too long.

"We've got a DIC going here!" Westus cursed. "Her blood clotting factors are all used up, and I can't stop this damn bleeding!"

Alex Westus looked up and saw Dana Lewis shaking her head. "She's going, Dr. Westus. She's…"

Sheila Gray had just taken a long, shuddering breath. "I can't breathe… Oh, God… save my baby…" Her pupils began to widen even more than they already were. The end was right in front of her, and she couldn't look away from it. "Save my baby…"

Suddenly, there was a little cry from the side of the delivery room. It was her baby girl. Mitch had been fast enough with his endotracheal tube. Sheila Gray's prayer had been answered. Her little girl was going to make it.

"Give me that needle!" Mitch barked.

He left the baby warmer and came up to the delivery table almost like a man possessed.

"Get out of my way!" He almost pushed Dana out of the way. Grabbing Shiela's right collarbone, he shoved the large catheter needle straight in, aiming right for the top of her breastbone. He knew he had to be in the large chest vein, but no blood came back into the attached syringe.

"I can't feel her pulse…" Dana whispered.

Mitch grabbed a scalpel from Dr. Westus's instrument table.

"God damn it all to hell!" he cursed. "This friggin' thing isn't over yet! Give me that damn IV line!"

He cut deftly down on the large veins in Sheila Gray's right antecubital fossa. Squeezing the elbow as though his fingers had eyes, he threaded the large IV catheter into its dry vein.

"Here, Jenny!" he ordered the other nurse. "Pump that saline hard!"

He jerked a unit of whole blood out of the just arrived blood bank supply and hooked it to the IV line besides the saline.

"Dana! Push this blood in! I'm going to cut down on her other arm!"

"Cool it, Rice!" Westus ordered. "She's gone! We're too late!"

"No, we're not, you arrogant son-of-a-bitch!" Mitch exploded. "Get out of my way! She wants to live!"

Westus drew back, stunned by the violence in Mitch's voice. He saw that all of the bleeding from the vagina had stopped and knew that Sheila Gray was out of blood. He was too defeated to even protest Mitch's affront. He just stood back and let Mitch have the space he wanted.

"There! Give me more blood!" Mitch demanded as he pushed in another IV catheter, this one in the other arm.

"Breathe! Damn it, Sheila! Breathe!" He slammed his fist down onto her chest in a huge precordial thump. Grabbing an endotracheal tube, he wrenched her mouth open and shoved the airway into place.

"Breathe, Sheila! Your baby needs you! Breathe!"

"Oh, to hell with it!" Alex Westus shuddered. "Here, Jenny. Give me that blood! Start another unit!"

Westus looked at Mitch. The old man knew the angel of death was in the room with them, demanding his due. But Westus saw Mitchell Rice wasn't going to give in. Westus watched Mitch'e eyes grow even wider than Sheila Gray's fixed-pupil death stare. They were on fire. It was almost as if this Mitchell Rice was pouring his own life into her. Westus knew the woman was already dead, but somehow this crazed young man wasn't letting her soul leave. Westus saw Mitch curse, sweat, plead, and swear viciously. And for all that time, Westus heard the new little girl in the warmer adding her own voice. It was a cry for her mother's touch, a wail for the embrace that was her birthright.

It was a struggle like Dr. Westus had never witnessed before in all of his years. Mitch pushed unit after unit of whole blood into the near corpse. He pushed air into her defeated lungs, refusing to let them deflate. He pounded and pumped on her exhausted chest, refusing to let her heart run empty. Westus and the nurses all helped, but it was Mitch who wrestled with the dark angel. The longer he worked, the wider and wilder his eyes grew. Mitch stood, not with grace or dignity, but with just utter, sheer stubbornness. And standing there, seeing the visions of the lives and deaths of his past, he fought death to a standstill.

After that, all that was needed was for Sheila Gray to hear the wailing of her newborn baby that needed her touch. It all amounted to such a clamor that her spirit had to listen.

"I think I can feel a pulse!" Jenny gasped.

They had just finished pumping in the fourth unit of whole blood, and Sheila Gray's young, strong heart was starting to respond.

"Good God!" Dr. Westus exclaimed, almost fervently. "She just moved her right hand!"

"And she's blinking!" cried Dana. "She's coming back!"

Several minutes later, it was all over. Sheila Gray was breathing on her own, her circulation once again supporting itself. More blood was still needed, but the red river running from her wounded womb had stopped. Her arms and legs moved as they should, and her voice, even though hoarse and full of tears, sounded true. And most wonderfully of all, her newborn baby girl was now peacefully silent, content in her mother's arms.

Death was forced to depart the delivery room just as it had entered, empty-handed. Those it left behind basked in the sudden glow of two special lives—one, new, and the other, reclaimed.

The next several minutes were for celebrating. Sheila Gray, her husband, Dr. Westus, the nurses—everyone rejoiced, grateful for the spared victims. Mitch smiled as best he could, but after just a few minutes he had to excuse himself. He was chilled, spent, almost empty. His eyes, scant moments before dilated full with visions of life and death, were now tightly constricted—hollow and drained from what he had done. Two lives had been saved, but the victory had cost him pieces of his very soul. It had been a good trade, one he was happy to have made. But he still needed time to recover, time to fill in his emptiness.

So as everyone in the delivery room celebrated, Mitch slipped out to the hall, trying to put away the sights, scenes, and faces of death that had again been his.

As he did so, it seemed he could hear an old woman's voice from the past reminding him that all life was connected, all of it being just a long chain. And then suddenly it struck him—life did come from death! Nothing was ever wasted! Everything was sacred!

And suddenly it all made sense. Victory did come from defeat! Salvation was possible! And with this discovery, Mitch's chilling stopped. He slumped into a chair behind the nurses' station. The voice of long ago had filled in his emptiness and made him whole again.

Nicki opened her car door and more or less fell in. She was beat. It was almost 10:30 in the morning. She had worked the entire evening shift, and then she'd had to double back because the charge nurse who was scheduled for the night shift had called in sick.

The floor had been crazy, and Nicki had worked her butt off. GI bleeders, cancer patients in various stages of disaster, and even an attempted suicide had all been part of the mix. And when the morning finally came, she'd still had to go to the special staff meeting.

"Well," she said to herself, "maybe, for once, Mrs. Wilcox actually got her money's worth."

Nicki was thinking of the hospital's nursing administrator who had been in charge of the staff meeting. At the meeting Nicki unloaded all of her professional indignation on the woman. Nicki spared nothing, explaining how the previous evening's near-suicide had happened just because the floor had been understaffed.

The unfortunate man in question, a terminal melanoma patient, had attempted to kill himself by disconnecting his IV and back-bleeding onto the ward floor. Nicki had been very lucky and had seen the pool of his blood seeping out under the door. She had been quick enough to reconnect all his lines before a code was necessary. Another fifteen minutes, however, would have told a different story. Adequate nursing personnel could have prevented the whole event. All the frightened, dying man had really wanted was attention, someone to talk to, and the dramatic gesture had seemed to him the only way he could get it.

Nicki had been livid with the administrator and had made her point even more poignant by throwing her blood stained uniform right on the woman's desk. (Nicki had slipped and fallen in the pool of the man's blood.) From the stunned expression on Mrs. Wilcox's face, the gesture might have worked. Nicki hoped so.

In the parking lot her faithful Chevy turned over on the first crank.

"Come on, girl. Take me home. You know the way."

Nicki always said her old car could find its own way home, and this morning she wished it was really true. She was one tired girl.

"Mitch, I hope you're home," she whispered. "I really need a back rub."

Mitch slipped his old Dodge into its space in the apartment complex's parking lot. It was late morning, and he should have been dead from the previous night. Somehow, however, the memory of Sheila Gray cuddling her new, little girl was still too fresh to let him be tired. The whole event had been—what had the chief called it?

"Oh, yeah, '… a life focusing event'," Mitch muttered.

Well, maybe it had been just that. Mitch got out of the car and looked around. Nicki's car was nowhere to be seen. Disappointed, he mumbled. "I guess she had to work another double shift. Damn that VA!"

He felt just like a little kid, wanting to tell her his whole story and feeling rejected because no one was home to hear him.

"Oh, hell," he mumbled, pouting. He kicked at a piece of gravel on the asphalt. "I guess she has waited on me more times than I can count," he muttered. "I'll just have to cool it 'til she gets back." He kicked another rock. He really was a disappointed little kid. "She'll probably be too dead to do anything but sleep anyway."

Mitch jogged up the sidewalk and bounced into the apartment. His running shoes, ever faithful, were right where he had left them two days before. Nicki wasn't there, and he had to unwind somehow. It was either that or explode. So he grabbed them, threw on his running gear, and took off. For a while the shoes and the wind would be all the listeners he would have.

Mitch's ritualistic purification runs usually lasted at least an hour and covered nine or ten miles of rural Iowa back roads. Nicki had come to expect them whenever he was getting too up-tight. It had taken two years of marriage for her to learn that there were times when she couldn't push him for explanations. Mitch always eventually told her what was on his mind. And his running, she had come to realized, was somehow his way of quieting the beast he had inside so he could talk to her. So she had learned to be patient… even when it hurt.

Nicki pulled her car into its slot next to Mitch's old Dodge. Looking up through her windshield she saw the familiar old towel on the porch handrail. It was Mitch's signal telling her he was out on the road, running again. She had once complained of his always being so drenched, dripping sweat everywhere, after his long runs. So now he was more considerate and always left a towel outside to dry off with before he came in.

"No, Mitch! Don't be gone! You're supposed to be here for me today!"

She got out of the car, almost crying, and started to go inside. Today, Nicki had really hoped Mitch would be here waiting for her. She wouldn't even have minded if he had been soaking wet. After last night, she needed some TLC. And anything else he might have wanted to give her would have been okay too. He was really blowing it.

Lots of times lately Mitch had been almost detached when he and Nicki had been together. The family practice residency was frustrating him a lot. Nicki knew he wanted to be a caregiver, and that's what family practice was all about. But she knew he was also a competitor, and always being at the back of the pack, right on the bottom of medicine's pecking order, was a hard pill for him to swallow. When he was frustrated, he ran. Sometimes miles and miles. It blunted his frustration, but it also dampened his spirit.

The end result was that the running contained his shadows, but it also dulled his sparks. Nicki didn't miss Mitch's dark ghosts. She had already spent too much energy learning to live with them. But she did miss his fire. And today, more than on any day in recent memory, she *really* needed that fire.

Nicki dejectedly unlocked the front door and went in, knowing the place was empty.

"Hey, lady! Welcome home!"

Nicki nearly jumped out of her skin.

"What the… !"

Mitch took no notice of her sudden surprise. He came right up to her, and his arms swallowed her whole. He had on his running shorts, but his muscled frame wasn't sweaty at all.

"Where'd you come from?" she gasped, recovering from his long hug. "I thought you were out running!"

"Sorry about that," Mitch said, sort of sheepishly. "I started to go out, but I knew running just wasn't going to cut it today. So I waited for you."

"Oh," she said. "I see." She pulled back a little, starting to smile. "What's on your mind, marine?"

"Oh, I was hoping the hot little lady who runs this place wouldn't be too tired for a little workout. What do you think?"

"I don't know," Nicki said with a bigger smile. "That might depend on what kind of workout you had in mind. You'd have to ask her."

Mitch slipped his arms down Nicki's form and lifted her right off the ground.

"I was thinking first about some light calisthenics," he deadpanned, putting her back down so he could lift her arms upward to free her of her top.

"And then maybe a little weight training."

He picked her back up and kissed her hard.

"And then I thought we might try a little aerobics."

Several minutes later both of them were panting.

"That was a pretty good warm-up," Nicki teased. "When does the real show start?"

"Right about now," Mitch answered as he gathered her totally nude form up into his arms. The bedroom was just in front of them, and a candle was already burning.

A long kiss later he gently deposited her onto their bed's smooth sheets.

"I was thinking a good back rub would be the best way to get started," he said.

"I don't think so," Nicki smiled, slipping back over to face him. "What I think this girl needs is a really good front rub." She pulled him down on top of her and snuggled into his chest, kissing him fiercely.

Mitch's answer was lost in her blond hair which suddenly surrounded him.

A few hours and a delicious nap later, Nicki stirred in Mitch's arms. He was really quite an eyeful, and she didn't hesitate to take in all of his lean form. Even his scars didn't lessen his beauty. She stretched upward and gently kissed him on each eyelid.

"Hi, lover," she said.

Mitch blinked himself awake. "Hi back at ya." He yawned shamelessly. "How'd you sleep?"

"I slept fine," she said, snuggling in close to him again. "I was just thinking about what you said earlier, Mitch. Maybe it *is* time for us to be thinking about a family."

He didn't say anything at first. He just stroked her face, first her cheeks and then her lips. He had a different look on his face.

Nicki cocked her head to one side. "I liked what you did this morning, Mitch. Setting me up like that. I thought for sure you were out on the road running. When you came up to me at the door, you scared me something awful…"

"But you liked it?"

"Uh-huh. I like it a lot when you get a little assertive. It makes me all goose fleshy inside when you really focus on me."

"You mean like now?" Mitch was taking his turn at staring. He was taking in her whole shape, from top to bottom.

"Yeah." She felt herself starting to glow. "Just like now."

"Good." He gathered her in closer. "I like it too."

He suddenly chuckled.

"What?" she asked, surprised by the amused look on his face.

"Oh, I was just thinking. I haven't felt quite like this since that afternoon up on 5-East in Columbia when I maneuvered you into canceling that other date so we could go out."

"Excuse me?" Nicki pulled back. "That's not quite the way I remember it."

Mitch smiled an impish grin and ran his hand down her throat onto her chest. "And just how do you remember it?"

Nicki was puzzled. She remembered the tongue- lashing Jane Chapel had given her over her initial refusal of Mitch's invitation, but she had never told Mitch about that.

"You don't really know what happened that day, do you?" Mitch said.

"I thought I did." Nicki said, frowning a little. "Why don't you tell me what I don't know."

Mitch turned over onto his back and folded his hands in behind his head. He looked smug.

"You remember how Jane Chapel gave you such a hard time over your turning me down in the elevator?"

"Yeah." Nicki turned on her side and rested her face in her cupped hand. "But I never said anything to you about that."

"I know. Jane did that for you."

"*What*?"

"Sure. She came up on the surgical floor right after morning report."

"Jane came up to 5-East? In the morning?"

"Yeah. She came up there and threatened my life. She said I was dead if I didn't wait for you to come and take back your refusal."

Nicki blushed several shades of red all at the same time. She rolled over onto her front and buried herself into the covers.

"I always knew Jane wasn't to be trusted! The rat!"

Mitch reached over and started playing with her shoulder blades. "Well, you might as well know it all."

Nicki rolled her face out of the pillow. "There's more?"

"Yeah. I wasn't totally sure that you'd come. So I talked to Mary Peters..."

"The lady med student? I thought her name was Aspers."

"Same person. She was married to Bob Peters by that time."

"Oh."

"Well, I didn't want anything to get fouled up if you did come by. So I had asked her to sort of hang close by. We more or less laid out a little plan to make it easy for you to ask me out. I thought if I made it seem like you were doing me a favor by reconsidering and all, you'd feel better about the whole deal, and things would get started on a better foot."

Nicki snapped right up off the sheets. She clutched a pillow in her hand.

"You mean all that talk about you being a basket case over my rejection was just bull?"

She cocked the pillow back over her shoulder.

Mitch threw up his hands to fend off her threatened blows.

"Actually, I *was* pretty disappointed when you said no, Nic. But I could still think. I knew I wanted to go out with you, and Mary was willing to help. The bit about me being worthless and her covering me was her idea."

Nicki drew the pillow back even farther.

"I think Mary and Jane were a lot alike. Both of them liked to think of themselves as real matchmakers," Mitch went on, taunting her, daring her to use the pillow.

"But you know, Nic." His face suddenly softened. "Jane was wrong about one thing."

"What? It looks like she knew more about the whole deal than I ever did! How else did you guys set me up?"

Mitch dropped his hands in surrender.

"I would have asked you out again—over and over—until you finally had said yes."

He smiled his wonderful, special smile that was just hers. "I knew what I wanted, lady, and I was willing to work for it. You just made it a lot easier than I expected."

Nicki let the pillow fall behind her, unused. Inside her a glowing sense of surprise was settling down to a firm, wonderful purpose. She lowered herself out of her threatening, upright kneeling position, and slowly let herself melt right on top of Mitch's torso. Locking her arms around him, she nuzzled in tight.

"So, marine, are you still willing to work hard for what you want?"

"Yeah," he answered. "Real hard."

"Good," she whispered. "Hard things are good."

Chapter Twenty-Three

In April, 1979, Mitch had just three months of residency left. His year as senior resident was almost finished. Life as an actual practicing physician was just ahead. It was a change he was ready for.

Nicki was ready for a change too. She had just four weeks to go in her pregnancy and could hardly wait to meet the new person inside of her. All kinds of exciting things were happening all at once. It was a time of new beginnings.

Nguyen Xuay awoke in the still dark hours of the Iowan dawn. He was a little disorientated. So much had transpired in the last ten or eleven years that he could hardly remember it all. Some of it, however, was as clear as the sunrise, which was just coming through his window.

Xuay closed his eyes, and once again he was dragging the lifeless form of General Truong back into the entrance of the underground Cambodian bunker complex. He remembered waiting for another of the assassin's bullets that would have let him join his general. He remembered how his ears had rung with the three fatal slaps of the silently launched bullets. And he remembered the emptiness he felt when that last bullet did not come.

It was the emptiness of total defeat, exactly the same as he had felt weeks before outside the wire at the Americans' Delta base. Failure had started to burn a hole in his soul all those years before. And now a decade later, his spirit was just ashes, all of it burned away and gone just like his long-absent left arm.

Xuay remembered the horrible days that followed the Cambodian assassinations. The Tet offensive had already been organized to the last detail, and the first part of it played out just as General Truong had predicted. They had overrun cities and bases all over Vietnam. It should have been enough to have driven the Americans completely out of Vietnam. But that's not what happened. Not only had the Americans not been driven into the sea, they had risen back out of their ruin and laid waste to whole divisions of North Vietnam's finest troops.

Hue, liberated intact on Tet by the North, had stayed free only for days. The Americans and their South Korean dogs had streamed back across the Perfume River Bridge like a wildfire and had retaken the city. It had taken house-to-house combat, just like the European cities of World War II, but the Americans had proven they were still capable of such things. And just like those European cities, about all that remained in the battle's aftermath, had been the burned-out hulk of a previously beautiful city. Hue, the Paris of the East, was left an incinerated corpse.

Xuay had not been in Hue for the great battle. He was then in disgrace following both his lost command at the Delta firebase and the disastrous assassinations of his three generals in Cambodia. It mattered little to General Giap that Xuay had lost his left arm and almost his very life on the wire at the firebase. (In fact, only the impromptu transfusions from his men's own arms had saved his life.) General Truong's sudden death at the hands of the "ghost rifle" had left Xuay unsupported and suspect. His next assignment, one to head up a suicide bomb squad for the attack of the U. S. Marine base at An Hoa, had come as no surprise.

Fate, however, had surprises of its own. Xuay's new command had been successful. An Hoa had been overrun and the proud U. S. Marines disgraced. Xuay, who had carried the last explosive charges right into the mouth of the final command bunker himself, had somehow survived its blast with only a severe concussion.

Xuay should have been decorated, but in the aftermath of the horrible American counterattacks that followed, his superiors looked for scapegoats. Xuay had been an obvious target for their dissatisfactions and consequently, in the months that followed, he had been given steadily worse and more hideous assignments.

Gone were honorable attacks and honest combat. In their place, Xuay was ordered to orchestrate terror. Murder, rape, and atrocity became his daily assignments. In the end, the blood lust had become so heinous that even Xuay's own tremendous need for vengeance had finally run dry. Even his final assignment, a six-month effort to find the "ghost rifle," had left him empty. Not even the posting of a $50,000 bounty, the largest ever offered for an American death, had bought him any peace. In the end he had neither honor nor vengeance.

Xuay's failure plus his subsequent opposition to the commanders' senseless campaign of terror were his undoing. His superiors had court-martialed him and sentenced him to years of hard labor in the same POW camps that held the very Americans he had helped capture. It was strange irony that those Americans, his sworn enemies, became first his cell mates and finally his allies.

When the war had finally wound down to its disgraceful end in 1975, those POW camp connections proved strong enough to give Xuay a way out of Vietnam. His name was changed to Cham, a fake medical record invented, and a whole new past created to explain his life. A long, tortuous course from refugee boat, to relocation camp, and then to America itself had followed. When it was all over, Nguyen Xuay had become a ward of the very country whose defeat he had once been willing to die for. Truth was indeed stranger than fiction.

Nguyen Xuay, now Nguyen Cham, looked out at the early morning sun that was now fully up in the sky. Today, he would return to the American flour milling company where he worked as an assembly line cleaner. As he looked up at the sun, he felt another of his awful headaches coming on. These headaches had been his curse all the months and years he had toiled in the POW camps. In recent days, they had become more severe, and this one would be the worst ever.

As Xuay looked at the rising sun, he suddenly felt his head almost split open, ripped from back to front, by a horrible, piercing pain of white-hot light. He fell, convulsing wildly, onto the small bedroom floor, knocking furniture and clothing everywhere.

The convulsion lasted for several minutes and then left him a limp, unconsciousness wreck. Two hours later, when he finally regained consciousness, he was without both his eyesight and much of his voice.

He could still speak and understand Vietnamese, but all of his English was gone. He was in a post-seizure state of confusion, and he was lost.

Several times before in the prison in Vietnam and a few times since coming to America, Xuay'd had times when his vision had temporarily blurred and his voice had become a little garbled. But his sight and words had always returned. This time was different. This time there was no return to normalcy. Xuay, already a refugee in a strange country, became a permanent prisoner of a dark, brown world where there was no color, no light, and no understandable words. He didn't even have his own real name. He was now Nguyen Cham, a blind, mute beggar trapped in an enemy's homeland.

The rest of Nguyen Cham's day was filled with shrill sounds of sirens and strange American voices. His head pounded mercilessly, and his neck stiffened to the point of absolute rigidity. His world was only a brown mist full of voices whose words he could no longer understand. Disembodied touches and unyielding restraints came at him from every direction, shaking him with a terror that made his first seizure seem almost nothing. He was coming undone, one sense at a time. And all the time he was disintegrating, the pain in his head worsened.

Mitch was on call as back-up resident for the ER at Mercy Hospital when they brought Nguyen Cham in. The ER's first-year resident, a conscientious woman named Jessie Felts, could make nothing of Cham's situation. She tried but got nowhere with the shaking, quaking oriental who understood nothing she said. Consequently, she called Mitch, her back-up, for help.

When Mitch hit the ER, he saw a Vietnamese male, a mid- shaft upper-arm amputee, who was obviously in the grasp of some sort of organic dementia. Mitch examined the fear-struck man as gently as he could, but the degree of central nervous system dysfunction was astounding, and made the exam difficult.

"Mitch, do you think this guy has had a subarchnoid hemorrhage?" Jessie asked.

"Could be, Jes. Something certainly has hit his squash hard, but I don't think a stroke would explain his fever. His nuchal rigidity is more like what I would expect from a meningitis or an encephalitis."

"Yeah, I thought about that," she said, "but his whole body was so stiff that I couldn't even think about doing a spinal tap. I was scared if

I did it, he might herniate his brain stem right in front of me and die on the spot."

"Does he have papilledema, Jes?" asked Mitch, inquiring about Cham's intracranical pressure.

"I don't think so, but he was so hard to examine that I wasn't sure."

Mitch looked at the writhing, trembling figure before him.

"Okay, Jessie, this is how we'll do it. We'll hit him with some IV Valium to relax him. Then we'll double-check his retinas, and if there is no sign of increased intracerebral pressure, we'll go right on to the spinal tap. That has to be where the answer is."

"Okay, Mitch, but I've never done an LP before on someone this sick."

"All the more reason why you should do this one then." Mitch gave her a reassuring grin. "It'll be all right, Jes. I'll be right here to help you."

Mitch looked back at the desk where the residents did their chart work. "Just let me call Dr. Williams so I can tell him what we have going down here. You get the Valium and LP tray set up while I clear everything with him."

Dr. Dick Williams was the chief of the residency. He and Mitch were a lot alike, both a little aloof and sometimes outspoken. Consequently, the two were not really friends and sometimes were just barely allies.

Today, however, the chief could find no fault with Mitch's plan of action, and he agreed to it all. Hanging up the phone, Williams rubbed his forehead. These Vietnamese boat people that now were settling into Cedar Rapids were presenting entirely new types of pathology that neither he nor his residents had ever seen before.

"Rice is probably the best man for this," he muttered. "He's been over there with all these weird tropical diseases. Let's see what he can come up with."

Dr. Williams had never delved much into Mitch's military background, but he knew Mitch was a stubborn dog who wouldn't scare off easily. Drumming his fingers on his desktop, he said, "Let's see what the spinal tap shows."

"Oh, God!" gasped Jessie Felts. "This spinal fluid is bloody!" She started to withdraw the needle.

"Don't, Jessie! It's just blood tinged! Wait a second for it to clear!" Mitch ordered.

The spinal fluid kept dripping from Nguyen Cham's back, turning from pink to a turbid, yellow color.

"You got a little bit of a traumatic tap, Jes, but that's not this guy's problem. His spinal fluid should be crystal clear, not junky and yellow like this."

The young Dr. Felts nodded her agreement and went on to finish the procedure, ordering a full slate of lab tests on everything she drew.

"Good job, Jes," Mitch said. "Get all this stuff down to the lab, and I'll get him admitted."

"Okay, Mitch. Thanks."

Mitch turned to head back to the main part of the hospital. "What do you think we have here, Jes?"

"I don't know, Mitch. It almost looks like some sort of meningoenchaphalitis."

Mitch nodded. "Yeah, I think so too. Write up a good set of orders, and I'll check them on the floor. Be sure to put him in isolation. This could be something contagious."

Jessie looked at her blood stained gloves. She hadn't thought about this being something transmissible.

"Mitch, whose service should I admit him to? I'm stuck here in the ER this rotation, and I don't get up on the floors very much."

"Admit him to me, Jes. The chief expects me to take this case anyway. I'll let you know all the answers when they come out."

She nodded and flung her gloves into a hazardous waste container. She was glad she didn't have to do anything more with this case. It was all kind of scary. She was happy to let "icemen" like Rice and Dr. Williams worry with it. Life was too short for this kind of stress.

Mitch was knee-deep in his family practice clinic, the same one he had run out on earlier to help Jessie Felts in the ER. He had used up a lot of time getting a room for his new patient, checking the orders, and getting the nurses squared away on the whole situation. It was time he really didn't have. So now he was working double-time to catch up.

Mitch was scheduled in the clinic all day long, and his schedule was pretty full. He had been in the program now for almost three years, and now commanded a pretty loyal following of patients. Happily, they were a pretty tolerant lot and seemed to understand that their doctor would get them treated as fast as he could.

Mitch enjoyed his patients a great deal and double- booked or not, he tried to do right by them. Consequently, the late morning passed pretty smoothly, and by early afternoon, he was caught up.

Mitch was in the cafeteria, grabbing a quick bite when his beeper started squawking. “Dr. Rice! Code blue! Room 5215! Code blue! Room 5215!”

“Oh, shit!” Mitch muttered under his breath. “That’s that Vietnamese guy! Here we go again!”

Mitch flew down the halls, out of the newer portion of the hospital, and into the older wing where the charity cases went. He burst into the room and saw Nguyen Cham shaking as if he were in the jaws of a big dog.

“Dr. Rice, his temperature is over 106! He was shaking so bad I couldn’t do a thing with him! I didn’t know what else to do but to call a code,” explained the floor nurse, a girl that Mitch didn’t know. “Is this some sort of seizure?”

“It might be,” Mitch answered. “Is that IV still working?”

“I think so! I had just finished giving him his first dose of ampicillin, and all this started! I thought he was having an anaphylactic reaction so I shut off the infusion! But I’m pretty sure the line is still good!”

“This doesn’t look exactly like any anaphylaxis I have ever seen,” Mitch said. “Let’s relax him with a bit of Valium, and I’ll go over him again. Be sure we maintain good infection control procedures.” Mitch injected the sedative himself. “We’ll need more blood cultures, and be sure we get a peripheral smear for malaria.”

“For what?” asked the shaken nurse.

“That’s right… malaria. This guy’s home was full of bugs we’re not used to around here. We have to check for it all. And we’ll probably need to get him into cooling blankets. I don’t want him cooking his brain from that fever. He already has enough problems in there.”

“Yes, doctor! I’ll get the lab down here right away!” said a new voice.

Mitch turned to it and saw it belonged to Sister Mary Stephen, the head of nursing. Mitch suddenly remembered that this floor was her personal stomping grounds. “Well, at least I have the ‘A’ team,” he thought to himself as he rattled off a whole string of orders. With Sister Mary Stephen on his side, Mitch had unlimited clout.

The next thirty minutes saw a lot of improvement. The Valium took hold and Cham's rigors went away. With that, the temperature fell quickly and was soon registering only 102.

"Sister, is there any lab work back from the spinal tap that we did this morning in the ER?"

"Yes, doctor. It just came in. Here it is."

Mitch took the reports that she handed him. He stopped when came to the chemistry report. What it said was totally unexpected.

"What do we have, doctor?" Sister Mary Stephen asked. She saw the wheels turning in his head.

Mitch hesitated. "Sister, I'm not sure. I have never seen anything just like this before. But this guy has a positive serology for syphilis. Since this thing started after he got his ampicillin, I think I have just seen my first Jarish-Herxheimer reaction."

"A what?"

"A Jarish-Herxheimer reaction, sister." Mitch repeated. "When someone has syphilis gets a big blast of penicillin, sometimes a lot of the germs die all at once. A lot of their intracellular contents are spilled *en masse* into the patient's circulation, and a severe reaction that looks a lot like a gram negative sepsis and an allergy reaction all wrapped up together can happen. I've never seen one before, but this is the way the textbooks describe it."

"Okay," sister answered. "What do we do now?"

"Just what we are doing, sister. We stabilize his aberrant symptoms, and then continue his antibiotics. It's only the first dose that can cause this. After that, everything is back to the routine." Mitch looked at his Asian patient. "But, sister, have the lab get me an FTA to make sure that this really is neurosyphilis."

By the next morning, Mitch's diagnosis was confirmed. The FTA was positive both in blood and spinal fluid, supporting the positive VDRL reports. No more rigors occurred, and as the rest of the lab analyses proved negative, Mitch switched to big doses of aqueous penicillin G. Now that he had a diagnosis, the treatment was cookbook. It was the recovery and the epidemiology that would likely be different stories.

Mr. Cham's neurological deficiencies were severe, and the prospect of doing a good infectious disease investigation was not a happy thought. Mitch knew the explanation of how a thirty-five-year-old emigrant had entered the country with active, undetected neurosyphilis was sure to make for a lot of good reading. It was the kind of stuff that would cause Mitch to "rub elbows" a lot with "city hall". Unfortunately, the bureaucrats who ran "city hall" weren't his favorite kind of people.

"So, Mitch," Dr. Williams began, "Sister Mary Stephen told me that you have a really wild case in the back wards. What did she say? Neurosyphylis? And a good old fashion "Jerxheimer" reaction to boot? That ought to be a grand rounds case if I ever heard of one."

"Oh, hi, chief," Mitch said, looking up from the chart he had been reading. "I like you too." Mitch grinned at his boss. "Oh, by the way, since I was officially in clinic when this whole thing started, you're actually my attending."

Dr. Williams' face stiffened a little. "So that's why Sister Mary Stephen was so insistent that I know every blow-by-blow detail of your little encounter with the spirochete. She knew I was already on the hook, didn't she?"

"I guess so, chief. You know you can never get anything by the sisters on their home turf."

Williams grimaced again. Mitch was quoting his own words back to him from the first year orientation lecture Williams had given all the new residents.

"Be careful, Rice. I still can bite if sufficiently provoked."

"I'm sorry, chief. I just couldn't resist."

Mitch paused.

"What is it, Rice? You're not one to hesitate about anything. You might not be right, but you're always goddamn certain!"

It was Mitch's turn to grimace. He and the chief always seemed to rub each other the wrong way.

"Well, it goes like this, chief. This Vietnamese guy really has neurosyphilis. That makes him a reportable case."

"So what? You've had lots of reportable cases. What's the problem?"

"The problem, chief, is that he should have been screened for this before he entered the country. He obviously had to have converted his serology before he hit our shores, or he couldn't have been this far progressed in his illness. So how did he get through undetected?"

"I don't know, Rice. Maybe someone made a mistake."

"Or maybe someone was bought off and the record falsified."

"Have you seen his immigration physical?"

"Yeah, it came in this morning. That's what I'm reading now. It reads lily white."

"Rice, I still don't see what the problem is? Just report the case, and get on with the treatment."

"Chief, if I report this thing and it turns out to be some sort of buy-off, this guy could get deported."

"So?"

"So… if he's sent back to Vietnam, he'll be killed. Chief, I don't feel right about reporting this just yet. At least, not until I know more about him."

Mitch looked straight at Dr. Williams.

"Boss, will you let me call this a nonspecific meningoencephalitis for now? It really is… sort of. Then I could have a little time to figure this whole thing out."

"Rice, what's up with you?" Dr. Williams asked. "You're my straight arrow, 'the iceman'. What's with this sudden interest in this guy?"

"It's just a feeling, chief," Mitch answered slowly. "I think I've seen this guy before. I want to figure out where that was before I send him off packing."

"Rice, you're nuts! Where would you have seen this Mr. Cham before? Timbuktu?"

Mitch took a long pause, trying to evade his superior's question. Realizing this wasn't a workable tactic, he slowly answered. "Vietnam, chief, or maybe even Cambodia."

Dr. Williams had seen the scar on Mitch's right side.

"Okay, Rice. We'll play it your way, but only for a while. So figure this thing out fast. Hospital administrators like Sister Mary Frederick don't stay fooled for long. I won't jeopardize either one of us to protect this guy's immigration status. Got it?"

Mitch smiled. "I got it, chief! Thanks! I won't take too long! I promise!" He was already heading down the hall as he spoke.

Mitch's schedule was really full for the next four or five days.

Early mornings were full of surgical procedures. Private practice was less than three months away, and Mitch wanted all the OR time he could get.

Mid-mornings and afternoons were full of clinic duties, ER coverage, and hospital rounds. At the top of this last list was Nguyen Cham.

The Vietnamese national's neurosyphilis was responding to Mitch's antibiotics, and he had already recovered all of his sight and some of his expressive language skills. But even though Mitch monitored his progress like a hawk, not enough of the language barrier had fallen to allow Mitch to learn much of his past.

Dr. Williams pushed Mitch hard to formally report the case to the state health department but had not yet completely forced the issue. Mitch knew, however, that the time left to solve his patient's mystery was running short.

Mitch's evenings were full of Nicki and the new life that she carried. She was just about three weeks away from delivery, and both she and Mitch were excited and nervous at the prospect of their quickly approaching parenthood. It was a special time, and Mitch relished it. The only fly in his ointment was the partially mute Nguyen Cham and the vague feeling of *deja vu* the man evoked every time Mitch walked into his room. Mitch just couldn't put aside the feeling that there was unfinished business between him and this speechless patient. Just before time ran out, Sister Mary Stephen came to the rescue.

"Dr. Rice?" she asked.

"Yes, sister?" Mitch answered as he worked his way through Mr. Cham's chart.

"Dr. Rice, what's your special interest in this case? I've read your notes, and, while you haven't lied about anything, you have really left a lot unsaid. Dr. Williams's attending notes are just as vague. You two are driving the utilization and review people crazy. Why won't you just say that Mr. Cham has neurosyphilis?"

Mitch sized up the nun. She had a reputation for being starch-stiff so he decided not to beat around the bush with her.

"Sister, there's a good chance that, if I call Mr. Cham's condition by its real name, he'll be deported. If he goes back to Vietnam, he'll be imprisoned and probably killed. I'm just not ready to set those kinds of wheels in motion. Nothing about all this feels right."

Sister Mary Stephen continued to stand quietly beside Mitch. "Would it help you if you had a reliable translator?"

"It sure would, sister. The other Vietnamese nationals who usually help us seem all to be unavailable, and I don't know why. If I could find someone else who spoke Vietnamese, then maybe I could figure out where I've seen this guy before."

Mitch looked up, but it was too late. His tongue had betrayed him.

"So that's it?" Sister asked quietly. "You think this man was an ally in your past, and you want to protect him?"

Mitch took a really big breath. His slip required that he give the nun an explanation.

"Sister," he started slowly, "have you ever heard of something called the 'brotherhood of arms'?"

She shook her head.

"Well, sister, it's an honor code of sorts. It requires soldiers to at least be honest with each other. Sometimes it's the only thing that makes any sense at all when the whole world is blowing up." He was chilling. "Sister. all the suffering, dying, and killing doesn't make any sense at all most of the time. Without some sort of honor, all the bleeding just becomes a mockery."

He saw that Sister Mary Stephen wasn't going to draw back.

"Normally, sister, none of this is much of a problem. It's usually pretty easy to be straight with the guys who fight with you."

She cocked her head a little to the side. "But?" she asked.

"But…" he said slowly, "but for some time now I've had the thought that this brotherhood probably includes your enemies as well as your friends."

As he spoke an image that had haunted his dreams for the last three nights ran through his mind's eye. The crosshairs of his scope were settling onto the forehead of a NVA general outside the bunker entrance in Cambodia. At the edge of his field of view was a one-armed man who looked a lot like Cham.

"You see, sister. I've come to believe that sometimes the men I fought had more honor than the men who gave me my orders. I won't see this guy Cham deported until I know how he and I are connected."

Sister Mary Stephen spoke without any hesitation. "You mean that, even if Mr. Cham has once been your enemy, you think now he's your brother?"

Mitch nodded slowly. "I guess so, sister."

"Well, Dr. Rice, if that's the case, then maybe it's time we spoke to Sister Elizabeth. She's one of our older sisters. She's had some mission experience in Southeast Asia, and she said she would help with translation if she was needed. I'll ask her to come visit with Mr. Cham. Perhaps she'll be able to help you with your problem."

Mitch was stunned, but he accepted the offer. "Thank you, sister. As usual, you're a lifesaver."

"No. Thank you, doctor. You see, we in the orders understand loyalty too. We'll be happy to help the two of you define your brotherhood."

And with that Sister Mary Stehpen spun on her heel and left. Mitch was left alone with his thoughts and Mr. Cham's chart.

The next evening, when Mitch finished with his clinic duties, he returned to Nguyen Cham's ward. Outside of his room, Mitch heard a gentle but older feminine voice fluently moving though the verbal rhythms that he had first heard at Mother Marie's orphanage. When Mitch closed his eyes, he could see Mother Marie. The memory was too real. He couldn't even enter the sick man's room. He couldn't because the face he had been seeing in his dreams, the face at the edge of the Cambodian crosshairs, was suddenly very, very clear. It was Nguyen Cham.

The next day was Saturday. Mitch had no clinic duties. He was supposed to have the weekend off. But he had come in to make rounds anyway. As he came down the hall, he saw that Sister Mary Stephen was waiting for him.

"Hello, sister. Are you on duty again today?"

"No, doctor. I'm supposed to have today for a time of recollection, but I thought that you would want to know what Sister Elizabeth has discovered about our Mr. Cham."

Mitch stopped in his tracks, not certain if he wanted to know or not.

Sister Mary Stephen went on. "Sister Elizabeth has learned that Mr. Cham has quite an interesting story. From what sister could piece together, it seems he originally came from a Catholic family from northern Vietnam."

Mitch maintained his neutral face.

"His family had taught him to hate the foreign invaders who controlled his country, and Cham thought the North was less corrupt than the South."

Mitch's face still did not move.

"He was a good soldier, Dr. Rice. He fought any number of battles and rose through the ranks. Eventually, he even became an important aide to one of North Vietnam's generals, a man named Truong."

Mitch winced.

"Is that a familiar name, Dr. Rice?"

Mitch took a slow breath. "Yes, sister, I know that name from a long time ago."

He felt like he was lying. How could he tell this nun that the face at the center of his cross- hairs, the first general he had killed almost ten years ago, had been this same General Truong?

"Our Mr. Cham had a different name then," Sister Mary Stephen said. "Sister Elizabeth couldn't get him to say it, but..." She caught Mitch's eye and held it. "But she did get him to talk about an opponent, a nemesis that haunted his life for most of 1968. It seems that this man, probably a Marine sniper, someone whom Cham calls the "ghost rifle," killed most of his company, almost two hundred men, as they attempted a night attack on an American Marine Corps camp. This same marine apparently also later killed this General Truong and several other generals."

Mitch didn't even blink.

"Sister Elizabeth is pretty sure these last killings were illegal assassinations in Cambodia."

Mitch still didn't blink.

"Our Mr. Cham dedicated his life in Vietnam to finding this American and killing him, but he never found him."

Mitch was stone-cold inside. All of his feelings were turned off. He knew no other way to deal with what Sister Mary Stephen was telling him.

Slowly, he asked. "Did she find out anything about how our Mr. Cham got his syphilis?"

"Sister Elizabeth isn't the shy type, Dr. Rice. She was quite specific with him about that. It seems likely that after the elusive marine sniper had shot off Cham's arm at the firebase, the blood Cham got after that in a transfusion must have been contaminated."

Mitch finally blinked. "That's quite a story, sister. Do you believe it?" His voice was very distant.

"I'll answer you this way, doctor. Sister Elizabeth says that there is as much truth in what Mr. Cham is saying as there is truth in what other people, such as yourself, aren't saying. So, yes, I believe his story." She looked down the hall towards Mr. Cham's room. "Isn't it strange, doctor, how so often mortal enemies can really become brothers if they just manage to get to know each other?"

Mitch looked away. "Sister, that's an irony that has haunted me for years."

His voice was distant. He was seeing visions of things long past.

"So, sister, what do we do about our patient now?"

"Dr. Rice, Sister Elizabeth took it upon herself to speak to our mother superior, Sister Mary Frederick. Sister Mary Frederick has told me to tell you that, if you are agreeable, she, as chief hospital administrator, will personally apologize for the laboratory error that indicated that Mr. Cham had been a victim of syphilis. As far as Sister Mary Frederick can see, your original diagnosis of a nonspecified meningoencephalitis was actually correct."

Mitch started to speak, but sister stopped him with a hand gesture.

"And Sister Mary Frederick has already spoken to Dr. Williams, and Dr. Williams has agreed that this case is not reportable to the state board of health."

She smiled a gentle smile.

"So you see, Doctor Rice, all we have to do is to complete the course of therapy that you have already begun and trust in the good Lord that our patient's recovery will be complete."

Mitch couldn't believe what he was hearing.

"Dr. Rice, sometimes the truth really is spoken ever so eloquently by an appropriate silence. All of the sisters, myself included, feel very strongly that this is the right thing to do."

Her smile grew a little more serious.

"We also think that no formal introductions should ever be made if Mr. Cham and his old enemy, the marine sniper, should ever cross paths."

Mitch didn't know what to say.

"Doctor, we have all prayed most of the night about this. Sometimes brothers should be officially introduced to each other only by their Father, and then only on the last day. Mr. Cham is coping with too many things now. To open up an old hurt would do him no service. Surely anyone who really is his brother would understand the wisdom of all this."

The nun's words bore into Mitch, leaving him both humbled and wonderfully unburdened.

"Yes, sister, I think you're right. Right now our Mr. Cham just needs to get well."

Sister raised her arm and touched Mitch's shoulder.

"And so do you, doctor. So do you."

She let a long, silent moment pass.

"Besides, Sister Elizabeth said the bounty that was offered for the death of this marine was never claimed and is still an open offer. Blood money is never a good thing, doctor. We would all feel devastated if somehow an old vendetta was allowed to revive."

She made sure she had Mitch's attention.

"Let the dead bury the dead, Dr. Rice. Life belongs to the living."

Mitch felt naked before this woman, but it was more like the nakedness of a small child rather than that of a shamed adult.

"Thank you, sister… for everything." He smiled at her. "Like I've said before, you're a lifesaver."

She smiled back and slipped her hands back into the sleeves of her habit.

"You and I do make a pretty good team, don't we?"

Mitch shrugged in agreement. "If you say so, sister."

"Well, I do."

She drew back and stood a little taller.

"But right now I need to return to the convent, and you need to finish rounds so that you can get back to your lovely wife. She is almost due, isn't she?"

"Yes, sister. Just two weeks to go."

"Well, get going then," she ordered and then she started to leave. Two steps later, however, she turned back and asked, "Oh, Dr. Rice?"

"Yes, sister?"

"See you in church?"

Mitch smiled sheepishly. "Yeah… okay, sister… in church."

"Good. You should go more often, you know. It would make your life a lot easier." And with that she was gone.

Months later Nguyen Cham marveled at his new life in this strange land called Iowa. He had fully recovered from his illness, regained his English, and even found a new job. He now worked as one of the chief cooks in the hospital cafeteria. It was a job he really enjoyed, and he was pretty good at it. In fact, he was so good that now everyone called him "Chef Cham." Some of the doctors were even talking to him about fronting him the money so he could start his own restaurant.

Life, Nguyen Cham realized, did come in cycles. Now he was on the upswing side of it. He hoped he could stay here for a long time.

Chapter Twenty-Four

The daytime sun was hot in the Nevada desert, even in December. It didn't matter if the wind blew or not. The sun burned down mercilessly and baked the ground barren. Normally, only the nighttime brought out the desert's life, but this time of year the ground couldn't hold its heat. Consequently, the lifeless, bright day slipped quickly into a bone-chilling, dark deep freeze where nothing moved. So the only lives the desert held stayed underground… day and night-prisoners of darkness, trapped in a land of brutal, burning light.

That was the way all the desert's inhabitants lived, both the natural and the unnatural ones. The only difference between the two was in the respective depths each called home. The desert's natural denizens lived just under the harsh surface. The unnatural occupants lived in places much deeper.

The latter places were much more threatening and forbidding than anything the surface's inferno had ever forged—huge, dark canisters warmed not by the sun, but rather by nuclear reactors. The desert held many such places, but the biggest was *El Armario,* the desert's "kitchen pantry," and that was where Jacob Wade was going.

El Armario had already been Jacob Wade's home on several previous occasions. He had been here in the 1960's when the place had been built. In those years he had watched and guided the complicated construction of this living tomb. He had even been the one who had coined the place's name. He still chuckled over the irony of calling this place a kitchen cabinet. He chuckled because all the *staples* stored here were meant only for *last meals*... or maybe last rites.

After his initial stint in the 1960s, the one cut short by Marilyn's ultimatum, Wade had returned here for a very brief time in 1974. That time he had returned with two marvelous little viruses, one called Ebola and the other, a mysterious retrovirus -- something that one day would be called HIV. He had just barely begun his work of marrying the two when the damnable Wilson Strong and his bitch, Sarah Thornton, had tricked him into showing his true colors.

In 1974, the prospect of the sweet, quick vengeance for Marilyn's death had been too alluring. He had smuggled his wondrous little viruses out of the *kitchen*, thinking he was giving them to the same Iraqi government he had tried to find two years before. But he found only that he had placed them right into the hands of the very CIA he wanted to destroy.

Many years had passed since 1974, and Wade had paid for his impatience many times over with years of semi-imprisonment, first in several CIA-sponsored psychiatric rehab programs and later in worthless appointments to no- name colleges scattered all over the country. The CIA had made a nomad out of him. But it was now 1981, and things had changed. He had learned patience.

Two presidential administrations had come and gone since Jacob Wade had last ridden the elevator down to the lab. Then the government was staggering under the aftermath of a presidential betrayal and resignation. Then everything in government had been suspect, and the conniving likes of Wilson Strong had found a way to pull Wade out of this sanctuary.

Now the country was reeling from the impact of its first ever oil embargo. People from coast to coast were stymied by their local gas pumps, and they were once again looking to Washington for answers. Consequently, the present president and everyone under him were groping for any new weapon they could find to reestablish a flow of cheap oil.

This new president, really only a stupid actor already teetering on the edge of senility, had easily been duped. Not even the debacle of the Iranian hostage crisis of his predecessor's doing had taught him anything. And so Jacob Wade was coming home, and *El Armario* -- the dark, hidden kitchen pantry dedicated to death -- was about to be his again.

El Armario was a cylindrical structure buried deep under the desert's surface. If erected on the surface of the desert, it would have stood nearly 200 feet tall. As it was, it was firmly rooted in the rock of the desert floor, hundreds of feet under the surface.

The research station possessed seven levels—the top three for administration and living quarters and the bottom four for biological weapons research and storage. Each of the four successive deeper levels was designed for more and more virulent microorganisms until finally the seventh level was reached. It was there that type four organisms were being studied, and it was here that Jacob Wade truly felt at home.

Type four organisms were the scourges of humankind. Included in this class were small pox, bubonic plague, anthrax, botulism, and rare tropical viruses that didn't even have names. They held two things in common. First, they were uniquely contagious, infecting by touch, ingestion, or inhalation. And second, they were all mercilessly lethal. So great was their threat, that *El Armario* was equipped with a small but extremely effective thermonuclear fail-safe sterilization device. The nuclear warhead was periodically upgraded, and living atop it was enough to make anyone paranoid. For Wade, however, it was all just one great compliment. His viruses could even hold a hydrogen bomb at bay.

As the elevator slowed, Wade realized there were only two problems with his situation.

First, no one in the outside world had any idea of the magnitude of his genius. And second, Wilson Strong and his kind still freely roamed about the surface.

Wade knew the first injustice would one day be remedied if he only remained patient enough. The world was destined to feel the weight of his virus.

Smiling, he realized this same destiny would be enough to also solve the second injustice automatically. Wilson Strong, Sarah Thornton, Mitchell Rice—all of them would be crushed by the same virus.

In the end, he would have his vengeance for Marilyn's death. All he had to do was bide his time and wait for the opening he knew fate would give him. The elevator opened, and all of *El Armario* was his again. Wade smiled. It was a world of endless opportunity.

Chapter Twenty-Five

"Wilson, get the hell in here!" David Helsey bellowed.

Helsey was no longer the Director of the CIA. He had left that position almost seven years before. President Ford, weakened by the remembrance of the Watergate scandal and frightened by the specter of what Wilson Strong had laid before him, had asked for Helsey's resignation. He smiled grimly. Wilson had won that round.

"Now! Goddamn it, Wilson! Get in here now!"

But now was a different time. The replacement Ford and the peanut farmer Carter, were both gone. Ronald Reagan was now in control, and the worm had turned. Victory and the weapons that victory required were now the order of the day. Helsey might not now be the director of the Central Intelligence Agency, but he was its new Special Projects Director, the SPD. He grinned without smiling. This position was actually even more powerful than his previous one. This one didn't require congressional approval, and it was his for as long as he wanted it. He couldn't have asked for more.

"Not tomorrow, Strong! Today!"

Wilson Strong, unshaken by his rival's bullying, entered David Helsey's inner sanctum at his own pace. He and David had not traded blows for years, and Strong had promised both himself and Sarah this confrontation wouldn't last long.

With a toss of his hand, the SPD dismissed the secretary that had escorted Strong to Helsey's inner office. Strong heard the click of the door locking when Helsey's other hand activated the "secure mode" status. Helsey's office was now a black hole that would frustrate anyone trying to spy into it.

Helsey motioned Strong towards a chair and got up from his desk to sit beside his old adversary.

"Wilson, what in blazes is this letter of resignation?"

"Just that, David. I'm resigning. You know the two of us are oil and water. Now that you're back, it's time for me to go. This will never work the way it is. I want out."

"Come on, Wilson. You know you can't just get *out*. What's bugging you?"

Helsey loved these games. Only this time, he would win. It was payback time.

"David," Strong said, "I've been here now nearly ten years. Before that, I had been a soldier for more than twenty. Over thirty years in this man's army is enough for any man."

"Don't give me that, Wilson! You're not just *any man*. I've been in this racket for as long as you have. I know burnout when I see it, and you don't have it. You're still just as sharp and deadly as you've ever been. Is your ass still hanging out over that SNAFU in the Iranian desert and those hostages? Or are you just scared of being under my thumb again?"

Strong was quiet for a moment. Some months before he had not been quite so reserved. In fact, he had been pretty much outspoken. The whole Iranian hostage extraction effort had been set up wrong. The people had been wrong. The helicopters had been wrong. The whole plan had been wrong. Strong had said so before the whole thing started, and he had continued to say so as the whole thing went down the tubes. He had said enough to get sideways with both the old administration and the current new one.

"David, you know as well as I do that disgrace could have been easily avoided. We bloodied our own noses, and had to beg our people out of hock. It was a FUBAR, as we used to say."

"Wilson, you're still an eloquent son of a bitch, but someday you're going to learn that sometimes you just need to keep your mouth shut! I had to use up every favor I had on the Hill to keep you from being shipped out to Greenland! So don't give me this shit about quitting! I want you here, and you owe me!"

Helsey stared warily at Strong.

"Wilson, you *do* owe me! A hell of a lot! So don't go on telling me that you want out! I won't let you go!"

Strong said nothing. He got up out of his chair and walked away from Helsey. It wasn't the response the SPD had expected. Moments later Strong turned back to Helsey.

"David, we know each other pretty well. We may have come from the same place, but we've been walking on different sides of the road almost from the beginning. For old time's sake, if for no other reason, let me out before we destroy each other."

"That almost sounds like a threat."

"No threat. Just a simple statement."

Helsey pushed back from his desk. This wasn't what he had expected at all. He wanted his payback, but he had also expected to have his old classmate in the game when he needed him. Wilson Strong might be an old anachronism, but he was a comforting one. When the fur got short, there had never been a better person to push into the fray. Helsey didn't want to lose that option.

"Come on, Wilson! Enough of this sparring! Are you that shook up over the little bit of retribution I'm likely to bring down on you for your getting me canned seven years ago? I never knew you to be one to back down from something as harmless as a little professional vendetta."

Strong snorted with disgust. "David, you're not even a shadow of the man I used to know! Then you were just a pig- headed, arrogant fool! But at least you weren't malignant!"

Helsey's face flushed.

"But now you're absolutely dangerous! You've lost your soul to the game, David! I don't want to be here for the end!"

"You can't talk..."

"Shut up, David! I'll say whatever I want! And you'll listen!"

Helsey's face got even redder.

"Where's Jacob Wade, David?"

"Who?"

"Jacob Wade, Mr. Special Projects Director. You know, the fair-haired genius of your most precious special project. The reason you have this position to start with. Where is he?"

Helsey started stuttering. "G… G… Goddamn you, Wilson! How would I know where the jerk is? It's been a long time since Munich! You can't still hold that against me!"

"David, you used to be a better liar. You know as well as I now do that he's been in Nevada in that secret hole in the ground for months now. I know you've been told to build the most god-awful biological weapons in our planet's history. I don't want to be part of it, David. Let me out. Or I'll kill us both."

Helsey spun around so that he was looking away from Strong. He was too angry. Strong could always do that to him. He had to regain composure and the upper hand. All the trump cards were his. He couldn't lose this hand on a bluff.

"Okay, David. Then let's talk about misinformation. You know… that thing which of late has become one of our primary functions. First you decide on your goal. Then take the facts, twist them, distort them, deny them, ignore them, and just generally discredit anyone you have to until the desired perception is had. We've become pretty good at it, haven't we?"

Helsey turned back to Strong but said nothing.

Strong pushed on.

"The peanut farmer never even knew about *El Armario*, did he? Whose idea was it to tell Ronnie about it?"

Strong walked up to Helsey's desk and put his hands on its top.

"Who's in charge now, David? I want to know so I can give my resignation to him. You've obviously kissed too many butts to be the boss!"

Helsey jumped out of his chair. He had murder in his eyes, but Strong gave him no room at all.

"What have we become, David? A bunch of prostitutes for oil company executives playing ball with the world marketplace?"

Helsey was too angry to even sputter.

"And what about Nixon and Kissinger selling all that military gear to Iraq through that Saudi arms dealer, bin-what's-his-name? How many millions did they make? Aren't these Iraqi the same people that Wade has tried twice to sell his viruses to?"

"Yes, Wilson. They are," Helsey answered, finally finding his voice. "But *El Armario* is different now! You have to know that! There's no way Wade could get any of his stuff out of there now!"

"Bullshit, David! Bullshit! I know no such thing!" Strong literally spat the words out.

"Whose boys have we become, David? Whose gospel are we selling today? Have we twisted the truth so many times that we don't even recognize it when it takes a bite out of our own asses?"

Helsey sat back down in his big chair.

"So what do you want me to say, Wilson? The world stopped being a nice place a long time ago. Hell, right and wrong became obsolete a long time ago!"

"Maybe in your world, David… not mine."

Helsey shook his head.

"I was wrong a while ago, Wilson. You *are* burned out. You just hide it better than most. Take some time off. You certainly have it coming."

"And then what, David? Come back and rejoin the game? What are you guys calling it now? *TEGWAR?* You know, "the exciting game without any rules." It's just chaos for its own sake! Even the brotherhood of arms rings false when chaos is the final goal!"

"Wilson, cool your jets. You've been a player too long not to know the rules. You can take some time off, but you can't just quit. You're just like me. You're *in* until you die."

"Well, Mr. SPD, that's where you're wrong," Strong said calmly. "Do you remember Yang Que Baick?"

Helsey paused, checking his memory.

"Isn't he one of those aggressive South Korean industrialists?"

"Yes. And he was also one of my executive officers in Hue. He has just offered me a position helping some of his family in Peru with an experiment in government. Something about right versus wrong. I think I'm going to take the job."

"Over your dead body you will!" Helsey exploded.

Strong didn't even budge.

"David, I'm going to make this real easy. I'm not going to betray any of my country's interests. I'm not going to break any laws. I'm not going to compromise any security clearances. I'm just going to retire after more than thirty years of service. My insurance policy is a large number of photos and documents showing you as a key player in the heroin export business that used to be centered in Vietnam."

David Helsey's face paled.

"You see, David, I know to whom Sergeant Davis was delivering his junk from the Delta firebase. His Manila connection—it was you, David. I have your picture taking delivery at the firebase and lots of film in Manila showing you distributing it. They're good pictures, David. Good enough to be a great insurance policy."

Helsey couldn't believe it. Wilson Strong had to die.

Strong read his mind.

"If something unexpected were to happen to me, David, an unstoppable chain of events would begin that would expose both you and a lot of your cronies in this government. A lot of heroin left Vietnam under your direction."

"You're bluffing, Wilson! There's no way you could have what you say! Those pictures don't exist!"

"Trust me, David. You know that I don't lie, and you know that I've never played poker. A lot of good men and women have died over a lot of years getting what I have. I figure it's about as good an insurance policy as anyone could ever have."

Helsey tried to recover.

"That was a long time ago, Wilson."

"You're right, and I know that somewhere there are documents confirming that you were really in deep-cover or some such thing during those long ago, dark years. But I also have a computer disc that has been copied several times over showing your secret Swiss bank account. Some people might still question just how good a businessman you really were in those days. The profit margins were astronomical, weren't they? There's no way you can lie your way out of this one… even if you did it all for the *right* reasons."

"Goddamn it, Strong! Just what in blazes do you want?"

"I've already told you, David. I just want to retire and to be left alone."

Strong met Helsey's stare.

"Look. I don't want your head. Whatever the indiscretions of your youth, I don't think of you as being a *bad* guy. It's just that you have lost your soul to *TEGWAR*."

Wilson paused.

"David, I'm not even appealing to your sense of fair play. This is just about basic survival. Stop me, and I'll stop you. We'll both be dead. You can't live with me, and your controllers won't tolerate exposure. You can live without me. So just let me go, and you can keep playing your games."

"So that's it then? A stand-off?"

"Isn't that what we do best, David? Hide behind the truth? The beauty of this deal is that it doesn't really cost either of us very much."

Strong took a long breath.

"Take the deal, David. It's the best one you'll get today."

"Goddamn you, Wilson Strong! Goddamn you!"

Helsey got up from his chair and walked to the back wall.

"Wilson, didn't you ever wonder why all you got in Vietnam were the ROKs? We all knew you were an inflexible bastard even then! Well, go sleep with your Korean friends! Hell, screw with them all you want! I'm through with you!"

Strong turned to head for the door.

"Thank you, Mr. Special Projects Director. I appreciate that you have accepted the terms of my retirement so gracefully."

"I'll see you in hell, Wilson!"

"Yes, David, you probably will," Strong answered.

And then he slammed the door.

"Is it over, Wilson?" Sarah asked.

Strong looked up from his desk.

"Yes, princess. It's over. We're history around this place."

"Good. I'm already packed."

He looked up at her. She was still amazing.

"Sarah, what did I ever do to deserve you?"

"You made love to me, you big jerk." She smiled her special smile at him. "You made my bells ring all at the same time, and I haven't been able to get enough of you ever since."

She saw he wasn't in a playful mood so she went up behind him and started to rub his shoulders.

"And you made me grow up and see the world for what it was. You made me see that the whole world would sell its soul for a few dollars.

You showed me that a whole government could be perverted to sell its sacred trust to the highest bidder. You showed me that whole wars, senseless deaths, and entire societies could be sacrificed in the name of a global economy and a world marketplace. And you showed me that we can even invent a virus that's the end of our very race, all in the name of profit."

She rubbed his neck muscles firmly.

"After all that, what else could I do but to hold onto the most honorable thing I ever found?"

She kissed him on the top of his head.

"That's you, my precious general. You're mine, and I won't let go."

He reached up and pulled her around to his lap.

"I've never deserved you, Sarah. Not before and certainly not now."

"Who cares, Wilson? I sure don't. Let's just be happy we have each other." She started to get up. "Come on. Let's go."

He started to let her up, but pulled her back just as she got to arm's length. She thought she understood his gesture, and she responded with her best snuggle. He answered back with a long, deep kiss. But then before anything could progress any farther, he held her out away from him.

"Sarah…"

"What, Wilson?"

She had never seen the expression he had now.

"Wilson, what's wrong?"

Strong got up from his desk and left her standing there. After three strides, he turned back.

"Sarah, I have always tried to be a man of honor.

I…"

"I know, Wilson. So what's…"

"No, Sarah. Let me finish." He seemed lost. "But there's one place where I've never been honorable, and I need to fix that before we go any farther."

She hesitated. "I don't understand."

He came back to her and took both of her hands into his.

"Sarah, I've held your hands in every way possible, starting all the way back to our days in Vietnam."

She looked at him, both puzzled and scared.

"But there's one way I've never held them, and I need to fix that right now."

"What are you talking about, Wilson?"

He took her chin in his right hand.

"Sarah, I need to hold them as the hands of the woman who is my wife."

He looked deeply into her face.

"Sarah, please marry me."

She stepped back, stunned. But the retreat was just momentary.

"Of course, you big jerk! Who else would I marry? You're the general, and I'm your princess. Besides, the whole world already knows I'm yours."

She giggled a little girl's laugh.

"It's probably redundant, but sure… I'll let you make an honest woman out of me."

Her eyes were starting to tear.

"Of course, I'll marry you! I had given up thinking you'd ever ask!"

"Sarah, I'm a jerk. I know that now. I've always tried to live by a code of honor… a code I thought was important than people. But I was wrong. The code only had honor because of people. Only people have value, not sterile words or some lifeless principles. I *do* know that now."

He took her into his big arms.

"And princess, you're the most precious thing I've ever found."

Sarah looked up and reached for his face. What she saw and felt there was both a salute and a caress. A long, tender moment followed. Then she stood up and walked with him out of the CIA. They were side by side. There was no reason to look back.

Chapter Twenty-Six

Sweetwater was an old, mid-Missouri town and the county seat of Big Bend County. Its history reached all the way back to the Civil War when the Confederate army rolled over General Sherman on the way to its bloody victory in the Battle of Lexington.

In more modern times, it was known more for its rich soil and its crops. Most of its fabulous soil was in the northern portion of the county whose boundary was the Missouri River. In the southern portion of the county was the northern-most tip of the Ozarks. There oak and walnut trees ruled the hills and valleys.

All in all, the county was a beautiful one, and it was only one hour to either west or east to reach either Kansas City or Columbia. It was here that Mitch and Nicki settled down and began the next chapter of their lives.

Those first years of the 1980s were busy times for the whole Rice family. Mitch had persisted in his idea of having a traditional family practice, and "Big Bend country" was certainly a place where he could use the full scope of his training.

His days there were full of the maladies that befell modern man, and he dealt with them by blending modern, medical science with Hippocrates' age-old code. But his old-fashioned approach branded him as an anachronism, just a dinosaur whose time was quickly passing.

In the 1980s, medicine was fast becoming a business. Medicine, just as predicted to Mitch in medical school, was quickly falling from its lofty place as an honorable profession.

But somehow Mitch either ignored or endured medicine's changed direction. He still remembered an old nun's words about things that had true value, about shared purposes and preserved honor, and about shared destinies.

So he continued dealing with each patient, one life at a time, as if each person that entered his office was the sole object of his attentions.

And the patients came. They appreciated this "sit-down doctor" who would settle into a chair and take the time to listen to their complaints. Mitch took little offense that both his practice peers and patients often took him for granted. He was a constant in their lives. They opened their souls to him, and he helped them get well.

Consequently, Mitch's medical life in central Missouri turned out in a lot of ways just to be a continuation of all of his earlier days. His patients and peers used and relied on him, but not many really got to know him. Fewer still realized all his efforts were still motivated by the need to keep his nightmarish conscience at bay. Lastly no one, not even Mitch, understood that all his time in medicine was just a time of his own special healing -- a time when his spirit could rest in a special cocoon, filling in its scars and defects, preparing for a new time that was coming.

These same years, however, were of a different flavor for Nicki. By 1986 she had added three new lives to hers and Mitch's legacy. Little Will had arrived just as they were arriving in Sweetwater, and Maria and Stephanie came along over the five years that followed.

Nicki was a dedicated parent, as was Mitch. But like a lioness protecting her own, she frequently rebelled at and resented the sacrificial role Mitch seemed to assume so naturally. Mitch may not have thought of himself as being anything special, but to Nicki and the children, he was everything.

Over and over again in those years, as Mitch slipped out of the house at odd hours to go to the office, the ER, or the delivery suite, she remembered what she had said to Wilson Strong at her wedding. The general's command had always been one of duty and honor, a place where self-sacrifice was the expected. Nicki's command was more one of love and preservation, an effort that cherished and enlivened.

The general's way was probably more selfless, but he was just Mitch's brother. Nicki was his wife, and her path was about selfish preservation. She was the one who shared Mitch's soul, seeing both his nightmares and his daydreams. Even when she pushed him out of bed in the cold of night to answer his patients' calls, she clung to the hope that one day he would finally count his old debts paid.

Consequently, Nicki's time in Sweetwater was both a time of joy and complaint. She reveled in the passion and purpose she found there with Mitch, but she recoiled from the burdens those same feelings brought. Through it all, however, she grew. Just as Mitch's soul healed in the place he shared with her, she matured—slowly learning lessons of the spirit… lessons of sacrifice that she had not yet even imagined.

It was a hot Monday evening in July, 1987. Mitch had been on call for the whole preceding weekend and had been out of the house nearly the whole time. Nicki had been left a single parent, and the kids hadn't cooperated. They always acted up whenever Mitch was gone for prolong periods, and over the last weekend they had been particularly difficult. For the moment she was really tired of being a responsible mom. She had slept alone for too many nights in a row, and she was ready to have a husband again.

Mitch, really bushed, slipped out of the car and started walking around to the back of the house. The weekend had been really full. Two car wrecks with assorted orthopedic injuries and multiple lacerations, six deliveries (two of which were C-sections), and a lot of normal walk-in ailments had used up all his energies.

But no one had died, and by the weekend's end, everyone had either been treated, delivered, or transferred to some appropriate referral center. He had even managed to finish the three-and-a half-day-long shift with a still fairly friendly face in place.

But now he was home. He had had enough of disease and pestilence. Now he just wanted a night's rest and a chance to "mend fences" with Nicki.

Mitch had just barely closed his old jeep's door when he heard the thunder of paws on the driveway pavement. It was the old Brittany spaniel, Jake, the household's canine patriarch.

"Hi, Jake. How's the pup?" he asked.

The dog wagged his tail joyfully and gave Mitch his best, wholehearted welcome home.

"Yeah, I know, boy. Come fall we'll chase those quail birds again. You'll be in heaven again, won't you?"

Jake seemed to understand and gave a quick, little bark. Mitch rubbed him behind his ears.

"You're amazing. You're always happy with whatever time I can give you."

Mitch was feeling guilty for his long weekend's absence from the house. The kids were becoming quite a handful of late, and he knew Nicki had to be fed up. He walked around to the back patio and was surprised by a smoking charcoal cooker. Lifting its top, he saw the grill was empty.

"Hmmm… I guess I'm cooking," he said, squinting at the afternoon sun. He turned, slipped through the back door, and ran right into Nicki.

"Where'd you come from?" he blurted out, surprised by her sudden appearance.

Nicki was smiling at him. "Right from a sailor's dream, hubby."

Mitch stopped and took half a step back. He saw that she was wearing one of his old, blue oxford shirts. The top couple of buttons were undone, and the long shirttail was hanging down unfettered. He had the very definite impression that, under the soft, blue cotton, a lot of other things were equally unencumbered.

Nicki put the glass of wine she was holding down on the kitchen counter-top and snuggled up close to him. Mitch realized immediately that his impression was very much correct.

Minutes later, when they finally broke from a long, shameless kiss, Nicki looked up at him.

"Hubby, it's good to have you home."

"I think I just forgot how tired I was," Mitch answered with a grin.

"Good because your day's work isn't over yet."

She handed him a glass of wine, and he sipped it gratefully.

"Where are the kids, Nic?"

"They're at Mom and Dad's in Tallis. I took them down there during the day. They haven't seen their grandparents for a while, and the folks were willing."

"Oh… I guess that's why no one answered when I called at noon."

"Uh-huh."

"This is sounding more and more interesting all the time, wifey."

"I would hope so," she flirted, loosening his necktie. "Now, go back out there and cook our steaks. I'm really hungry."

Mitch took the platter of uncooked meat from the kitchen counter and slipped outside.

"You know, Jake," he said as he slid the two fillets onto the hot grill. "Sometimes life is really good. You come home expecting to get keel-hauled for being gone all weekend, and instead you're met by this hot, young thing who just wants to nibble on your ear."

Jake just wagged his tail.

Mitch pinched off a piece of the tender meat and flipped it towards the faithful pooch.

"You always were a good listener, Jake."

The meat never touched the ground.

"Whose steak was that?"

Mitch turned, caught red-handed. It had been Nicki's steak.

"You're out here like that?"

"You bet! And if you keep giving my steak away, I'm likely to stay out here!"

She bent over to rub Jake's neck, giving Mitch a long look through her shirt's partially opened front.

"Besides, I'm all covered."

"Nicki, you may be covered, but you certainly aren't decent!"

It must have been the wrong thing to say because he saw Nicki's eyes suddenly snap.

"How would you know, Mitch? You haven't been around here enough lately to even know what *decent* is!"

Mitch grimaced at her sudden reaction, but then he relaxed when he saw her smile return.

"The salad and vegetables are ready whenever you are, hubby. And so am I." She turned to go back in, brushing her hands at her shirttails. For an instant her bare backside basked in the afternoon's light. "I really am ready."

That was all the incentive Mitch needed. He scooped the just-finished fillets off the grill and followed her in.

"Nicki," he mumbled, "sometimes you're the most shameless flirt I've ever seen!"

Nicki turned and caught him just as he entered the door.

"Mitchell Rice, you know that I don't flirt." She unbuttoned his shirt. "And I've never been ashamed of *anything* that I've ever done with you."

She took the meat platter from him and put it aside. "Come on. I'm hungry."

Sometime later, Mitch was sipping his wine, floating away on an easy wave as Nicki gave him a back rub. The evening had been a wonderful, animated fantasy, and now he was in heaven, floating away with Nicki's gentle, rocking motions.

"What the hell!" Mitch suddenly gasped wildly, his world jolted off its moorings by a sudden flood of ice water.

Nicki was above him, crying. She held the ice bucket that had been cooling the wine.

"Damn you, Mitchell Rice! Damn you! You just see if I ever try to seduce you again! You can't even stay awake for an hour!"

She was shaking, chilled both from the ice water that had splashed back on her and from the raw edge of her passions. Her sobs were coming from somewhere deep inside.

"Mitch, sometimes I really hate what you do!"

Mitch wiped the icy water off his chest. He looked up and saw that Nicki's eyes were bloodshot.

"How long have you been crying?"

"Long enough! What do you care anyway? You always have your patients!"

Mitch suddenly felt torn in half. The practice often did take nearly all of him, and it hurt him that Nicki saw him running on empty so frequently. In the next instant, his sudden hurt was replaced by a flash of silent anger. "Always the chump at home!" he thought to himself. "Never the hero!"

Nicki turned her back on him, ignoring the conflict that flared across his face. She stomped off to the bedroom, leaving him to stew in his own juices.

Mitch took the next few minutes to calm himself down. He knew the next move was his. Wrapping a towel around his goose bumps, he followed Nicki into the bedroom. He found her standing beside their bed, still sniffling loudly.

Nicki had seldom cried in their marriage, but her nerves were still too naked for any other response. Mitch went to her and wrapped his arms around her. She kept sobbing, shaking like a frightened, little girl.

"I guess we both have our own demons to cope with, don't we, lady?"

She remained in his arms, neither resisting nor yielding.

"I always have to push it as far as I can. You know that."

He stroked her hair.

"You know that if I don't push it, I feel like I'm not worth anything. And then I feel lost."

He tightened his arms around her.

"But when I do push too far, I always end up hurting both you and the kids. And then I really am lost."

He buried his head into the back of her neck.

"I'm sorry, lady."

Nicki sniffed.

"So okay, martyr. We all know what your demon is."

She sniffed again.

"What's mine?"

He turned her around slowly so he could look into her wet eyes. His were moist too.

"Nicki…" He took a shuddering breath. "Nicki, it's me… I'm your demon." He dropped his arms from her and turned away. "For some god-only-knows-why reason that I'll never understand, you love me."

He turned back to her and sat on the edge of their bed.

"Because you love me, you try to fill my world with joy, excitement, and emotion. It's like you're always trying to pump life into me."

He shrugged his shoulders in hopeless surrender.

"Nic, sometimes I guess I don't transfuse very easily—I'm sorry."

Nicki looked at Mitch and saw that his tears were real. It was only the third or fourth time she had ever seen him cry. She reached down to her bedside table for a tissue. Blowing her nose and wiping her eyes, she motioned for him to come to her. When he hesitated, she went to him. She saw that his soul was as exposed as hers was. She slipped into his arms, smiling gently as her jangled nerves began to glow.

"You always take yourself too seriously, Mitch. I'm sorry too. Come on, smile for me again."

She felt him still hesitate so she nestled in even closer.

"Squeeze me, Mitch! I promise I won't crack up again! I'm sorry I overreacted! But sometimes I don't know how to get your attention without totally unloading on you!"

Mitch, still confused and dazed by the sudden rush of changing emotions, did just as she asked. He pulled her in close, crushing the air out of her. She didn't seem to mind a bit.

And suddenly all of his confusion went away. Nicki was his, not by his choice, but by hers. He didn't understand it, but he really didn't have to. Her being here with him was enough.

"Here," she was handing him a bottle of body lotion. "I *do* want a back rub tonight, and I *don't* want you getting too relaxed again."

"Can I rub anything else besides your back?"

"Whatever you think you're man enough to handle, hubby."

She pulled him down onto the bed and showed him where she wanted to be touched. The time for flirting and hysterics was gone. Now it was time for something much more real.

"Take it easy, Nic. This might take a while."

She loosened her grip but still kissed him eagerly.

"Promises, promises," she whispered, turning over. She wiggled her bare bottom at him as she nestled down into the sheets.

Mitch started to answer but on impulse gave her a playful slap on the backside instead.

"Ouch! What was that for?"

"That," he said as he settled over the back of her outstretched legs, "was for the ice."

He reached up, taking her by the tops of her shoulders.

"And this," he said, starting a deep, strong massage over her shoulder blades, "is for everything else."

Nicki wiggled her bare bottom again so he could settle down even farther. Mitch could feel her skin tingling.

"You're right," she said. "I *do* want this to take a long time."

"Whatever you want, wifey. Tonight I just aim to please."

And with that Mitch let his hands slip down around her ribs. He touched the sides of her breasts and felt her catch her breath. Grateful little groans and quiet little gasps soon followed. The massage and everything else that went with it really did take a long, long time.

Later, in the early morning hours, Nicki awoke. She was lying just covered by the sheet. Mitch was snuggled in behind her, still holding her. His breaths were coming softly and steadily. Nicki turned over ever so gently so as not to wake him. She wanted to see his sleeping face.

As she moved, an emotion came over her like a strong wind blowing across a field of grain. She ached inside for this man. If only he could see himself the way she saw him. If only he could love himself even a fraction of the way she loved him. Maybe then he wouldn't be so willing to give himself up.

She reached out and gently touched his face. But then he wouldn't be Mitch, she thought, feeling a sudden chill. And maybe then she wouldn't be so totally petrified by the thought that one day she might have to give him up.

She reached out and gently touched his face again.

"You awake?" Mitch asked, opening his eyes.

"Uh-huh. I need some more of your godlike, Grecian body."

Mitch turned over, gently snorting.

"Nicki, sometimes you're so full of bull!"

She pulled him back so he was facing her.

"Yeah, I was… a little while ago."

She reached up to his face, this time a lot more purposefully.

"And I hope to be again, real soon."

She saw Mitch's face come alive with a hungry, knowing smile. He had gotten the message that the rest of his sleep would have to come later.

Chapter Twenty-Seven

Jacob Wade was lost in thought. He sat at his desk studying a computer printout.

It was 1989. For some time now, he had possessed the mythical doomsday weapon, the pathogenic converting virus, his PCV. Of course the military establishment knew this, and they were keeping Wade's baby under tight lock and key. And they would continue to do so until he gave them a vaccine to control the thing. Doomsday, by Washington D. C. standards, wasn't an acceptable option when the home team was going to die too.

Wade turned another page of his printout.

What Wade's keepers didn't know, was that he had already perfected the immunization. Wade held the key, and Washington didn't know it. The day of Wade's vengeance was quickly approaching.

Six years had passed since Jacob Wade had returned to *El Armario*. The six years had seen a lot of people come and go in the underground lab. Most of them had kept their distance from him. The circumstances, having him both as their prisoner and their boss, made for some odd relationships. But overall, the resulting isolation suited Wade just fine. Being a pariah made him a lot harder to be tracked by his captors. They frequently missed things.

The supreme example of their oversight had occurred just six weeks before. No one had even been in the lab when the professor completed culturing his latest crop of CCR-5 enriched T cells. Likewise, no one had been around to witness him use those T cells to create a special blocking antibody.

Consequently, no one realized that the secret of controlling the PCV, or even HIV for that matter, was not a vaccine against the virus itself. Rather the secret was a vaccine, a protein really, that mimicked a portion of the surface of the plague bacillus.

Strangely, the Black Death of the Middle Ages had used the same cellular entry site, this CCR5 portal, to extinguish half of Europe's population. Only those who lacked this site on their T cells, like Mitchell Rice's ancestors, had proven immune to its ravages. Wade had discovered this fact while reading the research of a husband-and-wife research team named Jonathan and Mary Lou Mann. All he had to do was to configure a protein that could couple permanently with the CCR5 receptor, and the PCV was rendered harmless. Wade cared little that he had also discovered a true cure for AIDS – death, not life was his purpose.

The concept of a blocking antibody was a completely new paradigm, a simple and yet profound discovery that had the power to be the death warrant of everyone in the complex and nearly everyone else in the rest of the world.

Wade turned another page.

It all was so simple really. In fact Wade had almost had the answer all the way back in 1970 in his little lab at UMR. Even that long ago, Wade had realized that a perfect plague could be perfect only if it was actually part of human chromosomes themselves. That's what his tissue cultures, the ones that Mitch had crashed into in Wade's lab, had been all about.

It had been that summer when Wade had modified the killing part of Ebola and learned how to connect it to human chromosomes. It had taken an understanding of meiosis, the peculiar unraveling of DNA that occurred in the human gonads, but Wade had been up to the task. What he had created that summer was the prototype of the HIV/ Ebola amalgam that now was the PCV. Sure, thanks to the harassment of the CIA, it had taken Wade eighteen years to fully marry the two devastating illnesses. But now that he had accomplished it, Wade was certain that he had the whole world "by the balls." That realization was a taste of real power.

Wade smiled at his little play on words. He always enjoyed remembering Mitchell Rice's little orchitis event, the sudden mumps-like infection that had caused Mitch's testicles to swell after the "'lab accident." Revenge was a sweet thing, something, according to the Good Book, that belonged only to God. But that's what Jacob Wade was now... the PCV had made him a *god.*

Wade sighed with satisfaction. Soon, with no one being the wiser, he would carry out of *El Armario* enough PCV and enough CCR-5 blocking vaccine to change the destiny of the whole world. He would have Judgment Day in his coat pocket. If that wasn't the same as being a god, then the word deity needed to be redefined.

It was December. The holiday season was bearing down hard, and even buried hundreds of feet under the desert sand, the occupants of *El Armario* were feeling the anticipation of Christmas.

This year, Wade, for the first time in a long time, was also on the list to leave the facility. He had not seen his daughter, Katie, for years. After Marilyn's death he had ignored the little girl, knowing that his Mormon in-laws would raise her. But in more recent years Wade had reclaimed some of his fatherhood via a long series of letters. Now this holiday season, the girl was getting married. And he was going to her wedding.

It had been years since Wilson Strong had filed his and Sarah's report listing the high degree of threat to national security that Jacob Wade's very existence represented. Since that report had been filed, Wade had worked so hard and so well and had been such a willing captive that his captors had forgotten the general's warning.

Wade's letters to Katie, always thoroughly censored, had been thought to represent that he was finally recovering from his paranoid ideations. The situation was a perfect ending to a long melodrama. A young woman was about to be reunited with her long lost father on the same day that she was getting married... it was a story that anyone would want to believe.

In fact, it was such a great fairy tale that not even one of the censors saw anything strange in Wade's request for Pamir Dannah, a chemistry professor friend from Wade's days at the University of Missouri/Rolla, to come to the wedding. No one remembered that Dannah's original visa had been issued in Baghdad. As far as the keepers were concerned, nearly two decades in America had made Dannah as native as apple pie, and no one paid the man any attention.

"Are you anxious to see your daughter, professor?" asked Dr. Shirley Jecker, Wade's front line lab assistant.

Wade put down his computer printout and was rubbed his old shoulder wound.

"Yes, Shirley, I am. It really has been a long time since I last saw her. Now she's all grown up and about to become a wife."

"It all sounds so perfect, professor. You're going to have a great holiday season."

Wade stopped rubbing his shoulder.

"Yes, Shirley. Yes, I am."

He was smiled, looking at the repository's air locks.

"Dear, would you bring me that last batch of synthesis reports over there?" he asked.

"Sure, professor, but I'm sure they could wait until you get back after the New Year."

"Yes, I'm sure they could, but I'm not leaving until this afternoon. The work will go smoother after the New Year if I finish those reports now."

Shirley shrugged and went to the computer terminal. She knew that the professor had toiled in this burial vault for years, always sitting atop a series of ever more efficient nuclear sterilization devices. Just that had to be enough to warp anyone. She was glad the professor was finally getting out for a breath of air. His sentence had been long enough.

The seventh level and the lab it contained was truly a world unto itself. One passed through a series of air locks from the upper levels to get to it, and once inside, a person was totally separated from the rest of the facility.

The workstation where Wade and Dr. Jecker worked held three desks, the computer terminals where Shirley was now gathering the synthesis reports, several gas chromatographs, and a myriad of high tech chemical analysis equipment. Also nearby were the microbe and animal host workstations, their maintenance facilities, and several electron microscopes. And beyond all that, just in front of them, lay the "holy of holies," the repository vault that held all of the PCV.

Each of the lab areas was maintained with its own atmospheric environment. Each was sealed from the next work area by two air locks in a series, and each area had a progressively lower atmospheric pressure. The "holy of holies" had the lowest air pressure of all so nothing inside of it could ever ride the breezes to any other part of the lab. And on top of all that, the exhaust air from all of the areas was separately funneled into a sterilization chamber in the core of the facility where gamma radiation sterilized everything. It was foolproof isolation technology.

The lab's security was likewise impregnable. Every area had its own alarms and sensors monitored by the central computer. In the central repository vault, invisible infrared lasers and the world's best weight-variation alarms added foolproof redundancy. No treasure anywhere in the world had ever been more zealously guarded than Jacob Wade's plague.

The only flaw in the system was that the actual research work still had to be done by hand. The viral inoculla were just too delicate to be handled by robotics. Consequently, all actual handling of the materials was done in specially sealed sialastic-glove workboxes, the best that had ever been built.

Wade had always acted flattered at how much his jailers valued his creations. With all of the technology around him, it was understandable that he might feel validated. In his long tenure in the place, he had seen all this sophisticated security come into being. In fact, he had actually helped orchestrate and install much of it. That was particularly true of the security systems in the repository vault.

The soul of all of the security system was for all of *El Armario* was a perfect blending of human and artificial intelligence. Every lab in every level was monitored by audio/visual monitors that were controlled by central monitoring personnel. As a backup, the facility's central computer was hardwired to double-check everything. Using a very sophisticated system of efferent and afferent electronic circuits, the central computer effectively had its own neural net or nervous system that constantly checked the well-being of the whole complex.

All this was done by a constantly changing code of electronic impulses that perpetually cycled from the computer to every peripheral instrument and lab in the whole facility. If there were ever any perturbations of these electronic frequencies that the security personnel couldn't explain, the computer could take its own action.

The whole security system was truly a blending of cyber and human abilities, so much so that sometimes it wasn't entirely clear just who was the overlord and who was the underling.

In summary, the entire security network was thought to be perfect. But, as was often the case, what was so very sophisticated and complicated, was easily beaten by something absurdly simple.

Professor Wade had been present when all of the alarm systems had been installed. He had been particularly attentive to those systems that protected his precious seventh level. All those years ago no one had thought too much about it when he had asked certain simple questions about the hard wiring of the alarms. And no one had noticed the little tags that had been placed on certain leads that ran through a conduit right behind the very desk where Wade now sat.

With everyone planning their Christmas breaks, no one noticed Wade slip under his desk to retrieve a pile of papers that he had carelessly knocked over. It took him only about ten seconds to remove the little access panel behind his desk and only another couple of seconds to pull out two sets of leads that ran there. After that it took only an instant for him to hook two little devices to the leads, effectively disconnecting the computer from the repository vault. The 'holy of holies" and all that it held was his.

Actually, it was just a little more complicated than that, but really not that much.

The last computer upgrades people had been very helpful. Wade had been taking them coffee when he overheard them discussing that the current program gave the computer five-second cycling time between each monitoring burst. Using that knowledge, Wade had just hooked a small voltmeter to the first efferent lead behind his desk. After the needle jumped, he had a full five seconds to make the four required alligator clip connections. That was two seconds more than he needed.

The little alligator clip contraptions were devices of Wade's own creation. Months before he had built the things using a very high-grade silver wire that ran between two of the clips. He had sealed this silver wire in a plastic tube, and in this tube he had placed a little quantity of hydrochloric acid in a crushable glass ampule. (He had already experimented carefully and had discovered just the right concentration of acid that would it would take to eat through the wires in exactly three hours.)

For the three hours the clips were in place, the monitoring system was effectively short-circuited in the vault, the efferent electric pulses being routed directly into the afferent lead without even reaching the balance or laser system.

But after three hours everything would instantly change. When the time was up and the silver wire was eaten through, the computer would automatically regain its usual clarity of vision. The computer would see that "something" irreparable was wrong in the repository, and it would activate *El Armario's* fail-safe device. Nuclear sterilization would follow, and *El Armario* would cease to exist.

When Wade sat back up with his printouts in hand, the three-hour countdown to nuclear vaporization had already begun.

"Do you need some help with all those papers, Dr. Wade?"

"No. I've got them, Shirley. I was pretty clumsy. I'm sorry."

Shirley turned back to her computer station, keeping herself busy.

"Shirley," Wade interrupted, "I guess I am excited about seeing my daughter. Maybe these printouts will wait until later after all."

"I think you're right, sir."

"Who's my escort out? You or Lieutenant James?"

"I hope you'll understand, Dr. Wade. James doesn't really have any family to go home to for the holidays. He's volunteered to escort you to the wedding."

"Oh..." Wade paused. "I didn't know you had plans for Christmas. I had hoped to introduce you to my daughter."

"I'm sorry, Dr. Wade, but I'm supposed to meet my family in the mountains in Utah for a Christmas ski holiday. We've been planning it for months."

"Of course you have," he answered. "I understand completely. Have a great time. You deserve it. This will be a Christmas season that you'll never forget."

She smiled back. "Thanks, professor. I'm pretty excited about it."

"That's good. You should be."

Wade pushed back from his desk.

"Now, dear, would you be so kind as to call up the lieutenant and tell him I'll be ready to check out in about an hour. I suddenly feel like a kid who's about to get out of school for the summer."

"Sure, professor."

"While you're doing that, I'll go inside the repository and close everything up."

"Will you need help in there?"

"No, I don't think so. There really isn't that much to do. It'll just take me just a moment or two to make certain everything is secure. I'll be right back out."

He grinned at her.

"Besides, you know I can't leave until I sign off on the final inspection. You can sign off at the end of your shift later today."

"Sure, professor. I know you're anxious to go. I'll call James now, and you'll be on your way to your daughter before this shift in finished."

He smiled at her and started to go into the air lock that led into the repository.

"Shirley?" he said.

"Yes, professor?"

"Shirley, you have always been a good lab assistant. I really couldn't have done without you all these last many months. Thank you."

She caught an odd tone in his voice and gave him a questioning look.

"Don't take an old man too seriously, dear. Just have a wonderful holiday." Turning into the air lock where he would don his protective air suit, he muttered to himself. "I know I'm going to."

Once inside the final vault, Wade deftly slipped a scalpel out of his bio-suit's outside pockets. No one had seen him slip it there earlier in the day. Likewise, the monitoring crew who were having a little pre-Christmas party, didn't see his quick slice that opened the sialastic sleeve in the laminar flow hood. No one heard the little hiss of air the cut caused, and no one saw Wade take the six little vials from their storage niches. It all took about four seconds.

The vials of PCV and the vials of vaccine were replaced by six identical looking vials of brown sugar. They weighed exactly the same as the originals. The sialastic sleeve, which was self-sealing, closed behind the professor's hand when he withdrew it. His phonies might or might not fool the computer, but human eyes would never know the difference.

No one was even looking at the monitors when Wade walked back into the air lock and took off his suit.

"Everything okay, Dr. Wade?"

"Sure, Shirley. Nothing could be better. It's all battened down in there, and I'm off to see my daughter."

He smiled broadly.

"You can double-check me when the shift is over."

"I'm sure there will be no need, Dr. Wade. You're always very thorough."

Wade stepped across the room.

"Shirley, I'm going to step into the restroom. I guess my coffee's cycling through."

Shirley shrugged acknowledgment. She had always hated that he was always even asked permission for that. She was glad he was going on parole.

Wade stepped into the little cubicle. From his left pants' pocket he took out six little wax suppositories. Into each pellet he pushed one precious little glass vial that came from his right pants' pocket. One by one he pushed each suppository up his own rectum.

It took only about a minute for the professor to finish his toilet. Leaving the restroom, he hugged Shirley, said his farewells, and stepped out of the work area to meet Lieutenant James. He was heading out.

Checking out of *El Armario* was always a chore. All of Wade's meager belongings were thoroughly searched, both by hand and by fluoroscope. He himself was thoroughly strip-searched and even his rectum was digitalized. The medic who did the exam was just a corpsman and when Wade winced with discomfort, the man abbreviated his exam a bit. The wax pellets felt just like stool. The corpsman had no idea what he was touching.

Shortly after that, just about an hour after he had left Shirley down on the seventh level, Jacob Wade was breathing fresh air topside.

"Lieutenant?"

"Yes, professor?"

"Lieutenant, could you pull over to that gas station over there. I need to use the men's room."

"Sure, professor."

Lieutenant James pulled the government-issue Chevy into the crossroad's little way stop. Wade got out of the car and walked around the side of the building where the men's room was located. James stepped out from behind the steering wheel and looked over the nearly empty lot. Nothing stirred inside the dusty station, and only a nondescript old Ford was in view at the far end of the asphalt. Everything looked very peaceful.

Minutes passed, and Wade did not return. The lieutenant began to feel a little uneasy. He left the car and walked around to the rest room.

"Professor Wade? Are you all right?" he called out at the door.

In the next instant, Lieutenant James felt his arms being jerked behind his back. In the next instant, he felt a cold metal pressure at his right ear. In the next instant, he felt nothing at all.

The little. 22 slug exited from the silenced Walther and entered Lieutenant James's right auditory canal, plowed through his auditory and vestibular structures, and finally lodged in his brain stem. Being a low velocity slug, it went no farther, but it had gone far enough. James was dead before he could even spasm. He didn't even lose one drop of blood.

Minutes later the nondescript Ford was gone. So too was the government motor pool Chevy. Lieutenant James's lifeless form was on its way to disposal, and Jacob Wade was on his way to Baghdad, still carrying his precious deadly cargo in his rectum.

It had been nearly three hours since Professor Wade had left his workstation at the bottom of *El Armario*. Shirley Jecker was still about an hour from the end of her shift. She had just finished with her terminal work and was walking by the professor's desk. There, under the desk, she caught sight of a piece of paper. It had to be one of the papers that Wade had dropped. Without thinking too much, she bent down to pick it up. Just as she started to straighten up, she caught sight of something shiny behind a small wall panel. She crouched back down and reached forward for the panel. Removing it, she saw the two little plastic tubes, each connected to wires that were pulled out of a conduit.

"What the hell is this?" she muttered.

She moved a little closer and saw that each little tube enclosed a slender wire that was nearly eaten away by whatever liquid bathed it.

"Oh my God!" she gasped with sudden insight. "Professor Wade!"

She jerked from under the desk, nearly cold-cocking herself on a drawer. She ran to the air lock of the repository. Throwing on her air suit, she plugged her headset into its connection.

"Control! This is Jecker!"

There was a second of hesitation, followed by a masculine reply. "We have you on the screen, Dr. Jecker. What's going on down there?"

"I'm not quite sure, control, but there are some strange little connectors attached to the security circuits that monitor the repository. I've never seen them before."

"Come again, Jecker. This is Captain Adams. What kind of connectors are you talking about? Where are they?"

Shirley moved into the vault area. "I can't talk right now, captain, but I'll know if there's really a problem in just about a minute!"

She entered the little work area. Everything looked normal. She went to the first workstation in the laminar flow hood. Everything checked out. Checking the contents of the storage niches, she saw that everything was in its place. She then went to the second workstation and reached into the two sialastic gloves. There was a little hiss from the left glove. Her eyes began to dilate. Her hand slid right through the slit.

"Dr. Jecker, what the hell is going on in there?" Captain Adams demanded. "I need answers right now!"

Before Shirley could utter a word, a throbbing bell came to life.

"Dr. Jecker, what have you done?" Adams yelled, his voice instantly quaking. "I'm showing complete security systems breech in the repository! The facility is switching to auto self-destruct mode! What's happened in there?"

Shirley reached forward and took one of the PCV vials. Something about it wasn't quite right. Turning it over in the light, she realized that the lyophilized crystals in the ampule were a slightly different shade of brown than they should be. She replaced the vial and straightened up.

"It's Wade!" she screamed. "Wade has the PCV on the outside!"

"What did you say, Jecker? This is Colonel Wilcox!"

Shirley was running out of the air lock as she was responding to the facility's commander.

"Colonel, Professor Wade has sabotaged security and has stolen his PCV and a trial vaccine he was working on! He's got them both on the outside!"

Colonel Wilcox was silent for just a second. The bell, just fallen silent, had been replaced by a wailing siren that pierced everything.

"Is she right, captain?" he asked the captain at his side.

"I don't know any other explanation for all of this, sir! The central computer is dumping its core into NORAD! I can't get a line to the outside while it's doing that! And I can't shut off the nuke downstairs! It armed itself when the computer started the core dumping!"

"How long do we have before it goes off?"

"Thirty seconds, I think, sir—after the core dump is complete!"

Both officers looked at each other. They both knew they were already dead.

"Colonel, this is Jecker! Wade *really* does have the bad stuff on the outside. Can we get word to NORAD before this place lights up?"

The colonel looked at the captain and then at the figure of Shirley Jecker on his monitor screen.

"We might have thirty seconds after the computer has finished the core dump, Dr. Jecker. Can you tell NORAD what it needs to know in that time?"

"I'll sure try, sir. I'll…"

The siren fell silent.

"There, Dr. Jecker!" Adams yelled. "I just hooked you 'plain voice' to Cheyenne Mountain in the Springs! Tell them all you can!"

Shirley Jecker keyed her mike. "This is Dr. Shirley Jecker in *El Armario*. Professor Wade has sa…"

Shirley Jecker never finished her words. Her mouth was still moving, but her voice was hushed by a flash of pure light. Her mind's eye looked outward and saw her own hands and everything else evaporate in the heat of the nuclear fireball.

She'd had only three seconds, not thirty, to speak her final message.

Chapter Twenty-Eight

Wilson Strong put the telephone receiver back into its cradle. His movement, thoughtful and measured, said very plainly something had just happened.

Sarah looked up at him from the pile of papers that covered her desk. She was across the room in their shared office at the presidential palace in Lima, Peru. They had been here together, organizing President Len Chi Baick's government, ever since they had exited the CIA together five years earlier.

"What is it, Wilson?" she asked.

Strong didn't seem to hear her question. His face was a blank wall, and its emptiness told Sarah more than words ever could that whatever had just happened was bad, very bad.

"Wilson?" she asked again.

Strong looked up at her. She was still his princess, the woman who had done his bidding and held his secrets from here to hell and back. His expression softened.

He and Sarah had endured all the way from the killing fields of Vietnam, through the moral morass of Washington, to this beautiful South American country. Sarah had been faithful to him even when she had had no reason to do so. Even when he had known there was no honor left, she had stayed with him, seeing his truth when even he was blinded to it. She had even become his wife.

Strong sagged visibly. Suddenly all they had accomplished together here in Peru, the social and political engineering they had done to put an honorable, selfless government in place... all of it seemed to evaporate.

Sarah got up from her chair.

"What's going on, Wilson? You're scaring me!"

Strong looked up at her.

"It's David Helsey, Sarah."

She saw him hesitate.

"He's dead, Sarah. He's been found on a country road in Maryland. His neck's broken."

Sarah felt her breath go away. Wilson and David Helsey had marched, both together and apart, all the way from West Point, through the Korean War, past Vietnam, all the way to their separation in Washington when Helsey had tried to stop her and Wilson from coming here.

"How did it happen?"

Strong looked away.

"He had a *bicycle* wreck, Sarah."

He shook his head.

"On a back road in Maryland, the Special Projects Director of the CIA, a man who hated bicycles with a raw passion, died in a ditch after falling off one."

Sarah felt totally lost.

"Wilson, I thought you once said Helsey wouldn't go near a bicycle ever since that bicycle bomb almost killed him in Saigon. You said he was almost phobic about it."

"That's right, Sarah. He was."

Sarah went over to where he was seated.

"You mean it *wasn't* an accident?"

"What do you think? You know about as much about 'the company' as I do. You tell me what to think."

She wrapped her arms around his big shoulders.

"Why, Wilson? Why would the agency turn on one of its own?"

He turned, stood up, and wrapped his arms around her in a protective, answering embrace.

"*El Armario*, Sarah," he said. "It's *El Armario*."

He squeezed her tight.

"There's been an *accident* out there. I don't know all of the details yet, but David apparently tried to buck the way the administration was covering it up what has happened. And whatever it was, it was enough to get him killed."

She pulled back from him.

"Are you sure, Wilson? Who was that on the phone?"

"That was Yang Baick, Sarah. He's on the way over here from South Korea right now."

Strong pulled her back into his arms.

"Sarah, think of the worst fears we ever had about Jacob Wade. They've all come true."

She looked up at his face in disbelief.

"Jacob Wade?"

Strong said nothing. He just pulled her face into his chest, right on top of his heart, right where she could hear it break.

Two days later Sarah was walking on a quiet, Peruvian beach. Wilson was walking at her right side, holding her hand. On her left side was their old friend, Yang Baick, Wilson's old exec from the days of Tet and the uncle of the Peruvian president they now served.

"Miss Sarah, do you remember the last time the three of us walked together on a beach?"

Sarah chuckled. "Walked, Yang? The way I remember it you two bruisers were running like hell, and I was being tossed around like a sack of potatoes."

"Well, a lot of people were shooting at us, Sarah," Wilson interjected.

"Minor details," Sarah countered.

"Yes, those were scary days," Baick admitted.

Baick remembered the sting of the flying sand from the NVA bullets. He and Wilson had been hustling the protesting Sarah to a departing landing craft when the NVA had started chewing up the sand around them. The Tet Offensive had still been in high gear, and Vietnam had been no place for a confused, idealistic young woman who needed vengeance for the killings and atrocities she had endured.

"Yang," Sarah said, "it took me a long time to figure out that it had been you who was bringing all those vegetables to the orphanage. You looked and acted just like a native."

She took his hand.

"If Dannie hadn't explained it all to me that day before we pulled out of Vietnam, I'm not sure I would ever have known."

Yang nodded a little acknowledgment.

"And it took you even longer to forgive me for being Mother Marie's intelligence contact for the colonel, didn't it?"

She nodded.

"Yeah. You know sometimes, even now, I still can't believe she actually did it."

She felt Wilson squeeze her hand a little harder.

"In a lot of ways I still can't quite believe she's really gone."

"She was a special kind of warrior, Miss Sarah. I've never found the likes of her since," Baick said simply. "Perhaps she is still here, watching out for you."

Baick stopped and looked squarely at Sarah.

"Miss Sarah, I was coming for the three of you the day before Tet. But they blew the jeep out from underneath me. I couldn't get to you."

"I know," Sarah answered. "Wilson told me."

She reached out from her position between the two men and slipped her arms around both of their waists.

"It's okay, guys. That was a long time ago… a whole lifetime."

Baick pulled up short and stepped away from his old friends.

"Yes, it was. But…"

"But what, Yang?" Wilson asked quietly. "You've never been one to reminisce much. What's going on?"

He turned to face Baick.

"What's happened to pull you halfway around the world? It's a long ways to come for a walk in the sand."

Baick felt Strong's stare and returned it without flinching.

"Wilson, we go back a long ways, you and I."

"Yes, we do, Yang."

"Back in Hue you were the commander, and I was your executive officer. You gave the orders, and I saw they were carried out. We were a good team."

Baick saw Strong shift his weight.

"And now you're the boss, Yang. And Sarah and I do your bidding," Strong said.

Baick laughed gently.

"No, I don't think so, Wilson. You may have helped my nephew with all that he has done in this country, but you did it because you believed in it. I'm not so foolish as to think I have any real authority over you. You always answered to higher powers than I could ever hear."

"If you say so, Yang." Strong shifted his weight again. "But enough of the past. What's going on today?"

"That's the problem," Yang said. "The past is still with us."

He paused for a minute.

"Miss Sarah... on the day of Tet the colonel and I were both devastated that we couldn't come for you at the orphanage. We wanted to, but we couldn't."

Wilson started to speak, but Baick waved him silent.

"The victory that day didn't belong to us."

Sarah gasped. "It's Mitch!"

She suddenly couldn't breathe.

"Yang, you want Mitch again, don't you!"

She started shaking.

"It's Jacob Wade, isn't it! That's what this is all about! Wade has escaped from *El Armario* again, hasn't he?"

Baick stared right into Sarah's eyes.

"Miss Sarah, no one could ever hide the truth from you when it was about those you love. Yes, this is all about Mitchell Rice."

"Damn it, Yang! Don't' go there!" Wilson swore. "We talked about this years ago! That crazy genetic quirk Mitch has on his white blood cells, that thing with his CCR5 receptor sites. We all agreed Mitch was too valuable a resource to ever risk again. What's going on?"

"Wilson, I know, but that was then." He shook his head. "And this is now."

Over the next twenty minutes Yang Baick recounted a tangled web of intrigue and scientific accomplishment. He told them how the biology people in the Defense Department had perfected their tissue culture techniques, making living reservoirs like Mitch unnecessary. He told them of the nuclear disaster that had befallen the Nevada desert.

He told them of the U. S. government's desperate, failing efforts to find Jacob Wade. Finally he told them of the confirmation that Wade and his PCV had reached Iraq, the same haven he had sought more than sixteen years before.

"Yang," Strong asked when Baick ran down. "Why are you here? Who has sent you?"

"General, your government is organizing an effort to take back the virus. The mission is being called "Desert Wind"."

"Okay?"

"Three days ago William Avery came to Seoul."

"The director of the CIA?" Sarah asked incredulously.

"Yes, Miss Sarah. The director himself." He turned to Strong. "General, your government believes it needs Mitchell Rice to be part of the strike team. They have already approached him twice, but he has turned them down flat both times."

"Good for Mitch!" Sarah exploded. "He's finally learned to say no!"

Strong wanted to applaud with Sarah, but he knew better.

"But what, Yang?"

"The problem, my friends, is that this thing that Jacob Wade has given the Iraqi is the most hideous weapon humankind has ever invented. And your government doesn't have a vaccine for it."

All three of them were silent for a long minute.

"Wilson," Sarah finally asked, "they'll have to nuke Iraq before Wade can use the thing, won't they?"

"I guess so, Sarah, unless…"

"Unless the "Desert Wind" mission is successful," Baick replied. "My friends, Mr. Avery said he knew you would never talk to him, especially after David Helsey's death."

"The bastard!" spat Sarah. "Wilson, we owe the son of a bitch Avery nothing! Screw him!"

"Miss Sarah, I have always admired your ability to speak so eloquently," Baick said with a sad smile. "But even though I agree about Mr. Avery's dubious parentage, the fact remains that this mission is the only way to avoid a nuclear holocaust. And for the mission to have its best chance, Mitchell Rice must be there. He's the only man in the free world who might be at least partially immune to what Jacob Wade has created."

"And we're the only people in the world who Bill Avery thinks can talk Mitch into going," Strong said quietly.

Yang Baick just nodded.

Sarah felt her world crumbling.

"Wilson, I won't do it! I did it for you in '72, but I won't do it again! Mitch's got Nicki and the three kids now! He's done enough already! I won't do it!"

She felt Strong wipe the tears away that were welling up from deep inside of her. She could feel the sadness in his touch.

"Yes, Wilson," Baick said. "This is just like Hue all over again. Both of us would gladly go, if we could. But once again, we are not the right men. Just like it was in Hue, this battle doesn't belong to us. Once again it belongs only to Mitchell Rice."

Strong looked up at his old friend.

"Yang, back in Hue you called Mitch "a tiger," but that was twenty years ago. Mitch hasn't been in a firefight in years."

Yang Baick took two steps away, stopped , and turned around.

"Wilson, in all the years before and after Tet I have never seen eyes like Mitchell Rice had that night. They were fire!"

Baick took a step back to them.

"The fire I saw that night was his very soul, and that kind of flame doesn't go out! Mitchell Rice may be a husband and a healer now, but underneath all that, he is still a tiger!"

Baick was speaking with urgent authority.

"Wilson, just as you will always be my colonel, Mitchell Rice will always be one of our world's final warriors. I saw that then in Hue, and to the depths of my soul, I know that is still true. It is his destiny."

"And, my friends," Baick said slowly, "this is one time when the whole world truly needs such a man. The situation *is* that bad!"

Sarah felt Strong looking at her. She didn't want to speak, but she knew she had to. Slowly, she nodded.

"Yang's right, Wilson. I saw Mitch's eyes that night too... in the chapel."

She shuddered, and her voice grew distant.

"When I was tied up on the altar, about to be raped, I was crazy out of my head with fear, but something made me look up. I saw something black, something huge, fly across the back of the chapel."

She looked at Baick.

"It wasn't a tiger, but it did have *burning, red* eyes! That's when all the VC just started dying! It was Mitch! When it was all over, I thought I had hallucinating because I had been so scared, and I never told anyone about it. But that's what I saw, and I've never forgotten it! Mitch's eyes *were* fire! He was a huge black angel whose eyes were fire!"

Strong stared at Sarah. She had never told him that part of Hue before.

"Yang," he said, "I'll talk to Mitch, but I don't know how it will go. He made me swear after Munich that I'd never ask him to do anything like this again."

Strong's voice changed its tone.

"But if he does agree, tell Avery that it'll work only if I get total command of the whole operation—no compromises and no exceptions! "Desert Wind" will be completely mine, and I *will* have the final and complete say! Tell Avery that anything less than this will see us all burning in hell together!"

Sarah came up beside Strong. Standing there she could see out over the Pacific. On the far horizon she saw a dark cloud. In the next instant, several bolts of lightning shot out from its base. And just like that, the drums of war were beating again.

Chapter Twenty-Nine

Wilson Strong pulled the unmarked FBI-issued cruiser into the parking lot across the street from Mitch's clinic. The lot was crowded even though an early March snow had begun to fall. The general sat there with the motor running in the gray afternoon and replayed the events that had brought him there.

Strong had already, years previously, gone on record that Jacob Wade and his virus were curses on humanity that needed to be snuffed out. But he had lost in his final efforts to make that happen. The siren song of destructive power had been too much for his superiors. The ability to control the entire existence of any people by power of plague had been too seductive for the accountants to pass up.

Only now the game had turned. Now the powerful had become the hunted, and they trembled at what their actions had allowed to transpire in the Nevada desert. In short, the lion now felt the awful power of something so much smaller than a mouse, a virus that could kill them all.

The general had not gone easy on his old peers. He had lobbied hard and had won total control of the mission to extract both Wade and his PCV from Iraq. The thought of the PCV flying a thousand miles either out of one of Jerry Bull's super cannons or atop a SCUD missile was just too horrible to accept.

Strong's authority had been made equal to that of the Joint Chiefs for the mission's duration. That effectively made him at least a four-star general, but the usual pecking order of military rank really meant nothing. Strong had just required that the bureaucrats would have no say at all in what was about to happen. The fact that he was given this kind of sway confirmed all by itself just how desperate the situation really was. It really wasn't a victory at all.

Strong knew the hardest part of all was just ahead of him. He now had to confront Mitch and convince him to go on the mission. As the snow continued to fall, he wished he could have been any other place in the world.

Strong sat in his idling car for almost half an hour. He saw patient after patient come and go from Mitch's clinic. Watching those people, he felt all the pious arguments he had organized evaporate. He had no idea how he could face Mitch with what he had to ask. On the one side he was being squeezed by the honor of his old Munich pledge to leave Mitch as a noncombatant. On the other side he was being crushed by the threat of what he knew was in a desert, half a world away. The strain was intolerable, and the only answer he could come up with bore but a simple name… Nicki.

Thirty minutes later Strong stood at the front door of Mitch's home. He had called Nicki from a pay phone and had asked if he could come. Almost as though she'd been expecting him she had said "sure." But Strong knew he wasn't really welcome. He raised his hand to ring the doorbell, but the door opened right in front of him.

"General…" She looked pale. "Come in."

"Thanks, Nicki," he said simply. "But it hasn't been "general" for some time now."

"If you say so, general. But I know you'll always be that to Mitch. If you weren't, you wouldn't be here now."

She took him into the family room.

"This is still about Jacob Wade, isn't it?"

Strong nodded.

"It's really bad, Nicki."

He watched her slowly sit down.

"Wade has escaped from a secret government research station out in the desert Southwest. When he escaped he was carrying the worse biological weapon ever created, and he got away clean."

He saw that he wasn't surprising her at all.

"Mitch and I pretty much figured that it had to be something like that. Those FBI goons that came here wouldn't say just what was going on, but we knew it had to be something like this."

She didn't even flinch.

"General, I don't know why you still want Mitch. It's been so many years since Munich..."

She stared at him.

"But whatever the reason is, he won't go!"

Her eyes snapped.

"He swore to me that he wouldn't kill any more, and he won't! No matter what you say, he won't do what you want!"

Strong heard what Nicki was saying, but somehow his ears were suddenly full with another conversation, one that he had had with Nicki years before.

"Nicki, do you remember when we danced?'

"What?"

"Do you remember when we danced at your wedding?"

She hesitated.

"Yes..."

"Do you remember saying that we, you and me, were a lot alike?"

She still hesitated.

"I guess so..."

"You said that you and I commanded "the bravest soldier that ever lived."

"I don't understand..."

"Nicki," he said slowly, "I haven't been Mitch's general for years now, not since Munich."

He smiled sadly at her.

"I passed that responsibility on to you."

Her face clouded with confusion.

"Nicki, you're right. He won't listen to me. He'll only listen to you."

She jumped up, almost bolting.

"You've gotta be crazy, general! You can't think I'll be the one to talk him into doing whatever you're talking about!"

"Nicki..."

"No!"

She turned on him like a great cat.

"No, general! He's mine! You can't have him again!"

She had real menace in her stride.

"You'll kill him! I won't let that happen!"

"Nicki," he said, not retreating, "in all the years since your wedding, I've thought a lot about what you said. Up to that point, I had always thought that honor and duty were the highest values I could live by. But what you said that day, about loving Mitch and giving him a reason to live, taught me that I was wrong."

Her advance toward him slowed.

"Nicki, you know Mitch better than anyone else alive. You know he'll try to live by his pledge to stay with you, but you also have to know that the government won't stop coming after him. They'll keep coming and coming, and finally someone will say things just the right way. The logic of the situation will win out, and then he'll go with them."

He saw her stop.

"He'll go because this time the cause *is* just, and in the end, he won't be able to deny what's right."

Strong felt his own eyes clouding.

"But, Nicki, if it plays out this way, he'll go to his death. He'll have broken his word to you, and he'll quit trying to live. Sure, he'll probably go out in a big blaze of glory, but he'll go out just the same."

Nicki stepped backwards, suddenly completely lost.

"You know I'm right, don't you?"

She started crying quietly.

"General, I always knew somehow it would come to this! I'm going to lose him, aren't I?"

He went over to her and took her in his arms, a lot like he had at her wedding.

"Nicki, listen to me. Sarah and I have talked about this for days. If I or Sarah or even the president himself talks Mitch into doing this thing, he'll do it out of a sense of duty. You know that's true."

She nodded.

"But if you're the one who convinces him to go, he'll go out of love. And that love will be the thing that will keep him going when there's nothing else left."

He reached up and took her by the shoulders.

"Your love is Mitch's best, maybe his *only* chance for survival."

Nicki started shaking violently as the terrible truth hit home.

"You know I'm right, Nicki. He'll die for the whole, miserable world. He'll only live for *you*!"

She kept shaking, rattled by great, jarring sobs.

"He gave you his life all those years ago, Nicki. Since then, you've treasured him and healed him. Now, if you have enough courage to live up to the things you've said, if you love him enough, *you will* send him to do what has to be done."

He pulled her chin up so he could see her face.

"If you can do this thing, Mitch will go believing in what he has to do, and that'll be the difference between his living and dying."

He touched her cheek.

"You see, I read somewhere that the greatest command was love! That's the kind of commander you have to be now! You have to love him enough to send him! Otherwise, he's a dead man!"

A couple of hours later, Mitch pulled into the driveway. He got out of the car and looked around. Ever since the last batch of FBI agents had come calling, he felt uneasy every time he came home. But tonight everything looked okay as he let himself in through the back door.

"Nicki?" he asked.

She was sitting on the family room couch. Her back was to him. Something about the way she sat seemed wrong.

Nicki didn't really reply, but rather she just motioned for him to come around to her. Mitch did so, and as he walked around the couch, he saw the rifle in her lap. It was his SSG, the Austrian sniper rifle he used in his long-range target matches.

Mitch looked at the rife for a long second, not understanding. Then, as he looked into Nicki's eyes, he saw what she was seeing… his past was still his future. The deepest sadness of his life ran him all the way through. Mitch saw Nicki. Her eyes were full of the greatest terror he had ever seen. She was raising the rifle up to him, offering it to him just as if it was her soul.

Mitch understood, took the rifle, and put it aside. He said nothing because there was nothing to say. He just took her into his arms with an embrace that had to last forever. When everything else had passed away, they would still have their love.

Chapter Thirty

Il Ibrahim was one of the highest points in Iraq. The mountain was very close to the Iraq-Iran border and not too far from Turkey. Legend had it that it was at the foot of this mountain that Father Abraham had made his original home. The ancient mountain that stood before Mitch had seen the beginnings of the Arab, Jewish, and Christian worlds. The shadow of its history was about to grow longer.

It was September, 1990. Six months had passed since General Strong went to Sweetwater to ask Mitch to take on this mission.

Mitch spent the entire spring and summer working himself into rock-hard condition. He shot, drilled, studied, and exercised as a man driven by one fearsome purpose, and by summer's end he had achieved it. By summer's end Mitch had rediscovered himself. He was again a warrior. He might not have been the strongest or the fastest or the smartest, but he knew he was the one who would endure longer than thought possible. He was the one who would carry more payload than could be imagined. And he was the one who would deliver it with more accuracy than was believable. In short, he had once again become a human weapon, the tip of the spear, and this time the spear was called "Desert Wind."

General Strong had persevered in maintaining absolute command of the whole recovery operation. Mitch was not privy to much of what the general planned, but on the home front, Mitch found a way to close down his medical practice—first the obstetrical part of it and then, by mid-summer, the whole practice.

His patients were very upset at his practice's passing, and his partners tried their best to talk him out of his decision. Of course, none of them knew anything of the true story, but on the surface, Mitch's known disagreement with their business-orientated practice style seemed more than enough to give credence to his leaving. Everyone knew he had pretty much used himself up there in Missouri so the cover story rang true.

The general made some of his CIA people help Mitch research the opportunities for another practice site. And after the appropriate, visible efforts, Mitch had picked a medium-sized community named Manhattan in northeastern Oklahoma for his future home. If Mitch survived the mission, he would have a new place to practice medicine. If he didn't, the general would see to it that Nicki and the kids were cared for and kept safe. They would even be given new identities so that none of Mitch's "ghosts" could ever haunt them.

Nicki, with Sarah's help, made the big move south in August so the kids could be in place for the start of the school term. While she was settling into Manhattan, Mitch made a much different journey east. Everyone in Missouri thought he was in Oklahoma, and everyone in Oklahoma thought he was still closing out the practice in Missouri.

The reality was that Mitch was in Turkey, working with an international medical relief unit that was offering care to Kurdish refugees from Iraq.

Mitch arrived at his Turkish station without any pomp or circumstance. Except for an American woman who was both a nurse and a linguist, he was the only American there in the twelve-man unit. The rest of the team was English. For all effects and purposes, they all were there to give aid to the displaced Kurds who had no home in Turkey and who faced annihilation in Iraq.

The Kurdish refugees' needs were real, and the team worked hard for them. But the team's truer mission was to make note of Saddam's current method of genocide, and for this service, a large number of world governments secretly paid a handsome price. It was a biological weapons listening post.

But all this was just a second layer of the cover. The relief team was actually the best biological weapons strike team ever assembled, and they were just waiting for General Strong's orders to go south into Iraq to retrieve what Jacob Wade had stolen.

The team consisted of three doctors, three male nurses, and three female nurses/physician assistants (who were necessary for the care of the Kurdish women who lived under the rules of the traditional mullahs). The tenth person was the ramrod of the outfit, a colonel named Gerald Smythe, M. D. His immediate executive was the American nurse/linguist whose name was Nancy Franklin. Mitch was the twelfth.

All of the team, except for Nancy and Mitch, were of what had once been called the Special Air Services, the SAS. Nancy Franklin, the sole surviving daughter of an American oil company couple who had been murdered in Lebanon, was one of the premier Arabic language specialists in the world and was one of the most effective operatives the CIA had in the Middle East.

And that left only Mitch who was, with his strange immunity, the mission's rear guard specialist and last-ditch hope. Together, they were the best mission team General Strong had ever assembled.

August dragged on slowly while the team waited for its orders to enter Iraq. The days were full of caring for the Kurds, spying on the Iraqis, and appeasing the Turks. The nights were full of rehearsals for the imminent mission.

Mitch worked right along with all the rest. During the day, he was a caring, competent doctor. At night he was a high-grade techno-warrior completing his training in bio- warfare. He also spent his time familiarizing himself with a big. 50 caliber sniper rifle and a special sighting system, something called the Livermore device, a device that General Strong had pulled out of the military proving grounds just for this mission.

The Livermore sight was an amazingly compact conglomeration of micro circuitry, lasers, and infrared detectors that allowed its user to track incoming projectiles right back to their source in any light or weather condition. When it was mounted atop Mitch's big rifle, he became sudden death to anyone shooting in the team's direction.

While Mitch acclimated to his mission role, General Strong kept his finger on all possible concerning Saddam Hussein and his various war machines.

Jerry Bull, the Canadian artillery specialist who had provided the Iraqis with the best and longest-range cannons in the world, was taken out of the picture. Presumably the hit was done by the Israeli Massad forces. His masterpiece, a cannon with a one-thousand-mile range that had still been under manufacture, was located and sabotaged.

Unfortunately, it proved a lot harder to keep track of Saddam's collection of SCUD missiles, and harder still to track down Jacob Wade.

The general had huge numbers of operatives in Iraq, all trying to find the professor and his PCV. Finally in late August, one of his agents, a sergeant in Saddam's elite Republican Guard, came through.

This man was actually assigned to the secret unit that worked with Wade as he prepared his virus for its first test. The man relayed to Strong that Wade was in the northern Iraqi city of Irbil, and by the first of September, he managed to supply Strong with the timetable and routes that Wade's first field test would take.

The first use of the PCV virus was to come from a launch of a virus-loaded missile from the slopes of *Il Ibrahim*. It wasn't clear whether the missile would be sent east into Iran, say to Mahabad, or southwest to Israel. Likewise, it wasn't known whether the missile was one of Saddam's short-range weapons or one of his SCUD's. And the SAS team was never told exactly why the mountain had been chosen by the Iraqis as the launch site. Perhaps it was the mountain's eleven thousand foot height, or maybe it was its location on the Iranian border.

Whatever the reason, it seemed ironic that the very mountain that had sired all of those who populated the region would be the place that caused their deaths.

On the night of the third of September, Mitch was still up in his tent. Earlier that evening the whole team had been briefed on the mission. Only five of them would be going -- Smythe, two of his lieutenants (men named Potter and McNab), Nancy Franklin, and Mitch.

The five would hitch rides on specially modified attack helicopters that would fly on the deck, probably under one hundred feet. The choppers would fly by wire, guided by global positioning satellites.

Mitch remembered his wild ride out of Cambodia more than twenty years before and was glad they would be flying in the dark before the birds of the area woke. General Strong had seen to it that no debacles like the botched Iranian hostage rescue attempt would be repeated, such as sand killing the helicopter engines. Mitch knew a vulture up the pipe would be just as disastrous, so he was thankful for the darkness.

In some ways, Mitch realized, warfare had become much more high-tech than it had been in Vietnam. But some things had not changed. Someone still had to go in and do the job. Technology could only get them there.

The whole thing was to begin at 0400. The choppers would lift off from outside their present campsite of Cukurca, fly generally east to a point southeast of Semdinli, and then head south into Iraq and Abraham's mountain. Time was short.

Around midnight, Mitch finished writing a letter home. As he folded it into an envelope, he heard Nancy Franklin knock on the flap of his tent.

"Dr. Rice? Dr. Smythe said you wanted to see me?"

"Yeah, I did, Nancy. Come on in."

She slipped into the little walled tent that had been Mitch's home for the last two and a half weeks.

"What do you have there?" she asked.

Mitch was turning his just-finished letter over and over in his hands.

"It's a letter home."

"You have bad feelings about tomorrow morning, Dr. Rice?"

Mitch's expression seemed to brighten. "What's with the formality, Nance? We're all just about family by now, aren't we? Mitch will do just fine."

She smiled in agreement.

"Look," he said. "I know you are a real pro in this spy business. General Strong thinks you're just about as good as they come."

"That's high praise. I hope I deserve it."

"Well, I know the general doesn't give his endorsements easily, and he definitely has put his seal of approval on you."

Mitch shrugged.

"So I'm going to ask you to do something for me… something personal."

"Okay?"

Mitch handed her his letter.

"I've been away from all of this for a lot of years. When I last worked for the general, I had no family and no real emotional attachments."

He took a slow breath.

"This time, it's different."

She looked at him. She had already been briefed by Wilson Strong himself on the circumstances of Mitch's recruitment.

"If it's any consolation to you, Mitch, General Strong has put his seal of approval on you too." She smiled.

"And on your family. Your Nicki must be something pretty amazing."

Mitch smiled back at her.

"If the truth be known, Nance, she's the real stopper for this mission, not me. I wouldn't be here if it wasn't for her."

He was silent for a little while, but then he went on.

"I guess that's what this letter is all about. I've always been a stickler for cleaning up all the details of a situation. If something happens to me so that I can't go home, I need this letter to get through to her. There are things in it that I need her to hear. If things get messed up, would you see that she gets it?"

Nancy reached out and took the letter.

"I'll take it for now, Mitch, but I'm giving it right back to you tomorrow afternoon. Whatever's in here, your Nicki needs to hear you say it to her in person."

She slipped the letter under her jacket.

"Besides, the general will have my ass if this thing goes sour enough for you to actually get in the thick of it."

Mitch nodded.

"I hope this is a cakewalk too. Your ass is much too pretty for our beloved general to get any portion of it."

Nancy was surprised by Mitch's sudden change of tact, and her face showed it.

"The general said you were full of your own sort of surprises. No one has made me blush in years."

She couldn't help but laugh.

"But you'll still have to give your wife your letter yourself. That's one job I don't plan to have any part of."

Mitch nodded again.

"Nance, the address on that envelope is for real. General Strong has been pretty sticky about covering up anything that links me to you, the team here, or anything about this place. Once this is over, I was never here, and no one knows a thing about me."

"No one but me, huh?" Nancy answered.

"Yeah, I guess that's right. At least it is if you are still willing to be my mailman."

"I said I'd do it."

"Even if it puts you on a collision course with the general?"

"Dr. Rice… Mitch… I know quite a bit about you… a lot more than you know about me." She paused. "I said I'd do it. So I will, if it's necessary… but it won't be."

Mitch smiled weakly. But in the next breath, his face turned to stone.

"Nance, tomorrow, I'll give you and Smythe *whatever* you need."

Nancy flinched as he spoke. For the second time in seconds she seemed to be feeling emotions she normally didn't allow herself. Something in Mitch's face suddenly mirrored for her so many sadnesses she thought she had buried. What she saw on Mitch's face was enough to make her voice stick in her throat.

"I'll see you in a few hours," he said simply.

"Ah… right," she answered.

Linguist that she was, she could find nothing else to say. She stepped out of the tent, making sure the letter was safe under her Kevlar vest. Its delivery was *definitely* one duty she didn't want to have to carry out.

The flight into Iraq was quiet. The black muffled helicopters flew in tight formation, and not even the wild sheep of those mountains realized something was passing just seventy-five feet over their heads. When the rotor wash hit them, it was too late for them to react. Mitch hoped that would be how the whole mission would go.

The incoming scrambled messages from Strong in the AWACS confirmed that Wade's column had left Irbil in the night and was following a road that more or less paralleled the Greater Zeb River. Intelligence indicated the column, which included tanks and a variety of armor, would continue until it was near *Il Ibrahim*. Then a smaller contingent of vehicles would break off along with the disguised fuel truck that was really a SCUD missile launcher. This smaller convoy would climb a road on the western side of the mountain, and set up for the launch of Wade's virus. It was there, on a switchback on the mountain road, the team would attack.

The helicopters were to land and hold on a plateau about half a mile from the point of contact. Potter and Smythe were supposed to plant the satchel charges in the face of the cliff that rose on the side of the twisting road. At just the right moment in the gray of morning, those charges would go off, separating Wade from the rest of his column. The blast was also supposed to destroy the missile launcher and its SCUD.

Then Nancy and McNab were to hit Wade's jeep. By that time, Wade should have already been eliminated by the driver, the sergeant who was Strong's Iraqi eyes. The three would extricate the PCV from the jeep while Mitch stood watch with his. 50 caliber and his Livermore device.

Then everyone was supposed to scamper up the small cliff to the waiting Cobras and fly home under a tight cover of F-18 Hornets. It seemed like a workable plan.

The helicopters landed on Iraqi soil without incident and the strike team hit the dark ground on the run.

"Colonel, this cliff is a lot steeper than it was supposed to be," said Potter who was on point. "I don't think we can get down it without the ropes."

Smythe, fully clad as they all were in an anti- biological air suit, looked over the dark cliff edge with his night vision goggles.

"You're bloody right!"

Nancy piped in immediately. "McNab and I will hump it back up the hill to the choppers and get the rappelling gear we brought. We'll hustle!"

"Good! Go! Potter and I'll find a tie off point for the ropes while you two are gone!"

As Nancy and McNab took off, Mitch looked over the edge. He wasn't too uncomfortable with the night vision equipment. The technology had improved immensely since Vietnam and the days of the "big eye" in the firebase's watchtower, but the effect was the same.

"Colonel? Can all of you guys rappel down the face of this cliff with all this germ warfare stuff on?"

"Sure, Dr. Rice. Don't worry. We'll show you how it's done. It's no different really than the usual drill," Potter answered for his boss.

"Okay," Mitch answered, but there was a strange note to his voice.

"Is there something else, Rice?" Smythe asked.

Mitch looked at both men. "I've been thinking about the actual extraction of the virus, colonel. I think I should be the one who does it. I don't trust Wade. He'll have planned for something like this, and I'm the one who supposedly has the immunity for the virus. I think our odds will be better if I go for it instead of Franklin and McNab."

The colonel looked at Mitch with an expression of surprise that was hidden by his suit. He just had argued for the very same thing with General Strong a few days ago, but the general hadn't bought it.

"Do you play cards, Rice?"

Mitch slowly replied. "Yeah, I used to play pinochle with my grandfather. He taught me that sometimes you had to lead with your ace of trump instead of protecting it if you wanted to catch the other guy's ace."

"You bloody, arrogant, American bastard! You read my mind, and you're right! We *will* lead with you! Give the Livermore to Franklin. She's almost as good with it as you are."

"I'm sure that's right," Mitch answered, reaching for the. 45 on his hip. It was still his insurance. That was another thing that hadn't changed.

Nancy and McNab returned moments later. They tied off the ropes, and everybody went over the side. Mitch was the third one down the rope, suit and all. Once at the bottom, Smythe and Potter went right for the cliff and planted their charges. Mitch switched off his night vision goggles as the sun was just beginning to lighten the sky. Nancy and McNab did the same.

"Do you hear it?" Mitch asked.

Nancy stopped for a moment and strained her ears. In the far distance, somewhere below them, came the growling sounds of trucks making a hard climb.

"Colonel, Rice just heard Wade's column. It's probably about a mile and a half down the road," she said into the little mouthpiece at the side of her face.

Smythe's curt reply came back in the little earphones they all wore in their left ears.

"Good! The charges are set! Potter and I will take our positions! You three up there get into yours! And, Ms. Franklin, we'll be doing this Dr. Rice's way! You take his. 50! He and McNab will make the retrieval from Dr. Wade's jeep!"

Nancy glowered at Mitch, but somehow she wasn't surprised.

"Yes, sir, I'll set up shop in these boulders until they get back here with the stuff."

She made a little gesture in Mitch's general direction with her right middle finger.

"Tsk, tsk, my but we're touchy," muttered Mitch as he turned his high tech sniper rifle over to her. "Take care of my baby. I'll want her back in a minute."

Mitch and McNab moved down the slope to the edge of the road where they thought Professor Wade's jeep would be when the satchel charges went off. Nancy stayed in the boulders about seventy-five yards away. The Livermore device was turned on and gave her quite a view of the whole scene. She felt a bit of a chill go up her spine. Through the device, she could see the shielded headlights of the professor's convoy below them. It was nearly time.

The first vehicle was a jeep command car. The column's commander was in it with two underlings. Professor Wade and General Strong's sergeant were in the second. The missile launcher was several yards behind them, and two armored personnel carriers brought up the rear. The first APC had a heavy machine gun mounted on its roof, and the second one had a large recoilless rifle up top. They were all approaching the bend in the road where the charges were set.

"Get ready, chaps," said Smythe into his mike. "This tea party is about to begin."

Moments later the dawn's gray light was ruptured by fierce blasts of plastique. The face of the cliff that hung over the road broke free, crushed the missile launcher, and threw its mass between the leading jeeps and the trailing APC's.

At the moment of the blast, the Iraqi sergeant in Professor Wade's jeep reached for his service automatic, but he never got it out of his holster. Wade had been expecting something like this for months, and little more than startled by the blast, he already had his nine-millimeter auto in his hand when the sergeant just started his reach. Wade shot the man in the face.

While all this was happening, Smythe and Potter hit the lead jeep hard with automatic weapons fire from the AUGs they carried. All three Iraqis died in their seats. From there, the two ran on to take on the guardsmen who were trying to climb over the wreckage of the SCUD launcher.

At the same time,Mitch and McNab were in full run, heading for Professor Wade's enclosed jeep. They heard the shot from its interior and were running to complete the extraction of the PCV when the jeep door opened on the passenger side. It was Wade, not the Iraqi, and he started firing at them with a vengeance. Only luck and Wade's poor marksmanship saved them.

"Nancy, can you get a bead on him?" Mitch whispered into his headset as he huddled down in the rocks, dodging the sparks that ricocheted all around him from Wade's bullets.

"Negative, Mitch! He's slipped down behind his truck where I can't see him! But that's okay! I'll just blow holes through the whole damn thing!"

"No, Nancy! Don't even try! Wade'll probably be wearing the virus right on his chest! He'll have planned on something like this! If you can't get a head shot, don't take it! We don't want that virus to get loose after all this!"

Mitch motioned to McNab.

"Geoff, you go right and I'll go left! Remember! Head shots only!"

"Right on, old chap!" McNab replied. "I'd have never thought the bastard could be so cheeky!"

"Neither did I," Nancy Franklin said under her breath. Maybe she was glad Mitch was on point. He seemed instinctively to know what Wade would do. It was an edge they needed.

"Hurry on, chaps!" ordered Colonel Smythe. "I hear the APCs behind the rock slide. "We're soon going to have a lot more company!"

"Colonel, should I switch to yours and Potter's position?" Nancy asked.

"Negative, Ms. Franklin! Aaron and I will take care of the Iraqis that scamper over the rocks! You cover Dr. Rice and Geoff until they have the professor neutralized!"

Mitch and McNab were moving in high gear as she and Smythe spoke. They did not see the professor as they dashed towards him. Mitch's thumb slipped the safety off his. 45. He only had a few yards to go.

Suddenly, Jacob Wade jumped out of the shadows, right in Mitch's path. Wade's automatic had fire on its muzzle. Rolling to his left, Mitch still felt one of the professor's slug rip the. 45 from his hand. Ignoring the stinging pain in his hand, Mitch came up lunging for his old professor who was just four yards away.

At that moment everything suddenly slipped into a horrible slow-motion dance that Mitch had so often seen proceed violent death. Wade had a different weapon in his left hand. It was a pneumatic pistol. In it was a dart full of the PCV. If the professor couldn't free his virus one way, he would do it another.

The air pistol was almost leveled at McNab who was trying to bring his AUG to bear. Mitch saw that Wade would win the race with the Englishman. It was a race that neither would finish.

Mitch slammed into Wade, yanking the air pistol down with everything he had. The professor responded by convulsively yanking the triggers of both of his weapons. Nine-millimeter slugs slammed into the ground all around Mitch, but none of them found their mark.

Wade's dart, however, was better aimed. It buried itself into Mitch's left thigh. Both men went down in a tangle of arms, legs, and Mitch's bio-suit.

"Get out of my line of fire!" Nancy screamed.

She couldn't tell who was who as Mitch and the professor wrestled in the roadway seventy-five yards away. Suddenly, she saw one of the figures slam something into the other's head. Red sparks flew from whatever the rock struck.

"That's Mitch's night vision goggles!" Nancy screamed to herself as she turned the big rifle on the other figure. Just as she squeezed off her round, the Livermore device found the professor's eyes. They flashed an eerie green stare in the light of the Livermore's lenses.

And suddenly, it was all over. The professor fell atop of Mitch, his head ripped off at the shoulders. The round Nancy had fired had been explosive, and it had been right on target.

"Rice! Are you hit?" McNab yelled as he rounded the side of the jeep. "That bastard had me in his sights!"

"I'm still functional, Geoff," Mitch said as he got up.

McNab's face was full of horror. "My God!" he gasped. "The bastard has shot Dr. Rice full of the damn virus!"

"What's that?"

It was Smythe. The air around him was full of angry bees as several Iraqi had topped the rock slide at the same time.

"Nancy, take those guys out for your boss!" ordered Mitch. "McNab and I'll get the virus!"

Nancy Franklin lived up to her billing. All six of the Iraqi home guardsmen who had come over the rock slide died in their tracks.

Mitch went right for Wade's chest. Sure enough, there was a harness that still held two intact ampules of the PCV. Mitch tore off Wade's blood-soaked jacket and found all three ampules of vaccine.

"Here, Geoff! Take these and go! I'm right behind you!"

With that Mitch reached down and pulled the now empty injection dart from his leg.

McNab hesitated.

"Put that stuff in that sample case and cram it under your Kevlar vest!" Mitch ordered. "Then take off! We're still a long way from home!"

McNab did what Mitch ordered and took off at a dead run, and Mitch was right behind. Not far behind them were Smythe and Potter. Just above all their heads hummed a swarm of. 50 caliber slugs that Nancy was furiously slamming into the Iraqis who were trying to come over the top of the rock slide.

The Iraqi executive officer who was in the last APC saw his men fall back from the top of the rock slide as if they were running into a solid wall. He ordered the drivers of the two vehicles to back up. About eight hundred meters back down the road was another switch back that would bring the heavy guns atop his vehicles open to engage the raiding party.

While the two armored vehicles navigated the treacherous downhill backing, the exec called word of the attack to his superiors, and they in turn called up the Mirages fighter jets already on alert. They would be overhead in minutes.

"Rice! Where are you hit?" Smythe demanded.

Blood ran down Mitch's left leg.

"Nancy!" Mitch barked. "Give me my rifle! It's time for all of you to go back up the ropes! I'll give you all the cover I can!"

The whole team focused on Mitch's leg. Beneath them, the two APCs growled backwards towards the switch back.

"Look people!" Mitch yelled as he tore off his bio suit. "You all know what I've been shot full of, and you know I can't go home!"

He threw the pack of the. 50 caliber clips onto his back.

"I figure you all have about ten or twelve minutes to be back up on top that cliff before all hell breaks loose around here! Those Iraqi Mirages are coming! So shove off! I'll buy you that long!"

"You heard our mate!" Smythe snapped. "Back to the ropes!"

"Nancy?" Mitch was looking for her eyes. "You did a good job with Wade. Get these guys up the hill with our cargo and..."

Mitch sent two rounds downhill.

"... remember what I said last night. Tell Nicki I did my best."

Nancy nodded to him as he looked at her out of the corner of his eye. Mitch smiled at her. She understood and took off after the three Brits. Mitch turned and settled back down behind the Livermore device. He would buy them the time they needed to reach the helicopters atop the plateau. The Mirages were just a few minutes away, and that meant that Strong's F-18s were inbound too. The air on the mountain would soon be an inferno.

Mitch focused carefully into the high tech sight. The pain in his leg was beginning to get intense. Nevertheless, he found the last Iraqi guardsman who had been returning fire from the cover of the rock slide. The big. 50 roared, and the Iraqi soldier died.

Mitch looked over his shoulder. In the still-murky gray of the dawn, he saw his teammates at the ropes. Two were already on them and the other two were about to begin their ascents. He couldn't tell who was who.

Focusing back on the Iraqi forces below him, Mitch ran thirty or forty yards to the right where he thought he could get a better view of the two remaining APC's. His leg had started to swell viciously, but it didn't matter. Mitch knew the guns on top of the two vehicles would soon send their heavy shells his way. He had to find a better firing point.

The Iraqi gunner atop the last APC had been instructed where the raiders would likely be. As soon as his truck cleared the curve, he sighted on the boulders and sent a heavy shell off. Just as he did so, he was slammed backward into the night by Mitch's armor piercing slug. The artillery shell plowed into the rocks where Mitch had been just moments before and turned everything into gravel. But Mitch wasn't there.

The Iraqi executive officer was perched behind the heavy machine gun atop the second APC. He was trying to give directions to his driver who was having trouble navigating the downhill backing. From his position on top of the vehicle, he saw the gunner in the second APC go down. Knowing the others in that last APC were only fair with the recoilless rifle, he jumped down and ran to the unmanned cannon.

Mitch saw the officer's flying form go across his field of sight and sent another round on its way. The bullet found the Iraqi, but hit lower than Mitch wanted. Being an armor-piercing round, it drilled right through the young commander's left calf, throwing him to the ground.

The sergeant left in the second APC took his commander's place behind the machine gun. The vehicle had just come around the curve, and the sergeant could just make out the forms of climbers some eight or nine hundred meters away. He turned the barrel of the machine gun towards the cliff and opened up.

McNab, who still carried the PCV, had just reached the top of the cliff on the first rope as had Potter on the second. Smythe and Nancy were only about half way up when the first volley of tracers hit the cliff a few feet beneath them.

The Iraqi sergeant had underestimated the range in the gray light, but he compensated and began walking the bullets right up the cliff's face toward them.

Mitch saw what was happening and switched targets from the recoilless rifle to the machine gun. The pain in his leg was overwhelming, and violent chills racked him. Even so, he still managed to turn on the tracking laser function of the Livermore and picked up the flight of bullets from the Iraqi machine gun.

In the next millisecond, the quaking inside Mitch's body and the blurring of his vision disappeared. For that brief instant, he was once more himself. He squeezed the big 50's trigger and sent off his best round, this one explosive.

The reaction that occurred when Mitch's bullet plowed into the works of the heavy machine gun was instantaneous and devastating. The machine gun blew up. The sergeant was cut in half by the weapon's disintegrating fragments. The gun's rain of fire that had been scorching the cliff half a mile away stopped, its last round hitting the rock just beneath Smythe's boot.

"By god! Rice got the bastard!" Smythe yelled.

"Right!" Nancy yelled back. "But we're out of time! Get to the choppers!"

The first two helicopters were already airborne. Nancy and the colonel sprinted across the plateau and threw themselves into two of the three that remained.

"Get this thing off the ground!" Nancy screamed. She knew the Mirages had to be close now.

"Where's the American doctor, ma'am?" asked the pilot as he threw his craft upwards.

"He bought it for us! Get us out of here!"

From the inside of the AWACS, General Strong saw the GPS readouts that told him that all five helicopters were airborne. Sarah was with him, and she saw the same thing. He'd been monitoring the team's headset communication, but that communication had broken up halfway through the battle and left him in the dark. As the helicopters took to the air, he and Sarah began to piece together what had happened on the ground.

The AWACS radar showed three Mirages screaming towards Abraham's mountain from the south. Strong had already vectored in three Navy F-18s behind them. With the helicopters in the air, he turned Hornets loose. The Iraqi fighter pilots never saw the Sidewinders that took their lives.

Meanwhile, Mitch was racked with horrible rigors and violent nausea as he struggled to hold his big rifle upright. Two other Iraqis had taken their places behind the cannon on the first armored personnel carrier and were blasting away in Mitch's direction. Mitch managed to take one of the gunners out, but his place was filled by the limping young executive officer who had crawled up the vehicle despite of his wound.

The young Iraqi settled the gun's sights on Mitch's hiding place. Just as he was about to fire, the man at his side crashed into him, propelled by the impact of Mitch's last shot. The cannon went off sending its shell uphill, but its aim was ruined. Instead of striking Mitch's boulder-reinforced position, it plowed into the loose talus and shale on the steep slope yards above Mitch.

As the Iraqi commander regained his stance, he saw the wave of loose rocks come down on Mitch's position as a thunderous avalanche. It was the last thing he ever saw.

One of the Hornets, fresh from its kill of its Mirage, was also responsible for any hostiles on the ground. The Hornet's cannon shells obliterated the Iraqi APC and all of its personnel where they stood.

Mitch heard the roar above him, but his head was already roaring with the PCV. He never saw the wave of rocks that the mountain sent down to cover him.

It should have all ended right there... with the very mountain that had spawned the father finally taking back the son. But it didn't. Fifty feet above Mitch was a large boulder. When the avalanche plowed down the mountain's side, the boulder held. Instead of covering everything in their path, the rocks parted, flowing both to Mitch's left and right.

The fourth plane General Strong had in the air, an Air Force F-15 Strike Eagle, knew its mission. It carried a full load of liquid-air-fuel bombs. Its job was to terminally sterilize the site of the just-completed raid.

First, the pilot knew, he was to come in at low speed to survey the situation, and then he was to torch the whole place. No PCV could be allowed to escape the mountain.

The Eagle glided in. The sky above it had been cleared of all the Mirages.

"Big Eye One, this is Eagle One," the pilot spoke into his helmet's mouth piece. (He was flying in a cumbersome bio- warfare flight suit.) "There's been a big avalanche down there. Most everything is covered up."

"Eagle One, this is General Strong. Are there any survivors?"

"Can't be sure, general. This bio-suit hampers my vision. I'm going around for another pass."

"Don't do it!" ordered the general. "Your job is to sterilize the whole area! That virus is too dangerous to take any chances with it getting into wind! We'll never be able to control it if it does! All of our choppers are in the air!"

"Acknowledged," the pilot answered. "I will pull up and then make my run. I'm…"

The radio went silent.

"Eagle One, come back," demanded Strong. "I say again, respond."

"General, there's someone on the ground! I got a good look at him! He standing right in the middle of the rock slide, dressed all in black, holding some kind of rifle! I think he's one of ours!"

In the AWACS General Strong turned to Sarah. She suddenly had a look on her face that he hadn't seen since the angry times after Vietnam.

"*It's Mitch!*" she gasped. *"He stayed behind to cover everyone else!"*

In the next moment Strong saw Sarah's face explode.

"You didn't order him to do this, did you? You didn't order him to stay behind?"

Strong, surprised, said nothing.

"*No! You couldn't have, could you?*"

Her right hand caught Strong square on the side of his face. Her slap had all the force of a woman betrayed.

"*You bastard! I'll never forgive you!*"

She swung for his face again, but his big hand caught hers in a tight hold.

"No, Sarah! I didn't! Something must have happened on the ground! Mitch was supposed to come home like everyone else!"

Sarah hesitated. Anger, disbelief, surprise, and grief all battled for control of her face.

"Sarah!" he said. "*By all that is holy, our marriage, everything we've been through, and even Mother Marie's own grave, this wasn't part of the plan! Mitch was supposed to come home!*"

"*So let's go get him then!*" she almost screamed. *"He's still alive!"*

The general dropped her hands and turned away.

"You know I can't do that!" he answered, his voice cracking. "You know the sterilization protocol as well as I do! He's been exposed to that damn virus. If he comes home, he'll expose everyone to it. As of this moment, Mitchell Rice doesn't exist anymore!"

Sarah slumped forward. She had written the protocol herself. The PCV was a death sentence for the whole world. One man, not even Mitch, mattered in the face of that.

"Big Eye One, this is Eagle One. What are my orders?" came the voice of the Eagle pilot. "What am I supposed to do, general? That guy is still standing down there."

General Strong spun around. He first looked at Sarah and then at the Air Force major beside her. He was looking at them, but what he saw was a young, bloodied, black-suited marine lying in a Vietnamese alley. The twenty-two years between then and now no longer existed.

"*To hell with the damn protocol!*" he cursed. "*To hell with it!*"

With a quick motion he keyed his headset mike. "Hold, Eagle One! Hold!"

Strong focused again on Sarah and the Air Force major.

"Emerson, we still have that air rescue team in the Osprey, don't we?

"Yes, sir! We do!" the man answered.

"And they're trained in bio-warfare rescue techniques, aren't they?"

"Yes, sir. They are. They have their suits with them. That's standard protocol."

"Okay, then!" yelled Sarah, suddenly seeing hope. *"So let's go get him!"*

"Sarah," Strong answered, suddenly hesitating, "anyone who steps on the ground down there will have to be quarantine for weeks. We could lose the whole crew."

"General!" Major Emerson interjected. "I recognize your concerns, but you need to hear this!"

He stood up and looked at both of them.

"Sometimes, sir, one man *does* make the difference... sometimes one man makes *all* the difference! Right now there is just one man left on the ground, and he is the *one* who has made all of the difference! Let's go get him! We have what it takes. *Let my guys go!*"

Strong's eyes were still dim, still uncertain.

"Sir!" Emerson pressed on. *"We're all the same! We all live by the same motto... "we leave no one behind!" NOT EVER! Sir! Let the Osprey*

go! That's what its men live for! It's their duty! Let them be proud of who they are! Mrs. Strong is right! Let's go get this guy!"

Strong hesitated no longer. The fire in his eyes came back.

"*You're both right!"* he said, nodding. "*You are both right!"*

He was the general again.

"Eagle One! This is General Strong! Continue your orbit! DO NOT, I repeat, DO NOT launch your weapons at this time! The Hornets will fly cover! We have another bird coming to bring our guy home! This isn't over yet! Your fire will have to wait! Mitchell Rice is coming home!"

Chapter Thirty-One

On the fifteenth of October, Nancy Franklin sat in a car outside of Mitchell Rice's home in Oklahoma, a home he had never seen. Lying on the seat beside her was a simple white envelope, the same envelope Mitch had given her in Turkey. The address on it was correct.

"I don't know if I can do this, Mitch," she said to the empty car.

It had been just over six weeks since she'd had her last glance of Mitch, a quick, over-the-shoulder glimpse of him from the floor of the helicopter that took her and Colonel Smythe out of harm's way. Mitch had just saved her life, and she was just able to make him out as he continued his deadly duel with the Iraqi armored personnel carrier. And then everything on the ground had been covered up by the avalanche. And then he was gone.

Nancy reached up to her own chest. Her heart felt again the heat of the PCV vials where she had cradled them between her breasts. She knew what she felt then and what she was feeling now wasn't real. The vials she had taken from Geoff McNab for safekeeping generated no heat. But her heart ached anyway. She could scarcely breathe for the empty pain. Today she was going to have to deliver Mitch's letter to his Nicki, his *last* letter.

She reached up and wiped a tear from her eye.

The letter was why she had jumped into the car as soon as she had left the bio-decontamination/quarantine facility in Arkansas where she and the strike team had been kept in isolation. The letter was why she was here. She hadn't even taken the time to go to her quarters, check her email, or to talk to anyone. She had especially avoided General Strong.

"*Oh, Mitch!*" she whispered. "*I really can't do this!*" Several more tears ran down her cheeks. "*I really can't!*"

"Can I help you with something?" a voice came through her car window. "Are you okay?"

Nancy looked up and saw a young woman with medium-length blond hair and striking green eyes. In an instant Nancy knew who it was… it was Nicki Rice.

"I'm sorry," Nancy heard Nicki say. "I don't mean to intrude, but you've been sitting out here for a long time. And I think you've been crying non-stop."

Nancy sniffed as quietly as she could and wiped away more tears.

"I wasn't trying to snoop… but you are parked here in front of my home," Nicki said. "I really would try to help you, if I can."

"I'm sorry," Nancy began. "My name is Nancy Franklin. I… "

"I know you!" Nicki interrupted. "You were with Mitch!"

"Oh, God forgive me!" Nancy whispered to herself.

"Yes, I was," she said aloud.

Nicki reached through the open car window and pulled up the lock button.

"Please come in, Nancy. The kids are gone with Sarah. It's just me. Mitch would want me to bring you into the house."

Nancy felt herself pulled out of the car. She knew she somehow should be resisting, but she couldn't. All the rehearsals she had done over the last six weeks had been a waste. She wasn't following any of her scripts.

"Come on in," Nicki said, smiling an impossibly warm smile.

"How can you be so welcoming?" Nancy stammered, picking up the white envelope at the last moment. "After everything that has happened?"

Nicki put her arm around Nancy's shoulders and steered her toward the front door.

"I'm sure I don't know everything that happened over there," she said. "But I know enough to know that Mitch thought you were pretty special. That's enough to get you through the front door any time you want."

Nancy pulled back. Every fiber in her being wanted to run away, just as far away as she could.

"Then... do you know about this?" she asked, holding out the letter.

Nicki took the letter.

"Is this for me?"

Nancy nodded. Her throat was closing off, and she could barely breathe.

"The night before the attack... Mitch asked me to see that you got this..." Nancy whispered. "*I am so sorry!*"

And then she put the envelope into Nicki's hands.

Nicki's face suddenly blanched. After a long moment , she opened the letter.

Sept. 3, 1990

Dear Nicki,

It's fairly late, here in Cukurca. I guess it's about midnight.

I've been here in Turkey for more than two weeks now. The trip here was a bit hairy. Turkey is a tough country. The closer I got to the Iraqi border, the worse it got. But after I finally made it here to the rest of the team, things settled down.

The crew General Strong has assembled here is pretty amazing.

The official boss is a Brit named Smythe. He's a real operator. I'm sure the general hand-picked him for all this. The rest of the "relief team" are also English, very spit- and-polish. There is just one other American. Her name is Nancy Franklin. She's the real linguist of the place, and, I think, probably the real boss if things ever get really tight.

The whole outfit was waiting for me to get here, and they put me to work as soon as my feet hit the ground.

Nicki, I'm seeing more patients here in a day than I ever did there at home. The medical needs of the people here are very third-worldish. I guess ignorance and malnutrition are the biggest problems, but I must say that the Kurds have really impressed me.

They are a proud people, Nic. Even displaced and persecuted as they are, they're good to be around. They try to take care of themselves and don't seem to be looking for pity. One of them the other day said to me that it wasn't too bad to have one's back to the wall. He said that at least if there was a wall behind you, you couldn't be attacked from all sides at once.

Nicki, I don't know what the future will hold for these people, but I like them a lot.

So, okay. Enough of the preliminaries.

Tomorrow, we're going for Wade and his virus. The word is that he is even now in a troop convoy, heading for an old mountain near the Iraqi-Iranian border. We're going to intercept him as he climbs that mountain and take both him and his virus. We'll take him alive if we can, but it's more likely we'll have to kill him. I know no one here will hesitate if he resists. We are slated to load into the general's special choppers in just a few hours. So, I guess time is short.

Nicki, I've been here before. The night before battle has always been hard, but I have to admit that this time it's a lot worse than it has ever been before. Before, I never really had anyone at home who really needed me. That made it easier. Now, knowing that you and the kids are there, it's really hard for me to get myself together. Every time I close my eyes and try to concentrate on the mission, I just see you and the kids. I miss all of you more than I can say.

I guess right now I'm just lonely and feeling sorry for myself, but I really do have a bad feeling about tomorrow. There'll be just five of us that will hit the deck come daylight. I don't know how many Iraqi Republican Guard will be against us, but probably a bunch. And, of course, Wade will have his PCV, and I know he plans *nothing* good with it.

So, I guess it is my fear that is making me write this letter. When I have finished it, I'll give it Nancy Franklin. I'm sure she's the hottest agent we have, or else General Strong wouldn't have her here in the first place. She has promised me to get this through to you if I can't be there for you. If I can't come back, I'll do my best to see that she does.

Nicki, whatever happens tomorrow, know these things.

First, you and the kids are the best that I have. I have never done well fighting for politicians or for their causes. I have always done well when I fought for people. Tomorrow, I will fight for you and for our children. I think that will give me the edge.

Second, know that I will do everything that I can to survive and come back home to you. I don't want to die tomorrow. Mother Marie, all those years ago in Hue, said that I needed to find something to live for rather than something to die for. When I close my eyes now, all I can see is you. So I must have found what she wanted me to find. I will come home to you, no matter what it costs.

The third thing, Nicki, is this. You have been mine for these last fifteen years. During that time, you have mended my wounds, given me your joy and passion, and helped me find my own to give back to you. You have loved me, given me my children, and taught me more about honor in your day-to-day, honest courage than I've ever known before. Know that even though half the world separates us, I know that it will be you who will be covering my backside when it all comes down tomorrow. And I will be well protected by your love.

Just then I thought I wanted to make a little joke about you covering my backside… just like we've always laughed about when we were together. But the feeling that you're behind me now is so powerful that I just *can't* joke!. It's all just too real! You must also know this! You are my other half! God made us for each other, and we will always belong to each other!

Tomorrow will be tough. But whatever happens, know that your light has brightened my soul, healed it, and, I think, saved it. I love you more than life! I will always be yours, and you will always be mine!

Lastly, I have finally come to realize something else.

We, all of us, will exist forever.

God is such a silly lover. He lets us begin as children who instinctively know that love is the thing that we need most. We all go through our lives in a crazy cycle until we are once again children who reach up again for love.

I have spent most of my life refusing to embrace love because I thought I wasn't worthy of it. And I wasn't. But it didn't matter. Love was always there anyway. It stayed after me, wearing me down, until I finally just had to reach out to it, just like a child. And when I did, I found you. And, from your love, I found peace. And from the children you have given me, I became something more than myself.

Isn't it amazing, Nicki? Think of it! Thanks to you, I've been part of creating new beings whose essences will last forever! God has given each of us such power, and we so seldom realize it! We're really little less than gods ourselves!

I'm grateful that I have realized this last thing before I came to the end.

Nicki, no matter what happens tomorrow, I will always be with you! I will always be your other half! Our love will always be! When times get really hard, think of our good times! Close your eyes, and I will always be there touching you just as you are touching me now! By God's good grace, we will always be! Oh, lady! I do love you!

Mother Marie once told me that, in the end, a person just had to do two things. First, one had to forgive oneself, and second, one had to say goodbye.

Nicki, somewhere, through our years together, I guess I have forgiven myself and have since then tried to make things right.

And if this is goodbye, then know that it is just a temporary and a partial thing.

General Strong was right about one thing. I have always been and will always be a guardian. If it happens that you can't see me with your eyes, then see me with your heart. That's where I always looked the best anyway. Please help the kids understand who their father was.

I have to go now, Nicki. It's time.

I do love you.

Mitch

Nancy saw Nicki lift her eyes from the last page. Her eyes were full of tears, but they seemed to see something that Nancy couldn't.

"You've been in isolation, haven't you." Nicki said.

Nancy nodded yes. Her voice was gone.

"And I guess some crazy CIA rule or debriefing requirement has kept you from talking to anyone except your handlers about the mission…"

Again Nancy could only nod.

"Then I love you more than I can say," Nicki said, getting up from her chair.

In the next moment Nancy felt herself locked into the warmest embrace she had ever felt.

"I know what it has cost you to come here today," Nicki whispered into her ear. "But I've already heard it."

Nancy pulled back enough to look into Nicki's eyes. The tears she saw there weren't tears of grief.

"Nancy, Mitch has told me all this himself." Nicki smiled a wonderful smile. "In fact, he has told me all this every day for the last six weeks."

Nancy felt her mouth fall open.

"Mitch made it, Nancy!" Nicki pulled her into her arms again. "*He made it!* I guess, for some crazy, horrible reason, you were never told what happened after you and that Colonel Smythe were extracted, but *Mitch made it, Nancy!* In fact, he's coming home today!"

Nancy slipped into a porch chair. Every gear in her head was slipping, spinning a hundred different directions all at once.

"*He made it!*" she heard again.

Just then a government-looking Chevy Suburban pulled up to the front of the house. Out of the two front doors stepped General Strong and Sarah. Next the back passenger door opened and out popped three kids, Mitch's kids.

"*HE'S HERE, MOM!*" they all screamed in unison. "*DAD'S HOME!*"

And then there was Mitch standing on the sidewalk. He had a cane in one hand, but he wasn't bearing much weight on it. Nancy heard Nicki's breathing stop.

"Hi, lady," Nancy heard Mitch say through a smile. "It was the kids' idea to surprise you. The general and Sarah weren't too crazy about it, but the kids wouldn't have it any other way."

Nancy saw Mitch drop the cane and hold out his arms to catch Nicki as she flew down the steps. And then they were all there together… the three kids, Nicki, and Mitch… arms all tangled up and everyone laughing and crying at the same time.

Nancy reached up to her own face, stunned by the smile plastered all over it. Mitchell Rice, she realized, finally had come home. It hit her that she had just witnessed the end of his tour of duty. This truly was his final homecoming.

"Hi, Nance," Nancy heard. It was Sarah. "It's wonderful, isn't it? Seeing them together like that."

"Yes, it is… it really is," Nancy answered.

She turned toward Sarah who was now at her side, offering her a hand. Out of the corner of her eye Nancy saw the general pick up the letter where Nicki had dropped them on the sidewalk.

After several long moments and several hard hand squeezes from Sarah, Nancy saw the general look up. He had just given Mitch's hand-addressed envelope a long look.

"Is this letter why you were so difficult in your post-mission debriefing?"

Sarah nodded.

"The psych boys told me you were PTSD'ing in the worst way. You had gone through a lot out there."

"Yeah, I did… and maybe I was," Nancy answered, now suddenly calm. "Mitch gave me the letter to bring here before the mission. He thought he wasn't going to make it. He had decided to make himself the mission's stopper. And he knew he was going to lay it all on the line to get the rest of us out."

"So you hid this letter from me, thinking I wouldn't let you bring it here?"

"Damn it, Wilson!" interjected Sarah. "You didn't even tell her that Mitch was alive, did you!"

"How could I?" he answered Sarah sharply. "She was acting weird! She had been on site with the worse bio- weapon ever invented! God forgive me, she had even carried it home nestled right between her breasts! How could I risk compromising Mitch and Nicki when I didn't know how stable she was?"

"God, Wilson! Even after all these years, sometimes you are just unbelievable!"

"That's not fair, Sarah! That's not fair at all! She *was* acting weird!"

Nancy pulled her hand out of Sarah's grasp and turned to walk away.

"Stop right there, Ms. Franklin!" the general barked. "*STOP!*"

Nancy felt her feet freeze right to the concrete.

"*And you can stop, too!*" he ordered Sarah. "It's time you both hear what I have to say!"

Nancy felt the general's stare burn right through her. She suddenly felt completely naked. One glance at Sarah confirmed she was probably feeling just as exposed.

"Nancy, you were recruited to the CIA after your family was killed in Lebanon. Your profile was that of a severely traumatized young woman who had to have vengeance!"

Nancy squirmed under his gaze.

"Vengeance is an okay motive," the general continued. "But I have realized the psych boys were wrong. You didn't really want revenge. What you wanted was for someone to kill you. You wanted to die so you wouldn't feel so guilty for surviving when your parents didn't!"

Nancy heard the general, but she couldn't look up. All she could hear was a roaring in her ears.

"And do you know how I knew that?"

Nancy couldn't move.

"I knew it because I had spent half an adult lifetime with a woman who had been nearly raped, who had watched a woman whom she loved more that her own mother die, shot full of holes. And she was so angry that she couldn't even imagine that it was her GUILT for surviving, not vengeance that was the center of her life!"

Nancy looked up. Sarah's face looked like a broken mirror in which Nancy saw herself. There was so much pain there.

"*Wilson...*"

"NO, SARAH! You're going to hear me out this one time!"

He stepped forward and handed Sarah Mitch's letter.

"*Or better yet, you're going to hear what Mitch had to say. READ THIS!*"

Nancy felt her feet starting to move.

"And you read it too!" the general ordered. *"Both of you do it! NOW!"*

Over the next several minutes Nancy and Sarah stood side by side and read the last words Mitch thought Nicki would ever hear from him.

At first the words chilled Nancy so severely that she had to clench her teeth to keep them still. She could feel Turkey and its fear all around her.

But the chill soon passed and then all she could feel was warmth growing in her heart. Her heart remembered what it was like to feel love even when her head had utterly forgotten.

And finally, something clicked inside Nancy's soul, something wonderful... *forgiveness of one's self... peace... and that a good-bye was just a temporary thing.*

Nancy looked up from the paper. First she looked long and hard at Sarah. The mirror she saw there wasn't so shattered anymore. Then she looked at the general.

"*You see, you two, sometimes one man does make all the difference,*" he said. *"That's who Mitchell Rice has always been... the one who always made all the difference."*

Nancy saw Sarah move toward her husband with outstretched arms.

"And that's who you are too, Wilson! I've always know that!"

Her voice was quaking.

"*After all these years, can you forgive me? I never meant for you to always have to stand in Mitch's shadow!*"

Nancy saw the general gather Sarah into his huge arms, and Nancy saw that the mirror that was Sarah's face had no more cracks in it. It was crystal clear.

"General," Nancy said, *"now I understand why I've always heard you two described as the prince and the princess."*

"Mitch was always the prince, Nancy. Not me," the general answered through Sarah's brown hair.

"Mitchell Rice may be a prince, general. He really may be that and a lot more."

Nancy took a big breath.

"But if he is, then he's the third in line, not the first or second. Those places will always be yours, not his."

Nancy smiled.

"*And I'll always be proud to have followed the three of you.*"

She paused.

"It's been a hell of a tour of duty, general... a hell of a tour of duty for all of us!"

"Yes, it has been," he answered, momentarily breaking free of Sarah's embrace.

Nancy saw Mitch and Nicki and the kids coming up to them. In a moment they were all enmeshed in a tangle of arms and hugs. It was noisy and wonderful, and no one could really tell who was who. But then over the din, Nancy heard Mitch speak.

"Come on," he said. "Let's go in. This time we all have finally come home."

Epilogue

(Excerpt of lecture given at the Chicago Museum of Science and Technology, June, 1985, by Isaac Eloi)

"Perhaps the oldest piece of written literature in the world is the epic of Gilgamesh. This work is actually a compilation of a large number of folk tales and legends put to the written record prior to 2000 BC.

"The origins of these stories are so shrouded in antiquity that it boggles the mind, and almost certainly predates the time of the great flood. In fact, Ethiopian monks, experts in the old legends, frequently claim that the story even predates the legend of Atlantis and is more contemporary with the mythical Book of Troth from which much of the legends of the pyramids arise.

"Whether this all is true or not and whether or not the story is truly a documentation of the "progenitors" is, of course, open to speculation. But the fact remains that the story is truly ancient. Distributed as it is throughout all the countries of the Middle East and Eurasia, the epic remains as one of the cornerstone works of all human culture.

"The story comes to us as a long narrative of the life and times of one King Gilgamesh, a king of the city-state Sumeria that lay in ancient Mesopotamia.

"Gilgamesh, a rather enigmatic rogue, ruled his people with an iron hand. He was said to have had a strange ability to make his eyes glow with an eerie green light whenever he was angry, and this phenomenon made him an object of fear by all of his subjects.

"After years of oppression and abuse, the inhabitants of Sumeria petitioned their gods to send a savior to free them from the "green-eyed one." A certain warrior-queen goddess (whose name is lost to us) was said to have heard the peoples' pleas, and she sent down to the people her own son, Enkidu, who was to battle the evil one.

"Enkidu was an interesting personage. Apparently a warrior supreme, he was one who chose to talk more often than he chose to fight. This tendency did not immediately endear him to the long-suffering citizens of Sumeria who wanted quick relief from their heavy-handed king. But Enkidu's persistence and patience eventually won the hearts of both the citizens and of Gilgamesh himself.

"The fact that the young man generated his own colored aura, apparently a deep red one, whenever he was stressed or angry probably had a lot to do with his success. But whatever the origin of Enkidu's strange ability, he was recognized as being a counterbalance for the formidable Gilgamesh and was thought to be of divine origin.

"The legends tell us that Enkidu's powers of persuasion were so great that Gilgamesh ultimately chose to mend his ways and sought the young champion's friendship. The two men became companions, almost brothers, and shared adventure after adventure right up to the time of a "great flood" when, according to one version, Enkidu died, or, according to another version, the two were separated by a huge wave.

"The epic, depending on its version, ends in different ways, but the most striking conclusion finds the prediction that the two opponents/friends will find each other again only at the time of the "great fire."

"All this written record has been brought to us from the excavated library of King Ashurbanipal who ruled Assyria from 668 to 627 BC. Other copies, varying in their content and less complete, have also been found in Syria and Turkey. Given all these documents' utter antiquity, this story certainly rates as being one of the most widely distributed legends of the prehistoric world, truly the first and most aged of all 'best sellers'.

"The most poignant aspect of all this, however, to all of us here today is not the antiquity of the story, nor is it the riddle of the archeology that salvaged the texts. Rather, the fact must be recognized that, even thousands of years ago, our ancestors were plagued by conflicts with their fellow man. Out of all this unwritten death and suffering, our forefathers chose to record their first written story as one of salvation.

"In it, two men, enemies from birth, were shown to find friendship and allegiance with each other by simply first coming to know each other before they attempted mutual destruction—a most cogent theme for any age—even ours which may be some fifteen thousand years distant from the time of the story's origin.

"Isn't it strange how little we have changed in all this time? Our past is still our future."

28708805R00209

Made in the USA
Lexington, KY
28 December 2013